Masques

Freda Bright was born in Boston, Massachusetts, into a family of writers. She began her career as a concert pianist after studying at the Conservatoire in Paris. She subsequently became an advertising consultant to the film industry, working in London and New York, and wrote her first novel, *Options*, while living in London. Her published works also include *Futures, Decisions, Infidelities, Singular Women, Consuming Passions* and *Parting Shots*. She has one daughter and lives in Montclair, New Jersey.

Also by Freda Bright

Options
Futures
Decisions
Infidelities
Singular Women
Consuming Passions
Parting Shots

FREDA BRIGHT

Masques

PAN BOOKS

First published 1994 by Macmillan

This edition published 1995 by Pan Books
an imprint of Macmillan General Books
25 Eccleston Place, London SW1W 9NF
and Basingstoke

Associated companies throughout the world

ISBN 0-330-33309-7

1 3 5 7 9 8 6 4 2

A CIP catalogue record for this book is available from
the British Library

Typeset by CentraCet Limited, Cambridge
Printed and bound in Great Britain by BPC Paperbacks Ltd

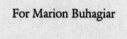
For Marion Buhagiar

PART ONE

The Sixties

MARIVAL

AT THE WATER'S EDGE, THE WOMAN SITS ALONE. SILENT.
BROODING. HER FACE IS HIDDEN BENEATH A MASK OF
BANDAGES.

Alix Bryden leaned out of the belvedere, the sun-baked wood rough against her elbows, and gloried in the panorama. Below her, a profusion of yellow flowers ('baskets of gold,' the gardener called them) garlanded the path that led down to the shore of Lac Leman. The grass was improbably green, the sky an equally unlikely blue. Here and there, atop the glassy surface of the lake, a white sail glistened, crisp and innocent as a nun's wimple. On the horizon, the snowy crest of Mont Blanc shimmered in the summer heat. The whole world was a-dazzle.

Alix shielded her eyes from the brightness and marveled. The setting belonged in a fairy tale. Each detail was perfect, from the picture-book clouds to the enchanted castle nestled in the hillside. And she was the princess of that castle, lovely and tender and languorous.

At the shore, a majestic white swan broke the silence to trumpet the arrival of her hero.

Alix felt a rush of blood. In her brain, Wagner's music blared, roiled, swelled to a tumescent climax. A host of violins announced that—

Lohengrin! Yes, it is he! The white knight, agleam in shining armor. Her *chevalier sans peur et sans reproche* come to claim his beloved for eternity. To marry her, carry her off to paradise. *Breathless, the fair maid sweeps back the veil and raises her face in expectation, waiting to be ravished with a kiss. He alights. Calls her name.* Elsa. No – not Elsa. *Alix!*

Rapturous, Alix too tilted her head and let the sun caress her

3

face, felt the hot breath of an immortal lover against her cheek. The music rushed to her throat, then—

'Idiot!' she scolded herself.

Damn fool idiot. What kind of rubbish was this? Princesses and castles and magic swans and Alix, with her pathetic alto, about to burst into song. *Lohengrin*, for Pete's sakes, which had to be one of the goddamn silliest operas ever written. Worse yet, she didn't much care for Wagner.

She flushed, embarrassed, even though there was no one in sight, for Alix would have preferred crucifixion to being caught out in such romantic blather. She hated mush.

Anyhow, Marival wasn't a castle at all, she reminded herself, but a Swiss château, too sunny to house even a ghost. And she, to be sure, was no princess. Rather, she was Miss Alix Spencer Bryden of Pride's Crossing, Massachusetts and Wellesley College. A clever (Dean's List), sensible (note the classic shirtwaist and low-heeled shoes), gangly ('a long drink of water,' her father would say) young woman bearing not the least resemblance to anyone's image of a story-book heroine. As for the swans that dotted the lake (and fouled the shore with their droppings), far from being magical creatures, they were – according to Mlle Mercier in Reception – filthy, vicious scavengers who bit the hands that fed them, and parasite-ridden into the bargain.

So much for princesses and knights and swans and fairy tales.

And yet. And yet . . .

Gingerly, Alix rubbed her fingertips against her cheek. The skin felt fine and smooth as a newborn babe's. Now *that* was magic. The ultimate fairy tale. Because in this place so full of wonders, Alix Bryden had herself become newborn. Had undergone, at eighteen, a second miracle of birth. Been granted a second chance at life.

I will always remember this summer, she vowed, *as the happiest time of my life*. Then with a self-conscious grin, she amended herself.

The happiest so far! For surely, the truly happiest times lay

4

ahead. For the day must come when *he* – the still undiscovered *he*, her own nameless Lohengrin – would declare his love, then enfold her in his arms . . .

Yes! Why not dream? Why not succumb to romantic reveries? For the first time in her life she felt entitled to indulge in fantasies. Perhaps they weren't fantasies at all, but portents of the future. She was reborn. Anything was possible.

Shamelessly, Alix·shut her eyes and gave herself over to the moment.

Images clustered, crowded, tumbled over each other. She was Sleeping Beauty, Rapunzel, Guinevere, Isolde, all the heroines of myth and fiction. She was Anna Karenina, exquisite in velvet and diamonds, about to captivate Prince Vronsky. She was Cathy, arms full of heather, surrendering to Heathcliff on a windswept moor. She was Scarlett, Helen, Milady, Scheherazade. She was by turns a Parisian courtesan . . . a Borgia princess . . . a Hollywood star. She was riding tandem on a motorbike with Steve McQueen, her hair flying in the wind. She was taking Marcello Mastroianni with her to the Senior Prom. No image was too outrageous, too incredible. With her face to the sun, Alix drifted. Dreamt.

'Yoo hoo!' The voice pierced her reveries like a dentist's drill. Alix tried to block it out.

May I have the honor of this dance? Yul Brynner was cutting in on Marcello. Amazing that a bald man could be so sexy . . .

'Yoo hoo, Alix. C'mon, kiddo. We're waiting!'

The image of Yul began to fade. In its place, across the swath of lawn, Bette West had materialized on the château terrace, waving furiously. Even at this distance there was no mistaking the figure in the lipstick-red polyester pantsuit. There couldn't be two such garments in the world, let alone within the confines of Marival.

'I'm sorry, Yul,' Alix murmured to the movie star's vanishing image. 'But I have a prior engagement.'

Then, tucking away her dreams for future reference, she

walked across the spongy grass to the terrace where the Wests, mother and daughter, sat at a wicker table beneath a striped umbrella.

What a pair they were! Bette, shuffling cards and tapping her toes in a nervous tattoo; meanwhile, serene as a Buddha, her daughter Kim smiled and stared into space.

'Sorry!' Alix pulled up a chair.

'You oughta be,' Bette chided. 'Two sharp, we said, and it's nearly quarter past. Anyhow, you should know better than to stand in the sun like that. Dr Frankl would have conniptions. Remember what he said – no sun, no smoking, no stooping. It's a good thing I spotted you. What were you mooning about, anyhow?'

Could you moon in the sun? Alix wondered.

'I was admiring the view. It's such a perfect day.'

'Yes indeedy.' Bette dipped her head in the direction of the lake to give nature its perfunctory due. 'A perfect day. A perfect view. And speaking of perfection, I've asked the waiter to bring us a plate of – oh! what'd you call 'em? – those teentsy frosted cakes in different colors. They're divine!'

'*Petits fours.*'

'Yeah – like you said. And some nesselrode pie and a pitcher of lemonade.'

Alix laughed. 'I don't know where you put it, Bette. We just got up from a huge lunch a half hour ago.'

'I eat for the hunger to come,' Bette said unflappably. 'Like camels with water. That's something you learn when you grow up poor. Besides, the food is free. Well, not exactly free, but they don't charge extra for seconds. They wouldn't have the gall – not at these prices! Jesus, Kimmy and I could bunk for a year in Oklahoma for what these three weeks set me back, so I figure, we may as well get everything we're entitled to in the chow department. I've got half a mind to ask for a doggie bag when we leave on Saturday. Maybe pack a nice ham for the plane, a couple of cheeses . . .' Looking at Alix, she chuckled. 'I bet you

6

don't even know what a doggie bag is, Alix. I can't imagine Lucius Bryden's daughter thinking to ask for one. And while I'm about it, maybe I'll liberate a couple of those nice big bath towels and a terrycloth robe. They'll never miss 'em.'

Kim, who had been sitting quietly until then, broke in with an embarrassed 'Oh, Mom!' It was as close to outright defiance as she was likely to come.

'*Oh, Mom!*' Bette mocked. '"She was poor but she was honest" – that oughta be my daughter's theme song. Anyhow, gals, time's a-wasting. So what'll it be? Five-hundred rummy? Hearts? Shame there isn't another American here, we'd have a fourth for bridge.'

'How about Scrabble?' Alix suggested.

'Yeah . . . sure. Broadens your mind. Kim honey, nip inside and get the set from the game room and while you're up, find out what happened to the waiter with our cake.'

Bette watched the girl glide off with patent satisfaction, then, leaning toward Alix, fell into the kind of confidential whisper that could be heard twenty feet away.

'You know who that was sitting next to us at lunch? The gal with the aviator glasses?'

Alix nodded. The Italian movie queen's arrival had been the week's hottest rumor.

'They say' – Bette's voice rang with admiration – 'that she is personally responsible for the extinction of some kind of rare Siberian tiger.'

'She shot them?'

'She bought them!' Bette lit a cigarillo. 'Got the world's largest collection of fur coats, our little lady – leopards, tigers, the rarer the better, insured for over three million bucks. I read it in Leonard Lyons' column. My God, the woman must have closets the size of a house.' Bette cased the terrace, examining the occupants of other tables. 'And see that little Chink over there, having tea with her so-called male secretary? Well, for secretary, read bodyguard. The guy packs a gun.'

Alix followed Bette's gaze.

'You mean the man sitting with Mrs Smith?'

'And for Mrs Smith, read Madame Chiang Kai-Shek. Who went to Smith College,' she emphasized, 'which explains the alias.'

'Madame Chiang went to Wellesley, actually,' Alix said with a surge of collegial pride. 'And I don't think—'

'She's had her eyelids westernized, but definitely Chiang. I got a load of her close up. She travels everywhere with her own silk sheets, even has her toilet paper custom made. Class – huh? Now, see that evil-looking old guy playing croquet? Thick lips, greasy hair? Well, my bet is . . .'

Bette gave herself over to a favorite pastime, speculation about the rich and famous.

Rich and famous. To Bette West, they were the two most beautiful words in the language. All her life she had been a passionate consumer of fan magazines and gossip columns, wallowing vicariously in details of their extravagances, lovers, scandals, most intimate secrets. Such tidbits had seen her through a thousand wearisome days and dull nights. But never before had she been so privileged as to observe the mighty at first hand. Here they were on every side, the very folk who constituted the life's blood of the tabloids. It was all Bette could do to repress a shudder of ecstasy.

Being here was worth it. Worth the money and cheese-paring and planning and sacrifice, worth the pain and suffering that these weeks at the château had cost.

Though the pain and suffering, to be sure, hadn't been hers.

'Smaller than a palace, larger than a jewel box,' says *Fodor* of the Château Marival. It rates three stars in the *Guide Michelin*, which cites it as 'a prime example of Palladian-style architecture.'

Built in the 1760s by the banker André Busschère, and

named after his children Marianne and Valentine, the château is, above all, a monument to fiscal and political prudence.

A cultivated Parisian, Busschère had amassed a fortune financing the wars and whimsies of Louis XV. Yet even as the wily banker encouraged his monarch to indulge in a thousand follies, he tempered his allegiance with a healthy self-interest. When Louis declared 'Après moi le déluge,' Busschère nodded in silent accord. It was too good to last. The time had come to secure a haven abroad, some quiet peaceful place where, come the revolution, the banker's treasure and his person would be safe.

Busschère opted for Switzerland, thus setting an example of 'flight capital' for generations of millionaires to come.

No expense was spared in Marival's construction. It was to absorb the bulk of Busschère's fortune. From all over Europe, the finest artists and craftsmen were recruited to give each of its forty-five rooms the stamp of luxury. Capability Brown was called in to create gardens that rivalled the most magnificent in England. Watteau was commissioned to embellish the walls of the Salon des Quatre Saisons (now the dining room) with pale-eyed nymphs and dewy shepherdesses. The marquetry floors were inlaid in complex patterns with rare and precious woods from six continents. And if God, as has since been remarked, was in the details, then He was everywhere in Marival.

The château soon became a gathering place for artists and intellectuals. Voltaire was a frequent visitor, as were Mme de Staël and Edward Gibbon, who reputedly sketched the early chapters of *Decline and Fall* in the belvedere above the lake. Benjamin Franklin mentioned Marival in his diary ('excellent wine, comely women') and to this day, distinguished American visitors may be put up in the Franklin Suite. Château Marival was enjoying a golden age.

By the mid-nineteenth century, however, the family fortunes had dissipated, Busschère's descendants having manifested a greater knack for spending money than for earning it. Little by little, the furnishings were sold off, the superb collections found their way into museums and private homes and pawnbrokers' shops. Weeds flourished where roses once had bloomed. By 1900 all that remained of its former glory were the painted shepherdesses on the walls of the Salon. Shuttered and abandoned, Marival's sole occupants were mice, voles and spiders.

This state of affairs continued until 1934 when it was acquired by a British Rothschild who combined a love of Watteau with a passion for party-giving. Employing the resolve for which his family is renowned, the new proprietor set about restoring those architectural features which were salvageable, then proceeded to add those luxuries the modern world had to offer: central heating, all-weather tennis courts, an indoor swimming pool. The bedrooms were fitted out by Syrie Maugham to reflect the ultimate in luxury. The ballroom completely redone in art deco designs by Serge Chermayeff. The gardens re-planted *à l'anglaise*, with turf from Somerset.

For a few giddy years, Marival enjoyed a second golden age. Once again, the rich, the famous, the merely notorious flocked through its massive wrought-iron gates with nothing more serious than pleasure in mind. Throughout the thirties, Marival's house parties were the talk of the Champagne Circuit. The coach house now sheltered sleek Lagondas, Daimlers and Bugattis. In the ballroom, millionaires fox-trotted with movie stars to the latest Cole Porter tune, as Jean Cocteau rubbed elbows (and possibly more) with Hemingway and Cecil Beaton while Garbo sulked. And, in a shadowy corner of the terrace, a sharp-eyed observer might glimpse the Prince of Wales stealing a kiss from Wallis Simpson.

Then Hitler invaded Poland and the party was over. Its owner returned to England, where he died two years later in an air raid. Marival once again shut its gates.

Shortly after the war, Rothschild's daughter Emmy donated the estate to the International Rescue League, with the proviso that it be used as a rehabilitation center for survivors of Nazi 'medical experiments.'

History has already chronicled the perversions practiced on the Ravensbrueck Rabbits and other human guinea pigs; the details are too gruesome to recount. Now it fell to the staff of Château Marival to reverse, so far as possible, the process. To make whole what other doctors had made monstrous.

To this end, a superb medical team was assembled: surgeons, dentists, dermatologists, psychiatrists, physiotherapists. The north wing was converted into a state-of-the-art hospital, with facilities for plastic and reconstructive surgery. The south wing provided living quarters where, as much as feasible, all sense of 'hospital' was banished, for it was Miss Rothschild's hope that the beauty of the surroundings might help countermand the past sufferings. 'One must treat the soul as well as the body,' she often said.

Thus the luxurious furnishings were maintained in their pre-war charm and elegance, as were the saunas, tennis courts and pool. Fine art dotted the walls. In the kitchen, Swiss chefs worked with nutritionists to create meals that were both healthful and delicious. Each night, a string trio arrived from Lausanne to play dinner music; films (with an emphasis on comedy) were shown in the grand salon. On occasion, world-famous visitors (Artur Rubinstein and Marcel Marceau among them) volunteered their talents. Nowhere else in the world did patients live in such splendor.

But it was in the operating theatre that the château made its mark. By 1950, the name Marival had become synonymous with the most advanced surgical techniques of the day. Miracles were performed here, medical history was made – most notably through the achievements of a young Swiss physician.

Dr René Frankl was (and remains to this day) the marvel of his peers. The stout young Zuricher was among the first to explore the possibilities of microsurgery, to employ lasers in treating skin deformities, to develop viable synthetic bone. Yet even more than a surgeon, Frankl was an artist, a Michelangelo who sculpted in human clay. Now and again, a colleague would joke about his virtuosity and call him 'Dr Frankenstein.' The fact that the fictional doctor conducted his experiments in nearby Geneva only heightened the jest, but Frankl took the ribbing with good grace.

'Frankenstein created monsters,' Frankl would reply mildly. 'I create beauty.'

By 1954, the last Ravensbrueck Rabbit had been discharged, in the knowledge that whatever could have been done *had* been done. Its mission at an end, the château was offered for sale, to be snapped up by a consortium of European investors. Henceforth it would function as a 'for profit' center of plastic surgery, with Dr Frankl at its head.

'At last,' quipped one investor, 'the expertise so long enjoyed by the poor and stateless will be equally available to the rich. Now *that's* what you call democracy.'

One of the clinic's first private patients, and its most passionate spokesman, was Vanni Moretti. The socialite-sportsman had been virtually incinerated when his Formula One Fiat burst into flames at Le Mans. One could smell the charred flesh from the stands. Yet within a year, Vanni was back in the social circuit, making new romantic conquests, handsome as ever (some say handsomer), a model of health and virile beauty.

'A miracle,' his friends would exclaim, enviously.

'A Marival miracle,' Vanni would acknowledge, thus chalking up another new client for the enterprise.

By decade's end, the clinic had won for itself an international clientèle, ranging from the merely vain to the disfigured and desperate; the sole common factor was wealth. Secure in its success, Marival never blew its own horn; discretion was its stock in trade. Word of mouth, and the occasional mention in gossip columns, sufficed to keep the eighteen bedrooms filled.

Most patients treasured their anonymity, for during those

early years, plastic surgery was considered a matter every bit as unmentionable as embezzlement or incest. Thus at any given moment, there was an assortment of 'Mrs Smiths' and 'Monsieur Duponts' on the premises. Yet those who knew, knew; in certain circles, the remark that 'I'm going to a spa in Switzerland for a few weeks' rest' was properly taken with a grain of salt.

For, as the Princess von Sturm und Deitmund (alias Mrs Jones) pointed out, 'You never know who you'll run into there.'

You never did. Marival swarmed with notables. Bookings were often made months in advance. The minimum stay was three weeks, with more complex procedures (complete body resculpting, for example) taking much longer. But once the inconvenience of surgery was over, you could easily pretend that you weren't a patient at a clinic, rather a welcome guest at a luxury resort.

His apprenticeship with war victims had taught Dr Frankl that healing was as much a matter of mind as of body. The word 'patient' was never used; staff were instructed to employ the term 'guest' and treat them as such. Ignore your black and blue marks and bandages, this attitude urged. Imagine instead that you are holidaying in an exclusive resort.

Thus, diet or dine as you choose. But if you choose to dine, enjoy cordon bleu cuisine with desserts by a former pastry chef from Fouquet. And though alcohol was forbidden (it delayed the healing process), there were compensations galore. Self-indulgence was the order of the day. Entrust your new face to expert cosmeticians; entrust your new body to golden-fingered masseuses and herbal baths. Relax and permit yourself to be pampered, for happiness is the best therapy.

Once on the road to recovery, you might leave the grounds to enjoy the amenities with which the district abounds. Concerts, sailing, jazz at Montreux, pique-niques at Chillon, roulette and *vingt-et-un* at Divonne-les-Bains. Best of all, a shopping spree in Lausanne or Geneva. And what better therapy for milady than a *petit rien* from Cartier? Mr Fritz, the Travel Steward, is on hand to arrange such pricey 'extras.' Given funds, one need never be bored.

But perhaps unique among the comforts provided were the services of a house psychiatrist. Indeed, they were deemed so essential as to be included in the basic cost.

'Waking up to a new face is a traumatic experience,' Frankl observed. 'Adjustments must be made.'

In order to ease the transition from age to instant youth, Dr Peter Mainwaring (Cambridge, Bart's) was on hand to dispense comfort and advice. An attractive Englishman with an infectious laugh and ready smile, he had half the female patients in love with him. In four different languages.

Not all Marival's patrons had come in pursuit of youth. Some, like Vanni Moretti, had been accident victims; a few, like Alix Bryden, had been disfigured from birth. But in most of the battles being waged and won at Marival, the true enemy was age. The pouchy eyes, turkey wattles and crows' feet, the pendulous breasts and sagging thighs – these were the foe to be eradicated. 'Make me young again,' the anguished cry went up. 'Make me young and beautiful.'

So they flocked to Marival as to a latter-day Fountain of Youth: wizened heiresses, Latin playboys, fading movie stars, rising politicians, desperate homosexuals, fortyish first wives terrified of losing their husbands to younger prettier women, and – a few years down the line – the frightened second wives, no longer quite so young and pretty. An endless parade of notables, masquerading as Miss Smith, Herr Braun and Mme Dupont.

For of all the diversions afforded here, the most intriguing was the guessing game of Who was Who. And no one was better equipped to meet the challenge than Bette West.

Her knowledge of celebrities was encyclopedic. 'Not just movie people either,' she was quick to point out. 'That's too easy,' though show-biz folk remained her favorites.

Bette (the orthography was in honor of her idol, Bette Davis) knew everybody, at least by repute. She reveled in lists and ratings. Oscars, Emmys, Golden Globes, Golden Bears. The Annual Ten Best-Dressed. New York's Fifty Most Eligible Bachelors. The Baseball Hall of Fame. Medal of Honor Winners. Hollywood *Variety's* Twenty Top Box-Office Grossers. *Forbes'* Four Hundred. The *Fortune* Five Hundred. She committed them to memory, for one never knew when the odd bit of data might come in handy.

She had pegged Alix the first time they met, though the girl was hardly a public figure. 'Bryden? Bryden?' Bette scrunched up her eyes. 'You any relation to Lucius Bryden of Bryden Electronics? The daughter, maybe?'

Alix nodded shyly, and Bette could barely contain her glee. Lucius Bryden: the eighty-second richest man in America.

Thus far at Marival, Bette had been the first to spot the Queen Mother of Greece (who would later die having her eyelids lifted, though not at Dr Frankl's). Bette alone had uncovered the nature of the Panamanian playboy's operation. ('He's here to have his you-know-what enlarged,' she told an embarrassed Alix. 'Well, it *is* how he earns his living!') She was the first to be rebuffed by the Italian movie star (but by then, Bette had been rebuffed by everyone except Alix). Possibly the first to smoke out Madame Chiang. By now, nearing the end of her stay, Bette had assigned identities of all of Marival's guests with a single exception. The sole holdout was 'that woman' – the woman who sat by the lake. Solitary. Aloof. Mysterious.

'She's gotta be someone really important,' Bette said. 'A super-celeb. But I can't get a peep out of the staff. Plus which she takes all her meals in the room. It's so frustrating. What d' you think, girls?' she polled Kim and Alix. 'We talking Dietrich here? Liz Taylor? Garbo? She vants to be alone.'

Garbo was front runner until one day when Bette announced: 'I got a good look at the hands this morning. Too young and she bites her nails. I would guess Jackie O, but I see in the *Trib* that she's in Hyannis all summer, sailing with Caroline and John-

John. And Princess Anne is out, too. Bardot? God knows you can't tell much from those clothes. Woman dresses like a nun. Which makes me think that she's hiding from someone. On the run from the Mafia, could be. Or a Russian spy. Maybe she's wanted by the police.'

Alix laughed, without admitting that she too was intrigued. The lady of the lake struck her as ineffably sad. 'Perhaps just a very private person,' Alix said. 'Let her be.'

Today, however, on the terrace, with the mystery woman nowhere in sight, Bette was more absorbed in the matter of the Italian movie star, she of the tiger coats, and who did Alix think was better looking – Loren or Lollobrigida?

'I'm no expert,' Alix said. 'They're both lovely.'

At the far end of the terrace, Kim West came towards them with the Scrabble set, moving with the gawky grace of adolescence, her hair brighter than the sun. Bette's face lit up.

'Tell you one thing, Alix. With all these famous so-called faces in this joint, there isn't one who can hold a candle to my baby. Am I right or am I right?'

She was, quite possibly, right.

The Wests were amazing, Alix reflected as Kim set up the board. Mother and daughter. Darkness and light. Salt and sweet.

Except for the yellow hair (and Bette's locks owed more to Miss Clairol than to nature), the pair made for a striking contrast, both in looks and temperament.

The mother was short and sturdy, with thick wrists and ankles. When she thrust her head forward, she resembled a pug dog worrying a bone, hot and feisty and tenacious. She had gray crafty eyes and a humorous mouth. Some part of her was always in motion. Bette darted, sniffed, circled, engaged in bits of 'business,' swung her handbag, tapped her feet, punctuated her speech with jabs and puffs of the pungent black cigarillos she favored, invaded your personal territory. Her conversation was peppered with money references, mostly phrases from an earlier era. 'Another day, another dollar,' she

16

would say each evening. Or 'Go ahead, talk. It's your nickel.' Or 'I wouldn't give you two bits for that dress.' Her favorite adjective was 'wealthy,' pronounced with a naked relish that made Alix wince.

But if Bette was a pug, her daughter derived from a more elegant breed. The father must have been handsome, Alix concluded, for already at fourteen, Kimberly West was statuesque, with a strong well-formed body and fine, even features that gave the promise of great beauty. She had violet eyes, remarkable for their color and depths. She also possessed – by virtue of Dr Frankl's skills – newly heightened cheekbones ('Suzy Parker-style,' Bette said), sleek ears ('They used to stick out like Gable's') and an Ava Gardner dimple in the middle of her chin.

'My Kim,' Bette stated, 'is going to be famous. Movies . . . Broadway . . . on the cover of magazines. You wait and see!'

Bette West was manufacturing a star.

Alix Bryden was horrified. Kim West should never have been brought here. Her 'Before' was what most women hoped for as 'After.' Such tampering with nature struck Alix as not merely unnecessary but downright criminal. Yet Kim had submitted to the surgical procedures without a whimper. Good-natured and utterly guileless, she had the knack of sitting quietly, hands folded, while her mother catalogued her accomplishments.

'Look,' Bette would buttonhole any listener who offered as much as a polite hello. 'Just feast your eyes on this.' And before her victim had a chance to escape, Bette had pulled out a scrapbook from the depths of her tote bag and begun a guided tour of the clippings.

Bette tended to speak about her daughter in the first person plural, as though she and the girl were one. 'Our prizes . . . our press clippings . . . our age category.'

'This was Miss Tiny Tots in Santa Cruz . . . this was when we took second place in the Kute Kiddies Kontest, Eugene, Oregon. Kimmie sang "Good Ship Lollipop." Oh, sure, she sings. Been taking lessons since she was four. Dances, too, you

17

bet. Ballet, modern and tap. Oh, look at this! Isn't this darling? The Littlest Mermaid competition in Pasadena. Swims like a fish, a regular Esther Williams . . .' continuing until her prey moved off, never to return.

How the Wests – so clearly people of modest means – had managed to afford Frankl's services was an enigma. But the snubs they endured had to do with matters other than money.

With her polyester pantsuits and ten-cent cigarillos, Bette looked worse than poor. She looked provincial. And though young Kimberly appeared to be unaware of her mother's vulgarity, Bette West became something of a joke.

As one of her fellow guests commented: 'Who on earth would name a child after a diamond mine?' 'Someone who wanted that child to be a diamond mine,' came the response.

Given their closeness, it was impossible to befriend Kim and ignore the mother. Alix alone befriended the pair. Partially it was because they were the only other Americans in the establishment. Far more important, Alix knew, better than most, what it was to be a pariah.

In fact, she liked Kim enormously, who could be great fun when her mother wasn't around.

Sometimes, when Bette took an afternoon nap, the two girls would climb the hill to the little belvedere, where they could admire the view and exchange confidences without being overheard. Kim, punctiliously demure in her mother's presence, proved to be as chatty, as silly, as eager to share bits of dreams and gossip as any normal teenager.

'Do you really want to be a movie star?' Alix once asked.

'Yeah . . . I guess,' came the equivocal answer. 'It would sure make Mom happy. But what I'd really like is for someone fab to fall in love with me. Like Dr Mainwaring only not so old' – Peter Mainwaring was almost thirty – 'and I'd fall in love with him too, and he'd just sweep me off my feet.' Kim stopped, flushed. 'Do you believe that for every girl there's a Prince Charming?'

'Not really,' Alix lied.

'Well, I guess I do, sort of. I definitely do. And one day we'll meet, just like in the movies, and we'll get married and live in this huge ranch house in Colorado. I love Colorado, we spent a couple of weeks there when I was in the Little Miss Dogie Contest. Boy, was that dumb! The guys try to rope you in like cattle, and everybody got drunk, but the countryside was so pretty. Anyhow, him and me, my Mr Wonderful, we'd have this lovely home, with dogs and ponies, plus at least three adorable children. I'm an only child, you know, and I kind of missed having brothers and sisters. And I wouldn't have to take dancing lessons any more. Or elocution or voice or go to acting class, because my Prince Charming will think I'm terrific as is.'

Then she buried her nose in the flowering vines that had overgrown the balustrade. 'Mmmmm . . . jasmine,' she sighed. 'We had a jasmine bush when we were living in Santa Cruz when I was small. It was real beautiful, then we moved to Bakersfield, or was it Oakland? No, Bakersfield, 'cause that's where I went to First Grade.'

'You certainly have moved about a lot.' Alix didn't know whether to feel sorry or envious.

'You name it, we've lived there,' Kim went on, 'except for the East Coast. I guess that's next. My mom says we're gypsies. She says rolling stones shouldn't gather any moss. Though I don't know what's so awful about moss. Well, after California we moved to KC where I was runner-up Miss Corn-Fed Girl . . . then Odessa Texas where I learned how to ride . . .'

It struck Alix that each relocation served some particular goal in Bette's agenda: a contest, a vocal coach, a chance to study tap with a retired Rockette. The operation ran on a shoestring, with Bette struggling to support them both on her earnings as a beautician. As Kim rattled on, Alix had a vision of tacky salons and the stench of peroxide. Places where, when business was slow, Bette would burrow into tattered fashion magazines or

19

years-old issues of *Town and Country*, whipping up her own vision of high-life.

Eventually, their travels brought the Wests to Tulsa and it was there that Kim's mother caught the fancy of an elderly widower. 'My real father died in Korea,' Kim said, and Alix caught a sad, doubtful quiver in the girl's voice. 'So Mom married Uncle Ed. We stayed in Tulsa nearly three years, the longest anywhere, but I'm not sure we're going back . . .'

Feel sorry, Alix decided, not envious. The girl was being pushed and molded like a hunk of clay. She felt outraged on Kim's behalf.

'If you'd like to stay put, Kim, why don't you tell your mother? Say that you're not really interested in being a star. After all, you have rights too.'

Kim's pupils contracted as though stung. 'Oh, I couldn't. She's worked so hard, made so many sacrifices. I mean, she's doing all this for me.'

Alix's heart went out. Poor thing, she mused. Though it did seem odd that, given Alix's own history, she should feel sorry for someone so blessed with beauty.

Several times, Alix had been on the brink of speaking up to Bette, even offering her money to let Kim be. But she squelched the impulse. What business was it of Alix's, after all? And it wasn't as though Kim were unhappy. Instead, she continued the daily routine: taking her meals with the Wests and whiling away the empty hours with card games or, as on this sunny afternoon, a round of Scrabble on the terrace.

The waiter came with tea and pastries. Tiles were dealt out, laid down. Alix, who was near-sighted, put on her glasses to play. There was intermittent talk and the occasional groan. 'Double word, double letter.' 'I never get any vowels.' 'How do you spell *scion*?'

They played through the warmth of the day, engrossed, content, when a shadow fell between them and the sun.

'It's her!' Bette whispered, as the woman glided past their

table, an elusive figure in a long black dress. Play stopped. All three watched as she descended the marble steps that led to the shore.

'Our mystery lady. She's going down to the lake.' Bette sprang to her feet. 'Well, kiddies, I'm going down there to ask her if she plays bridge. What the heck, we need a fourth and it's a good opening. All she can say is no, and at least I'll find out what language she speaks.' Ten minutes later, Bette was back, unaccompanied. She looked ready to burst.

'Well, she's English or American – that's for sure. I mean she was reading Shakespeare, right? If she can read that stuff, she'd have to understand what I was saying. So I asked her if she wanted to join us in a game of bridge. At first, she didn't even lift her eyes from the book. It's like she was deaf. Then I said it again, really clear and simple. *Do? You? Play? Bridge?* You coulda heard me in Lausanne. Like I was not going to leave till she gave me an answer. Well, she finally, *finally*, raised her head – got the most piercing blue eyes, gave me the willies. That was all you could see through the bandages, those eyes. For a moment, I thought she was going to say something like "Get lost!" maybe. But she just blinked and went back to her book. You know what I think, kids? I think she can't talk. I mean she's bandaged down to there. Like maybe she's had her throat cut or something.'

'Or maybe she just wants to be left alone,' Alix said.

'Yeah, well so much for bridge and Wonder Woman.' Bette sat down and poked through her tiles, trying to decide if she should waste a perfectly good 'S' to make a plural or whether she could fake some kind of word to get rid of that lousy 'X' she'd been stuck with.

She pondered another minute, then placed her letters on the board with a triumphant smile:

LADY X

PRIDE'S CROSSING

Alix Bryden came into this world a murderer.

No pardon was possible. Her very existence proved her guilty, not just of murder but of other crimes as well. By the act of being born, she had, at a stroke, robbed her mother of her life, her father of his bride, and Boston society of its most exquisite ornament.

To be fair, Lucius Bryden never charged his daughter with these offenses – not in words. But in his eyes, Alix read the full indictment. *Murderer. Home-wrecker. Thief.* His loathing for her was instinctive, apparent in every gesture. Coming across Alix in some unexpected corner, or switching on a light to find her in a darkened room, Lucius could barely suppress a shudder of his lanky frame.

'Oh, Alix!' he would say with a visible struggle for self-control. 'I didn't know you were in here.'

Never once did he touch her, except by accident. Alix was careful never to take him by surprise.

Sometimes, when they were playing chess in the library, Lucius would glance from the chessmen to the Bouche painting above the fireplace. It was a portrait of Alix's mother, radiant in a shell-pink Charles James ballgown, a double strand of matching pearls at her throat – the pearls that had been Lucius Bryden's wedding gift. Then he would bite his lips, glance at Alix in mute comparison and return to the game without comment. Mostly, though, he kept his eyes on the board.

However, Alix scarcely required this reminder of her delinquencies. She need only look in the mirror. There it lay, like the mark of Cain – the red, raging birthmark that proclaimed her guilt for all to see. Blighting her face as it blighted her life.

The disfigurement began just below her hairline, gripped the right cheek in its bloody hand, then wound a ragged path down her throat to end at a point just above her collarbone. The left half of her face was unmarred.

Hideous though it was, the birthmark exerted a fascination. When Alix was small, she would sit for hours before her mirror studying its contours, like an antiquarian seeking a figure in a carpet. In the lines and blotches, Alix could variously make out a map of China or a ruby goblet or a burst-open pomegranate or a quetzal bird devouring a snake.

As she grew older, a new and better pastime took its place. At ten, Alix devised an elaborate game of Let's Pretend. Seated before the mirror with the lights dimmed, she would arrange her thick brown hair to hide the blemish, then twist her neck this way and that, until she could catch a glimpse of her 'good' profile in the glass, untainted by its fellow.

What greeted her was a visage which, though it lacked her mother's classic features, might yet be accounted good enough. A face, in fact, much like her father's: strong-featured with a high forehead, wide-set brown eyes and an aquiline nose. A nice face. A perfectly decent, serviceable, ordinary, *normal* face that strangers would neither stare at nor shrink from. Imagination did the rest.

'Let's pretend,' Alix would murmur, then conjure up visions of herself surrounded by playmates and girl friends and increasingly, as she neared adolescence, the company of boys. But above all, she dreamt of winning her father's approval.

'How nice you look, Alix!' In her fantasy, he would smile. Then, tucking her arm under his elbow, take her with him wherever he went. To his office, to restaurants, to Washington on business. They would snuggle together in the back of his Rolls, laughing and intimate. Close as paint.

'Let's pretend.' And as she daydreamed, the real world fell away. All too briefly. For it took but a turn of her head for the mirror to jolt her back to the truth.

If only! If only she could go through life half in light, half in

23

shadow. If only she could cut the evil half of her away. But that was impossible. The game palled, and she ordered the servants to remove all mirrors from her room.

She had a habit, developed in early childhood, of hiding her face in her hands. Public places and brightly lit rooms were to be avoided when possible. In school, she always sat in the back row. When a teacher fired her imagination, she suffered agonies of indecision, torn between the itch to flex her intellect and the desire to remain invisible.

As a teenager, her greatest solace was music, and she was happiest drinking up huge drafts of Bach and Brahms and Mahler in the privacy of her room, where 'real life' never intruded.

In her sophomore year at Rosemary Hall, Alix decided to become a nun, going so far as to take instruction from the Archbishop of New Haven. She said nothing to her father who harbored a profound dislike of Catholic ritual. Nonetheless, she felt it was a sensible decision. Alix would take the veil, both literally and figuratively, and spend her life in a cloistered setting.

As it turned out, however, this plan was derailed by a total lack of mystic sensibility. She was too skeptical, too intellectually independent to relinquish her will in favor of a prescribed set of beliefs. She wrangled constantly with Monsignor, often quoting her father to support her conclusions.

'You must make the leap of faith,' the priest urged. But that was asking the impossible. Had she not, as a child, wished on stars, chanted abracadabras, prayed for miracles? Faith had let her down every time. There were no miracles. There was no god. She knew this as fact.

Regretfully, the Archbishop gave up on her; irreverence was as ingrained upon the girl as was her birthmark.

In this respect, too, Alix resembled her father. She had inherited, along with his bone structure, Lucius Bryden's drive and brains. Both possessed tough, tenacious minds. Both shared an appetite for intellectual sport coupled with the inability to suffer fools gladly, or indeed in any way at all.

Thus, whether Lucius liked it or not (and clearly he did not), Alix was truly her 'father's daughter.'

Descended from a long line of Boston blue-bloods, Lucius Bryden was a maverick. As a boy he built his own radio sets, grew crystals, constructed a cloud chamber in the garage. Eschewing the Harvard education traditional in his family, he attended MIT, graduating first and youngest in his class, after which he moved to Berkeley to study physics under E. O. Lawrence. For relaxation, he played tournament chess.

Bryden's studies were interrupted by World War II. He served as a cryptoanalyst in the Signal Intelligence Service, achieving the rank of major. The war over, he returned to California just long enough to claim the most popular debutante in San Francisco as his bride. She was the only girl who ever made him laugh.

Persis Spencer was a born charmer: slender, athletic, with a sparkling sense of humor. 'The rich man's Carole Lombard,' a gushing columnist declared. She was also an excellent horse-woman, with a string of show-jumping trophies to her credit. By all accounts, it was a genuine love match.

After a honeymoon in Switzerland, the newlyweds settled in a Boston suburb and Lucius Bryden turned his talents to serious money-making. Though comfortably fixed, his means were insufficient to support Charles James gowns and pink pearls and a spacious new home in Pride's Crossing with stables for his wife's show-jumpers, Castor and Pollux.

His wartime work had fired the young engineer with a profound faith in the future of computers. In time, he was certain, the cumbersome UNIVACS and MANIACS then extant must give way to a line of mass-produced computers. These new machines would be fast, compact, sophisticated, yet easy to operate, a boon both to business and government. Clearly, these streamlined new computers would require streamlined programs to run, as surely as Castor and Pollux needed oats.

Lucius bought an empty warehouse on the outskirts of Boston, hired a dozen of the brightest grads from MIT, and proceeded to build what is now Bryden Electronics International. In time, his Route 128 address would be universally synonymous with high-tech.

The early days were exciting. Scarcely a month went by without a new patent being issued, fresh ground being broken. BEI services were sought by the Pentagon, Wall Street, the IRS. Prospects were splendid, and to complete his happiness, Persis was expecting a child.

The Brydens had names picked out, the nursery decorated, an exquisite layette ordered. But by the eighth month of her pregnancy, Persis was chafing at the bit from inactivity.

'Like my horses,' she wailed.

Each morning she spent hours in the stables, mucking out, currying Castor and Pollux with her own hands, regardless of what that stuffy obstetrician said.

The exact sequence of events on that fateful morning was never determined. Had Persis, on impulse, mounted one of her favorites? Had she been thrown? Kicked? Or had she succumbed to some completely unrelated medical crisis? Whatever the cause, she had lain unconscious for hours before a stable boy found her. She was rushed to St Elizabeth's, comatose.

Only two outcomes were possible, the doctor told Lucius: the mother or the child.

'Save my wife!' Bryden pleaded, hoarse with grief, but the choice was not to be his. Massachusetts was a Catholic state, St Elizabeth's a Catholic hospital, and the medical ethics of the day were specific. The infant's interests must come first. Persis Bryden died without ever regaining consciousness.

That night, Lucius went to the stables and shot the horses where they stood. Had it been possible, he might have shot Alix too.

Instead, he refused to acknowledge her, consigning her

welfare to nannies and tutors. Father and daughter saw each other only in passing. Alix accepted this as the norm.

To say that Lucius Bryden was destroyed by his loss would be hyperbole. Only in fiction do people die of broken hearts. But he ceased to be a lovable man. Ever a perfectionist and work-aholic, he became even more so. Nonetheless, he was still a relatively young man, the head of a dynamic company, and considered a 'catch' by any number of attractive women.

When Alix was six, Lucius remarried. It was a good marriage, if not an epic love affair, and came to be blessed with two healthy boys.

Dorrie Bryden was raised to be a rich man's wife. A Boston socialite, cheerful and kind, always immaculately dressed, she also was a conscientious step-mother. Lucius's abandonment of his daughter offended Dorrie's sense of propriety. The girl was a Bryden, after all, and should be integrated into family life.

Thus, Alix was promoted from solitary meals in the nursery to the dining room, where, to be sure, her father continued to ignore her presence. Yet Dorrie continued to do the right thing. Though her own boys came first in her heart, she saw to it that Alix was well-dressed and well-tutored. She wanted to make the child happy, preferring sunshine to gloom.

'Alix is very clever for a nine-year-old,' Dorrie said to her husband one night. 'And she's dying to learn to play chess. She's taught herself the names of the pieces and how they move. I'd love to help, but you know me, darling. I'm just hopeless with that sort of thing. Wouldn't you . . . couldn't you?' she wheedled. 'It would be nice for you to have someone to play with.'

After some weeks of gentle nagging, Lucius conceded.

'Very well,' he said. 'Tell her to be in the library Wednesday evening at eight.'

When Alix arrived at the appointed time, the room was dark

except for a lamp focused on the table where the chessboard had been set up.

'Good evening, Daddy.' Her voice shivered with awe.

Lucius mumbled something unintelligible, then moved his queen pawn forward two squares.

'The Ruy Lopez opening,' he announced.

Two hours later, he concluded the lesson. The child *was* clever, as Dorrie had stated. A remarkably quick study.

'Next Wednesday, same time.' Lucius got up to leave. 'You will learn the Sicilian Defence.'

The weekly sessions were to prove their most enduring form of contact, with conversations that ranged far beyond the confines of chess. In the soft shadows of the library, Lucius might drill his daughter on Latin verbs, discuss Russian novels or Restoration plays or cold war politics, expatiate on current theories of artificial intelligence. Her grasp of detail delighted him.

Had she been a boy . . . Lucius would think. Hell! had she been anything other than a gargoyle, he might have groomed her for the firm. Then the memory of Persis would make him sigh.

The child might as well be clever, he conceded, for she would be nothing else. Regrettably, business deals were not conducted in the dark.

Alix crammed for these sessions like a college student gearing for final exams, boning up on philosophy, logic, current events: whatever she thought would beguile his capacious mind. She devoured every chess book in print.

When Alix was twelve, she beat her father for the first time using a variation of the Nimzowitsch–Larsen Attack. She could barely smother a squeal of delight.

'You're very pleased with yourself,' Lucius observed.

'I like to win.'

He nodded thoughtfully. 'Don't we all.'

*

28

As part of her plan to give Alix a normal life, Dorrie enrolled her in a girls' boarding school. Alix did well at Rosemary Hall, graduating at sixteen, then going on to Wellesley. She enjoyed the academic work and made a few friends.

At college, her days were full and not unhappy. But in those late night sessions, when the girls sat on their beds cross-legged, gossiping about dates and dances and getting 'pinned' and whether or not to go 'all the way,' Alix excused herself and buried her nose in a book. She needed no reminder that 'normal' though she might be in a single-sex environment, there was no place for her in the male–female world beyond. *Well, well*, she thought wryly her first year in college. *I wound up in a nunnery after all. Could be worse.*

But no such logic ruled her dreams, which were violent, passionate, erotic. In her dreams there were no faces, only bodies. Hot thrusting bodies, needy and naked. Hers open and vulnerable; his strong and virile. He would enfold her, this Demon Lover. Possess every atom of her being. *Darling, beloved* – he whispered honeyed words into her ear while her body liquefied with joy.

Then Alix would wake up to find that her hand had crept under her nightgown and insinuated itself into the forbidden reaches, coming away moist. She felt disgusted.

'You sure were thrashing around last night,' her roommate Patsy once commented.

'Yeah. I was dreaming about the French Lit exam. *Quel* nightmare, *eh, mon amie*?'

Never, Alix vowed, would she parade her weakness to the world. She refused to be an object of pathos.

One day, in Alix's sophomore year, Dorrie returned from the country club a-bubble. Remarkable news! she gushed to her husband. Simply splendid! There was a clinic in Switzerland . . . Marion Cabot just got back from there . . . couldn't stop raving . . . a really super plastic surgeon who was working miracles with lasers or some such . . . a veritable sculptor of the flesh.

'Who knows!' Dorrie crossed her fingers. 'He might be able to turn our Alix into a regular Pygmalion.'

'Galatea,' Lucius corrected. 'Pygmalion was the sculptor. You really should bone up on your mythology.'

But he promised to look into it.

The night before her departure, Alix and her father played chess.

'You won't recognize me when you see me next,' she said. Which was an odd remark, since he had hardly 'seen' her in all her eighteen years.

Lucius's eyes wandered up to the Bouche portrait.

'Your mother and I went to Switzerland for our honeymoon. We ate at a splendid restaurant in Glovier, not far from where you're going. Best pheasant I ever had. You might try it if you get the chance.'

'Oh, Daddy!' Alix's heart overflowed with love. Instinctively, she reached across the table to kiss him. Just as instinctively, Lucius recoiled. Briefly their hands touched, then he sprang to his feet.

'Have a pleasant journey,' he said.

BY THE LAKE

The night before Kim and Bette flew back to the States, Alix invited them out for a farewell dinner.

'My father recommended a terrific restaurant about an hour away. I don't know about you,' she said tactfully, aware that the Wests had not been off the grounds since their arrival, 'but I've developed a case of cabin fever. You'd do me a favor by keeping me company.'

Though her own stay was nearly over, Alix was sorry to see them leave. She would miss the tête-à-têtes with Kim in the belvedere. Even miss Bette's badgering in a way. No parent had ever fussed over *her* in that manner.

Alix planned the evening scrupulously, from the chauffeured Mercedes to a detailed phone consultation with the chef at Glovier. Though playing hostess was an unfamiliar role, she determined to do everything 'just so,' as a preview of the glamorous life ahead. Exit the recluse. Enter Miss Alix Spencer Bryden: woman of the world.

'Will you feel this upholstery!' Bette exclaimed as they climbed into the limousine. 'Real classy, Alix – like you. Something tells me this'll be a night to remember.'

She was decked out like a Christmas tree trimmed with gobs of costume jewelry. Kim looked fetching in a flowered cotton dress. As for Alix, she had chosen a subtly draped 'little black dress' by Donald Brooks, which made her feel both elegant and self-conscious.

The meal began with *pâté aux truffes* and tiny ravioli stuffed with wild mushrooms. Then a velvety lobster bisque sprinkled with coral, followed by *perches du lac*. Alix opened a notch on her belt. She felt insanely happy.

The waiter cleared the fish plates and brought little dishes of lime sherbet sprigged with mint.

Bette's face fell. 'Dessert already?'

Alix assured her it was only to refresh their palates for the next course.

At last – and one could almost hear the trumpets – the pheasant arrived. Three gleaming roasted birds on a silver platter garnished with ornamental feathers, accompanied by a symphony of sauces. Even Alix, hoping to look worldly, could not suppress an adolescent 'Yum!'

Bette laughed. 'Couldn't put it better myself.' Then leaning across the expanse of white linen, she tapped Alix's wine glass with her fork. 'This calls for a toast, honey. Something special. I wonder, could we order champagne?'

'Absolutely,' Alix said, embarrassed she hadn't thought of it herself. A conference with the sommelier resulted in a Bollinger '52. With a grand flourish, he popped the cork.

Kim clapped her hands with delight.

'Un p'tit souvenir de cette soirée charmante, monsieur?' Kim said with a perfect accent. The girl had a remarkable ear.

'Bien sûr, madame.' He handed her the cork.

Kim giggled. No one had ever called her *madame*.

'Am I allowed champagne, Mom?'

'A teentsy bit, this being a special occasion.'

Their glasses filled, Bette surveyed the scene with satisfaction: the napery, the silver, the flower arrangements, the number and attentiveness of the staff.

'Real ritzy,' she declared. 'I could live like this year round. Oh to be rich! Well, Alix, since you're the one who pays the freight, you get to propose the toast.'

Alix blushed. What to say?

Unaccustomed as I am to public speaking? But this was no time to be arch. It *was* a special occasion, one that summoned up intense and lofty feelings. The joy of youth. The miracle of change. The pleasures of friendship. If only Alix could voice her happiness. Seeing a reflection of her face in the ice bucket, she picked up her goblet. The words came of themselves.

'A toast, then. A toast made in gratitude. Here's to the magicians and artists of Château Marival. In particular, our miraculous Merlin, otherwise known as Dr Frankl, for granting each of us our heart's desire. To Kim, a face the angels could envy. To Bette, a gateway to fame and fortune. And to me' – she fought down the urge to blubber – 'a second chance I never believed possible. For all of us, these weeks have been a turning point, a supreme gift—'

'A damned expensive gift,' Bette muttered, though Alix, carried away by the emotion of the moment, scarcely heard.

'A gift of the future. Of limitless possibilities. Of dreams come true —' She stopped, appalled at her effusions. For if there was anything Alix hated, it was making a spectacle of herself. Best to end simply. 'Finally, a toast to the three of us. Here's to our new lives.'

'Better lives!' Kim whispered.

'Famous lives!' Bette had the last word.

There was a moment of sacred silence, each of the three entranced in a private vision. Then Bette broke the hush.

'Skoal, lachaim, and down the hatch.' She drained her glass in one gulp. The waiter poured her another. 'Jesus, this stuff is good. Bubbles go right up your nose. How about another toast? To Switzerland. I guess it deserves a blast too — great scenery, great chow — though I tell you one thing, I'll be glad to get back to the good old US of A.' She cleared her throat. 'Now for an important announcement, like they say on the radio. Kimmy and I are moving to Miami. We'll be there tomorrow in time for a midnight swim. You're gonna love it there, honeybunch. Sun and sea and palm trees. Plus I've got fantastic plans.'

'What about Tulsa?' Kim asked. 'What about Uncle Ed?'

'What about him?' Bette shot back a dangerous glare, then turned to Alix. 'Yuppers, we're heading for the Sunshine State and the Junior Miss America contest. That's the biggie in our age category, you know, and sometimes they show the highlights on TV. We win that, baby, and we're on our way. After which, the sky's the limit. New York . . . Hollywood . . . Though we may have to do some more work on the cheekbones first. But Junior Miss is crucial. *Crucial!* Talk about gateways. Say, did I ever tell you about when we were in the Littlest Mermaid Contest . . .?'

Alix winked at Kim and dug into her food.

The pheasant was superb, followed by a *bombe au chocolat*

blanc. By the time coffee arrived, the diners had overdosed on champagne and calories.

Alix paid the bill with her father's American Express card, then reached into her bag and slid another twenty francs under the plate.

'I thought tip was included in these foreign restaurants,' Bette said.

'Yes, but it's customary to leave something extra for good service. Shall we go?'

They were halfway out the door when Bette spun on her heels. 'Damn!' she said. 'I left my lighter. You kids wait in the car. I'll be right out.'

She scurried back to their table, looked around, then pocketed the twenty francs. Quick – before the waiter had a chance to clear. *What the hell!* Bette thought. *We'll never come this way again.*

The girls were still giggly when the driver deposited them at the front door of the château.

'I'm too excited to sleep,' Kim said. 'Such a gorgeous night, and a full moon too. Anybody for a walk?'

'You kids go ahead,' Bette said. 'I'm gonna do a little packing. But not late, huh, Kimbo? We need our beauty sleep.'

The moonlight had turned the world silver, giving sharp pale edges to the cypresses, bleaching the tiles of the terrace, gleaming hard and cold down the hundred marble steps that led to the lake. Every line, every contour was clear but drained of color, like black-and-white photographs in a coffee-table book.

The girls strolled through the gardens, then settled on their favorite bench in the belvedere.

'Well,' Kim said, tucking her legs under her, 'it looks like I've seen the last of Tulsa. I smelled it coming. Mom just can't stay put. Too bad. I kind of liked it there, and he's okay, Uncle Ed. Lord knows he was always nice to me, and just nuts about Mom.

He used to call her "Miss Personality." She got a kick out of that. She always wanted to be in show-biz herself, you know, though Uncle Ed thinks it's pretty silly stuff. He's a periodontist.' Kim grew thoughtful. 'He told me I had wonderful gums and showed me how to floss and all that stuff, though I don't know how he'd feel about my having my upper molars extracted. Well, actually I do know . . .'cause when Mom once asked him to take them out – it's for the cheekbone line, you know. Lots of models do it. Anyhow, she asked him, he went bananas. They had this terrific argument. I mean you could hear 'em a block away. My mom may be short, but she's got big-league lung power. Like Ethel Merman, she says. And then . . .'

And then, after the blow-up, nothing. All sweetness and light for months and months. Until one day six weeks ago – 'Mom collected me from school in the middle of English class. She had our suitcases and everything, and the next thing I knew, we were on our way to Marival.'

'So you never said goodbye to Uncle Ed?'

'Nope.' Kim shook her head. 'Isn't that weird?'

Not to Alix. She had already divined the reason for Bette's last-minute return to the restaurant. The woman was not only a liar but a thief. In which case, the 'get-away' from Tulsa made sense. Bette must have bided her time until the arrangements at Marival were firm, then cleaned out her husband's bank account and decamped.

In the moonlight, Alix scoured Kim's face for any sign of rebellion, of anger. But there was none. Only puzzlement. Kim never thought to question her mother's motives. Like God, Bette moved in mysterious ways.

'So Miami it is,' Kim brooded, 'but who knows where we'll wind up. Maybe one of these days we'll come to New England and look you up, if you're still there. Think you will be?'

'Mmmm-hmmmm,' Alix murmured. Then she brightened. 'I've decided to go to law school, especially now that Harvard is taking in girls. It'll be fun. After that, I want to work for my father at BEI. He already has an in-house legal department, but I think my being there would please him.'

'Join the family business,' Kim said. 'Wow! I'm impressed. You'll be a lady tycoon. You'll do it too, I bet.' Kim squeezed her arm. 'You're so smart.'

For a while the girls lounged in silent felicity, listening to a nightingale. Suddenly, Kim jerked to attention.

'Did you hear that?' she asked.

'Hear what?'

'A sort of splash?' She was on her feet. 'Look, Alix! There in the lake! Just beyond the dock.'

Alix stared at a vague shape bobbing across the water's surface. Dark with a blob of white.

'Jetsam from a boat, probably. Or maybe a swan. I can't tell without my glasses.'

'A *black* swan?' Kim was shaking her head. 'No way. It almost looks to me like . . .'

'Oh no! Couldn't be!' Alix strained her eyes, comprehension wrangling with disbelief. 'You don't think—' But by then, her friend was off and running.

'Mother of God!' Kim cried as she tore across the grounds, trampling flowerbeds. She bolted down the marble steps that led to the dock, stopping only long enough to kick off her shoes at the water's edge. Alix, panting, lagged far behind.

Couldn't be! Couldn't be! The words reverberated in her brain. Kim's vision was a trick of the moonlight. *Trompe l'oeil.* By the time Alix got to the water's edge, heart slamming against her ribcage – *couldn't be! couldn't be!* – Kim had dived off the end of the dock and disappeared.

'Kim!' Alix screamed. 'Come back!'

The moon dipped behind a cloud. For one nightmare moment, she could see nothing in the water – neither the murky object that had lured them nor any trace of Kim. The lake, so sparkling and benign in daylight, had turned into a black and sinister expanse veined with hidden whirlpools and cross-currents. A death-trap.

Then, simultaneously, the moon came out and Kim's head broke the surface. She was swimming outward with powerful strokes, certain of her course. Alix froze.

Kim had hit the water with a shock. It was cold. Far colder than it had seemed on those sunlit afternoons. And the moon was playing hide-and-seek among the clouds. But Kim, who had, after all, battled the surf at Monterey, who had been dubbed Littlest Mermaid at Pasadena, who – in Bette's words – was another Esther Williams, refused to panic.

She trod water till her eyes adjusted to the speckled light, then she gazed around her, all senses on alert.

There! There it was, perhaps twenty yards away, for distances were hard to judge. An area of turbulence roiling the surface.

'Right!' Kim sucked in a lungful of air and began to swim. From a distance, she could hear Alix yelling. She shut out the sound. Nothing must spoil her concentration.

Steadily, Kim plowed through the featureless water in long firm strokes to the spot fixed in her mind, but when she got there, there was nothing to be seen. Nothing to be heard but her own heavy breathing. Too late – too late! the water mocked.

Dear God – Kim prayed – don't let me fail. Then she saw it a dozen feet away. A patch of white floating up to the surface. A hand? A handkerchief? Kim willed herself forward. Reached for the ghostly object. Grabbed. It came away in her fist. A length of bandage.

'Lord, give me strength,' she cried and jack-knifed in a surface dive, down, down, until her ears popped. A second later she was battling for her life.

The woman was smaller, lighter than Kim, but informed with a desperate fury. Arms and legs flailed out like tentacles, pulling her rescuer back down beneath the surface. For what seemed an eternity, the two figures locked in primitive combat, as Kim tried to break the grip.

If I drown here tonight – the notion flashed through her head – my mom will kill me. The thought emboldened her. With a mighty heave, she pushed upward, dragging her nemesis with her.

'Okay,' Kim gasped. 'You asked for it!' Working her right hand free, she reared back and let loose with a powerhouse punch. The tentacles went limp and Kim, locking one arm beneath her opponent's jaw, began towing her back to land.

By the time they were ashore, Alix had disappeared. Gone for help, Kim supposed, then wasted no time in speculation. She had her work cut out.

With effort, Kim pulled Lady X – for no doubt it was she – on to the grass. Then straddling the supine body, she poised herself for administering mouth-to-mouth resuscitation.

Impossible! Impossible to get through the waterlogged mass of surgical dressings that masked the face. Impossible to find the mouth, to give the kiss of life.

Kim caught her breath and began to unwind the bandages.

What to do?

Alix stood on the dock, staring at the spot where Kim had vanished. She wanted to jump in after her, be noble and brave and strong. Instead, she stood there and cursed herself, for never having learned to swim.

Get help!

Behind her, the Château Marival loomed dark and remote. Far beyond earshot. How many minutes up? How many down? A hundred steps. Dare she leave Kim while she went for aid? Perhaps Kim had already drowned? She felt helpless, impotent.

Then, as though fired by the devil, Alix ran toward the château, screaming at the top of her lungs.

*

38

By the time Alix returned with the night porter and Dr Mainwaring, Kim had the situation in hand.

'It's okay!' she waved, then crouched down. 'What is it?' Kim asked, placing her ear against Lady X's mouth. 'I can't make out what you're saying.'

To Alix a few feet away, the croak that emanated from the woman's mouth sounded scarcely human. But Kim must have grasped the words, for she was shaking her head vehemently.

'Oh, no!' she cried. 'You mustn't say such things. Please. You're fine. You'll be all right. The doctor's here.'

Gently, Peter Mainwaring pulled Kim aside and felt Lady X's pulse.

'We'll take over now,' he said. 'You girls go back to your rooms. The orderlies are coming with a stretcher.'

But Kim and Alix lingered nearby, too excited to leave.

'What did she say?' Alix whispered. 'When you were leaning over her, what did she say? You looked so shocked.'

Kim swallowed. 'She said – you should have let me die.'

Alix's mind reeled. 'When I was coming back down the steps and saw you bending over her – well, I had the impression she *was* dead. The flowers on your dress, the dark clothes she was wearing – they looked like flowers covering a bier.' Alix rubbed her eyes to make the image vanish. 'It's Lady X, isn't it?'

Kim nodded.

'You saw her face?'

Kim nodded again, almost imperceptibly.

'And . . .?' Alix breathed.

'Oh, God!' Kim burst into tears. 'It was awful. Horrible. I've never seen anything like it, not even in horror movies. Her face was like raw meat. Hamburger. If whatever happened to her happened to me, I'd want to die, too.'

They watched from the steps as Peter cradled the woman in his arms, talking, giving comfort. Then the orderlies arrived and loaded her on to a stretcher.

'I guess we should go,' Alix said.

Still dripping, Kim collected her shoes and the pair headed up the steps. Moments later, Dr Mainwaring overtook them.

'You're a very courageous girl,' he said to Kim. 'And you, Alix, did the right thing in getting help quickly.'

'I should have done more,' Alix said. 'I should have jumped in after Kim. It's just that – oh, God! I feel like such an idiot. You see, I can't swim.'

'So you listened to your head instead of your heart.' Peter smiled. 'And a good thing, too. You should both be proud. Now, I'm going to ask you girls to do something that may be even more difficult than saving a life. It will require a great deal of will and self-discipline. I'm going to ask you not to breathe a word about what happened tonight. Not even to your mother, Kim. The poor young woman whose life you just saved has suffered enough already. It would be a kindness to spare her further humiliation. May I rely on your discretion?'

'Of course,' Alix said.

'I promise.' Kim raised two fingers. 'Scout's honor.'

A half hour later, they were ensconced in Alix's bedroom. Kim had showered and was sitting in her friend's terrycloth bathrobe, a towel round her hair, while her clothes were stretched out to dry on the balcony. Dr Mainwaring had had cocoa sent up.

'Wow!' Kim said between gulps of the steaming liquid. 'And triple wow! When my mom said this would be a night to remember, she didn't know the half of it.'

Alix managed a laugh. 'Quite a grand finale to your stay. Little Miss Mermaid!' Then her sober mood returned. 'You know, Kim, they say that when you save someone's life, you're bound to that person forever.'

'Forever!' Suddenly Kim shivered. 'That's crazy. Insane. How can I be bound forever to someone whose name I don't even know?'

MARIVAL

The Comtesse de Granz arranged herself on the couch with consummate care. 'I'm so worried,' she said, patting down the pleats of her Courrèges miniskirt. It was a ridiculous garment, more suited to a mannequin than to the plump widow of a Belgian brewer. Ridiculous dress. Ridiculous woman.

'So very worried,' she repeated with a flutter of hands. 'Don't you want to know why?'

Peter Mainwaring grunted on cue.

'It's because of Toto. I'm terrified my darling won't recognize me when I get home.'

Toto? Surely not her husband's name. A lover then?

'I see,' Peter said.

'He adores me, you see.' A flirtatious note crept into her voice. What now? Peter wondered. Having bought herself a new husband, a new face and a spurious title, did this dumpy widow with bad French and worse thighs plan to acquire Peter as well? He avoided her eyes.

Dear Toto, it turned out, was 'the most precious cocker spaniel, and what if he doesn't know his mummsy with her pretty new face? Will he think I'm an intruder, and bite?'

Some day, Peter vowed, he would write his life story. Entitle it *Memoirs of a Useless Man*. Meanwhile, he assumed his most unctuous voice.

'Dear lady. Be assured, nothing of the sort will happen. Our pets, bless them, don't judge us by our appearance. They recognize the people they love by—' By smell? The woman stank like a perfume factory. 'By our aura, our voice, our gestures. Toto will doubtless rejoice at your return.'

He uttered a few more platitudes, asked a question or two and let his mind drift. One needn't actually listen, thank God.

41

One need merely play the part. The occasional 'hmmmm' accompanied by the steepling of fingers or a solemn 'What do *you* think it means?' usually sufficed. And keep in mind – he consoled himself – these fifty minutes too shall pass.

By now, his patient had diverted to other 'problems,' something to do with her interior decorator. As she gestured, her miniskirt hitched up. 'You're fifty-six,' Peter wanted to shout. 'Act your age.'

Suddenly, the emptiness of his life swept over him. Four years. Four years of listening to the vacuous self-obsessed mouthings of shallow women and strutting men. Four years of listening to the long collective whine of the rich and spoiled. Psychiatrist? No. Wet-nurse was more like it. For this he had taken a first at Cambridge? Interned at Bart's? What a farce!

But Peter had done his duty, keeping his mouth shut and his manner professional. He needed the pay-check. It arrived once a month in solid Swiss francs to be deposited in his account at Barclays.

His father had taught him to scorn money and despise the rich. 'Any fool can make a fortune if that's all he wants of life,' he counseled his son. 'But only a man of taste can spend it properly.' Roger Mainwaring was that man.

A delightful fellow, charming and cultivated, Peter's father enjoyed a reputation as a linguist, sportsman and maker of epigrams. He was a third-rate painter and a first-class bon vivant. He died when Peter was in Cambridge, leaving his only son a legacy of good bones, a gift for languages, and a stack of debt.

Peter's decision to study medicine was pragmatic. As a boy, he had fancied himself a writer, living in a garret, turning out exquisite prose. Like his father, he was cursed with a romantic streak.

His mother blanched at the idea. 'That's all we need!' she said, rolling her eyes heavenward. 'Another artist in the family. And who will pay the butcher, may I ask?'

She was a small forceful woman, a Viennese Jew with a

refugee's sense of survival. She adored her husband without quite approving of him, and trembled at the notion that their son might follow his example. Peter must make something of himself, she urged, for his parents' sake as well as his own. Who else would support them in their dotage?

It was ordained that Peter become a doctor. At the time, it seemed a wise decision. He was bright, diligent, able to assimilate mountains of data and pass the course work with ease. He was not, however, deft with his hands.

'Go into psychiatry,' his tutor advised, watching Peter dismember a cadaver. 'You're good at dealing with people.'

'In other words, I'm a menace with a scalpel.'

'We must play from our strengths,' the doctor replied. There followed an inspirational talk about the challenge of healing psyches, bringing inner peace, binding up unseen wounds. 'And of course it's a lucrative field.'

Peter's mother was delighted. 'My son the psychiatrist' sounded even more distinguished than 'my son the doctor.'

'You know, darling, Sigmund Freud was a dear friend of your uncle Max's. And I believe your aunt Tilli was related to Adler. It runs in the blood. After all, you are half Viennese.'

Shortly after qualifying, Peter was offered the post at Marival, largely on the basis of good looks and linguistic skills. Everyone said he would be a fool to turn it down. The money was splendid for a newly minted doctor and he would be dealing with the class of people who were the core of a prosperous practice.

'Lucky bastard!' his flatmate congratulated him. 'All those oversexed birds stretched out on the couch, looking for enlightenment. And you get paid for it, to boot.'

'Dispensing inner peace.' Peter laughed.

In the event, he proved to be both conscientious and perceptive, though it struck him that he did little more than exercise common sense. At Marival there was no probing of psyches; the situation didn't call for it, his patients being mostly short term. Peter's duty was to listen and to soothe, not to inaugurate life changes.

To suggest that an aging dowager might be better served by a healthy diet than a 'tummy tuck,' to hint that a fading rock star's problems stemmed not from a receding hairline but from cocaine: such intimations ran counter to the spirit of Marival, which ordained that 'guests' leave satisfied. Peter soon realized that he had been hired as a kind of luxurious accoutrement, like the pastry chef from Fouquet's or the Roman hairdresser. The rich expected certain services wherever they went, and Marival was – first and last – a business enterprise.

Peter kept his opinions to himself. He had debts to pay, a mother to support, and at least he was following the primary tenet of the Hippocratic Oath: First, do no harm.

Then Kimberly West arrived at Marival.

Peter was horrified. He stormed into Frankl's office, shaking with rage. 'I can't believe you're going ahead with this! To operate on a healthy, attractive fourteen-year-old simply because she has a crazy mother! It's a breach of every medical ethic.'

'Now now,' Frankl crooned. 'If we didn't do it here, the mother would take the girl to somebody else. Someone a good deal less skillful, I warrant, so you might argue that I'm sparing the child unnecessary risk. Besides, I too have an ethical duty – to my stockholders. You do your job, Peter. I'll do mine.'

Peter hesitated. Calculated. Tried to balance the clinic's need for a multi-lingual shrink against his own need for a monthly wage. Nor could he deny the force of Frankl's logic. That dreadful West woman would, with no difficulty, find another surgeon to work her will.

He didn't quit. Instead, he consoled himself with the notion that there were occasional patients who might benefit from his guidance.

And one in particular.

*

As a young doctor should, Peter kept abreast of developments. Periodically, he attended conventions and seminars, listened to papers full of jargon. More often than not, he came away dissatisfied like a diner at a Barmecidal feast. Recently, he had begun to doubt the basic tenets of his profession – if it truly was a profession. Psychiatry, it struck him, was neither art nor science. The truly mad were often beyond help. The merely neurotic resisted anything that smacked of change. And he himself was drowning in trivia.

'. . . should do the bed in mauve,' the countess droned on. 'My late husband hated mauve. Is that significant?'

'What do *you* think?' Peter murmured, eyelids at half mast.

The time had come to leave Marival. His father's debts had been discharged. His mother had remarried. The sensible move would be to set up a private practice in London or New York. He had excellent contacts.

But would it be more of the same? Year after year buried in the minutiae of rich women's lives? Peter had his own mental health to worry about. He should have left long ago, in fact. Would have, if not for —

Peter checked his watch, counting the minutes. Soon she would be here. Their last meeting. This afternoon at five.

Lady X, those American girls had called her, investing her with continental glamour, though she was anything but a member of the aristocracy. The staff referred to her as Missy. Dr Frankl now called her 'my masterpiece.' Only half a dozen people knew her name.

She had arrived in an ambulance three years earlier, with nothing but a passport and a suitcase.

The next day, René Frankl summoned Peter for a conference.

'An interesting problem,' Frankl said, 'and one that will be as much yours as mine. American. Female. Twenty-one years of age. Fundamentally in fine physical shape – excellent heart and lungs – though I have been unable to obtain a medical history. However, as I say, a sturdy specimen, otherwise I would hold out no hope. So – the situation is this. Our young lady has been the victim of some terrible violence, a bestial attack. An animal, you might think to look at the wounds, but that would be a slander on wolves and jackals. They are incapable of such malice. No, my friend, a man. A madman with a knife. Perhaps a tire iron too, or a bicycle chain. A rich and powerful madman, you may be sure, for I saw no mention of the crime in the papers. The financial arrangements are being handled by a lawyer in Paris, a Maître Gustave Viarnet. He naturally declines to name his client. However, as M. Viarnet led me to understand, such information would be irrelevant. His client has diplomatic immunity and can't be prosecuted. I tell you, Peter, I haven't seen evidence of such savagery since my Ravensbrueck Rabbits.'

He shook his head, then pulled out a manila envelope.

'Of the circumstances, we know almost nothing. Apparently, the assault took place in the château country of the Loire, for she was transferred here from a cottage hospital near Chambord. Not much they could do for her there, beyond first aid. These were taken this morning.'

Dr Frankl spread a set of Polaroid photos on the desktop. Peter winced and looked away.

'As you see, Peter, there is almost no face left. The flesh has been sliced away. The cheekbones are smashed. Except for the passport photo – and you know what poor likenesses they always are – it is impossible to say what she looked like. So – we will have to start from scratch, building something out of nothing.' A ghost of a smile played about Frankl's lips.

'She is, you could say, a *tabula rasa*. A clean slate upon which one might write anything. This is an enormous challenge, Peter. Perhaps the greatest of my career. I will have to create everything: bone structure, skin, facial features. It could take years. By

46

some miracle, the eyes were spared, so there is a ray of hope – though I don't want her looking in the mirror for a very long time. Yes, yes, we'll have to keep her under wraps as much as possible.'

'Can she speak?' Peter asked. 'Or is she still in shock?'

Frankl sighed. 'Ah! There we have a problem. He cut her throat, our rabid gentleman, and may have severed her vocal cords. I've scheduled preliminary surgery for tomorrow to see if the larynx can be rebuilt. Even so, it may be months before she heals enough to speak. The worst of her suffering, I'm afraid, lies ahead, and that's where you come in. Your duty will be to instill in her the will to live.'

'The will to live? But how? What function can therapy serve if she can't speak, can't express her feelings . . . ?'

'How you do it is your business, not mine,' Frankl said. 'Find a way. Experiment. I don't care how. But if I am to succeed, then you must too.'

The next day, Peter was waiting when she was wheeled out of the operating theatre, tubes running in and out of every orifice. He took her hand and sat by her side in the recovery room until she awoke.

'Hello,' he said to the white mask of a face. 'My name is Peter Mainwaring. I'm here to help you.'

The blue eyes widened in fright.

'It's all right,' he said softly. 'I'm your friend and I promise not to leave you. Now rest.'

He sat with her until she fell asleep again, her hand in his. And still he sat there, profoundly moved.

As a psychiatrist, he had been trained to keep a physical and emotional distance from his patients. But from the moment he took her hand, he tossed the rules out the window. At this juncture, the poor creature was less in need of psychiatric treatment than of human contact. Of warmth and sympathy.

Did she know where she was? Probably not. How terrifying this must be: the pain, the strangeness of the surroundings, the staff jabbering away in French and German.

Did she have family? he wondered. Friends to be sent for?

Peter wanted to help, but the absence of data frustrated him. He had no details, no background. In this clinic filled with false Smiths and Jones and Brauns, the name on her passport was Johnson. All he could glean from the document was that she had been born in Chicago. How many Johnsons there were in Chicago, Peter wouldn't begin to guess.

The next day when she awoke, more fully alert, Peter was ready with a block of paper and a felt-tipped pen. 'I know you can't speak now, so don't even try. But if there's someone you want us to notify—'

Her response was a violent fit of trembling. The gaping wound that was her mouth forced itself into an 'O': *No!*

Peter didn't press the issue. 'No matter. I'll be here in their stead.'

Soon after, when she was well enough to sit up, Peter was back with paper and pen.

'Is there anything you want?' he asked.

For a long time she sat motionless, staring at the blank sheet, then formed the letters in a shaky hand.

I WANT TO DIE.

'Not on your life,' Peter said briskly. 'I won't permit it. In the first place, we're going to make you well, Dr Frankl and I. And in the second, I need your company. You see, I hardly ever get a chance to speak English.'

After that, however, he phrased his questions more cautiously.

'Can I get you anything? Books? Records? Would Bob Dylan cheer you up? Jefferson Airplane? Sinatra? Do you like jazz? There's a great new Ella Fitzgerald—'

The blue eyes filled with tears. He knew he had scored.

48

That afternoon he made a trip to Lausanne and came back with a dozen albums. She liked the female vocalists best – Ella, Sarah Vaughan, Nina Simone – and would listen to them late into the night in her room. Sometimes Peter stood outside the door, trying to read her mood from the music.

Each afternoon at five, he saw her for an hour, except on those occasions – thirty-seven in all – when she underwent surgery. Her physical endurance astonished him, yet her body language spoke of endless torment. Often, she would claw at the bedclothes, thrashing like a wounded animal. I WANT TO DIE, her whole being cried out. I WANT TO DIE.

During the early months, while her vocal cords were healing, Peter read to her: short stories, poetry, humor, Hercule Poirot mysteries in which he acted out all the parts.

Mostly, he sat and chatted, rambling on in seemingly artless monologues that touched upon a number of matters. But there was method to his meanderings. Peter was on a fishing expedition, trawling for those topics that would elicit a nibble of interest.

'I read in the *Herald Trib* that your Chicago Cubs are having quite a season.' Thus Peter might bait his hook. If the response was right – eyes widened, head alert – he would begin reeling her in, always taking care to leave slack in the line. 'They play the Giants today. A very important match, it appears. I'll let you know tomorrow how it comes out . . .'

His strategy was to pique her curiosity, then leave her in suspense until the next session. If he could keep her interest alive for another twenty-four hours, that day's battle could be counted as won. Baseball or fashion or the escalating war in Vietnam: whatever linked her to a life beyond Marival provided another slender reason for hope.

The topic that intrigued her most, he soon discovered, was Peter himself. How could she not be curious about him? He was her sole connection to the outside world. Shamelessly, Peter used this curiosity to advantage, regaling her with anecdotes about his father's eccentricities, tales of his boyhood in England, of theatricals at Cambridge, the year he spent in the National Service.

'I hope I'm not boring you,' he would say.

NO, NO! The eyelids fluttered wildly.

'Did I tell you about the time I was sent down from Winchester? Kicked out, I think you Yanks call it. I was fourteen and madly in love with the waitress at the Copper Kettle. She, as it happened – oh, damn! Six o'clock already. I'm afraid that particular tale will have to wait till tomorrow.'

Such personal revelations went far beyond what was countenanced by his professional code, but Peter didn't care. What worked, worked. His only concern was keeping hope alive.

'Dr Frankl is delighted with the results,' he announced after her fourth round of surgery. 'A speech therapist will be coming in daily to teach you how to use your voice again.'

Did he imagine a smile about the eyes? Was she pleased, despite the constant pain? Peter thought so. A few weeks later, she tried to drown herself.

That incident was two years and many operations ago.

In the interim, she had learned to confide in Peter who, she claimed, knew more about her than she knew about herself. She astonished him with the quality and range of her memory. She was able to recall the most trivial incident – what people said, what they wore; she could summon up places, dates, the pictures on the wall – in exacting detail. By all rights she should have made a superb witness.

Yet concerning the central tragedy of her life, her mind was a blank. She suffered from traumatic amnesia, rendering the events of that day (or more likely that night) as much an enigma to her as to her doctors.

'I don't remember anything, Peter. Not the town, not the weather, what I was doing there.'

She had buried the knowledge so deeply that nothing could

jar it loose – not even hypnosis. Thus, her assailant's identity was likely to remain a mystery forever.

The idea of 'that animal' roaming loose in society, perhaps hunting new prey, haunted Peter, but his first concern was his patient's welfare and, on balance, it was as well she couldn't remember. Her amnesia might have saved her sanity.

Despite his urging, she never socialized with other patients, preferring to sit by the lake and read, or throw breadcrusts to the swans.

'I left high school at sixteen,' she told Peter. 'Just a working-class girl. I'm not used to hanging out with duchesses and millionaires.'

'Fancy yourself too good for them, eh?' Peter teased.

In fact, she possessed a bright inquiring mind and it pleased Peter to recommend books and new music, or to take her on an outing, heavily veiled, to nearby churches and museums. To be, in short, a college of one.

One day for fun, he took her to the little casino at Divonne-les-Bains, where she tried her luck at the tables with petty cash. She was quick to figure the odds. 'Roulette,' she announced, 'is a sucker's game. But I do like that *vingt-et-un*. We call it blackjack where I come from. But *vingt-et-un* sounds classier.'

Peter laughed. 'Classy' was such an American word. Yet it struck him this high-school leaver was herself on the way to becoming a very 'classy' young lady. And as her scars began to heal, an attractive one as well.

'And this is my masterpiece,' René Frankl exulted.

On the day the final bandages were to be removed, the entire clinical staff had assembled to witness the miracle.

She sat in a swivel chair beneath arc lights.

'*Regardez!*' Dr Frankl turned the head this way and that. *Look! Look at the sub-ocular cavities . . . the re-alignment of the maxillary bone . . .* Item by item, he summarized the procedures, tapping relevant points on his subject's face with his index finger, as though dealing with a plaster model. Peter winced. Tact had never been Dr Frankl's forte. At last, the inventory was complete. There was a round of applause.

'Well, Missy' – Frankl switched into a heavily accented English – 'congratulations. Our work is complete.'

And so would Peter's be, this afternoon at five.

She came to his office on the stroke of the hour, wearing a blue silk-jersey shift that matched her eyes and made the most of the lithe body. She had been to the beauty salon an hour earlier. The chestnut hair was swept back in a smart Italian cut, light and gay as the wings of a bird.

Peter drank in the details with approval: the deft gray eye shadow, luscious red lips, the fingernails no longer bitten to the quick, but buffed and polished.

Self-consciously, she twirled and gave a nervous laugh.

'My going-away outfit,' she said. 'A gift from Dr Frankl. He's throwing me out tomorrow morning.'

'You look wonderful!' Peter said truthfully. 'And you'll never be readier than you are now. Just think! In twenty-four hours, you'll be back in the States. Home.'

'Sometimes I think *this* is my home, Peter. It's been so long—' Her voice trembled. 'Words can never tell you what I owe, what I feel. When I came here I was lost. Helpless. Filled with despair.' The beautiful eyes glistened with tears.

Peter sensed what was coming and tried to divert the flow.

'Yes. Dr Frankl has done a superb job.'

'Frankl!' She shook her head impatiently. 'He gave me a face. Nothing more. But you, Peter. You gave me a life. I survived it all – the pain, the shame, the loneliness – only for you. You were my reason to live. My whole world. I'll stay here forever if you let me. I'll go with you wherever you want. I love you, Peter. Desperately. Hopelessly. I know—' She choked back a sob. 'I

52

know it can never be, but that doesn't change what's in my heart. I will love you till the day I die.'

Peter felt heartsick. They had been through this before.

'That's not love, my friend,' he said. 'It's transference. It happens frequently between patients and psychiatrists, and it's healthy. A sign of healing. But now you're healed, both body and mind. It's time for you to get away from here and put the past behind you. Go make a life for yourself, and real love will come. One day you'll meet someone, Marga—'

'Don't call me by that name!' she burst out. 'That woman is dead, Peter. She died three years ago in a village in France. I can never revert to what I was before. As you say, I must go forward and build a new life. Well, you know me, Peter. I'm a survivor. I've survived pain beyond imagining, and I'll survive without your returning my love. I ask only one last favor. Promise me that if anyone ever asks for me by name, the name of the girl I was once – anyone!' she insisted. 'Whether people claiming to be friends or detectives or that lawyer who sent me here, say that she died under surgery. Which is true. My old self is gone forever. I look in the mirror and a stranger stares back. My best friend wouldn't know me. Why should she? I am someone else. Now do you promise?'

Peter promised, but he shook his head. 'You can't change what's inside you . . . your character, your feelings—'

'Oh, but I can! I shall! Step by step. I'm going to create another life for myself as surely as Dr Frankl created another face. I've given this a great deal of thought, Peter. You look surprised, but you see, there are some feelings I didn't share, even with you. When I leave I shall assume a new identity. That way, he can never seek me out.' She touched her hand to her throat. 'That beast! I don't know his name, but he knows mine. Or did. Well, no more! I shall build a fortress around me, a wall of money and power, so that he can never touch me. Neither he nor anyone. I swear, no man will ever hurt me again.'

Though disturbed by her vehemence, Peter understood. He nodded. 'There was a time when I was worried that you might try to hunt him down. But you won't, will you?'

Slowly, she shook her head. 'I used to brood about it night and day. Revenge! God, how I wanted revenge. But it's pointless. How do you hunt down a ghost? A question mark? No no, my darling. I shan't waste any more of my life.' As she spoke, she clenched her fists till the knuckles showed white. 'Yet if I ever come across him, by fate, by accident, I will recognize him. Of that I'm sure. My blood will scream out. My pain will shriek – *This is the man! Monster! Assassin!* And I will kill him. No power on earth could stop me.'

The ugly words hung like a pall between them.

'So you see why I don't want to be found,' she said softly. 'Not even by you. Past is past. Future, future.'

He held out his hand for a last goodbye. She clasped it tight for a few seconds, then walked out without looking back.

Stepping in the taxi that would take her to the airport, she paused and turned for a farewell glance.

For three years she had lived in this enchanted château. Marival had been her haven, her world, an island sheltering her from the storms beyond.

She had chosen a name. Her first name from Shakespeare. Her second, from the circumstances of her life.

Miranda Vee.

Miranda – after the island heroine of *The Tempest*.

Vee – for Victim.

The following week, Peter Mainwaring gave his notice. Professional burnout, he explained.

BOSTON

On an October afternoon in her second year at law school, something happened to disturb the tenor of Alix Bryden's life.

She had been to court observing trial procedures, then stepped out into Government Square to find herself in the midst of an anti-war rally.

A crude platform had been run up at the foot of the steps. Atop it, a muscular young man announced that his name was Sam Houston Matthews and that Government Square was about to become 'the battleground of the Second American Revolution!'

Despite the autumn chill, he was dressed in a cotton work shirt and jeans, as if to say 'I generate my own heat.'

Normally, Alix would have walked away, such demonstrations being a commonplace, but the drama of the setting intrigued her. By staging his protest on the courthouse steps, the fellow was thumbing his nose at the entire establishment.

He had a gift of polemic that top trial lawyers might envy, and a rich baritone voice that was, by turns, incisive, scathing, seductive, inspirational.

'Stop the war in Vietnam,' he exhorted, 'and bring it back where it belongs. On the streets. In the courts. In our hearts.'

Alix moved in closer, repelled and attracted, for he was saying what she never dared admit to herself: that the war was cruel and senseless. For the daughter of Lucius Bryden, such thoughts were heresy, notions best left unexamined.

Yet the speaker was compelling. In quick order, he stripped the skin off the corpus of American policy, held it up to ridicule, then flung it into the gutter in bleeding hunks. By the time his exposition was finished, Alix, along with others in the crowd, was eating out of his hand. Or, more literally, out of his clenched fist.

Suddenly he stopped, smiled, a glorious embracing smile, then began the rhythmic chant. 'Hell, no! We won't go!'

Over and over. *Hell, no! We won't go!* He flung his arms wide in an in-gathering gesture as other voices joined his own.

Half-hypnotized, Alix also mouthed the words.

'Let 'em hear you talking!' He laughed, cocking his head in the direction of the courthouse. *'Hell, no! We won't go.'*

Arms raised, he began a measured crescendo, drawing volume from the crowd like a Leonard Bernstein of the soap box until every stone in the square reverberated with the chant. Later, Alix was to learn that this skill was legitimately come by. But at the moment, yelling herself hoarse, she couldn't separate the man from the message. She was enthralled.

Sam Matthews radiated sexuality. His body seemed to reject the constraints of clothing. The powerful thighs, muscled calves, his very manhood – all strained against the skin-tight Levis. The clenched fist might have been sculpted by Rodin.

From her dreams, Alix knew that body. It had invaded her own times without number. Had ravished her in a hundred ways. Only now the body had a face. She inched to the front of the crowd. Her flesh sang.

Close to, the sense of handsomeness faded. No movie star, her hero. The face was rough-hewn with broad cheekbones, the skin pitted and coarse. A high forehead was half hidden beneath a thatch of black hair. (The latter, he would claim, was the legacy of his Choctaw grandmother, but Alix never knew if this was true, for Sam was a compulsive fantasist, and the 'Indian blood' might have been invented to fend off hecklers. When taunted that if he didn't like America he should go back where he came from, Sam could retort: 'I'm a native American, buddy. And you're treading on my turf.')

But that knowledge lay in the future and on this bright fall afternoon, Alix regarded him with uncritical awe.

He was standing, legs apart, watching the forces he had unleashed. Then, at the precise moment when voices would begin to flag and spirits falter, he raised his arms to the sky.

'You're great!' he shouted. 'Wonderful! But I want more from you than slogans.' He leaned forward, lowered his voice. 'Will one of you guys do me a favor, bring me a trash bin? Just grab one off the sidewalk.'

A couple of undergraduate types obliged him, dragging back a wire bin overflowing with Coke cans and newspapers.

'Great!' Sam Matthews said. 'Courtesy of the City of Boston. Thank you, Mayor White.' A few people tittered. He stooped down and ruffled the trash. 'Here it is, friends. Ready to burn. Genuine garbage. All it needs is a bit of kindling. Does everyone here know what an auto-da-fé is? In Spain, it was the test of faith, the burning away of iniquities.' He reached into his shirt pocket and pulled out a chit of paper.

'This is my draft card. It is an obscenity, an offense against everything this country once stood for.' From another pocket, he produced an orange Cricket lighter. 'And this, my friends, is the torch of freedom. Now – what I want from every man here today is more kindling for this fire. Give me your draft cards. Now is the hour, brothers. This is the day. Seize it, and set the world on fire. Let it rise and spread until they feel the heat in the White House. This is your moment of decision – when real men step forward. What's that? Do I hear someone mumbling something about a criminal act? No way. Just say to yourself – the only criminal act is cowardice.'

There was a moment's shocked silence. The word 'criminal' hit the crowd like a shower of ice water. This was, indeed, a moment of decision – when each young man present had to ask himself if he had the guts, the will to pay the price.

Draft-card burning was a federal offense. Few were unaware of the consequences. At worst: arrest, trial, a ten-thousand-dollar fine and five years in jail.

A hush fell. Suddenly, the fun had turned scary.

To underline the gravity of the situation, two dozen of Boston's finest were lined up on the pavement, fingering their billies. And should a law-breaker be lucky enough to avoid arrest, he couldn't escape observation. Common sense dictated that FBI plants also mingled in the crowd, making notes, taking names. It was a scenario to intimidate the stoutest heart.

Alix, still cresting on the tide of oratory, was the first to break the silence.

'I wish!' – the cry sprang from her throat – 'I wish I were a man with a draft card to burn. I'd set an example.'

A few feet away, Sam Matthews roared his approval.

'At least there's one person here who's got balls.' He bent down and extended his arm to pull her up on the dais. Alix tugged at her skirt. 'Come on, babe. Come up here and let everybody see what a real gutsy dame looks like.'

Before Alix could protest, she was hauled on to the platform with a flash of leg. She didn't care. She was intoxicated, drunk with the prospect of action. For once in her life, she was inhabiting center stage, not sitting it out in the library shadows. And she was ecstatic at the thought of pleasing *him* – this ugly-handsome lion with the white teeth and vibrant voice.

Instinctively, she found her style.

'As I said' – she raised her voice – 'we mere women don't have draft cards, but we have other assets to dispose of. Maybe some of you remember the story of Lysistrata. On the eve of war, the Greek women told their men, put down your arms and we will welcome you in ours. In other words, make love, not war. They were real women. Are we any less? We too have our hearts, our affections, our bodies. And we real women only sleep with real men. So to all you girls out there, I say – let's put it on the line with every guy we know. If you don't stoke this fire' – she pointed to the trash bin – 'we don't stoke yours.'

A wave of laughter rippled through the crowd. Sam Matthews flung his arm about her shoulder in a comradely hug.

'You hear that?' he said, beaming. 'All you gals out there?

Take a cue from our . . . our own Lysistrata. What's your name, by the way? Introduce yourself to our friends here.'

'I'm Alix Br—' she started to blurt out, then froze. In that second, time stopped dead. The enormity of who she was and what she was doing crashed down on her.

Alix Bryden? To identify herself in this milieu would be insane. Bryden, of Bryden Electronics?

The name that once opened doors, won respect, that had been her sole social asset, was now indisputably linked with Vietnam. Lucius Bryden was not merely a hawk: he was a major Pentagon supplier. For him, the conflict was a boon.

With each escalation of hostilities, BEI stock had climbed in lockstep. With each air-strike it soared. Bryden programs could be found in every B-52 bomber, every nerve center from the War Room in Washington to the loneliest outpost in Big Muddy. Only a month ago, *Ramparts Magazine* had branded Lucius Bryden a war criminal. He travelled in bullet-proof cars.

Alix's personal feelings were not the issue here. The man was her father. Her flesh and blood.

She pictured the headline in the *Boston Globe*: BRYDEN DAUGHTER ARRESTED IN ANTI-WAR PROTEST. Her hand flew to her face. Yet it was not the prospect of arrest that paralyzed her; it was dread of her father's wrath.

Then her inner clock resumed ticking. Alix was aware that Sam Matthews was studying her with puzzled eyes. What must he be thinking? That for all her fine words, she was a coward? A hypocrite? Alix wet her lips.

'Alix Brown,' she said, in a soft clear voice.

No sooner had the name been uttered than she felt a shock of recognition. *Brown. Smith. Jones.* A no-name. Ironic that she had chosen to hide behind a pseudonym so common in Marival. Sam Matthews, however, seemed satisfied.

'Well, Alix Brown.' He smiled and handed her his orange Cricket. 'How about lighting our fires?'

Alix stepped down, ignited the bonfire to a round of

applause, then, as others mobbed the platform, drifted back into the crowd to watch from the sidelines.

As for Sam Matthews, he was surrounded by admirers, mostly female. When the fire burned out, he chose the two prettiest girls, tucked one under each arm, and headed into the subway.

And that, Alix Bryden thought, was that. She took a cab back to Cambridge, secure in the belief that their paths would not cross again.

Only later, settled in her kitchen brewing tea, did she realize she had walked off with his Cricket. It was a cheap lighter, the kind that sold two for a dollar. She placed it on the table, poured her tea, then contemplated her new acquisition. Gaudy orange plastic and Limoges rosebud china: the contrast spoke volumes.

Alix felt uneasy.

She had always given herself high marks for honesty, yet today she had lied and equivocated, too spineless to speak the truth. The memory shamed her. Was she destined to spend her life in Lucius Bryden's shadow? Under Lucius Bryden's thumb?

She finished her tea, cleared away, then – without quite knowing why – hid the lighter in the bottom of her lingerie drawer.

Though it had not required the oratory of a sexy young man to alert Alix to the Vietnam agony, she had never before taken an overt stand – on the war or any political issue. She was accustomed to living in the shadows.

As a child, she had known only two realities: her disfigured face and her father's loathing. In her mind they were linked. They governed every aspect of her life. Why make noise? Why rail against fate?

Even after Marival, though outwardly Alix joined the ranks of the normal, she bore inner scars. She remained shy and insecure. The difference was, she cherished high hopes.

Dr Mainwaring had warned her against setting fanciful goals.

'Don't expect miracles,' he cautioned. 'At least not right away. Life is full of pitfalls and disappointments, even for the most favored people.'

But Alix, at eighteen, knew better. How could happiness elude her now? Or popularity? Or love? She had earned them, paid for them with eighteen years of misery. She could almost believe that every handsome young man in America was going to be waiting for her breathlessly, hat off and flowers in hand, when she left the plane at Logan Airport.

In fact, only her step-mother had been waiting.

'Don't you look wonderful!' Dorrie was genuinely delighted. Not 'beautiful,' mind you. Or 'gorgeous.' But wonderful was good enough. 'Your father couldn't come, darling. He's in Washington, being tycoonish. But I know he'll be as thrilled as I am. He promised to be home in time for dinner.'

Whether Lucius was thrilled or not, Alix couldn't say. Effusiveness was not his style. However, he seemed content.

'Yes, much better,' he acknowledged, then his tone soured. 'Now, I suppose, you'll be out every night, gallivanting around Boston, riding in cars with boys—'

'Oh, Daddy!' Alix flushed. He had zeroed in on her fondest expectations.

'And once you're back in college, I don't imagine you'll bother to come home on weekends.' For a moment Alix wondered if he preferred her the old way: isolated, hidden from view. But she dismissed the notion as absurd.

'Of course I'll come home. Every weekend. I promise.'

'And do you still remember how to play chess?'

'I haven't played in a month, but sure—'

'Very good. Friday night at eight.'

'Now, Lucius,' Dorrie said with a smile, 'Alix will have better things to do. I thought we'd go to the country club Friday, have fun. In fact, I had this terrific idea the moment you stepped off the plane, Alix. A brainstorm, really. I think you should come out next June.'

'Come out?' Alix's hand darted to her face. *Come out from under a rock?*

'Come out?' Lucius glared.

'What's the matter with you two?' Dorrie furrowed her brow. 'Don't you understand plain English? I'm not talking about indecent exposure, Lucius. I mean, come out in the Junior Cotillion. There's no reason Alix shouldn't make her debut. I did in my day. So did Persis. Didn't you meet her at a debutante ball? Besides, it'll be fun. Shopping for clothes ... all the luncheons and parties and dances. We'll throw our own bash, of course, a proper ball. But if we're going to book Peter Duchin's orchestra, there's not a minute to spare.'

'I can't possibly!' Alix's head reeled.

'I know what you're thinking,' Dorrie chirped. 'That you'll be nineteen next June and all the other gals will be eighteen, but I think the Junior League will grant some kind of dispensation. And it's the best place to meet eligible men.'

'Dorrie!' Lucius thundered. 'That's enough of this foolishness. I will not permit my daughter to be turned into a freak show or a curiosity piece. People will want to know where she's been all these years. I'll look like an ogre. No debut. No parties. And that's final.'

Alix didn't know whether to be relieved or furious.

She did attend dances that summer at the country club and, doubtless through Dorrie's intervention, got squired about the floor a few times. But she never chucked the sense of being a displaced person. Nothing in life had prepared her for the social whirl.

With the exception of her half brothers (and they were too young to matter), she had never carried on a normal conversation with a boy. Flirting, teasing, the common currency of dates and college dances: that lexicon was as alien as ancient Aramaic. She had no small talk.

'You've got great legs—' one young man told her as she

lolled beside the pool at the club. Alix didn't know what to do with the compliment. Thank him? Pretend she hadn't heard? Then he finished his thought. 'But do you have to be so damn serious all the time?' Alix, who had taught herself to smile by painful fractions, was crushed.

She returned to Wellesley that fall, determined to lose her virginity. Start with sex, she believed, and love will follow. Then engagement, marriage, all the rest.

The mechanics proved easy enough, although the earth never 'moved,' and after several desultory affairs, Alix lowered her expectations. Passion, romance, true and timeless love – such emotions were less likely to be found between the bedsheets than between the covers of a novel.

But if grand passion was hard to find, popularity seemed even harder to come by. She was gawky with boys. When the phone rang in the dorm (almost never for her), Alix took refuge in a self-deprecating humor. 'Castle Dracula,' she would announce. Or 'Lonely Hearts Club' or 'Vice Squad. May I help you?'

After Wellesley, she took an apartment in one of the leafier streets of Cambridge, a short walk from Harvard Law. It was all she could do to keep Dorrie from furnishing the place to the hilt.

'I don't want to live like a rich man's daughter,' Alix griped, while Dorrie unpacked crates of luxurious housewares.

'But you are, darling,' Dorrie said, opening a carton of Porthault linens. 'So don't go pretending you're just another indigent law student. You're a Bryden, lambchop, which means you have a certain station in life to maintain – oh! aren't these lovely! – and I know your father doesn't want you sleeping in hair shirts.'

Alix sighed and succumbed. She had wanted this apartment to be hers, not theirs.

'Well, I draw the line at sterling flat-ware.'

'Just a few pieces, for when you entertain. And some decent

china. Is this neighborhood safe, by the way? Your father worries.'

'Please, Dorrie. It's a doorman building. What's Daddy afraid of – that some guy is gonna break in and rape me? Hell!' she snorted. 'I can't even get a date for Saturday night.'

Yet despite the tart humor, she continued to yearn for romantic love as keenly as that day when she had stood in the belvedere at Marival.

Alix had never thought of herself as rich; the word 'heiress' made her flinch. In what mattered most – parental love, affection, a sense of self-worth – she was impoverished.

In fact, the Brydens never flaunted their wealth. Her father kept a low profile, especially now. Power was the spur that goaded Lucius Bryden, not fame, and certainly not luxury, for his tastes were simple. As for Dorrie, although a world-class shopper with a priceless collection of French porcelain, ultimately she subscribed to the Boston doctrine that one ought to live off the interest of one's interest. Capital was to be handed down to children intact.

Alix herself never gave any thought to the material prospects in store until her twenty-first birthday. On that occasion, Lucius gave his daughter her mother's pearls.

Alix felt honored. She had to fight back tears.

'They're quite valuable,' he said. 'Be sure to keep them insured to market value.'

She had them appraised at ninety-five thousand dollars, which she supposed was a good deal of money. But to her, their real worth was sentimental.

She wore them everywhere with everything: to school, to football games, to study sessions, when she went jogging along the embankment.

'Those aren't real, are they?' a classmate asked one evening as they tossed back beers in Patsy's Bar and Grill.

'Of course not, Jenny.'

'I didn't think so.'

Alix took them off only to sleep.

Her step-mother's gift was at once flashier and more fun: a racy black E-type Jaguar. 'So you won't forget to come home on weekends.'

Alix loved the car. It was fast, responsive. When she overdosed on work, her favorite release was to take the sleek black beast out on the highway and drive full throttle up to Newburyport for a cup of coffee, then turn around and speed back. At the wheel, she felt carefree, confident.

But after the rally in Government Square, she examined the Jag in a harsher light. It was a shameless toy for a student. It reeked of money and privilege. *Why, the licence plate might as well read RICH. Amend that to STINKING RICH.* Alix felt a stab of shame. From that day on, she let it sit in the garage, except for the weekly pilgrimage to Pride's Crossing.

For the first time in her life, Alix felt the burden of her position. Like it or not, she was rich in a world racked by poverty. Safe and protected in a world torn by war . . .

For years, Alix had shut out all criticism of the status quo, and her friends were too tactful to bring such matters up. The Vietnamese war in particular was a sensitive topic. For how could it be evil when it had treated the Brydens so well?

But that was before Sam Matthews's rhetoric unlocked her mind. Yes! – Alix could at last admit it. She hated the war. She hated all war. Hated poverty and death and destruction. Hated burned flesh and broken bodies, as she had once hated her own disfigured face.

'Hey, hey, LBJ, how many kids did you kill today?' the chant went. And how many kids had her father killed with the Bryden Electronic Bomb-sight? Hundreds? Thousands?

No matter how Lucius Bryden saw his role, Alix knew how it would look to people like Sam Matthews.

Several times that fall, she tried to discuss Vietnam with Lucius, in hopes that he would provide a rationale – something more than knee-jerk patriotism and the opportunity to make big bucks. He refused to take up the challenge.

'Stick to your law books, Alix. I should think you have enough on your plate.' Then Dorrie would jump in, all silky tact, and change the subject to 'something pleasant.'

Invariably, Alix went back to Cambridge feeling cheated. That damned Sam Matthews! He had robbed her of peace of mind.

On Thanksgiving, Alix drove to Pride's Crossing for the traditional meal. She dressed carefully for the gathering in a beige cashmere frock, elegant and unadorned except for her pearls and a small badge with hot pink lettering.

AMERICA OUT OF VIETNAM, it read.

Throughout cocktails and hors d'oeuvres, Lucius scrupulously avoided taking notice. There were a dozen people to dinner, and he was busy playing host. Nor did he comment when they were seated at table, while Bridget served the consommé. At last, with an almost audible blare of trumpets, Jeremiah, Dorrie's Jamaican chef, wheeled forth the turkey on a trolley. He posed for a moment so that all might admire, then placed the platter before Lucius. Dorrie offered a round of applause. 'A hundred ingredients went in the stuffing,' she announced to her guests. 'It's Jeremiah's specialty.'

Lucius sharpened the carving knives in a familiar ritual, and began slicing with swift sure incisions. He served his wife first, then his in-laws, his sons, the other guests, himself, then cut a plate of meat for the kitchen staff. Alix watched in amazement.

He's not going to acknowledge me, she thought. *I no longer exist.*

Finally, when the bird had been totally dismembered, Bryden turned to his daughter.

'Well, Alix,' he said. 'White meat or dark? Or perhaps you prefer communist red.'

Alix held his gaze. 'White meat, please, and no dressing.'

'I should think not!' Lucius plunged the knife deep in what remained of the breast.

'I would think you're dressed quite enough for the occasion. Overdressed, one might say.'

'Oh, Daddy,' her brother Ted intervened. 'Everybody wears badges and stuff like that at Choate.'

'This is not Choate,' Lucius said coldly. 'Nor Harvard Law nor Greenwich Village nor Hanoi. How dare you bring such propaganda into this house? With your mother's pearls, no less. Take that thing off.'

Alix felt a surge of fear. Then another of confusion. Should she stand her ground? Or get up and leave? Or remove the badge in the interests of domestic peace? But she couldn't knuckle under again! If Sam Matthews could brazen it out on the courthouse steps, then, dammit, she was entitled to a voice at the dinner table.

'Your friends in Washington are always saying that America is the leader of the free world' – Alix had risen to her feet – 'so why should I be constrained from stating my beliefs? I hereby exercise my right to free speech. The pin stays. It is protected by the first amendment.'

Lucius gripped the carving knife. His eyes were shooting daggers but his voice was ice. 'The first amendment stops at my threshold. This is my home and you are eating my food and I am not going to tolerate such insubordination within these walls. Who the hell do you think you are—?' His vocal temperature rose a hundred degrees. 'Jane Fonda?'

An awful silence ensued, then Dorrie piped up, ever the peace-maker. 'Now, Lucius darling . . . and Alix too. Here is this wonderful dinner that Jeremiah worked so hard over . . . I won't have it spoiled by wrangling. You won't settle anything by arguing and Jeremiah would be righteously offended. He spent nearly two days just on the stuffing. Well, I am not going to lose the best cook I've ever had over a mere difference of opinion.

Forgive and forget, darlings, and eat your turkey before it gets cold and gelatinous. It is Thanksgiving, after all. Good lord!' she exclaimed. 'We're practically out of wine. Bridget, bring in the Nuits St Georges.'

The rest of the day passed without incident. At eight, Alix excused herself. No, she couldn't stay over as planned. She had a lot of studying to do. Sorry 'bout that.

It was a relief to get back to her flat in Cambridge and bury herself in books. She didn't emerge the rest of the weekend, working at full tilt, sending out for pizza or Chinese.

Sunday afternoon there was a knock on her door. She had just finished washing her hair. Alix furrowed her brow. Had she ordered something from the deli? Must have. Still, the doorman ought to have buzzed . . .

She wrapped a towel around her hair and went to the door. And there he stood. Big as life and twice as arrogant. Leaning against the jamb with a cat-and-mouse grin.

'Hello, Bryden,' Sam Matthews said. 'I've come for my lighter.'

MECHANICSVILLE

'What is your goal in life?' he asked.

'To work with people,' she replied.

'Hobbies?'

'Patchwork and reading to the blind.'

'If you had one wish, what would that be?'

'I wish for world peace.'

'World peace,' he grunted. *Great bod* he wrote down in his notebook, followed by three exclamation points. Bob Tillman believed in Truth in Journalism.

And indeed, Kim looked fetching in a white halter-top dress, sitting on the porch settee, ankles crossed demurely. A few feet away, her mother glowered.

Bette had been expecting a reporter with clout, not some kid fresh out of college. Not that an interview with Miss Bituminous Coal constituted earth-shaking news, not even in the *Appalachian Times*; but out of courtesy to the coal industry, if not to Kimberly West, they ought to have sent a pro. Bette was sensitive on such scores. Hard work deserved good press.

Still, it paid to be nice to the kid for you never knew where the next Ed Murrow would spring from.

'And how do you rate your chances of being voted Miss West Virginia?'

'I don't know,' Kim said modestly. She had been through this drill a dozen times; the script was word perfect. 'Naturally I'd like to win, but whoever the lucky girl is, it will be a great thrill to represent our beautiful state in the Miss America pageant—'

'And an honor . . .' Bette mouthed along with her.

'—and an honor and a privilege.'

Satisfied the interview was running on automatic pilot, Bette relaxed. 'Can I get you some iced tea, Mr Tillman?' she asked. 'Or maybe a beer? I know what you journalists are like.'

'Tea will be fine, ma'am. Thank you. Now, Miss West . . . Kim. May I call you Kim?'

'Please.'

'Well, Kim, what will you do with the scholarship money if you win?'

Bette went inside. Kim folded her hands, prayerful.

'My dream is to study acting and make a contribution to the stage.'

'Classic drama? Modern theatre?'

'I've always wanted to play Joan of Arc.'

'Joan! Great! Now what's your favorite color?' Bob Tillman

looked around. The old broad was out of earshot. He lowered his voice. 'How about having dinner with me tonight?'

Kim smiled. She had been coached in that answer too.

'That's sweet of you, but I spend the evenings with my mom. We're very close. And my favorite color is pink.'

'I know a nice steak house down by the lake. Inch-thick sirloins and a pianist who sounds like Nat King Cole. My intentions are honorable by the way – more or less.'

His blandishments were wasted. With a simultaneous smile and an air of regret, Kim made it clear that no meant no.

By the time Bette reappeared, Tillman was back on the job.

'And what is it that made you and your mother decide to settle in West Virginia?'

Kim wanted to burst out laughing. If only he knew!

What indeed – but her mother's mad logic?

Immediately upon returning from Switzerland, Bette began scouting out Florida to find the optimum launching pad for the Junior Miss America title. They spent a week in Miami ('too many Cubans,' Bette declared); another in Key West ('too many fags'); and a few days in St Petersburg ('too many old farts') before zeroing in on Daytona Beach. With a furnished room as her command center, Bette began looking for potential backers.

Ice-cream parlors, bowling alleys, soft-drink bottlers, Jaycees, Elks and Kiwanis – wherever there was a chance of sponsorship, there was Bette, beating down the door. 'Let me tell you about my gorgeous daughter—' her spiel began. After which, she improvised wildly, depending on circumstance.

Thus, to the secretary of the American Legion branch, she confided that Kim's father had been shot down over Korea.

'Oh, yeah?' said the secretary, a Korean vet himself. 'What unit was he with?'

Bette down-shifted pronto. 'I never was good at numbers,' she said.

That same day, with a kosher hot-dog manufacturer, she

switched gears. 'My Kimberly sings, dances, recites, looks like a million bucks. Jewish too. The name is really Wasserman.'

'Lady,' said the hot-dog baron. 'Take your song and dance elsewhere. Blonde beach girls are a dime a dozen here.'

It was true. Florida was turning out to be almost as awful as California. It teemed with luscious leggy blondes, all teeth and tans, girls from whose ranks Kim could scarcely be differentiated. In any case, local businessmen preferred to sponsor home-grown talent. The final blow came when Bette learned that candidates had to be bona fide residents. Kim wasn't even enrolled in a Florida school.

'Maybe we should go back to Tulsa and Uncle Ed,' Kim ventured that night, but Bette hardly heard. She had her nose buried in the Rand-McNally atlas.

'I been thinking,' she said at last. 'You know, if I wanted to be a senator, I wouldn't run for New York or California, where the competition's fierce. No sirree. I'd pick some dinky little state that didn't know which end is up. Move there, put down a few roots and reap the benefits. Now in a couple of years, you're gonna be old enough for us to do Miss America, but we have to win a state contest to qualify. So first off, we gotta pick the right state.'

For days, Bette researched the problem, debating the merits of Little Rhode Island, Empty Idaho and West Virginia. West Virginia won hands down.

'It's inland, so no beach Barbie-dolls, like you'd get in Newport. Also, no fresh-faced cow-gals from the wide open spaces. You know what they got in West Virginia, honey? Coal mines. Which means we're dealing with Slovaks, Albanians, swarthy types. You can imagine what the girls look like. Thick ankles is my bet, probably half of them have mustaches. You're guaranteed to knock 'em dead. I can hear it now.' She cocked her head to imaginary music. 'They strike up the band. The announcer grabs the mike. *And here she is* – ta da! – *Miss West Virginia.*'

In addition to the state's divine shortage of Golden Girls, West Virginia had the virtue of being economically depressed and therefore affordable. Bette rented a furnished house in Mechanicsville for next to nothing. Then she got a job at a beauty parlor and enrolled Kim in high school.

Their lives soon fell into a pattern with Kim's hours all accounted for, even during school vacation. She had a talent regimen, a health regimen and a beauty regimen. Each day ended with a sixty-minute maintenance routine. First teeth, face and nails were tended to. Then her mother brushed her hair with one hundred strokes of the Mason-Pearson, after which the long blonde locks were put up in twenty tight rollers. Then Bette applied a face mask of her own devising. Kim was usually in bed by nine thirty for the mandatory nine hours' beauty sleep. 'And no reading in the sack,' Bette ordered. 'It puts bags under your eyes.'

In the morning the routine was reversed. Up at six so Bette could devote sufficient time to teasing Kim's hair into an air-whipped bouffant, then another day began.

Despite the routines (perhaps because of them), Kim flourished. She enjoyed the pace of small-town life, the folksiness. In due course, she made a dozen 'best' girl friends at school; adopted a more-or-less Airedale (okay, a stray mutt!) with huge soulful eyes whom she named Ringo; even developed a West Virginia twang. She had a gift for mimicry.

'Naow listen to yeeew,' Bette teased. 'A regular Loretta Lynn. Bet you could make it as a Country-Western star. I can just picture you in one of those cute denim minis and a hat with a fringe. By God, honey. C & W. Could be just the ticket.'

Henceforward, Kim spent two afternoons a week learning to hum and strum country style under the tutelage of Minnie Mae Jessup, who had actually appeared on *Grand Ole Opry* – twice!

'*There's a little wooden crate on the seven twenty-eight*' – Kim sang, a catch in her voice – '*bringin' my baby back home*.' Then she thunked her guitar, and Ringo howled on cue.

'Wrings the withers of my heart,' Minnie Mae said.

The tune was Kim's big number, her 'signature.' She sang it on Talent Night at Mechanics Hall and won first prize. Then again, when she was crowned Miss Bituminous Coal. By her senior year in high school, Kim had become something of a county celebrity. And though she missed being voted *The Girl Most Likely to Succeed*, she did win a secret ballot in the boys' locker room: *The Girl We'd Most Like to Succeed With*.

To which a number of jocks muttered 'fat chance.'

For though Kim participated in much of what Mechanicsville had to offer, from Girl Scouts to the Baptist Bowling League, she never dated. 'My mom won't allow,' was her answer when asked. Not that she was asked very often, for her beauty was too potent for most teenage boys to deal with.

Bette defended her strictness by declaring that all members of the male sex wanted 'just one thing.' This was followed by a lecture on virginity. It was a prize, a treasure. 'More precious than pearls, honey. And once it's lost, you can't get it back.'

Bette was particularly hard on the neighborhood youths.

'They're nobodies – on the way to becoming nothings,' she said, when Kim asked permission to date. 'Ten years from now, these yokels will be pumping gas or working at the 7–11. That is, if they're lucky enough to hold down a job. And you'll wind up with a thirty-inch waistline and a passel of kids.'

'But, Mom, I'm not planning to marry Karl [or Joe-Bob or Earl],' Kim would plead. 'Just go to the drive-in with him.'

'Yeah. And bundle down in the back seat and next thing you know, it's a shotgun wedding and a tar-paper shack. Anyhow, sex is wildly overrated. Take it from me, it's unpleasant most of the time. Anyhow – this is not why I took my baby to Switzerland, Kimmy. Not why I spent myself poor. Be patient, and when you're famous, you'll meet a hubbie worthy of you.'

Whose likes were clearly not to be found in Mechanicsville.

'*There's a little wooden crate*,' Kim sang on the night she was crowned Miss West Virginia. She was eighteen, the youngest competitor.

Bette was beside herself with joy. 'You're looking at the next Miss America,' she shouted from the sidelines, while on stage, Kim wept and promised to cherish the crown. The Lieutenant Governor himself shook her hand. The crowd went wild.

And this time, the West Virginia media sent out not some cruddy cub reporter but a proper camera crew and a popular television interviewer.

To Maggie Ross and to all the viewers, Kim confided her desire to work with people, pray for peace and study acting at the state university with her thousand-dollar scholarship.

'Would you say this is the most thrilling moment of your life?' the newswoman cued.

The question stopped Kim in her tracks. Suddenly, the violet eyes clouded over, the lips trembled. There was that most dreadful of pauses – dead air time – then she regained her equilibrium and shot the camera a dazzling smile.

'You bet it is! I can truly say that being named Miss West Virginia is a thrill and an honor and a privilege.'

Later, back home in Bay Street, Bette gave Kim's hair a hundred strokes, put it up in rollers and made cocoa, as though it were any other night. But she was beaming.

'Of course I expected you to win, toots, and you've done me proud.' She paused in midroller. 'But what on earth was going through your head when Maggie Ross asked that question about your big moment? You looked a thousand miles away.'

In fact Kim had been farther away than that. The honest answer, and it had almost spilled out right there on camera, was 'My most thrilling moment was the night I saved Lady X's life in Marival.'

Four years on, the incident continued to haunt her. Kim reckoned it always would. How could anything surpass the fact that she, Kimberly West, acting on nothing more than impulse, had once shaped the destiny of a total stranger?

She had kept her promise to Dr Mainwaring, never leaking a word to her mother. By now it was too late to confide. Besides, it gave Kim pleasure to hug this secret to herself. To know that there was at least one area in her life, consummately private, where Bette could not trespass.

Soon after her West Virginia triumph, Bette announced that they would be leaving Mechanicsville to take up residence in Philadelphia. There, until September, when it was time for the Miss America pageant, Kim could be coached by a professional trainer.

'So it'll be goodbye coal pits, and hello Big Leagues. What a relief to get out of this burg. Jesus, I stayed here any longer I would bust.'

Kim spent the final days saying her goodbyes and packing up a few sentimental treasures. She felt sad, yet exhilarated.

On the morning of their departure, Kim tore downstairs, the rollers in her hair. Then she swept through the house like a whirlwind.

'Gone!'

She spurted out the door, into the street, racing through the neighborhood, into the woods. Then she ran back to the house. Their luggage was piled on the porch.

'He's gone!' She burst into the kitchen where Bette was drinking coffee out of a paper cup. 'Ringo's gone. I looked for him everywhere.'

'Uh-huh.' Bette didn't blink. 'Put a kerchief on your head, hon. We'll comb out at the bus station. Cab'll be here any sec.'

'But we can't leave without Ringo.'

Bette shrugged. 'Musta run away. You know what mongrels are like, Kimmy. Hoboes at heart, only happy on the road. Now don't you worry your pretty head. Old Ringo can look after himself.'

'But his bowl is gone too!' The realization was too much to bear. 'You've given him away! You gave my Ringo to somebody else. Well, I want him back. Ringo's mine . . . mine! I'm not leaving till we find him.'

'I told you, he probably just took off . . .' Bette muttered. 'Ah, what the hell. I may as well lay it on the line. Now I want you to be grown up and try to understand. You knew everything here was only temporary. This isn't our home. From the start, I told you we were only going to stick it out until you got the title. Well, now it's time to move on. We gotta travel light, babe. We can't tie ourselves down with non-essentials. You shoulda known that the dog was only temporary.'

Kim was trembling with rage. 'Where is he? Did you take him to the Animal Shelter? The SPCA? We can still get him back. I'll call and tell 'em we're on our way.' She began flipping through the phone book with frenzied fingers. 'Lordy! I don't even know what number I'm looking for,' she cried. 'Where is it, the shelter?'

'Stop it! That's enough. You'll drive yourself nuts.' Then Bette's voice softened. 'He's not at the pound, honey. I'm sorry but . . . Well, Mr Buckley down the road, he's got a hunting rifle so I asked him as a favor—'

'*Nooo!*' The cry burst from Kim's throat. 'You had no right!'

Outside, their taxi was honking. Bette was shaking her.

'Listen, Kim. We got a bus to catch, we got a future in front of us. A big beautiful future.' She grabbed Kim's arm and pulled her through the door. 'Sometimes you have to be hard, just to get where you're going. That's life, doll. When you're rich, you can have all the dogs and cats you want. Thoroughbreds. Classy animals with pedigrees. Not some mutt off the street.'

Kim wept in the cab to the station. Wept through two changes of buses. Was weeping outside the Trailways Station while Bette counted their luggage. Was weeping when her mother piled her into a taxi.

'Look at you, Kimmy,' Bette said when they were safely stowed in the back seat. 'Eyes puffed out to here. Anyone would

76

think you'd gone ten rounds with Muhammad Ali.' She put her arm around her daughter and gave her a smooch. 'Can't have the next Miss America looking anything but sunny-side up. Smile, baby, smile. Today is the first day of the rest of your life.'

LONDON

'Tomorrow is the last day of the worst of my life,' Peter said. 'Or however the cliché goes.'

It was Sunday, and Peter Mainwaring was 'reporting to headquarters.' In other words, taking tea with his mother, a ritual reserved for the last Sunday of the month.

His mother furrowed her brow.

'Do I take that to mean you're leaving your post at Hawksmore?' she asked, then answered her own question. 'This makes the third hospital since you've been back from Switzerland. Really, darling, you can't hop from one post to another and expect to make a name for yourself as a psychiatrist.'

Peter laughed. 'I don't want to make a name as a psychiatrist. Perhaps I never did. Sorry to disappoint, but I'm simply not cut out for the work, despite Wienerblut and Uncle Max's having chummed around with Sigi Freud. To be blunt – I loathe it. It's all I can do to get out of bed in the mornings that I'm due at the hospital. Do you know what my rounds consist of? Prescribing happy drugs to lunatics for whom nothing more can be done. Do you hear voices? Three milligrams. Being persecuted by Martians? Three milligrams. Can't sleep? Can't eat? Can't go on living? Three milligrams. A pleasure talking to you, Monsieur Bonaparte. And give my love to Josephine.'

'You mustn't make fun of them, darling.'

77

'Quite right. That's why I'm calling it a day, before I wind up on the couch myself, boring the pants off some other hapless shrink. It's over. *Fini. Terminado. Kaput.*'

What Peter stopped short of saying, what the mocking tone was intended to disguise, was the fact that he could no longer bear the pain of other people's sufferings. He had returned from Marival with hopes of being buoyed by 'useful work' and found instead that his patients depressed him. Mental illness was contagious – he had come to think – like chicken pox.

For all his gifts, he lacked the ability to slough off his professional skin once the day's work was over. To shut the door of his mind as firmly as the door of his office, and walk away whistling. But could one go through life without whistling? He was whistling now.

Peter's mother pursed her lips, then cut him a generous slice of strudel which he gobbled down in two bites.

'Best strudel in London,' he said, holding his plate out for more. 'The National Health ought to prescribe it as a cure for anorexia. Three large doses, taken internally.'

She ignored the compliment. 'But what will you do, *liebchen*? How will you live?'

Peter put down his fork. 'Remember when I was ten and said I wanted to be a writer? Nothing's changed – which shows that I'm a ten-year-old at heart. Well, love, it's now or never. I've decided to give it a go.'

'A writer? Really?' Mentally, she tested the shift from 'my son the psychiatrist' to 'my son the writer,' savored it for several seconds, then frowned. It sounded dangerously like 'my husband the painter.'

'You will write novels?'

'Actually, I'm going to try my hand at comedy. A little revue with some friends for a night club in Shepherd's Bush.'

Her gloom deepened. 'Do they pay you for this, these friends?'

'It's a speculative venture. No money up front . . .'

78

'Oh, Peter!'

'. . . but that's before taxes, of course.'

My son the comic?

She scanned Peter's face. The 'elevens' were gone, she noticed – those vertical frown lines that had been a constant these last years. Suddenly she felt a lift of the heart.

'How like your father you are when you smile! Only be happy,' she said, and cut him another slice of strudel.

When Peter was at university, his keenest pleasure had been taking part in the theatricals for which Cambridge was celebrated. He joined the lofty Amateur Dramatic Club and the town-and-gown Mummers. But, above all, Peter relished being part of the Footlights revue, then as now famous throughout England. He had a flair for comedy.

As it had done for decades, Footlights signified fun, relief, release. The shows and 'smokers' – written, produced and acted by students – were an amalgam of skits and musical numbers, a mix of high-brow allusions and low comedy. The productions were raucous, irreverent, often bawdy, always outrageous, full of waggish satire and verbal pyrotechnics. Every sacred cow in the British establishment was milked for laughs. 'From the Queen on up,' as one contributor put it. The show managed to thumb its collective nose in a dozen different directions simultaneously.

For most participants, Footlights constituted a final carefree burst of youth, after which these clever young men (and occasional women) knuckled down and devoted their energies to making their mark within the same establishment they had so recently mocked. Footlights alumni can be found in the highest echelons of law, government, academia and the sciences. They include several MPs, a former Solicitor General, the provost of a major university, and a number of company directors.

Yet despite subsequent achievements, these old Cantabrigians look back on their youthful high jinks with affection and a sigh of regret. When one Footlights veteran encounters another years later, on a government commission perhaps, or in the VIP lounge at Heathrow, all other business is temporarily shelved while old nicknames are resuscitated, ancient punchlines snickered over. The routines may have been long forgotten, but the key phrases never. They have passed into folklore. *Those were the days, my friend, when we were young and witty. When we had punch, not paunch.* Then, sadly, it would be time to open their briefcases, shuffle papers and play at being grownups again.

'They're as bad as Masons,' the wife of a High Court judge remarked at a formal dinner, while her husband traded cryptic one-liners with an archbishop.

'Worse,' said the archbishop's wife. 'At least Masons shut up about it in public.'

Not all veterans of Cambridge theatricals entered the traditional professions. An astonishing number of them, spoiled irrevocably for other forms of endeavor, went on to create – or more precisely to maintain – the maverick topical humor for which Britain is renowned. For although Cambridge was the intellectual mother of Darwin, Russell, and Keynes, it was also the comedic mother of *Beyond the Fringe*, *Monty Python* and other stalwarts of the BBC. David Frost, John Cleese, Peter Cook, Alan Bennett: all had come up through Footlights.

That Peter envied these men went without saying.

'There's nothing intrinsically wrong with being a doctor,' he would console himself, writing out another prescription for lithium. 'Remember, Jonathan Miller was also a doctor.'

But Dr Miller had escaped to a more noble calling: he had managed to make people laugh.

Thus Peter was ripe for conversion when, the day before taking tea with his mother, he was strolling up Kensington Church Street, with nothing on his mind beyond a pub lunch and a pint, when a voice whispered into his ear.

'It was spring, and in the vicarage garden, the polyester were in bloom.'

80

'Ted Northrup!' Peter whooped with delight. 'You old bastard. I thought you were in Aden.'

'I thought you were in Switzerland.'

'I think we both ought to nip into the Swan and have a pint or two.'

'Or three or four.'

'I've always liked this pub,' Peter said as they made their way to a quiet corner. 'You know why? It's the local for the witches of Notting Hill Gate. There are a number of them in this area. Fully qualified, practicing witches. They meet here a couple of times a week and swap trade secrets. Recipes too, I warrant. I'm happy to say they extend me every professional courtesy. Why not? We're in the same racket. We both pretend to answer the unanswerable.'

Ted laughed. 'Do I detect a note of discontent?'

'Do you not!'

Over the first pint, Peter unburdened himself. Over the second, it was Ted's turn to bitch about the Foreign Office. Over the third, both men grew thoughtful. Did Peter remember Jim Stockle? Yes? Well, Jim had a girl friend, a Sally-something, who had bought a little club in Shepherd's Bush and wanted to turn it into a comedy center. 'Songs. Skits. Rather like Footlights, with everybody doing everything – only for a wider audience.'

Ted himself had chucked his job at the FO and he and Jim and Sally were trying to whip a show into shape. But they could use more material . . .

Over the fourth beer, it was a done deal.

'Right, then.' Ted pumped Peter's hand. 'Monday at ten.'

'Ten in the morning?' Peter was scheduled to do rounds at the hospital. Hearing voices? Three milligrams. Think you're Prince Charles? Three milligrams. He paused all of one split second. *Bugger the hospital.*

'I'll be there.'

*

'Doctor!' Sally Travis minced across the postage-stamp stage to where Peter was sitting behind a desk.

SIX PSYCHIATRISTS, NO WAITING read the sign.

'I have a problem,' Sally lisped, then did a take. The psychiatrist was wearing nothing but horn-rimmed glasses and a grave expression.

'You say I have a problem?' Peter echoed.

Thus the opening exchange in a rude send-up of psychiatry, doctor and patient switching roles to and fro. Who was crazy? Who was sane? Ultimately, it was the audience who went nuts.

Within weeks, the routine became famous throughout London as *The Naked Psychiatrist* (original title, *Jung at Heart*). In addition to laughs, it engendered speculation. Was the doctor wearing anything over that part of his anatomy the desk concealed? Was he really a doctor, as rumor had it?

Peter declined to answer, though when *Off the Wall and Into the Street* (the ensemble's final name) went on television a year later, Peter confessed to camera fright, preferring to write material that others would perform.

His mother, he explained, could live with 'my son the writer' but not with 'my son the nude.'

In fact, he was perfectly content to sit at the typewriter and dream up skits for the weekly show. It was an immensely fertile period. Ideas dripped from his fingers, outlandish characters sprang to his imagination fully formed. And while *Off the Wall* continued to be a collaborative effort, Peter was its driving force. To him, the only thing more gratifying than the clackety-clack of the typewriter was the sound of laughter.

At its best, it seemed to Peter, humor contributed far more to the happiness of mankind than did all the volumes of Freud. Humor liberated. It conquered pain. It gave joy.

His had been a tortuous struggle full of many wrong turns. But at long last, Peter Mainwaring had found himself 'useful work.' And in doing so, he had changed the direction of his life.

CAMBRIDGE

'. . . come for my lighter.'

And with those words he changed the direction of her life.

But Alix, unwitting of the future, stifled her surprise as best she could. 'Please come in,' she said to the man in the faded jeans and worn black leather jacket.

Sam Houston Matthews stepped across the threshold and swept past her into the living room. It was a brilliant day and the room was flooded with afternoon sunshine. Light glanced off the beveled glass and sparkling china, added luster to the sheen of the cherrywood desk.

'What a beautiful room!' she expected him to say. Most visitors did, before settling down for a drink.

Instead, ignoring her presence, he made a tour of inspection. Alix watched, stunned by his lack of manners as he scrutinized each object in turn like a tourist in a foreign bazaar. He read off book titles, examined prints, held an antique paperweight up against the light, fondled the English carriage clock, took his measure in the silver-gilt mirror. A bull in a china shop, Alix thought, expecting her treasures to come crashing down any moment. But her image was wrong, for he moved with the grace of a cat. His eyes too were feline, almond-shaped and green-gray with flecks of yellow. The big paws handled each bit of china with exquisite delicacy.

'What's this?' he asked, picking up a small ivory carving.

'A nineteenth-century netsuke. Japanese. It's an ornamental closing for a wallet.'

'I see.' Sam tossed his jacket on the floor, then collapsed on to the velvet sofa, more amused than impressed.

'So this is how the rich live. Nice, Bryden. Very nice.'

Alix, who had thus far refrained from buzzing downstairs and having him booted out – the man could turn violent for all she knew – teetered between curiosity and indignation. Curiosity prevailed.

'How did you get past the doorman? This is a high security building.'

'I'm good at slipping in and out of places unobserved.'

'In other words, you snuck in. Okay. Next question: how did you know where to find me in the first place? I never gave my real name that day.'

'You and Rumpelstiltskin.' He chuckled and lit a Gauloise. 'No big secret. Marcy Hendricks spotted you at the rally. And very surprised she was, by the way. Her exacts words were – "wonders never cease".'

'Good old Marcy.' Alix remembered her from Wellesley – a sexy blonde deb with a fabulous clothes sense and not much else. 'What else did she say?'

'That you were ferociously smart. The class wig, in fact. Which intrigued me. In my book, there's nothing sexier than a smart woman, except maybe a smart woman with sensational legs.'

Alix was skeptical. If she were that intriguing, why had he waited so long to get in touch? She fished for information. 'Marcy's such an attractive girl,' she fished. 'Really pretty. Do you know her well?'

Sam folded his arms and grinned.

'She gives good head.'

Alix flushed. 'Are you trying to shock me?'

'Did I?'

'No . . . yes . . . a little. That wasn't a very gallant remark.'

Sam snorted. 'Gallant! Now there's an antique word, even older than your carriage clock. I'm not a gallant man, Bryden. Get used to it. And we don't live in gallant times. However, since sex talk upsets you, how about you being a gallant hostess and making me coffee. Black. No sugar.'

Alix suddenly felt foolish, standing there in a floppy bathrobe with her hair wrapped in a towel.

'Sure, if you'll just wait while I slip into—'

'Something less comfortable?'

'—into something else.'

No point in saying 'make yourself at home' for her guest had already pulled off his sneakers and put his feet up on the cocktail table. She hung up his jacket. It had a male, musky smell. Then she went to throw on a shirt and slacks.

When she returned with a pot of coffee and biscuits, Sam was on the floor, prowling through her record albums.

'Are you looking for something in particular?'

'Clues to Alix Bryden.' He riffled through the stack with a practiced eye, sometimes humming approval, pausing now and again to render judgment. 'Good! Cruddy! Okay, but the Glenn Gould version is better.' He rose, resettled on the sofa and drew a deep breath. 'I see you lean to Bach and Mahler.'

'They're my favorite composers.'

'Bach and Mahler.' He folded his arms. 'Sublime order and emotional excess.'

'Is that meant as a diagnosis?'

'Merely an observation.'

'I ought to sue for invasion of privacy.'

He smiled. Despite the bluster, he had a sweet boyish grin *See?* it assured. *I'm really quite tame after all.* Alix smiled back and poured them both coffee.

If she had expected instant 'pounce,' she was first relieved, then disappointed. For the next hour, Sam Houston Matthews seemed more interested in talking about Life with a capital L than in seeing how Alix compared with Marcy Hendricks in the oral-sex finals.

His conversation rambled: Nixon, Mailer, Marcuse, growing up in Cleveland, Mexican food, the various merits of American symphony orchestras. He had opinions on everything, mostly outrageous but always intriguing. He liked to position himself off-center so as to view the world from a fresh vantage point. Never once did a tinge of doubt creep into his judgments.

'But surely,' Alix protested when he advanced some particularly outré notion – equating the Elgin Marbles with Andy Warhol's soup cans, declaring that Cardinal Cushing was a child molester, prophesying that World War III would be between the Soviets and China – 'surely you're joking.

'But surely,' Alix spluttered as Sam savaged one of her favorite films, 'you don't seriously believe that *The Graduate* is right-wing propaganda.'

'It is. And Mike Nichols is a pompous fucking phoney. I'll take a John Wayne movie any time. At least with the Duke, you know where you stand.' Sam gave a big burly laugh that welled up from the depths of his barrel chest. 'I bet your old man is a big John Wayne fan. Especially in *The Green Berets*.'

'My father never goes to the movies,' she countered.

By now, she suspected this verbal barrage was Sam's way of drawing her out. It made her fidgety. She disliked giving herself away in conversation. One never knew what people might do with personal data. But Sam didn't let up.

Whatever the topic, politics or art or the status of women, he stated his convictions, even the most preposterous, with a vigor that owed little to logic and even less to conventional wisdom. 'I'm right,' he'd insist with a good-natured smile. 'You know I'm right.'

Given his perspective, half of what he said made sense. The other half was pure nuttiness. But even his most off-the-wall speculations had the effect of shaking her up.

He was exciting. Fresh. And if she cringed at his ideas, she nonetheless loved watching his mouth move when he talked. The way his eyes danced. He was very male, very sexy.

If he makes the first overture, Alix decided, *I'll go to bed with him*. A one-night stand, most likely – he didn't seem the type to stick around – but even so, there was nothing lost.

She edged closer on the sofa, willing him to touch her, put his arm around her as he had in Government Square. But Sam seemed content to rattle on. Except for the occasional dramatic gesture, he kept those big wonderful hands at rest.

Along the way, Alix learned that he was twenty-eight, the son of a furrier, a former student at Juilliard where, he claimed, he had been a protégé of Leonard Bernstein. Despite his talent, he had decided to forgo a career in music. 'Too much sucking up,' he declared. 'I lack green-room manners.'

He lit a joint.

'Do you smoke grass?' he asked.

'Sometimes,' she said. 'Not often. I'm a law student. I have to be careful.'

'Why? So you can be a corporate lawyer? Go ahead. I swear not to tell.' He handed her the joint. Their fingers touched briefly. 'You know, Bry—'

'The name is Alix.'

'That's a boy's name. I'm not going to call you by a boy's name. I was about to say – what attracted me to you that day we met was that you had this reckless quality. Passionate. An air of do-it-and-be-damned. Sexually reckless too, I presumed. A wild woman – which always gets the juices running. Then it turned out, you weren't so reckless after all. Not so reckless as to give your real name.' The cat's eyes narrowed. 'I've thought about you a great deal these last few weeks. You'd be surprised how much.'

'In what way?' Alix felt a rush.

'I wondered what you'd be like in bed, though that's only part of it. I wonder that about every woman. But of you in particular . . .' He paused to collect his thoughts. 'I thought about how ballsy you could be. How intense. How your eyebrows arch when you get excited, like the wings of a gull. But mostly, I thought about *who* you were. A revolutionary or a rich man's daughter? I wondered how you could split yourself in two like that. I still don't know. You want it both ways, Bryden, don't you? Mahler and Bach. The rollercoaster and the balance wheel.' He folded his arms. Waiting for something. For her?

In the ensuing hush, she could hear her breath, feel the blood pulse in her veins. The last of the sun squeezed through the shutters, layering them in broad golden stripes. Then Alix rose, flipped through the pile of albums and put a record on the stereo.

Mahler. No need to identify the work. Sam would know – and understand. The slow movement from the Fourth Symphony issued from the speakers: poignant, sweet, voluptuous, sensual. The music of excess. With a glorious smile, he opened his arms.

Wordlessly, she slipped off her shirt and kneeling before him placed her head in his lap, feeling his maleness against her cheek. Her nipples brushed against the rough cloth of his jeans.

He buried his hands in her hair. It was still damp.

'Beautiful,' he murmured. Then raising her head to his, he sought out her lips with his own. 'Beautiful.' His mouth was honey, cinnamon, apricot, vanilla ice cream – all the luscious things of the world, as rich as the music that enfolded them. Slowly they undressed each other, then lay on the sofa bathed in the deepening twilight, their limbs entwined in infinite trickery, hands and mouths busy with discovery.

'Fuck these pearls,' he said as his fingers struggled to undo the ornate clasp.

'They were my mother's,' Alix said.

'Take them off. Where we're going I want there only to be us. You and me, Bryden. You and me.'

The music had stopped. It had stopped long ago. And somewhere, far out of sight and mind, a woman was screaming in transports of ecstasy. A mad woman. Alix had never heard such a sound before.

Then dimly Alix realized it was her own voice, her joy crying out. She loved him. She loved his body, his smell, his taste. She loved the words he whispered in her ear: sweet blessings, obscenities, endearments, a whole new lexicon of sex and tenderness. No one had ever spoken to her like that. Or loved her like that. To completion. To excess.

In Sam Matthews's arms, she had lost herself, found herself, been subsumed, incorporated. *If I die tonight*, Alix thought as she closed her eyes in sleep, *no matter, for I have known heaven on earth*.

LAS VEGAS

Flocked red velvet wallpaper, white baby grand, mock marble and rococo gilt, a plastic fountain running Jello-colored water – who could ask for anything more? Desert Paradise, the flashing lights proclaimed. If sequins died and went to heaven, this place might well be paradise. Otherwise, it looked to Miranda to be nothing other than a run-of-the-treadmill casino, one of an unbroken series on the strip. Not too big, not too small, but just right.

Miranda paused at the threshold of the gaming room, checked her watch, took a deep breath and headed over to the cashier's booth, where she bought a thousand dollars' worth of chips, mostly in tens, but some fifties. Slipping them into a large leather bag, she circled the room, past the slot machines, roulette wheels, chuck-a-luck and craps. At last she came to the blackjack tables. *Vingt-et-un* as it was called at the little casino in Divonne, but no matter the nomenclature, the principles were the same. So were the odds, Miranda knew, having spent the past three months doing calculations.

She spent a half hour taking the temperature of the two

dozen blackjack tables, noting the rhythm of the dealers, sizing up the pit bosses. Then, when a desirable chair fell vacant, she sat down and placed her stack on the table.

Everybody's got a system, casino owners say with a smirk. *That's why we're rolling in money*.

Miranda had a system, as simple as it was complex. Beyond the system she had a plan.

The Desert Paradise was her third hit in a week, her sixth since arriving in Vegas. Thus far, business had been good. She was smack on schedule, within striking distance of her goal. Only sixteen thousand dollars left to go. Today should be the grand finale. With luck, she'd be out before dark.

No, not luck, Miranda told herself. *With skill and smarts.*

The dealer shuffled the decks; the player next to her cut once; the dealer cut again, placed the cards in the shoe, then set them out with metronomic regularity.

Had the ceiling fallen in, Miranda wouldn't have noticed: she had cleared her mind of everything except what lay on the table before her.

. . . eight of diamonds, 34–16 . . . nine of spades, 35–16. . . eight of clubs, 32–16 . . . three of spades . . . sub-total, total and divide by sixteen, factoring in the house's 5.9 per cent edge . . .

By mid-afternoon, she had totted up a number of modest wins, her stack of chips growing steadily. Periodically she creamed off the top of the pile and slipped it into her bag. Yet though she had avoided big bets or flamboyant tactics, her play had nonetheless attracted an audience.

'Sure knows when to stick, when to fold,' someone said. 'You ask me, this little gal's got a sixth sense.'

Miranda ignored them all: the kibbitzers, the rubber-neckers, the side-bettors cashing in on her streak. She didn't give a damn whether they won or lost. Her concentration was total. In the universe there existed only 208 cards, of which fewer than a dozen truly mattered. Her own and the dealer's.

'Hey, pretty lady!' – a hefty Shriner clapped a paw on her shoulder. 'Does that lucky stuff rub off?'

Miranda turned to stare.

'Get your hands off me, thank you very much. And please don't interrupt my calculations again.'

She returned to the game, playing slowly, deliberately, winning a healthy 62 per cent of her hands. She pulled out the fifty-dollar chips, upped her bets. At this rate, she figured to be out of the casino by six thirty, mission accomplished in time for dinner and a good night's sleep, after which she would kiss Las Vegas goodbye.

She hated Vegas. In particular, she loathed the casinos: the din, the harsh lights, the stink of perfume and cigars, the women with their lacquered beehives and beaded sweaters, the polyestered men with a bourbon in one hand and a bimbo in the other. The smoke stung her eyes. One day when she was very rich, she would live in a clean and beautiful place, free of loud voices and glare and tobacco fumes. God willing, after today, she need never set foot in a casino again.

But, as Willy Sutton had observed about banks, 'That's where the money is.' Miranda arched her back and stretched; the houseman dealt another hand. Soon she'd be out of here. In the meanwhile – eight of clubs, two tens, queen of spades, which made the mathematical odds against her busting exactly . . .

'Hit me please,' she said. *Only eighteen hundred dollars shy.*

'I think you want to cash in now.' The voice in her ear was soft but insistent. It was the pit boss.

'I wasn't aware that I've exceeded the house limit,' Miranda said politely.

'Please, miss, don't make a scene.'

'I'm not making a scene, merely playing a little blackjack. Hey, my chips!' For he was shoveling them into her bag. 'What the hell do you think you're doing? Those happen to be my winnings.' She tried to snatch the bag back, but he was in full possession. Next thing Miranda knew, he had seized her elbow and began marching her toward the cashier's cage.

He was a well-built young man, with dark eyes and fleshy lips. Latino perhaps. But though his manner was casual, even civil, his grip was unyielding. No mistaking the pressure of his fingers. *Don't mess with me!*

Miranda felt her knees buckle, her flesh crawl. This wasn't the genteel environment of Divonne-les-Bains. This was Vegas – capital of America's criminal empire. A city founded on Mafia money, greased with enforcers. These guys meant business.

She was terrified.

What did it take for a man to maim a woman? Nothing but the will to cruelty. She knew – oh God, how bitterly she knew! – the sum total of a boot in the face, a knife at the throat. She clutched her stomach to keep from vomiting. *Take the fucking money!* her inner voice screamed. *Take it all!*

Adrenaline told her to run for her life. To get away from this man with the iron grip and the blue-black hair.

Suddenly a buried image surfaced to the fore of her brain. A dark country road, lined with poplar trees. A sliver of moon. A man with blue-black hair. And terror. Blind wild terror.

Miranda blinked. The road was gone. The moonlight. The trees. Vanished as quickly as they had appeared, leaving no shadow. Miranda braced herself.

Peter Mainwaring's words winged back to her. 'Conquer fear,' he had said, 'and you can conquer the world. Otherwise, all our years of work will be lost.'

Lost! Like the thousands of dollars she had been ready to jettison a few seconds ago. Lost, out of fear and panic.

But now, though Miranda's feet said *run!* her head said *stay! Stand your ground. Exert your rights.*

She gulped. Swallowed down the bile in her throat. What was needed was a swift evaluation of facts.

Look at the situation logically, she reasoned. Logically, she was safe. She was in the midst of a well-lit casino with hundreds of people about, and the management didn't want any trouble. Logically, no one was going to rub her out or rough her up over a few thousand bucks. Why, compared to the high rollers, the guys who bet thousands on a single roll of the dice, Miranda's winnings were peanuts. This wasn't some banana republic. This was America.

Remember, you have your rights!

Miranda squared her shoulders and turned to face Mr Muscle, who was piling her chips up at the cashier's cage.

'I demand to speak to the manager,' she said, a duchess addressing a stablehand. 'I insist upon knowing why I'm being treated in this insulting manner. I have done nothing disgraceful, disruptive or dishonest. And if you don't let go of my arm I shall call the police.'

The pit boss did a take.

A few minutes later Miranda was ushered through a door that said PRIVATE, into an office elegantly furnished in beige-and-blond woods. It reminded her of Dr Frankl's office at Marival. The sole clue to the nature of the establishment was a bank of closed-circuit television screens that monitored every inch of the casino floor.

A short sleek man in Brooks Brothers tailoring was sitting in an armchair watching the action.

'Please come in.'

He got to his feet – he was hardly taller than Miranda – and introduced himself as Walter Zaplinski.

Miranda didn't return the courtesy. Her name was her own business. 'I want to know what's going on,' she said.

He smiled and indicated a seat on the sofa.

'As you can appreciate, the management reserves the right to turn away customers. I assure you, Miss . . . ummm, it's nothing personal. Nevada law stipulates . . .'

His voice was warm and comfortable, more like a small-town banker's than a Mafia don's.

'But what have I done?' Miranda was honestly puzzled.

Walt Zaplinski spread his hands in wonderment. It was his turn to be befuddled.

'You're a counter.'

'A what? I don't understand.'

'A counter. A clocker. We've already had word on you from the High Time and Tropical Sands. You took them both for a substantial sum.'

Miranda shook her head, boggled by his terminology.

'I'm sorry, but could you tell me – what is a counter?'

Zaplinski studied her face for a moment, then burst out into a high-pitched laugh. Her naïveté touched him. 'You really don't know? You've been doing it all week and you don't know what it is? Sit down, young lady.'

A counter, he explained, was a player who tracked every card that had shown as a basis for calculating the odds of the draw. There was nothing intrinsically illegal about it, but the casinos denied such players entry. It shifted the odds.

'Though I'll hand it to you, you're the best I've seen. Good thing you weren't playing for serious money.'

He offered a drink, she asked for coffee. He ordered, then plumped down beside her on the sofa. 'Now,' he said, 'I'd like you to satisfy my curiosity.'

He was interested in how she had arrived at her system. She was very efficient, he remarked. He himself was a Wharton MBA and respected business acumen in others. By the time the coffee arrived, they were chatting away like old colleagues.

Miranda described her technique. Zaplinski professed his admiration, and told her never to show her face in his casino again.

'Once the house loses its competitive edge,' he explained, 'the system falls apart. The house never gambles. That's not our business. Our business is making money off those who do.'

He glanced at the monitors.

'Luck. Hunches. Rabbit's feet. The mumbo-jumbo of losers. See that woman on camera three, the jiggly one in the white sequinned top? She comes on the days when Jupiter is in the ascendant and only plays table number seven. She's convinced there's an affinity between the state of the heavens and chuck-a-luck. Now the gent at the roulette table with the cowboy hat . . . Watch. He'll rub it three times before each bet . . .'

It was Miranda's turn to be amused.

'How did you spot me?' she asked. 'Granted you were tipped by the other casinos, but how did you know what to look for?'

'Easy. Your clothes were a dead giveaway.'

Miranda looked down at the simple black twill skirt and tailored blouse.

'I thought this outfit was low profile.'

'It would be – anywhere but Vegas. Here everything's ass backwards. If you want to pass through these halls unremarked, your best bet is to dye your hair blonde and deck yourself in the shiniest threads you can buy. Silver is good, gold better. And black, gold and silver is best, preferably appliquéd with a king-size butterfly across the boobs. Now *that's* low-profile.'

They both laughed. Walter checked his watch.

'It's been nice talking to you, Miss . . .'

Miranda rose and collected her bag.

'What about my chips?'

'Why, cash them in, of course.'

'But I'm eighteen hundred dollars short. You see, I had planned to win sixteen thousand tonight. That's my quota.'

Walter's ears perked up. 'Considering what you took home at the other casinos, you must be about eighty, ninety grand to the good.' Then it struck him. 'You have a specific sum total in mind, don't you?'

Miranda nodded.

'And some particular purpose to put it to? But of course! You're a motivated woman. Out of curiosity, and it won't go further, may I ask how much you planned to win in all?'

Miranda named a figure.

'Such an exact sum. But why?'

Miranda smoothed her skirt and told him. He was a business-man. He would understand.

'That's perfect!' Walter doubled up with glee. 'You really *are* a gambler. I mean, this is only poor benighted Las Vegas, but what you're talking about – that's the big time. Well, we all have fantasies.'

'And now you know mine. But as I say, I'm eighteen hundred shy. And no one will let me play blackjack any more.'

Walter grew thoughtful.

'Give me a ten-dollar chip.'

Miranda did so. He handed her back ten silver dollars.

'You see screen number eight?'

'With the fruit machines?' She was beginning to tumble.

'If I believed in luck,' Walter said, 'I would take a flyer on the fifth machine in from the left. Maybe up to ten tries, just on the come. Who knows? It might be ready to blow.'

Miranda clutched the silver pieces in her fist.

'You're very kind,' she said.

'I like spunky women, I'll look for you –'

'Not here!' She rolled her eyes. 'I've had it with Vegas.'

'Then I'll look for you on the cover of *Fortune*.'

She was back in her hotel room by six-thirty, mission complete, although she kept the last silver dollar as a souvenir. It had taken but two pulls of the lever before the three red cherries popped into view. They had paid off handsomely.

By eight o'clock Miranda had packed, booked a morning flight out, slipped her winnings in a money belt, and prepared for bed.

Room service had sent up a steak with French fries, but it sat on the dresser untasted. Miranda was too exhausted to eat, too wound up to sleep. When she shut her eyes, cards danced behind the lids, figures crowded her brain, phrases rang in her ear. *Six of diamonds, king of hearts, 208 divided by 16, down for double, ace of clubs, hit me, nine of spades . . .*

Her body cried for a narcotic, a drug to numb the brain and stupefy the soul. She knew just the prescription: TV.

Miranda switched on the set and stretched out on the bed, arms linked behind her head.

'Now – live from the Convention Hall in Atlantic City . . .'

The Miss America pageant. God! Talk about sleep-making.

Through half-closed lids, she watched as the state finalists were introduced one by one.

'From the heart of Dixie, the magnolia state . . . *Miss Alabama*!' A pretty girl swirled into view and smiled at the camera. '. . . from the Sun Belt, the gracious *Miss Arizona*!' Another pretty girl swirled and smiled. Already Miranda was yawning. The rhythms of Bert Parks's incantation was soothing as a lullaby. '. . . pleasure to introduce – *Miss Arkansas*!' Swirl. Smile. Miranda's eyes grew heavy. '. . . from the shores of the blue Pacific, *Miss California*!' And heavier still.

By the time the alphabetical roster arrived at the rugged mountain state of West Virginia, Miranda Vee was enjoying the sleep of the just.

ATLANTIC CITY

'It's a fix!'

But Kim scarcely heard her mother's tirade. She was too busy throwing up the remains of her Farewell Brunch.

'The whole goddamn pageant is a set-up.' Bette pursued Kim into the bathroom. 'A fraud. You listening? Jesus, it sounds like you're barfing everything you've eaten since kindergarten. Well, I could puke too, just thinking about that Carole-person. Shoving that chest of hers in everyone's face and all the while pretending to be Miss Lah-Di-Dah, playing the fiddle, like she was Heifetz. How phoney can you be? Big boobs, big rear-end. Tits and ass, like they say in show-biz. That's what passes for talent these days. If there was any justice, we would've placed in the money. We did everything right.'

Kim raised her head from the toilet bowl, bleary with suffering. In fact, they had done everything wrong.

'You *young ladies* have so much to learn' – (Lally Goodwin eschewed the word *girls*) – 'from how to shake hands, how to eat, how to put on a swimsuit, how to breathe, how to wear the crown like a queen.'

Lally knew whereof she spoke. A former Miss Georgia, she had been a Top Ten Finalist a generation ago, and subsequently devoted herself to shepherding other aspirants through the ordeal. To her credit, she could point to having trained one Miss America, half a dozen runners-up and three winners of the not-to-be-scoffed-at Miss Congeniality title.

Lally ran a charm school in a Philadelphia suburb, but her work with candidates for Miss America was largely a labor of love. Or, as Kim might have put it, an honor and a privilege and a thrill. 'My American beauties,' as Lally called them, were members of a national elite, the fifty state-pageant winners. They had beaten over seventy thousand other applicants to get this far, but the true test lay ahead in Atlantic City. As did six months of hard work.

Kim was impressed with Lally's dedication. The older woman was a fount of wisdom and inside tips, preparing her young ladies for every contingency. Kim learned the correct way to eat spaghetti in a restaurant ('The answer is *don't!*'); what to do if your nose starts running when on stage ('Bury your head in your hands and pretend you're giggling'); the penalties of being seen in pink plastic rollers ('If you can ask that, you don't belong here in the first place').

Kim was alerted to the dangers of Fanny Overhang; memorized the Three Bs (Bust Out, Belly in, Butt Under); was instructed in the art of squeezing into a one-piece swimsuit two sizes too small ('Roll it up like a doughnut, pull it over the hips to the waist, bend over, ease it up to the bottom of the bustline, tuck your right breast up and slip it under, repeat on the left – then stand up and check for pubic hair').

Nor was her education limited to matters of grooming. Manners and etiquette were given their due, with tutelage covering such fine points as the only three occasions when it was proper for a lady to remove her gloves: 'Before eating, upon being received by a prince of the church, and when being introduced to a head of state.'

This last made Kim titter. 'Can you imagine *me* being introduced to a head of state?'

Kim proved an apt student, picking up instruction well, but from the start there was friction between Lally and Bette, who insisted on sitting in on all sessions.

Though Lally tried to fend her off, Bette was adamant. 'Kimmy and me have always worked together, and I refuse to be shut out.'

The two women clashed over make-up, posture, fingernails. They squabbled over the talent portion of the pageant, with Lally urging that Kim seek less dated material than 'Little Wooden Crate.' Their hardest battles were fought over questions of wardrobe, which represented the contestants' biggest financial outlay.

For months, Bette had scrimped, wheedled, cajoled and begged for money enough to provide the glamorous outfits that Atlantic City required. Kim had looked forward to a Cinderella spree. Here, Lally's guidance would be priceless.

But the shopping trips soon became a nightmare, with Bette complaining about cut, cost, colors; sequins versus chiffon; gold sandals versus satin pumps; and nobody was going to make Bette West, thank you very much, fork out over four hundred and fifty bucks for a gown in a shade of green that made her barf. That particular day ended with a tearful Lally stomping out of Nan

Duskin's and Bette purchasing an elaborate ballgown in fire-engine red. 'Just like Bette Davis in *Jezebel*.'

Caught in the midst, Kim felt like a femme fatale duelled over by rival suitors. The outcome was never in doubt. In any conflict between Bette's will and someone else's wisdom, Bette always prevailed, for the simple reason that what she wanted she wanted more desperately than her adversaries wanted what *they* wanted. As for Kim, she never dreamed of interfering. Domestic peace was more important than any prize.

The final rupture came over the choice of hairdos.

'Hair can be the make-or-break,' Lally warned. 'Let's play around, see if we can construct a more flattering style.'

'*We!*' Bette shrieked. 'What do you mean by *we*? Who do think you're dealing with, some amateur? Kim's hairdo is my own creation. So don't you presume to tell *me*.'

'But it's so busy, her features get lost . . .' Lally argued.

'Oh, yeah? Well, maybe you know how to eat peas with a knife, Miss Fancy-Pants, but you know zip about style.'

'Oh I do, do I?' Lally's southern gentility was slipping. 'And you're such a model of chic, you polyester prune.'

'Listen, you old hag, I happen to be a professional with twenty years' experience.'

'Well, you listen to me, you vulgar bitch . . .'

They traded insults for ten minutes before being separated by the school secretary who was terrified they'd come to blows. The upshot was that Bette removed Kim from the academy. 'You don't need some paid hack to show you the ropes. You got me.'

Henceforth Bette would be everything for her daughter: trainer, stylist, fashion director, talent advisor, chaperon. Who more capable, who more caring than a girl's own mom?

'Mother knows best, after all.'

The week preceding the pageant sped by in a breathless blur: a stream of luncheons, dinners, fittings, interviews, quick but intense friendships with other contestants. By week's end, Kim had taken the measure of her competitors and knew she would not make it into the final round. Not only were the other girls older and more savvy. They were far better educated.

They bore the fine gloss of professionalism. This one had studied modern dance at Juilliard, that one had spent three seasons in summer stock. Several were successful models. They were experienced performers, who had entered the pageant to boost careers that were already underway. Whereas Kim—

It was not, as her mother griped, a matter of 'tits and ass' – a phrase that made Kim cringe. It was a question of talent and poise and projection.

Kim sang a little, danced a little, strummed her guitar with the ignorance of the true amateur. 'Sounds good to me, pumpkin,' Bette said as her daughter rehearsed her old standby, and it dawned on Kim that her mother had a tin ear as well as an unsophisticated eye.

Despite her assiduous study of beauty magazines, Bette's sense of style was roughly ten years behind the times. Whereas the Miss America contest itself was, aesthetically speaking, a mere five years off the mark.

As for her prize contribution, the beehive so lacquered it could withstand a hurricane, it did not withstand the scrutiny of the network's make-up man. One glance was enough to send him grabbing for a hair-brush.

'Sorry, honey,' he said to Kim. 'But this isn't amateur night. Fifty million people will be watching.'

'I happen to be a professional beautician,' Bette broke in. 'And I'll have you know this hairdo was inspired by a spread from one of the top magazines.'

'Yeah,' growled the expert. *'National Geographic.'*

Bette was helpless. For once she was outranked and Kim emerged from the dryer looking ravishing.

*

But looks alone did not suffice. The contest had been lost not to 'tits and ass' or even to talent, but to something less definable.

Kim lacked that quality – charisma, star power, show-biz pizzazz – that made Marilyn Monroe, for example, who had also once been just another 'pretty girl' from California, pop off the screen and into your lap. Kim had a light pleasant voice that traveled a few feet, then took a nose-dive. Even a microphone didn't help. Her smile was sweet but shy, her movements self-conscious and slightly gawky. Strictly amateur.

'*There's a little wooden crate,*' Kim breathed at the talent preliminaries, achingly aware of her shortcomings. Did she imagine it, or had one of the judges tittered? Suddenly Kim wanted to laugh along with him. It *was* ridiculous.

That Kim got through the pageant without breaking up or breaking down was miracle enough. That she would place out of the money was inevitable.

'My moment of glory,' she said wryly after the telecast. 'At least I was on national TV.'

'Don't feel bad,' her buddy Nancy, another also-ran, consoled. 'Whatever happens, you will always be the Former Official Miss West Virginia. They can't take that away from you. Me, I'm going home to get married.'

That there would be no 'going home' for the Wests went without saying. The only question was – where next?

Two days after the contestants dispersed, they were still lodged in the hotel. The weather had turned unseasonably warm, and Bette told Kim to enjoy herself while she formulated plans and assembled statistics.

'A few facts, Kim. Thirty-six C, that bimbo who won first prize, twenty-four-inch waist. Not much we can do about the waist, so let's stick with the bra and bottom sizes.'

She reeled off figures for the top entrants and concluded that 'No question, they like 'em curvy. Well, that can be fixed. I had a nice yak-yak with Helen Enderby, the gal in publicity. That's where I got these figures, not the ones that are posted, but the real McCoy. Anyhow, Helen told me about this doctor in Richmond who does implants at half the going price. Kim! Pick your jaw up off the floor. It's absolutely painless, I guarantee. It won't be as posh as Marival, but then, we're not talking about major surgery. They shoot a little silicon into you, bim-bam-bang, and the next day, it's Jane Russell – move over! And we should do your derrière too. Build it up a little, make it curvier.' She nibbled on her pencil. 'Depends how we're fixed for dough. Let's see. There's the two hundred left over from the Mechanics-ville Jaycees. We could maybe get a refund from Saks for the suit, you hardly wore it . . . Listen, hon. You don't have to stick around. Go to the pool and enjoy the sunshine. I'll be tied up for hours.'

Kim went downstairs and swam forty laps. Usually exercise defused her, but not today. She felt angry, bruised. She collapsed into a lounge chair and let the sun beat down.

'I can't believe she's doing this,' she muttered to herself, her bowels quaking at the prospect of 'bim-bam-bang.' There was nothing bim-bam-bang about undergoing surgery. She hated it. Dreaded it. And yet . . .!

And yet, at a deep and near-unconscious level, some part of Kim responded to the prospect with a kind of sexual thrill.

To lie naked, defenseless, at the mercy of a stranger's hands, to have your body invaded and possessed, to surrender all will. In a way, not so different from standing on the stage in Convention Hall in a tighter-than-skin bathing suit while hundreds of men stripped you with their eyes, penetrated every inch of your being in their imagination.

Kim shuddered, in horror that she could even entertain such a fancy. Was she crazy? The thrill of surgery indeed! It was a form of mutilation, nothing more.

Kim was confused. If only she had a good friend to advise

her, someone who also had known both the pain and joy of these transformations. Alix Bryden, for instance. Smart, practical, kind-hearted Alix.

But recalling their afternoons in the belvedere, she knew what Alix's counsel would be: *Just tell your mother no*.

Easier said than solved. There was no hope of changing Bette's mind, once made up. Tell her mother *no* and then what? Run away from home? Kim had no home to run away from. Strike out on her own? Get a job? Doing what? She had no skills and – as the pageant had made bitingly clear – even less talent.

As she lay on the chaise perfecting her tan, her mind drifted through scenarios. Maybe she would hitch-hike back to Mechanicsville and look for work ... Maybe she would call Alix in Pride's Crossing and be invited to stay ... Maybe Prince Charming would come to her rescue ... Maybe ...

The sun was hot. Her eyes were heavy. Time slid by.

'You're going to get a third degree burn, young lady.'

Kim rolled over. Looked up.

'And such a teeny little string bikini! Why that's no protection at all.'

He was fifty, maybe (she was no judge of age), gray at the temples. Fatherly, with kind blue eyes. He wore a heavy gold chain and a terrycloth robe.

He introduced himself as Fred something, a doctor, a cardiologist from Baton Rouge, here for a medical convention. He had a daughter just about her age. 'Seventeen?'

'Eighteen last March.'

'Were you in the Miss America contest, by any chance? I bet you were, to look at you.'

'I didn't win, though,' Kim said quietly.

He laughed. The gold chain glittered against his chest.

'Which shows how much *they* know! My God, but it's hot for September. Would you like something to drink?'

'I don't drink,' she said.

'Good lord. I wasn't suggesting Scotch or anything like that, though I may have a highball myself. How about – I know just the thing, a southern specialty. It's like an ice-cream soda, only better.'

He went to the bar, came back with a Scotch for him, and for Kim a creamy confection in a tall slim glass. She sipped it warily – it was all he said – then polished it off in a gulp.

'Yum. Terrific. What is it?'

'It's called a sazerac. Would you like another?'

'Are you sure this doesn't have alcohol?'

'Just a smidgen. But mostly cream and sugar and nutmeg.'

'My mom would have conniptions if she knew.' Kim smiled. For the first time in days she felt good.

He laughed. '*Momma don't allow* . . .' he crooned a snatch of some old tune in her ear. He had a soothing voice. Kim let him talk her into another, and then a third – what the heck! She was eighteen, an adult, and he was a man of the world. A medical doctor. The liquor made her feel unafraid, voluptuous.

He said the heat rash on her thigh looked like sun poisoning. What it needed was a good antibiotic salve. He recommended acetyl-salycilate. It was just the treatment. He always kept a supply with him when he traveled.

'My mother would throw a fit,' she said, when he suggested they go to his room. 'Are you sure it's all right?'

'Trust me, I'm a doctor.'

He led her by the hand through the lobby.

In his room, the air conditioning was on full blast, the blinds drawn. Kim shivered, more from excitement than from the cold. Here she was in a man's hotel room. But it was okay. He was a doctor. She lay face down on the bed, the stiff yellow bedspread rough against her skin. His hands were smooth, though. Skilled. Eyes shut, she let her mind go white while he lathered some kind of cool salve inside her thighs, massaging slowly and in ever upward circles. It was very pleasurable. Little by little, he worked his way under the bottom of her bikini, oiling the crease between her buttocks, up and down, up and down. Such huge hands he had. Broad spatulate fingers, yet gentle too.

The tip of his thumb touched her clitoris. Kim felt an electric shock. Billy-Joe had done that to her once after school in the back of his dad's pick-up. It had scared her then, but this man was wise. Experienced. He was a doctor. Besides, what he was doing felt good.

'Your garment's in the way,' he said. He untied the strings of her bikini. 'Much better. You have excellent skin texture, my dear. I happen to be a dermatologist, you know.'

'Please, I'm a virgin,' she whispered, too numb to move. 'My mom would kill me if I got pregnant or anything.'

'Good lord, child,' he murmured. 'What kind of man do you think I am? I have a daughter your age, remember.' His fingers moved deeper inside her, front and back. 'I wouldn't hurt you.'

Then he was crouching on top of her. She could feel the hair on his chest. One hand slid beneath her belly stroking her clitoris – it made a slap-slap sound – even as his penis explored the cleft of her buttocks.

'What a nice ass you have. So round and sweet and warm. Now I'm going to give you a little internal examination. See if it's as sweet inside as out. I'm a gynecologist, you know.'

Suddenly he was snaking into her rectum, hard and strong as a surgeon's probe. Kim screamed in agony.

'Shut up!' he said. 'Do you want everyone to hear?'

Kim choked down her sobs. No fuss, no scenes. If the house detectives came, they would send for her mother. And Bette would kill her, if she didn't die of shame first. Better to bite her lips and surrender to the pain. Better yet, to go beyond the pain and seek the pleasure.

When it was over, the man said, 'You're a sweet girl. I hope you have a lovely life.'

Kim dressed and left. On her way out, she noticed that his 'antibiotic lotion' was nothing but Vaseline. She felt humiliated.

Her mom was right – this was what happened to girls who went to men's bedrooms. They got what they deserved.

But if what this Doctor Fred had done to her was awful, was it any worse than what awaited her in Richmond?

Pleasure and pain, pain and pleasure. They were linked.

In the lobby she discovered to her astonishment that the 'treatment' had taken less than fifteen minutes. She went back to the room to find Bette on the phone making bus reservations.

'Where were you, hon?' Bette hardly looked up. 'I didn't see you down by the pool.'

'I had a sandwich in the coffee shop.'

'Hey, you're shivering, kid. What's the matter – too much sun? Anyhow, we're checking out first thing tomorrow morning, catching a nine-thirty bus. And not a minute too soon. There's some kind of convention starting today. Doctors? No, sweetie. What gave you that idea? Record-business people, distributors, – and you can imagine what kind of creeps those guys are.'

CAMBRIDGE

It was heaven. It was hell. It was love as Alix had never envisioned in her pastel fantasies of white knights and Swan Princes, for Sam Houston Matthews was no Lohengrin. The sun could turn purple before he would submit to such basic civilities as opening the door for Alix or helping her on with her coat, let alone more dashing gestures.

When he was late, he never thought to call. When she accused him of neglect, he charged her with possessiveness. They argued often and sometimes bitterly, yet Sam always made it up in bed. 'Now,' he would say when he had fucked her into a stupor, 'isn't that better than some limp apology?'

In short, he made Alix happy, wretched, angry, euphoric, jealous, scared. But above all, he made her feel beloved.

'Bry,' he called her. On his lips it sounded erotic. And sometimes 'Brydie,' with its nuptial overtones, which set her thinking silly thoughts.

Yet despite the sex, which was sensational, despite the endless talk talk talk, Alix couldn't get a handle on him.

Sam was a wild card, a streak of mercury, zipping in and out of her life to stay a few hours, a few days as the mood suited, upsetting her plans. He arrived like a blast of wind, with a slam of the door, overwhelming Alix with love and kisses and passion and energy. Then at a stroke he was off – to a rally, a meeting, a sit-in – leaving behind a happy chaos of crumpled sheets, overflowing ashtrays, magazines, books and odd socks. He might pop up at a moment's notice or disappear for days at a time. He had no phone, and never felt obliged to account for his time away from her except to say he was busy with 'important things, babe, vital activities.' If there was a key to his character, it was a hatred of authority. Alix knew better than to try to rein him in.

At first, reeling from this great messy love of hers, she assumed that this erratic behavior derived from his status as a fugitive. Having burned his draft card, he was on the run. Then one night he let slip that he had been called up and rejected years earlier because of a heart murmur. Though delighted that he wasn't a criminal, Alix also felt betrayed.

'So that auto-da-fé in Government Square, me burning your card – it was just a bit of theatre? A charade?'

'It was a symbolic action, Bry. And symbolism can be the ultimate reality.'

But what troubled her most was Sam's credo that sexual fidelity was a bourgeois hang-up. 'Like the League of Women Voters and Lawrence Welk,' he scoffed.

She took this to mean that he was still sleeping with, or at least enjoying the services of, Marcy Hendricks. Those suspicions were enhanced when, a month into the affair, she ran into Marcy buying lingerie in Bonwit's.

'I hear you've been seeing Houston,' Marcy said, holding a frilly garment to the light.

'Houston?' It took a moment for Alix to grasp whom she meant, another to realize that Sam assumed different names for different people. In fact, he boasted of having a dozen phoney IDs. Before Alix could think of a response, Marcy laughed and put her purchase on the counter. They were peach-toned silk panties trimmed in lace. 'And the same in black,' she told the sales clerk, then turned to Alix with a satisfied smirk.

'Totally corrupt,' she said, 'but Houston goes bananas when I wear sexy skivvies. He says it makes me look like a Hollywood version of a high class French whore.'

'I wouldn't know,' Alix said stiffly.

The next time Sam came by, Alix was furious.

'How can you make love to that airhead and me? And how many others, I want to know?'

Sam laughed. 'Believe me, you don't want to know.'

But he was tender that evening, almost penitent. He told her he loved her, and went on to describe the relationship of Jean-Paul Sartre and Simone de Beauvoir.

'Two superb minds,' he amplified, 'a man and woman who enjoy total intimacy and total freedom.' He explained to Alix the difference between 'essential' and 'contingent' love. Thus, while Alix was essential to him, he was entitled to supplemental affairs.

What was true for men was also valid for women. People were not possessions. Freedom meant, among other things, the freedom to enjoy a range of sexual experience.

'So there you are.'

'Bullshit!' Alix said, tears streaming. 'That's just a fancy way of telling me I'm one of a crowd.'

'Why are women so fucking subjective?' he groaned, to which Alix replied hotly, 'I am not!'

But as always, Sam had the last word. He took her in his arms. 'Don't be jealous, Bry. I'm crazy about you. Let's put it this way. I fuck Marcy, but with you I make love.' After which they either fucked or made love until dawn.

And though he never revised his view about the incompatibility of radical politics and monogamy, he began spending most nights with Alix, leading her to believe that the peach-pantied Marcy had been routed.

One day, he took Alix to his 'pad,' an illegal squat in the old North End.

She was appalled. How could he live like this? The windows were encrusted with grime. There were roaches everywhere, and the stench of bad drains and week-old pizza. He shared the squat with a dread-locked 'colonel' in the Angolan Liberation Army, two college drop-outs, a Weatherman from Chicago, and a teenage runaway named Cathy who lounged about in an outsized man's shirt and little else and who, Sam admitted, would go to bed with a zombie.

Sam slept on a mattress in the corner. Alone, Alix hoped, though she wouldn't bet on it. She never went back.

The next day, she gave him a key to her apartment, and told him he might come and go freely, which he did.

'Hotel Bryden' he called it. Inevitably his first act upon entering was to luxuriate in a long hot shower and dry himself with her thickest towels, which he then strewed on the bathroom floor. For a radical, he relished bourgeois perks.

Alix asked him to move in with her. 'All the fresh towels you can eat,' she bribed. But as usual, Sam turned the tables.

'Why don't you come live with *me*, Bry? Lots of room. We can always throw another mattress on the floor.'

Alix gasped. 'You can't be serious.'

'Oh, yes, I can.'

'But . . . but . . .' she spluttered.

'But why? What do you think you'd catch there? Poverty?'

'Well, what's so great about poverty?' she shot back. 'It stinks

– literally and figuratively. Why should anyone prefer to live in a hole when they can enjoy a few amenities, like hot water and central heating? You enjoy them yourself, I've noticed. And it's not as if you grew up in the slums. This is not about political commitment, Sam. It's about common sense. Our living like squatters won't benefit society one whit. All it'll do is sap our energy. Move in with me, love. And if it's a question of pride, your not wanting to live off a woman, well – the rent is already paid for.'

'Living off a woman doesn't bother me in the least.'

'Then what's your objection? You won't be taking bread from the mouths of the poor.'

Sam snorted. 'I find that an extraordinary remark considering the source of' – he flung wide his arms – 'all this. Silk sheets and bone china . . .'

'I don't have silk sheets,' she broke in, but Sam ignored her quibble.

'. . . and silver tea trays, courtesy of the Bryden Bomb-sight. Each little nicety paid for with the flesh of innocent Vietnamese. Not that your old man's any worse than the rest of the fucking industrialists. Him. Dow Chemical. The lot of them. There is no such thing as clean money.'

When Alix protested that the firm made things other than bomb-sights, most of them useful, Sam shouted her down.

'You know your problem, Bry? You're an onlooker. You'd rather be an observer than a participant. A typical Limousine Liberal. You want to say the right words, think noble thoughts, then come home to your doorman apartment, crawl into your canopy bed, pull up the sheets – silk or otherwise – and feel good about yourself without getting engaged at gut level. Without risking minor discomfort, let alone pain or poverty. Now I don't claim there's anything uplifting about roaches or blocked-up toilets. They suck. But at least I'm not watching from the wings.'

'Hypocrite!' Alix was stung. 'That's a load of garbage –

111

especially coming from someone who likes to screw rich girls. Me, Marcy Hendricks with her imported lingerie —'

They screamed at each other till a neighbor thumped on the ceiling, at which point Sam grabbed his jacket and stomped out the door with an ominous 'See you around.'

For days, Alix agonized. She hated Sam. She missed him. He could go fuck himself. She'd give her soul to feel his hands on her body once again. In her irrational moments, she pictured herself moving into that dreadful hole of his – she would hire a cleaning woman, a plumber, a painter, an exterminator, make it habitable – only to have the actual memory of the place (and its inhabitants) quash the image.

She could never live in such filth! Never sleep on a mattress on the floor! Why should she? She was Miss Alix Bryden of Pride's Crossing.

A week passed without word from Sam. She suffered horribly. Finally, swallowing her pride, she flushed him out at an SDS meeting. Within the hour they were back in her apartment, falling upon each other like sex-starved wildcats. She didn't ask where he'd been or with whom. The important thing was that they were together. Never again, Alix swore, vowing to keep him close.

That winter, to prove that she was not an 'observer' but a caring and passionate woman, Alix flung herself into a round of activities: handing out leaflets, marching in demos. The first of each month, she donated most of her allowance to the civil rights movement. Reasonably, what more could Sam ask?

Yet she worried that her life had come to resemble a crazy quilt. Nothing connected any more.

In Harvard, she was the good student, on staff at *Law Review*. In Pride's Crossing, the dutiful daughter, appearing once a week for dinner and chess. With Sam, she was lover, helpmeet and partisan.

If only! Alix brooded. If only she could weave the disparate strands of her life into a harmonious whole.

For this to come about, there had to be a meeting of the minds between her father and Sam. Alix could scarcely envision such an event. The two men stood at opposite ends of the pole. They differed on everything. But since her father was incapable of change, the 'give' would have to come from Sam.

At first, she was optimistic. Why not? Sam was clever, fast on his feet and (Alix liked to think) 'tameable.' Besides, he adored her. She hoped that under her influence, he would eventually divest himself of his more outrageous opinions, don suit and tie, clean up his language, return to his middle-class origins and prove presentable as a future son-in-law.

Yet as the months passed, his moods grew darker, stranger, and their affair more claustrophobic. They rarely went anywhere together; mostly they stayed in bed and talked or read or made love. When the mood was on him, he could be extravagantly affectionate. For all her resolve about making Sam 'shape up,' she melted at his endearments. He could make her feel not merely beloved but even beautiful.

'"Had I the heavens' embroidered cloths,"' he quoted Yeats's poem to her, laying his head on her feet, and Alix was wrenched by the intensity of the moment. No one had ever loved her so.

Yet a few hours later, he might be off without a word.

Secretive by nature, Sam made no effort to introduce her to his circle, just as she too was wary of how this wild man might fit in with her Harvard friends. That he led a complex life apart from her could be inferred from the phone bills he ran up. He made his calls when Alix was asleep or studying, keeping his voice low and indistinct. Alix never asked for details. Had she done so, Sam's reply would doubtless have been, 'You don't want to know.' And he was probably right.

So much for the Sartre–de Beauvoir pact of total trust.

Alix blamed herself for this impasse. For crazy as she was about him, she was no more able to suspend her innate skepticism about the World According to Sam Matthews than she had been years earlier when taking Catholic instruction.

113

By spring she had given up all hope of Sam's making himself presentable to her father. The two men would hate each other on sight, she was certain. Instead, she continued to segment her life: Harvard, Sam, Pride's Crossing.

When summer came, instead of interning with a State Street law firm as planned, Alix joined the Cambridge Law Commune. The office consisted of a handful of idealistic attorneys and law students who provided free legal services for the indigent: battered wives, petty criminals, tenants facing eviction. It was a seven-day-a-week job and Alix flung herself into it with zeal. It amused her to think that she was being true to her roots. One ancestor had been an abolitionist preacher; another, a suffragette who had chained herself to the rails of City Hall.

Thus the commune struck her as a sensible compromise between her family's world and Sam's.

'It's volunteer work,' she told her step-mother on the phone, explaining her increasing absences from the Pride's Crossing dinner table. 'And very worthwhile.'

One summer's day, Alix returned from work to find her father's Rolls parked in front of her apartment, his chauffeur standing at attention by the door.

'Good evening, Miss Alix.' Billings tipped his cap. 'Mr Bryden is expecting you for dinner at seven.'

Breathing a sigh of relief that Sam wasn't present (what a joke he would have made of car and driver) and a sigh of regret for a wasted evening, Alix climbed in. She knew better than to resist a command performance. Yet she was furious. What right had Lucius Bryden to 'kidnap' her like this? Times had changed. And Alix, too.

The chess games and fireside chats, once the highlight of her life, had become an ordeal. In dealing with her father, she had only two choices: argue or lie. Which would it be tonight?

Scrunching down in the cordovan leather of the Silver Cloud, Alix wondered how much longer she could stick it out. How much longer could she suppress those critical faculties sharpened at Harvard, fine-tuned by Sam? Lately she had brought them to bear on Lucius Bryden, and the judgment was harsh.

Her father's opinions, once set in stone, she now saw as narrow and self-serving. Yet he could not admit to fallibility. In Lucius's view, money validated his every notion: to be rich was to be right. Ideas that in a poor man might be construed as ignorance or prejudice assumed the weight of gospel when subscribed to by a millionaire. But Alix, working with clients at the commune, had learned otherwise.

This realization that Lucius Bryden was not the World's Greatest Living Authority on everything from global politics to miniskirts had come to her painfully. Sam was probably right, Alix concluded. The only thing to do with authority was to kick it in the butt.

Still – the man was her father, and she hoped to get through the evening with minimum friction.

After the Thanksgiving fiasco, the topic of Vietnam was tabu. Now more and more issues had joined the list as too inflammatory to be discussed: civil rights, labor unions, tax reform, public housing, capital punishment. But while Alix didn't want to pick a fight with her father, she had a right to be treated as a thinking adult.

After dinner, she and Lucius went to the library for a game of chess. As they played – and he was in particularly fine form – Alix's resentment bubbled up.

'I'd rather you hadn't sent the car for me,' she ventured.

'Why not?' Lucius was absorbed in his next move.

'For one thing, it takes up half a city block, and for another – well, the Rolls is a fairly high profile example of, shall we say, conspicuous consumption. Most of my friends are students, without a lot of money. I doubt if they could even afford a Volkswagen bug. I mostly get around by bike, like everyone else. If they had seen me drive off in a chauffeured limo . . .' Her hands fluttered.

Her father looked up from the board. 'Are you telling me that you're ashamed to be Lucius Bryden's daughter? Bishop to queen three, and check.'

'Oh God, Daddy!' Since when had her father started referring to himself in the third person, she wondered. 'All I'm saying is – I want to live like a normal student.'

'And do what? Smoke dope? Throw Molotov cocktails? Crawl into bed with the worst kind of human trash? Your move, Alix.'

Alix felt a wave of frustration. How could you reason with a man who was never wrong?

'I'm twenty-three, Daddy, and considered intelligent. Give me credit for some modicum of judgment. I hope to be known as something other than Lucius Bryden's daughter. You make it sound like a job description. And I resent that crack about human trash. Simply because I don't show up for dinner every week doesn't mean' – with an abrupt gesture she pulled her king out of harm's way – 'that I'm going to hell in a hand-basket.'

'Now that, my dear, was an unwise move.' He looked up from the chessboard to engage her eye to eye. 'Don't deceive yourself, Alix. And don't think that you can deceive me. I'm not a man easily taken advantage of, as my business competitors can testify. I'm aware of exactly what is going on in your life at every given moment. I know the who and the what and the where. I know the vermin you associate with, malcontents who nibble away at the fabric of our society with their schemes and connivances. Misfits who can't hold a job. What do you think the attraction is for these people? Your beauty? Your charm? What else except the fact that you are my daughter, a young woman of vast expectations? Rook to bishop three' – he moved his castle so that it dominated the board – 'and check-mate.'

Alix got up and stalked out. She was almost at the front door when her step-mother stopped her, ignorant of the scene in the library.

'Alix, darling,' Dorrie chided. 'I've been meaning to speak to you. You're not taking care of yourself these days. Your hair is a wreck. And when was the last time you had a manicure? Tell you what. I'll make an appointment for a Day of Beauty at Elizabeth Arden, my treat, and then we can —'

But Alix didn't hear her out. 'How do you live with him, Dorrie? How does anyone live with him?' She was about to slam the door, her great dramatic exit, when she realized she had no way of getting back to Cambridge. 'Could Billings drive me home?' she asked sheepishly.

Later that night, recounting what had happened, she burst into tears. 'For all I know, he's having me followed.'

Sam's face grew black with indignation.

'Bastard! I ought to go there and punch him out.'

'Oh, Sam!' Alix hid her face behind her hand. 'Let's not talk about it any more.'

'He treats you like a shit. It pisses me off.' Sam was staring at her. 'You're doing it again, by the way.'

'Doing what?'

'Covering your cheek like a leper. You do it whenever you mention your father, are you aware? It's a nasty habit. Makes me wonder. Tell me, Bry, did your old man abuse you sexually when you were a kid?'

'Of course not! My God, Sam. What a mind you have! My father didn't even acknowledge me for years on end.'

'Well, that's abuse of sorts. My old man abused me. Not sexually but in every other way. He was a drunk and a scumbag. Well, fuck him. And fuck your father too.' Sam stabbed the air with his middle finger in the classic obscene gesture. 'Here's to those dirty old men! May the devils get their due.'

Precisely when it was that Sam made the transition from rabble-rouser to something darker, more dangerous, Alix was hard put to say. Looking back it struck her as a gradual process. At first the change appeared to be largely one of style as, step by step, the student uniform of tee-shirts and blue jeans was replaced by garments that projected a more violent view of life. Black turtlenecks, camouflage pants from the army-navy store, a broad leather belt fitted to hold an ammunition clip. The look frightened her.

'How come you're wearing combat boots?' she asked one August afternoon. 'It's ninety-five degrees out there.'

'They're comfortable,' Sam replied. 'Besides, they make a statement.'

'Which is . . . ?' She was almost afraid to ask, but instead of a direct reply, Sam began ruminating about what was wrong with student movements.

'Words, words, words,' he said, gesticulating wildly. 'What do you think? We're gonna solve the world's problems by running off at the mouth like some Ivy League debating society? Christ! What assholes they are – your SDSs and COREs and SNCCs and SNACKs. I'm sick of talk, Bry. Hot air, empty oratory. One good stink bomb going off in the lobby of the Ritz Carlton would get more of a rise out of the fascist establishment than any number of undergraduate bull sessions.'

Alix grimaced, but comforted herself that this too was 'empty oratory.'

'As long as it's only a stink bomb,' she said mildly.

One day he turned up in a Fidel Castro cap, which gave a pugnacious cast to his appearance. Alix hated it, but was afraid to push the point.

'Next thing I know, you'll be growing a beard.' She rubbed his chin. It felt rough. 'Or have you started on one already? In which case, you'll really have a revolution on your hands – with me.'

The feeble joke went right over his head. 'Do you know,' Sam mused, 'that Castro started with only thirteen men? One more than Christ had disciples.'

Now who was joking, she wondered.

But soon after, when autumn classes had begun, something happened that frightened her profoundly.

Alix and Sam had been walking along Memorial Drive, arguing about Norman Mailer's campaign to become the mayor of New York.

'What does he think?' Sam sneered. 'That he can beat the system by joining it? Fascist bastard.'

Alix bridled. 'That seems to be your favorite epithet these days. At least he's doing something positive to get his views across.'

'Bullshit! Mailer's idea of positive action is to beat up on his wife, then cry all the way to the bank.'

Suddenly he stopped and peered into the window of a parked Chevrolet station wagon. 'Look at that.' He turned to Alix with a grin. 'Some asshole left his key in the ignition. Hop in, Bry, and we'll go for a joy ride.'

'You're kidding!'

'C'mon, babe. It's like we've been invited.'

'Sam!' Her heart was doing jackhammers. 'That's crazy. Look, if you want to take a drive, we'll go to the garage and get my car. But this . . . ! You're talking Grand Theft Auto.'

'Will you listen to the lawyer?' he mocked, but his eyes flashed fire. 'Grand theft, my ass. For Chrissakes, Bry, is that how you're going to spend your life – defending private fucking property? Don't you know that property is theft – and vice versa? Or are you afraid your old man's spies are watching you? Well, I'm going, pal.' He had his hand on the door.

Alix reeled. There were people on the street.

'In or out, Bry? Decide. Right now. Right this second.'

She turned away and began walking as fast as her feet would take her, convinced he would follow on foot, praying that this nonsense was only bluster. A few seconds later, there was a screech of gears, then the Chevy roared past her with a *voom voom voom!* Sam had stuck his head out the window and was roaring with laughter, as though it were all a cosmic joke.

She spent an anguished night waiting for a call from the police station to tell her that he'd been arrested and needed bail. The call never came. And when he turned up at her apartment the following evening, he behaved as though the incident had never occurred. All he could talk about was the My Lai Massacre. He was horror-struck.

'Jesus, Bry. The world is coming to an end.'

CHICAGO

Whether being back in Chicago was good or bad after so many years, Miranda couldn't decide. It was definitely strange, for she was masquerading as a different woman.

Her first order of business upon returning 'home' was to petition the court for a change of name. She cited professional reasons.

'What's wrong with Johnson?' Judge Lipschitz peered down at her. He was a diminutive man with a shiny bald dome and glasses perched on the tip of his nose. 'Look at my name and yet I made it to the bench. What's in a name anyhow? As the bard once said, who steals my purse steals trash, but who steals Lipschitz . . .'

As he lectured, Miranda guessed he had made this speech to a hundred such supplicants. There was no malice in it.

'With respect, your honor,' Miranda replied, 'may I point out that there are over three thousand Johnsons in the Chicago phone directory alone. Over eighty listed as M. Johnsons, seven M. J. Johnsons, five Margarets. Projected nationally, that would indicate phone entries for approximately five thousand six hundred eighty M. Johnsons, four hundred ninety-seven M. J. Johnsons . . . well, you get the idea. Your honor, I hope to make a name for myself in business, not share one with hundreds of other women across the country.'

The judge grinned. 'What do you want to change it to?' And when she told him, his grin widened. 'Sounds Chinese.' It was, he added, a refreshing change from similar requests he had handled. 'I have changed a Jim Hanks to a Rasheed Olatunji, a Miss Newman to a Miss Newperson, and a Mieczslav Janusewitz to Mike Johnson. You wouldn't be interested in switching to Janusewitz, would you? There happens to be a vacancy at the moment.' Then pleased with his own humor, he rapped his gavel. 'Petition granted. Next case . . .'

Formalities over, she obtained a new passport, driver's license and Social Security card in the name of Miranda Vee. Next she set about finding an apartment.

Her requirements were strict: it must be neat, modern, convenient, and above all – safe. What had happened to her in France must never happen again. Had there been burglaries in the building? she inquired in each place. Assaults? Rapes? 'I live alone and I want to feel secure.'

Her search was rewarded with a smart but small sublet facing the lake in a building fortified along the lines of a crusader's castle. 'Lady,' the doorman assured her, 'a fly couldn't get into this place unannounced.'

It would do, she thought, until she had made her fortune. Which, God willing, would be soon. She signed a one-year lease. *Miranda* no-middle-initial *Vee*.

Next came a shopping trip to Marshall Fields where Miranda laid out an exactly budgeted three thousand dollars from her Vegas winnings on a business wardrobe.

The years spent observing rich women at Marival had taught her that in matters of style, less is more, and quality more vital than quantity. She bought two suits, some silk blouses and four pairs of Italian shoes.

One suit was a Chanel tweed in the rich purple tones of a stained-glass window, finished with a chain-weighted hem. The other was of soft English flannel, beautifully cut, sleek yet feminine. She had seen its mate on the Bryden girl, and admired its quiet elegance and breeding.

As the fitter darted about with busy hands, making minuscule adjustments, Miranda stood still as a mannequin and stared at herself in the three-way mirror. The mirror image stared back. 'You fake,' it declared. 'Who the hell are you pretending to be? You're Maggie Jean Johnson, remember?'

Giggly little Maggie, who never paid more than twenty-five bucks (more accurately $24.95) for any outfit. Who had never set foot in a designer salon. Who dolled up in peppy prints and hot colors that showed plenty of leg. Ah, those were the days!

And the nights.

Saturday Night Threads, she used to call her best duds: short kicky dresses with swinging hemlines, strappy sandals with three-inch heels, dangling earrings that shook when she danced. How she had loved to dance! – the Twist, the Madison, the Bugaloo, the Watusi. And Maggie herself jiggling and jangling like a one-man band, bracelets clanking, earrings bobbling up and down to the pulse of the Big Beat.

No more. No metallic costume jewelry. Nothing but sterling silver and gold next to the face, Dr Frankl had said. It was one of a dozen injunctions – no cigarettes or alcohol among them – to remind her that she was an experimental creature. Like her namesake, a woman concocted from art and air and fantasy.

Miranda.

Alone in the apartment, she would say the name over and over, hoping it would sink in by dint of repetition. Yet she could not shake the conviction that Miranda Vee was not a real person, was nothing other than the product of paperwork in triplicate.

She was pleased to be back in Chicago. It was home and she loved it all: the parks, the Polish restaurants, the South Side jazz joints, the fun of St Patrick's Day when the Chicago River ran green. This was her city: from the sailboats gliding on Lake

Michigan to the saucy lingerie boutiques on State Street to the august Chicago Board of Trade on Jackson Boulevard, whose landmarked façade afforded a grand contrast to the frenetic action that took place inside.

And it was in that handsome edifice that her future lay.

The fitter took the last of the pins out of her mouth.

'Thank you, Miss Vee,' she said, in the respectful tones with which seamstresses addressed their betters.

For a moment, Miranda wondered who the hell she was talking to. *Miss Vee, my ass!*

Once upon a time (was it only four years ago?), she had been part of a complex network. She had had friends here, colleagues, neighbors, landladies, dry cleaners, dancing partners, one or two young men she had fallen in love with – any one of whom might stop her on the street, clap her on the shoulder and say, 'Hey, Maggie! Where have you been all this time?' For despite the testimony of her mirror, it seemed impossible that she could pass through familiar streets without incident.

For the first time since leaving Marival, she weighed the gravity of her action. She had eradicated twenty-four years of her past. Yet though Maggie Johnson was no more, she had not fully evolved into Miranda Vee.

For weeks, she hardly left her apartment, except to go to the libraries. Her days were spent studying the futures market, analyzing, compiling statistics, reading everything germane from *Business Week* and the *Financial Times* to livestock manuals and the effect of Black Pod Disease on the cocoa crop in Ghana. Every morning at ten, she placed imaginary orders: soy beans futures, cocoa, pork bellies, number one wheat. At the end of the business day, she would check the closing prices on television to see how she had done.

Sometimes she lost, mostly she gained, and by the end of eight weeks, she had, on paper, doubled her investment. Yet though common sense told her she was ready to join the real world, she continued to dawdle, convinced that the moment she set foot in Jackson Boulevard, someone would recognize her as 'the little gal from the typing pool at Hershy and Kay.'

How often had she daydreamed of walking through the front door of H & K Commodities, sashaying past the pool into Jay Conklin's office and tantalizing him with a six-figure order. Jay Conklin who had fallen over laughing when she asked if she might try her hand at trading. Who couldn't remember her name two days running.

And while any brokerage would do, there was a sweet satisfaction in picturing herself a courted client in the company where she had been the lowest of the low.

'My girl,' Jay referred to her in his casual way, his feet crossed on his desk. 'I'll send my girl around with the paperwork.' Or he'd buzz the intercom: 'One of you girls bring me coffee. And snap it up.'

Only it would be Jay Conklin who snapped to when Miss Vee deigned to call. That dream had sustained her at Marival.

But now, back in the 'real world,' she was losing her nerve. As the weeks trickled by, Miranda kept picturing another scenario. She would walk into Hershy and Kay, Jay Conklin would see her and shrug. 'Well, if it isn't what's-her-name! What d'ya do, kid? Have a face lift?'

She didn't think she could stand the humiliation. Each day she grew more timid, more uncertain about achieving her goal.

One afternoon on a Michigan Avenue bus, Annette Grossman got on and plumped down next to her. Miranda practically jumped out of her seat.

Annette! She bit her lips to keep from yelling.

How could Annette not know her? They had sat three feet away from each other for years. Had swapped earrings, sweaters. Lunched together. Double-dated.

Annette! She screamed silently. *It's me – Maggie!*

Annette gazed past her out the window for a moment, as though Miranda were invisible, then opened a Sidney Sheldon paperback. She wore a wedding ring, Miranda noticed. Had she married Jack Rosenthal? Or somebody else? Did they have kids? Was it possible she didn't realize just who was sitting in the next seat, sweating bullets? Good God, they were thigh to thigh. At last Miranda could stand the suspense no longer. She tapped Annette on the shoulder.

'Excuse me,' Miranda said.

Annette looked up from her book, her expression a blank. Miranda was shocked. She had assumed her voice would register.

'Sorry to bother you, but would you tell me when we get to Randolph? I'm a stranger in town.'

'Stop after next,' Annette said and returned to her novel.

'Thank you very much.' Miranda exhaled.

And that was it. Maggie Johnson was finally dead.

The following morning, in her Chanel suit, Miranda marched into the office of Hershy and Kay and asked to see the Vice President in charge of customer services.

'My name is Miranda Vee and I'm a private investor,' she explained when ushered into the sanctum sanctorum, 'I wish to open an account. To start with, I have a hundred thousand dollars to invest. Can you handle it personally?'

'I'd be delighted!' A smiling Jay Conklin motioned her into a chair. 'Would you like some coffee, Miss Vee?'

'Thank you. Milk please, no sugar.'

As he reached for the intercom, his smile went the extra yard.

'I'll have my girl bring it in right away.'

She remained a Hershy and Kay client only briefly. For delicious though it was to flaunt her clout in the office where she had once been a lowly worm, a major beneficiary of her account was her old nemesis Jay Conklin. He stood to make a fortune on commissions.

One day, without warning, she notified him that she would be taking her business elsewhere. Conklin was flabbergasted.

'But why?' he asked. 'We've done so very well by each other. There must be some reason.'

Miranda grinned. 'You know what us girls are like. Just fickle little bubble-heads, the lot of us.'

In fact, she hated paying commissions at all. Within a year of confiding her goal to a total stranger in a Las Vegas casino, Miranda had fulfilled a dream. She had bought herself a seat on the exchange.

LONDON

The first sound he heard out of her mouth was the sound of laughter.

It rippled across the room, over the clink of cocktail glasses, the chatter of wedding guests, to find its home in Peter Mainwaring's ear.

The sound was infectious – by turns silvery, deep-throated, light as a celesta, rich as plum pudding, encompassing the full repertoire of happiness. Peter put down his drink and tried to discover the source. Failing, he headed to the bar for a fresh glass of champagne.

Whenever possible, Peter turned down wedding invitations. Weddings made him uncomfortable for the simple reason that they were all about marriage. And the prospect of marriage made him want to run for cover.

Of course, Peter expected that he too would marry one day. When he was fifty, perhaps – the half-century mark having struck him as the prudent age for such a life-shaping decision. In the interim, he cherished his bachelorhood.

Others didn't. That was the problem. Weddings were prime occasions for friends and family to twit him mercilessly about his single status, as though it were a kind of affliction. Worse yet, there was something in the air at weddings that made normally sensible females grow dangerously dewy-eyed and fall prey to unreasonable hopes. In short, they were an emotional quagmire, best avoided.

He wouldn't have been here today, had the bride been anyone other than Sally Travis. For Sally, he made an exception. She was a dear friend, a colleague, and how could Peter not be on hand to wish her well? Ever quixotic, she had married a 'civilian' – which is to say someone from beyond the ranks of the entertainment world. Thus, except for a couple of fellow *Off the Wall*-ers, Peter found himself amid unfamiliar faces. And that unfamiliar laugh.

A few minutes later, he heard it again, coming roughly from Ted Northrup's direction. What on earth was so funny?

Drawn by the sound, he picked his way across the room to where Ted stood, leaning against the piano, holding court. Ted was in his goofy television persona and had found an audience in a pretty young woman whose face was flushed with laughter.

Well, not so pretty actually, Peter determined. Not 'pretty' in the beauty-contest scheme of things, but attractive. Not so young, either. Thirty, maybe. Small, dark, with black fly-away hair and a crooked smile and dark eyes that looked ready for all sorts of mischief. She was wearing a soft woolen dress the color of apricots, and crystal earrings that tinkled when she laughed. Ted was treating her to the 'French waiter' routine that was a staple of the show.

'. . . zee breast of jellied eel,' Ted concluded amid another gale of laughter. Peter inserted himself.

'Is this waiter-person bothering you, miss? I can see that he is. They should never let him mingle with the guests.'

She giggled and dabbed at her eyes with a lace handkerchief. Then Ted did the necessary. 'Peter, meet Anne. Anne – Peter.

And now if you'll excuse me, I must find my wife or whoever it was I came with. Watch out for this man, young lady. He's a notorious child molester.'

'Are you?' She turned to Peter with a glowing smile.

'Only during office hours,' he crooned. 'And you?'

She was a cousin of the groom's, it turned out, an illustrator or some such, up in London for the wedding, and having a super time. That wonderful laugh, Peter realized, derived more from the sheer joy of living than from parrying jokes. They chatted for perhaps ten or fifteen minutes, small talk, eminently forgettable, before she was co-opted by other guests. Peter drifted off to fetch another drink. When he looked for her a short time later, she had left.

He felt briefly let down, but no matter. The world was full of delightful women. He finished his champagne and went home.

That night, however, to his astonishment, Peter couldn't sleep. Worse – he couldn't read or think or get the sound of her laughter out of his head. His elbows itched. His nose tickled. There were butterflies in his stomach. Half a dozen times he got up, switched on the light, glared at the clock. Switched the light off.

He tried counting sheep jumping over a fence, counting beagles doing the same, naming all the counties in England, the stations on the District Line, songs that had the word 'love' in their titles. To no avail.

Damn it! He hadn't even had enough sense to take her telephone number or jot down her last name. But now the omission loomed as near-tragedy. She'd come up to London, he remembered her saying. But come up from where? He had the impression of something with a G in it. Guildford? Glastonbury? Glasgow? John O'Groats? If she were truly from John O'Groats, he might never see her again.

But if he didn't find her, he might never have another night's sleep. Surely there were trains to John O'Groats.

I've fallen in love, it dawned on him. Not even with a woman. With a laugh. Which was patently ridiculous. However, common sense insisted – or was it Oscar Wilde? – that the only thing to do with an obsession was succumb to it. He would call the girl, take her out to dinner and that would be that.

Which would have been fine if he knew where to get in touch with Anne What's-her-name from the city of G.

At daybreak he made tea and waited until he could decently ring up Ted Northrup in hopes that his friend could supply the missing details.

'Do you know what time it is?' Ted bellowed.

'Seven?'

'Six fifteen. And in answer to your question, I never saw the girl before in my life.'

At eight o'clock, unable to endure the suspense any longer, he awakened Sally née Travis now Fleisher at the bridal suite of the Georges Cinq in Paris.

'I can't believe you're doing this, Peter. I'm on my honeymoon.'

But after a brief consultation with her groom, interspersed with heavy giggling, Sally vouchsafed the last name of Golovin and that Anne lived in the suburbs. Sevenoaks. No, of course there was no G in Sevenoaks. And no to his next question as well, Sally didn't happen to have the phone number on her – 'Good God, Peter, I don't happen to have anything on me at the moment!' – but he might try Directory Enquiries.

'Bless you, Sally. I live again.'

More giggling at the other end. 'Don't you want to know if Anne's married? If there's a Mr Golovin in the background?'

'Oh, my God!' Peter's heart sank. 'Is there? Is she?'

'No,' Sally crowed, delighted to have wreaked a minor revenge. 'Though you might ask her about this Morgan she lives with. The big ape.'

With immense self-control, Peter waited until nine fourteen

before ringing up. She was living with someone. Of course. Figured. Lovely woman like her. It explained why she had left the wedding so early. To get back to that big ape.

If a man answers, he brooded, *I'll . . . I'll . . .* He couldn't think how to end the sentence. But Anne herself answered and the first words out of his mouth were 'Who the hell is Morgan?'

'He's not an ape at all,' Anne told him that evening, after he had motored down to Sevenoaks. 'I can't think why Sally said such a thing. He's a mandrill, actually, a fictional mandrill, as in *Adventures of Morgan the Mandrill*. My bread and butter. Well, anyhow, my bread and marge.'

She wrote children's books and it was her dearest hope that Morgan would some day be to simians what Paddington was to bears and Babar to elephants. Although at present, her titles didn't sell awfully well.

'I can't tell you how relieved I am,' Peter said.

'That Morgan is a mandrill or that I have no money?'

'Both.'

She laughed with obvious pleasure, then showed him about the tiny cottage, which was little more than a sitting room, a sleeping loft and a studio. She had paint under her fingernails which he found absurdly endearing. She seemed glad to see him, which was a source of unbearable delight.

They went out for an Indian meal, chatted, dawdled, didn't leave until the restaurant closed, after which Peter drove her home, pecked her lightly on the forehead and floated back to London, bewitched.

Love, he mused later that week – by then, he had seen her on five successive nights – love had nothing to do with logic. And it struck from the most unexpected quarters. Why this one? Peter couldn't say. He had known prettier women, more elegant women, had had dozens of affairs, but only once before in his life had a woman ever touched him to the core.

*

One evening over jasmine tea and biscuits in Anne's sitting room, Peter poured out his heart.

Anne had asked him why he abandoned the practice of psychiatry. He was about to return some trifling glib answer, when, for the first time in his life, he found himself able to articulate the truth.

'I quit because I fell in love with a patient.'

Anne said nothing, merely cocked her ear and waited for the story to come, her bright eyes full of sympathy.

'She was an extraordinary girl,' Peter began. 'American. Brave. Courageous. With a thirst for knowledge.'

She had been born into a poor family, the kind that mocks grand aspirations. The father, a meat-packer, was killed in an industrial accident when she was in high school; the mother, defeated by the contest of life, died soon after.

But the girl was ambitious, independent. At sixteen, she left school to strike out on her own, driven by that most American dream of endless upward mobility. It's a free world, she had been led to believe. Anyone can aspire to any station. She determined to put that promise to the test.

For the next four years, she clerked in a Chicago trading firm, putting in sixty-hour weeks, learning the business, trying to better herself. At night, she took courses in shorthand, book-keeping, accounting and finance. Yet her efforts were in vain. She remained mired at the bottom of the pyramid.

For hard though it was to be a woman in a man's world, she suffered an added disadvantage. In a 'classless society,' she was hobbled by her upbringing. Speech, style, dress, and manners: each stigmatized her as coming from the wrong side of the tracks.

She might have stayed put, made a living, married some local bloke and raised a family. Yet she never gave up aching for more. She hungered to see the world, meet interesting people, have adventures, absorb culture through her pores.

At twenty, she went to Paris for a year to work as an au pair with a well-to-do French family. Her new employers were to serve as her finishing school. In their household, she learned by observation: how to enter a room, select a bottle of wine, do clever things with scarves, look at paintings and speak French. And not just French. At the Alliance Française, she took a course that taught English as a foreign language and finally learned to speak her native tongue properly. At the end of the year, newly polished and self-confident, she bought a bicycle and set off on a cycling tour of France, a last holiday before returning to the States.

What happened next was never ascertained, for when Peter first saw her at Marival she was traumatized, wishing only to die.

At first his quest for a treatment that would save her from suicide was a professional challenge, but it soon became a personal one as well. Seeing her daily, struggling with her against excruciating odds, he soon lost his detachment. This pathetic creature, this Miss Nobody from Nowhere, had taken full possession of his heart. And though they never as much as kissed, he felt bound by invisible ties.

'I could scarcely admit to myself how much I loved her. And God knows I could never tell *her*.'

'But why not?' Anne's brown eyes gleamed with tears. 'Doctors marry patients. It's not unheard of. And you say she made a good recovery.'

'Because there would be no equity between us, don't you see that? No balance of power. What kind of marriage would we have had? There would always be a residue of pity on my part and – how shall I put this without sounding arrogant? – hero worship on hers. She idolized me, Annie. She put me on a pedestal, as though I were a god. It would have been criminal to take advantage of those sentiments. Best that she find her own way in the long run. So I let her walk out of my life forever. I don't even know what name she goes by now. No matter. It's over, which is just as well, not just for her sake but for mine. You see, she never criticized me or found fault or questioned my judgment. Which was soothing for my ego, but very unhealthy. I need someone to tell me I'm a complete berk, from time to time.'

'You're a complete berk, Peter,' Anne said.

He looked up, surprised. 'Why?'

'Because you let what you wanted slip through your hands.'

She put her arms around him and kissed him full on the lips. A great rich lingering kiss. And at the touch of her lips, the ghost of his old love was laid to rest.

'You're right.' He drew her close. 'And I promise never to do it again.'

ROUTE 128

Rare though it was for such a magnificent car to grace such a mean North End street, Sam Matthews took it in his stride. He had a notion the 'call' would come one of these days.

'Mr Matthews?' The chauffeur touched his cap. 'If you'll get in, sir, Mr Bryden would like to meet with you.'

'As I would like to meet him.'

They drove in silence through the wet October night, arriving a half hour later at a pair of high iron gates. The chauffeur tapped a numerical pad on the dashboard and the gates swung open to reveal a broad oak-lined drive. Sam tapped the divider for attention.

'Sir?' The chauffeur's head tilted back.

'What's your name?'

'Billings, sir.'

'Billings-Sir. A splendid name. Tell me, Billings-Sir, how do those gates operate? Some kind of electronic gadget you have there?'

'Staff are not allowed to discuss security arrangements.'

Sam couldn't resist a jibe.

'I might be staff here myself one day soon. A paid employee or a member of the family, pretty much the same thing.'

Alix had described the house as 'comfortable,' but she was prone to understatement. A classic-revival mansion with its porticoed façade, it was modeled after Monticello.

A Filipino maid answered the door.

'May I take your jacket, sir?'

'That's okay,' Sam said. 'I don't think I'll be long.'

She led him down a central hall to a set of double doors. 'Through here, sir,' she said with her lilting accent. 'Mr Bryden is waiting.'

It was a handsome room, square, white and high-ceilinged, furnished with English antiques, oriental rugs and American primitive paintings. By the window in a Chippendale wing chair, one of a facing pair, Lucius Bryden was sitting, lean and erect in a dark business suit, hands linked in his lap. He had long thin fingers and immaculate nails.

Sam ambled across the room, insolence in every step. The mud of his boots left traces on the carpet. Bryden didn't wince nor did he greet him. Instead, with a dip of the head, he indicated that his visitor take the chair opposite. Sam sat down, crossed his legs and pulled out a pack of cigarettes.

Thus disposed, the two men silently took each other's measure. Like children in a playground, they embarked on a contest of wills: who would break the silence first?

Sam grinned and lit a Gauloise. Bryden grimaced but said nothing. As far as Sam was concerned, they could sit there forever, for he was damned if he would be the first to speak.

At last, Lucius Bryden grunted. 'Sam Matthews,' he said. It was a statement, not a question. Sam took a drag on his cigarette and let the ash fall to the floor.

They glared at each other for another minute, then Bryden folded his arms.

'How much?' he said.

The words sank like dead weight, from Bryden's lips to the Isfahan carpet. Sam wondered if the room had been sound-proofed, or whether it was the creepy quiet of the country. He was a city boy himself.

He smoked for a bit, looked thoughtful, then ground out his cigarette in a Jasperware bowl.

'Oh, I like that, Mr Bryden. You are a man of few words. Simple. Direct. How much? Just like Baron Scarpia in *Tosca*. *Quanto*? How much? Very operatic. I was a music student, you see. I appreciate theatrical gestures. But back to your question, I take it you're inquiring about my price list. Well, as with every transaction, the price depends on the services rendered -- or not rendered, as the case may be. I presume we're talking dowry here.' He grinned shamelessly. 'Or maybe we should call it a reverse dowry. How much will I charge *not* to marry your daughter, because she'd have me in a minute, you know. Of course you have the option of cutting her off without a sou, but it wouldn't make a damn bit of difference to Alix. She's quite willing to live on love alone.'

Bryden said nothing, merely refolded his legs.

'Well,' Sam went on, 'maybe I am too, but then again maybe I'm not. Anyhow, my bet is that eventually she'll come into money on her own. Surely, a man in your position would have set up a trust fund for her. It's a standard rich man's tax dodge. Money that your daughter -- my wife -- will get at a certain age whether you like it or not. So all I'd have to do is wait. However' -- he lit another Gauloise -- 'it could be that I'm not a patient person, in which case, we can negotiate.'

'I am willing to give you fifty thousand dollars' -- the words issued from paper-thin lips -- 'on the condition that you sign a document promising to leave the Boston area and never see my daughter again. My lawyers have prepared a contract.'

'You mean you won't take my word as a gentleman?' Sam sneered. 'It's a pittance for such a lovely young lady, but okay. Lucky for you I'm broke. Except I want the money *now*!'

Bryden nodded his assent.

'And in cash,' Sam added.

'Don't be stupid, Matthews. I don't keep that kind of money in the house. I'll give you a check.'

'Don't *you* be stupid, Bryden. You know my circumstances. Where the hell can I cash a fifty-thousand dollar check? It would take a week to get it cleared, by which time you'd have your chit of paper to show to Alix just what kind of low-life I am. And then what? You put a stop-payment on the check and I'm screwed. She always said you were a canny bastard. Nope. It has to be in cash or traveler's checks, properly endorsed. I'm told you keep a supply on hand.'

The two men haggled about the means of payment for a few minutes more, then Lucius Bryden went over to his desk. He pulled out a wad of American Express traveler's checks and three copies of the contract. Then he rang a bell.

Sam signed all copies with only a cursory glance. The parlor maid and the Jamaican cook appended their signatures as witnesses. The checks changed hands.

'I think our business is concluded,' Bryden said.

'Very satisfactorily. Now if you'll lend me twenty bucks, I need the cab fare back to town.'

Alix had already gone to bed when Sam burst into her room, very full of himself. He dumped the stack of checks on her night-table, then sprawled down alongside her.

'You won't believe what happened, so I'm going to tell you . . .' He spoke rapidly, swallowing words, erupting with laughter now and then, while Alix listened horror-stricken.

'. . . so I took the fucker for nearly eighteen thou. End of story. Whole business didn't take half an hour, including the time it took him to endorse the checks. After which, I went to the Jade Palace and ate Chinese.'

He stopped to wipe his eyes, then began howling again. 'Asshole! He acted like that goddamn paper was binding. What's he going to do – haul me into court for breach of contract? What a joke! Anyhow, he'd have to find me first. But this way, I get both you *and* the bread. Sweet Jesus, but it's good to be alive. Make me coffee, love – will you? There's a lamb.'

'Oh, Sam! How could you?' Alix burst into tears.

'How could I what? Rip him off? Come on, Bry. He asked for it. Son of a bitch! Trying to buy me for a few thousand bucks. I hate him for it. And you should too. Please, babe. Don't cry. The man isn't worth a single fucking tear.'

But Alix was devastated. The vision of the men she loved dealing, haggling, bartering away her future, was unbearable. 'How could you sign such a paper?' she cried. 'Why didn't you do the honorable thing, tell him to take his money and shove it. You should have stood up for me.' Then she turned her back to him and buried her head in the pillow.

Unrepentant, Sam took her in his arms, and began stroking her hair with gentle fingers. Alix felt her flesh melt.

'So I lied to him, babe,' he murmured in her ear. 'It meant zilch. I lie all the time, Bry. I have to, to stay alive. But I've never lied about loving you, I swear. My God, if not for you I'd have been gone long before now. As for the money, I don't give a rat's ass about it. It was just a chance to get back at your father. Here! You want it? It's yours. In fact, that would be a sweet revenge. Take the checks and donate 'em to your law commune. Wouldn't that frost your old man? No? That's okay too, 'cause I've always wondered what it's like to have money to burn.'

With that, he reached for his lighter and began torching the checks one by one. The bits of paper flared up briefly, and burnt themselves out in the waste-basket. Alix watched in mute fascination. Then the smoke alarm went off.

The sound galvanized Alix. She snatched the remaining checks and jammed them into his shirt pocket.

'Keep it, and buy yourself food, some decent clothes. Winter's coming, you don't have a warm coat. Oh, Sam . . . Sam! What'll happen when my father finds out he's been swindled?

One way or another, there'll be hell to pay. I must be crazy putting up with you!'

Suddenly they were in each other's arms, making love with a first-time ardor. Only later, lying in a tangle of limbs and lips and hair, Sam grew thoughtful.

'You don't think he'd put out a contract on me, Bry?'

'A contract!' Alix defuzzed her brain. 'Like in a gangster movie? My father isn't a mafioso! But you can bet he'll make trouble. You haven't exactly been a law-abiding citizen and he has all kinds of connections. Police . . . FBI. Plus he knows where you live. Maybe you shouldn't go back there.'

Sam mulled this over. 'Maybe not. Maybe I shouldn't even be Sam Matthews for a while.' Then he snorted. 'If it's games your old man wants to play, we'll play games.'

He left shortly before dawn, whistling the love music from *Tosca*. He was in excellent spirits.

He phoned the next night and left a message on her machine – 'I love you, babe.' She didn't hear from him for two more days. She resolved not to worry. Sam always turned up.

Friday afternoon, she was in the *Law Review* office when a call came through for her.

'Listen and don't talk,' Sam said in an urgent whisper. In the background she could hear the roar of highway traffic.

'Something's happened. No questions. Just do as I say.'

He instructed her to drive her car to the Waltham exit of Route 128, park twenty yards beyond the Exxon station where there was a wooded area. The trip should take less than an hour. 'And for God's sakes, Bry, drive carefully. I don't want you stopped for speeding.'

It was five thirty and getting dark when she arrived at the designated spot. She switched off the motor, locked the door and sat breathless. Ten minutes passed, twenty. She watched the cars come down the ramp. Commuters going home.

A man pounded at the driver's seat window. At first, she

didn't recognize Sam. He was coatless, but wearing a three-piece suit and white shirt. He had cut his hair. He had a striped tie on. She had never before seen him in a tie. She had the sense of being in a dream.

'Open up,' he mouthed through the glass.

She unlocked the door and slid into the passenger seat. He got in and turned on the motor. His hands were blue from the cold, his eyes preternaturally bright.

'You didn't bring a jug of coffee, did you, Bry?'

She shook her head.

'Shit!' He kissed her, then placed a finger across her lips. 'Listen, love. I don't have much time. Life's gotten dangerous. Like I said, something happened and I have to go underground for a while. It's that or jail. The cops will be on to me any minute, if they aren't already. Anyhow, the less you know the better — for both our sakes, believe me.'

'What happened?' she cried. 'Sam, what kind of games are you playing?'

'War games,' he said. His excitement was palpable: a mix of exultation and fear. Sam was high all right, but not on drugs or booze. He was running on pure adrenaline. His speech came out in spurts.

'Action, babe! Nothing in the world can take its place. You can only sit around and bullshit for so long, then you've gotta *act*!· I'm not sorry, you understand. Only there were problems, you see. Mechanical problems. So the safest thing for me is to split. Head for Canada, maybe. At least till this blows over. Brydie, if you love me—'

'Oh, God!' she burst out.

'If you love me, you'll help. I'm broke. I'm on the run and I don't have wheels. What's your cash situation?'

'A few dollars. You know I never carry much money. Here. Take whatever's in there.' She handed him her bag, fighting down hysteria, trying hard to think like a lawyer. Perhaps Sam was being dramatic, romanticizing his exploits. It wouldn't be the first time. 'Exactly how serious is it, Sam? Tell me. I have to know.'

He opened her wallet, took out two tens and a five, leaving the singles and the credit cards.

'How serious?' she repeated

Sam fixed his eyes on hers.

'Dead serious.'

Alix's heart stopped. *Capital crime* flashed through her brain. She might be aiding and abetting a killer.

Sam handed back her bag.

'Believe me, I didn't intend to hurt anyone, Bry, only shake people up, make some mischief. The fucking device wasn't supposed to go off until midnight.'

'Stop.' She clapped her hands over her ears. She couldn't bear to hear more.

'You're right,' he muttered. 'The less you know, the better for both of us. But I've gotta get away.'

'Twenty-five dollars won't get you very far,' she said.

'Plus I want your car, only for Christ's sakes don't report it stolen. I need a decent head start.' He took her hands in his. 'It's lousy, the way it worked out, but that's life. You're the only thing I'll regret. I love you, Bry.'

She nodded mutely, too stunned to speak. He gunned the car and began driving through the back streets of Waltham into Watertown, till he spotted a station stop on the MTA. He pulled up at the bus shelter but left the motor running.

'You can find your way home from here, can't you, babe? I won't be in touch for a while, you understand. I have to play it cool. No point in fucking up both our lives.'

'But, Sam,' she cried, 'what about us? I'll die if I don't see you again.'

They clung to each other in a long and desperate embrace. Sam was the first to pull away.

'I'll come back for you, Bry, when things calm down. I promise. One day we'll laugh about this. But meanwhile I have to go, babe. Take care, stay calm and remember – no matter what happens, I love you.'

Sam reached across her to open the door. She got out slowly, choking down tears. Then she reached up and unclasped her necklace.

'These pearls are the most precious thing I own, Sam. Sell them. And may they bring you safe passage.'

'A bomb went off at Bryden Electronics,' said the anchorman on *News at Ten*, 'causing widespread damage and maiming a maintenance man. The employee, Michael Mason, is in critical condition at Waltham General. According to police sources . . .'

There was a freeze frame from the video monitors that recorded the entrance of all visitors to the plant. The picture showed a tall man in a dark suit and white shirt, carrying a briefcase. Despite the grainy quality, the likeness was there. Recognizably Sam. Her father must have 'made' him by now.

Alix pieced together the facts.

At three that afternoon, carrying false identity, Sam drove up in what later proved to be a stolen car. He presented himself at the gate, saying he had an interview in personnel. He was promptly admitted, the appointment having been made the previous day in the name of Arthur J. Wassermann.

The applicant, who offered 'impeccable credentials,' according to the personnel man, purported to be a Stanford graduate with a Ph.D. in computer engineering. Once inside the building, the young 'job-seeker' was given a cursory tour of the facility, during which he managed to leave his briefcase in an area containing data banks. A few minutes later he excused himself, ostensibly to go to the men's room, and disappeared.

The explosion took place a little after four, blowing out windows, destroying a dozen computers, damaging others, and ripping the limbs off the maintenance man.

Alix never went to bed that night. She was terrified for Sam. Why was she sitting here, warm and safe? She should have gone with him, sharing his danger, his fate. It was like that night on the lake in Marival when she had been too timid to jump in to help Kim.

Once again she cursed herself for not being brave. Heroic. For what was true love if not the will to sacrifice everything for the beloved – even life itself?

Yet her anxiety was two-edged. Guilt mixed with shame. She couldn't free herself of the suspicion that Sam had used her.

It was no coincidence that the target of his violence had been Lucius Bryden's firm. Or that the whole scheme – clothes, briefcase and explosives – had been financed with Lucius Bryden's money. Could it be that her father was right? That all Sam had ever seen in Alix was her name and family power? If so, then their 'love' had been a lie.

No! She refused to entertain such heresy. Why, Sam's last words had been 'I love you.' If she didn't believe that, she would die.

She sat up all night drinking tea and listening to Mahler. Every hour on the hour, she switched on the radio to check the news.

Developments were not long in coming. By 5 a.m., the FBI had located the real Arthur Wassermann, who was a genuine Stanford Ph.D., working for Westinghouse in Texas. By seven, the culprit was tentatively identified as Samuel Harold Matthews. (So even the 'Houston' had been a fib, Alix thought without surprise.) Shortly after nine, Michael Mason died of his wounds. An all-points bulletin had gone out. Sam Matthews was wanted nationwide for murder.

Damn him! Alix wept. *And pray for him too!*

At a little before ten, there was a knock at her door. She opened it to Lucius Bryden.

'You're a very lucky girl,' he said, his eyes flashing.

'Lucky!' Alix thought she would faint.

'Extremely fortunate. I have spent the last three hours with my lawyers trying to keep you out of jail. Successfully, I may add. You're aware, of course, that you have figured in the FBI files for over a year. If not for my connections in Washington, you would be facing criminal charges. Conspiracy to commit a felony. Aiding and abetting a terrorist. Destruction of government property. Entire banks of data gone forever . . .'

He began outlining the extent of the damage. Totting up the cost. It ran into millions.

Alix listened, numb with pain, yet aware that never once in his catalogue of crimes did he mention that a man had died. His own employee, in fact. But what was life and death to Lucius Bryden? Instead, he seated himself on the sofa, and pinched the crease in his trousers. It was knife-sharp already. Alix waited for him to finish his speech.

'I had no knowledge before the fact,' she said simply.

Lucius's mouth narrowed to a single harsh line.

'So you say.' His nose twitched in distaste. 'That piece of human garbage was in this apartment last Monday. He visited you just hours after he took money from me on false pretenses. Your doorman keeps me informed. You made love. Your laundry woman keeps me informed as well. Tell me, Alix, did the two of you plan this outrage together? Was this your idea of a joke?'

A tide of wrath began welling up inside her.

'That's a vicious question.'

'It was a vicious act.' He paused, to let his contempt sink in. 'However, I will give you the benefit of the doubt. I prefer to believe that you were exploited by this fellow. A foolish girl, who squandered her affections on a man whose sole intention was to humiliate the Bryden family. That, at least, was the argument I gave my friends at the FBI. I convinced them to leave your name out of the investigation. So you have me to thank for your freedom and your continued good standing in Harvard. In turn, I demand my quid pro quo.'

'Quid pro quo?' She tried to suppress her inner rage and found it surprisingly easy. Years of rejection, of coldness and isolation had made her an adept at disguising emotion. 'What do you want – my gratitude? I'm glad I'm not in jail, okay?'

'More than that, Alix. Gratitude doesn't begin to compensate for such behavior. You've caused a great deal of misery. It has to be atoned for. Specifically, I have three considerations. First, you must tell me where Matthews is at present. If you don't know, then you must promise to inform the police, should he get in touch with you.'

In the dozen hours since she had said goodbye to Sam he might well have crossed the border into Canada. She hoped so, for his sake. Her face was a mask.

'Second,' Lucius went on, 'I want your solemn oath never to see him again.'

'And third?' she asked.

'Third – I expect you to beg my forgiveness.'

Alix's heart turned to steel.

'And if I refuse to meet your terms, then what?'

'You will have proven yourself a wicked and ungrateful child. Should you refuse – and I cannot believe you would be so reckless – then you can expect nothing from me. Neither your allowance nor rent nor tuition. Not the clothes on your back nor the food on your table. You will be a penniless girl with no home and no prospects, for I will cut you out of my will and out of my life! However, should you be sensible and accede to my conditions, then we can continue as before. As though this dismal incident never occurred. You will lead an orderly existence, finish law school and look forward to a brilliant future, your heritage intact. Do I make myself clear?'

'Perfectly.'

'So think, Alix. Think about what you have to gain – and to lose. You can have everything or nothing.'

'I don't need to think, Daddy. You leave me no choice.'

She folded her hands, head bowed as though in filial submission. Beneath half-closed lids, she saw the flicker of triumph in his eyes. It was all she needed. She rose to her feet. The flow of emotion could no longer be dammed. The words spewed out like molten lava, scalding, excoriating, laden with the accumulated wrath of years.

'Nothing!' she snarled. 'So Lucius Bryden will give me nothing, right? Well, I've had nothing from you from the day I was born. No love, no warmth. In twenty-three years have I ever had a hug? An endearment? When was I ever made to feel welcome in your presence? For twenty-three years you starved me out, treated me like a leper. For this I should be grateful? I should grovel at your feet? As for "that piece of garbage," as you so elegantly put it – at least from Sam I had love and affection. Two words I doubt you know the meaning of. But getting back to your demands, let me give you a formal response, because I know that's how you like to conduct business, isn't it? In terms that are crystal clear. The answers to your three conditions are No. No. And No. No! I will never betray Sam Matthews. No! I will never forswear his love. And no! I shall never beg you for anything! Forgiveness indeed! You would have done better to beg mine! But I will neither forgive nor forget! As long as there is breath in my body, I shall never forgive you for trying to purchase me from Sam. He burnt your money, you know. That's what he thought of it. Forgiveness!' She choked on the word. 'Keep your money, I want nothing from you. Nothing. This is how I value by heritage.'

She seized the pretty Spode teapot from the table and hurled it across the room. It crashed against the silver gilt mirror. Then she reached for the antique crystal inkwell. 'And this!' she shouted, as it shattered into a thousand gleaming shards. 'And this!' The Chinese ginger jar was next.

She felt sublime. Potent. Who would ever have thought that an act of violence could afford such satisfaction? This must have been how Sam had felt the day before – delirious with the joy of seeing things go bang. *Bang!* The English carriage clock. The celadon fruit bowl. The Imari vase. It was an orgy of rage, of uninhibited destruction, ending only when her arms grew tired, by which time almost everything breakable had been reduced to smithereens.

But by then Lucius Bryden was long gone.

Alix collapsed into a chair, exhausted. She lit a Gauloise from a pack Sam left behind. The pungent aroma made him seem alternately near and far away. She looked around to see if by chance an ashtray had escaped the holocaust. None had. She let the ash dribble to the floor.

Her father would make good his threat, Alix had no doubt. By now he was probably busy with his lawyers, canceling credit cards, rewriting his will. Turning her into a non-person.

Amazing, she brooded as she sat amidst the smoke and broken china. *Within the space of twenty-four hours, I have lost a lover, a father, and a fortune.*

NEW YEAR'S EVE

Times Square was jammed. A heaving, happy sea of thighs and breasts and butts and shoulders. A sonic barrage of shrieks and sirens and giggles and ghetto blasters. Let alone hear yourself speak, you couldn't move one millimeter, couldn't twitch your nose without getting positively intimate with a total stranger. Who was as thrilled as you were to be in this place at this time. At the heart of the universe.

The cold was brutal, but Kim scarcely felt it. All about her was warmth, gaiety. The wintry air held the perfume of promise. Because this wasn't your ordinary run-of-the-mill New Year's Eve. Tonight was special. In a few moments, the big white ball would begin its traditional descent, arriving at the stroke of midnight to announce the death of one decade, the birth of another.

'Hold on to my hand,' Bette shouted over the hubbub. 'You could be swept away!' But Kim was in heaven. She loved the sense of being part of a mass, of sharing this spectacular moment with a multitude.

TEN! the roar went up from the thousands of throats. *NINE! EIGHT! SEVEN!* – Kim shouted too – *SIX! FIVE!* – she clutched Bette's hand tighter – *FOUR! THREE! TWO! ONE!* – Bette squeezed back. Then came the final explosion –

HAPPY NEW YEAR!

'Happy New Year, honey.' Bette hugged Kim.

'Ditto ditto ditto.' Kim hugged Bette.

After which, their cheeks bright with cold, the two women pushed their way through the throng to welcome the new era with slabs of pepperoni pizza at Sbarros. New York pizza was better than pizzas anywhere else, they agreed. Spicier. More – well, more sophisticated. Like everything else about their adopted home. Bette licked the last of the sauce off her fingers, then ceremoniously hoisted a plastic coffee cup.

'So long, sixties,' she announced. 'They were a total drag. But the seventies? Like Bette Davis said – fasten your seat belt! – 'cause the seventies are gonna take us to the top of the world.'

Her impulse had been to turn down the Andersens' invitation for no other reason than that she rarely went to parties. However, Miranda respected obligations.

Joe was a friend and mentor, the grand old man of the commodities market who had helped her buy a seat on the exchange. His wife Ellen was sweet and hospitable.

'There'll be dancing,' Ellen promised, 'and plenty of nice young men on hand.' Eligible men – that went without saying. Well, why not? Miranda hadn't danced in years. As for those eligible men, Peter would have approved. He always told her she must get out into 'the real world' – presumably, the real world being a place where men and women laughed, flirted and fell in love. Thus Miranda was doing her therapeutic duty.

For the party, she had splurged on a sexy black crepe column by Geoffrey Beene, topped off with a satin evening wrap that matched the sapphire of her eyes.

'You ought to treat yourself to a sable coat,' her accountant said – it had been *that* kind of year – but Miranda couldn't bear the thought of wearing the skin of an animal. Cashmeres and satins would have to suffice. As it was, she arrived looking chic and very expensive.

And it was fun! Marvelous food, barrels of bubbly (though she limited herself to a single glass of champagne) and a raft of dancing partners, mostly nice, some delightful. One fellow in particular, an executive at Continental Can, was personable and attentive.

'Tom Wherry's a terrific catch,' Ellen confided. 'I invited him especially for you.' And, judging by the way Tom popped up at Miranda's elbow every time she turned around, the 'catch' seemed eager to be caught.

But as the old year drew closer to its end, she succumbed to an anxiety attack. At midnight, Tom Wherry would kiss her. It was standard procedure for New Year's Eve. It meant nothing.

Yet the prospect terrified her and the knowledge that her fears were unreasonable did nothing to allay them. He would take her in his arms and she'd be trapped. Caught like a bird in a snare, while an alien tongue forced its way between her lips, choking her, strangling her.

A dim memory stirred, painful and repellent. Her palms grew damp. In her ears, a rush of blood hammered out the primal message: fight or flight.

Flight!

Shortly before midnight, Miranda fetched her wrap and made her excuses, saying she had another party to attend.

'But can't I . . . ?' Tom said.

'No. Sorry.' And she was gone.

Twenty minutes later she pulled up in the garage beneath her building. She had missed the big moment. The new decade had begun without her tribute.

Miranda parked, then headed for the service elevator, alert for intruders as usual. Garages were notoriously dangerous areas, even this one, though it was on closed-circuit TV.

Suddenly, Miranda heard the rustle of paper. She tensed. In a shadowy corner, something was alive. Moving. Stalking her. Who would be in a deserted garage at this hour on New Year's Eve? Robbers. Rapists. 'Help me!' the scream rose to her throat, then subsided as quickly when, from behind a bank of trash cans, the mysterious intruder emerged.

'You idiot!' Miranda almost wept with relief. If anything the 'intruder' was more panicked than she was. The ears were pinned back. The stiff marmalade fur was standing on end.

Miranda got down on her knees.

'Here . . . kitty kitty kitty.'

She inched forward, crooning, trying to win its trust. The poor thing was skin and bones, and half frozen into the bargain. Noiselessly, she slipped off her wrap and pounced, swooping the kitten up in a whoosh of satin.

'It's okay, puss.' She cradled the kitten in her arms. 'You're safe now. We'll go up and have some nice warm milk.'

A few minutes later, the pair were comfortably ensconced in the kitchen. Miranda watched the kitten tackle a bowl of Half-and-Half, then take possession of a chair by the radiator. *Here to stay*, the stance announced.

'My big New Year's Eve date,' Miranda said wryly.

She supposed she ought to name it, but the kitten was too young to tell if it were male or female. Not that it mattered. She would call it OJ. That was unisex. Besides, Miranda had made a fortune on orange juice futures last month.

Then she brewed a pot of coffee, and thought of Peter.

Nearly two years had passed since they had said their farewells, yet tonight had made it clear: If ever she were to love, to marry and have children, it must be with him. If ever she were to entrust her future to a man, it must be to him.

When they parted, that appeared an impossible dream. What had she to offer him but her needs and her fears?

Now, however, the situation had changed.

Peter cared for her. That much she intuited. Only he had felt – she could quite understand it, since she had felt the same way – that she was a nobody. No breeding or background. Hardly a fit mate for a Cambridge-educated gentleman.

But she was no longer a nobody. She was Miranda Vee, a force in the Chicago financial world with a seat on the exchange. A woman of substance, respected, admired. A 'catch' herself, to use Ellen Andersen's term. As the situation stood now, she and Peter might meet on equal ground. The brilliant psychiatrist, the distinguished businesswoman.

Dr and Mrs Peter Mainwaring, she mouthed cautiously. Radiance lit her from within. It sounded so right. So natural. *Let's have the Mainwarings over. The Mainwarings – such a delightful couple. Miranda and Peter. Peter and Miranda.*

With Peter, she would never be afraid. Safe. Safe at last.

'Why not, OJ? Can you tell me one reason why not?' She scratched her new companion behind the ears.

Why not indeed? But she would have to take her fate in her hands. First, she had to find out where Peter was, how he was. Then proceed from there.

Monday morning, she would hire a private investigator to make inquiries. It was a simple problem, solved in a matter of weeks. Then, when Peter had been located, she would go to him.

She would arrive in a chauffeured limousine. Magnificently dressed. And he would be stunned to see how elegant she had become, how influential. A wife of whom the finest gentleman could be proud. And if he appeared to be intimidated by her transformation, Miranda would take the initiative and propose.

A bold move, to be sure. But life had taught her to be bold. Daily, she gambled in the futures of cattle and soy beans and wheat, staking vast sums on her skills and judgment. By nature, she was a plunger, a risk-taker. Yet what future was more vital than her own? What wealth compared to the happiness of reciprocated love? She would take the plunge, in both senses of the term. God willing, they would marry.

That night, Miranda lulled herself to sleep in a dream of white weddings and Mendelssohn marches. Dr and Mrs – or would he prefer Mr and Mrs? Mrs Peter Mainwaring. It had a lovely ring. Would they marry here? Or in Switzerland? Or in London? Big wedding? Small? Did it matter?

OJ snuggled up against her and purred.

The din was fierce. It always was at Adrian's parties, but tonight even more so, given that a new decade was about to begin. Old friends, old jokes, silly hats and crackers, plus enough champers and egg-nog to launch another *QE2*. On the stroke of midnight, Big Ben rang in a new decade, courtesy of the BBC, and everyone present linked hands and sang 'Auld Lang Syne.' Followed by a good deal of kissing.

A few minutes later, Peter, emboldened by eggnog, maneuvered Anne into a relatively quiet corner. He was determined to act upon his New Year's resolution. Now or never.

'Annie.'

'Yes, love?'

'There's something I want to ask you.'

'Yes, darling?'

'A simple question.'

Only it wasn't simple at all. He felt suddenly tongue-tied. And foolish. They'd known each other what – a few months? She'd probably think he was presumptuous.

Or kidding. Peter kidded all the time. In fact, it was a wonder that anyone ever took him seriously.

Suppose she did take him seriously? In which case, she might very well say no. Who was he to be so arrogant as to alter the style of life to which she seemed so happily accustomed? She was an independent woman, none more so, and would doubtless laugh at his cheek. For what on earth would a beautiful young girl like Anne – okay, not breathtakingly beautiful or ferociously young but so very remarkable – why should such a divine being wish to tie herself down with an old duffer like him? Thirty-four next birthday. Practically middle-aged. Pipe-and-slippers country, so to speak. Creaking bones, thinning hair. Geriatric ward coming up. Being pushed in a wheelchair. Pity. Handsome young woman tied down to an old fossil like that. Who drank too much into the bargain.

She would say no and that would be the end of it.

On the other hand – she might say yes, a scenario that struck terror in his heart.

Peter Mainwaring married! – with all the connotations that followed. Hair in the sink, yoghurt in the fridge, she would probably use his razor when he wasn't looking. Well, Peter liked to keep his razor just so.

But those were minor considerations. They paled beside the loss of freedom that marriage signified. What would become of the Friday night pub crawls, or his playing a bit of rugger at Hurlingham on a crisp winter morning? Of that most masculine pleasure – messing about with boats? All those joys gone forever. Scuttled in the swamp of matrimony.

Marriage. The noose. The ball and chain. The life sentence. Trouble and strife, in cockney. Being single was comfortable as breathing. Peter had been born in the single state; it was doubtless what nature intended for him all along.

'Peter?' Anne was eyeing him with naked curiosity.

'Umm . . . yes?' He shifted his weight from foot to foot.

'There was something you wanted to ask me?'

His mouth went dry. 'Ask you. Sounds like – askew, doesn't it. As in, my mind's gone askew.' He grunted. 'Bad joke. Was going to ask you if you want another eggnog.'

She shook her head and smiled.

'You were not. You were going to ask me if I will marry you, and to spare you additional embarrassment or suspense, I will give you my answer now. The answer is – yes.'

'Yes.' His heart skipped. Thudded with joy. 'You really . . . really . . . ?'

'Really!' She threw her arms about him. 'I decided that the moment I met you at Chris and Sally's wedding. Yes, I'd like nothing better than to be Mrs Peter Mainwaring.'

And in that moment Peter had an epiphany. After years of floundering, questing, pondering his goal in life, all was revealed. He had been put on earth to marry Anne Golovin.

She had sold everything that could be sold. The china – or what was left of it. The prints to a gallery on Mount Vernon Street. The carpet to an Armenian rug dealer. But selling items one by one was too time-consuming for a third-year law student. After a week scurrying from one dealer to another, Alix called in an estate liquidator to quote her a price for the contents of the apartment. 'Everything?' he asked. 'Down to the bare walls,' she replied, excluding only the kitchen table, two chairs, some bedding, a few personal possessions and her bike.

He poked around for twenty minutes, jotted down notes, then made an offer. Alix nodded. It never occurred to her to haggle, though, judging from the gleam in the dealer's eye, she knew she was being ripped off. No matter. It was sufficient to pay her last term's tuition and other essentials.

She had to finish school and pass the bar, that was the given. As for the rest, she looked forward to a simpler, more spartan existence. There was a perverse pleasure to be found in this new image of austerity, like probing a toothache with your tongue.

The problem was that Alix had been raised with no economic sense. She never asked the price of anything. Cost was irrelevant. She had had an allowance which provided her with pocket money; beyond that she had an inch-thick pile of charge accounts and credit cards. All bills went directly to her father. Lucius paid her rent, garage, grocery bills, cleaning woman, even her hairdresser. She had no idea what she spent.

That she happened to be a woman of relatively simple tastes was beside the point (in fact, her simply tailored suits and 'little black dresses' cost a fortune); what mattered was that no limits had ever been put on her expenditures.

Until now. Suddenly Alix found herself without the least notion of how to proceed. Where did one learn to be poor? Was there a special course at school, Poverty 101? A how-to manual for the newly impoverished? Were there *Cliff's Notes*?

Her first jolt of reality came when she inquired about the rent on her apartment. 'Per *month*?' she asked astonished.

Logic dictated moving into cheap digs, but Alix resisted. The apartment would be her last extravagance. For how could she surrender the rooms where she and Sam had passed so many rapturous nights and blissful mornings? The very walls resonated with memories. Besides, where would Sam reach her, if not here?

Though weeks had passed since the explosion, Alix had heard nothing from him.

Each day, Alix pounced on the mailbox, in hopes of a postcard at least. With a picture of a Canadian mountie, say, or Big Ben or a Stockholm street scene. No signature. Just 'Hi!' or 'Wish you were here.' That would suffice. Alix would read the unwritten and take comfort.

Sam was being super-cautious. Her phone might be tapped, the mails watched. These were reasonable assumptions. Yet sooner or later he'd be in touch. He had promised. Maybe he would even turn up in person, slipping past the doorman for a clandestine reunion. He still had her keys.

On New Year's Eve, Alix passed up the round of student parties. She was in no mood to celebrate and the thought of eggnog made her ill. (Could you get evening sickness, she wondered, as well as morning sickness?) Besides, she was certain that tonight would be the night she heard from Sam. The notion

154

struck her as right. Almost inevitable. Sam had such a sense of occasion. And what occasion more symbolic than the end of one decade and the start of another?

Alix settled down to wait it out with a volume of Prosser on Torts, a bottle of diet-Pepsi and two cans of Chef Boyardee. (Among her recent revelations: hamburger was cheaper than filet mignon, and canned spaghetti was cheaper than either.)

She studied till twelve, listened to Dick Clark doing his count-down from Times Square, then conceded that she would not hear from Sam tonight. But wherever he was, he was thinking of her, she had no doubt. As she of him.

'Happy New Year, darling!' She kissed the air. Then she undressed and went to bed. Or more accurately, lay down on the mattress on the floor. Funny, she mused, how sleeping on the floor had once seemed to her the nadir of existence. Funny, too, how quickly circumstances change. And how radically. Oh, the ability of the human brain to adapt!

As she lay there in the dark, listening to the sounds of merry voices in the street below, she wondered which would come first: passing the bar – or the birth of Sam's child.

PART TWO

The Seventies

BROADWAY

'"Can't sing, can't dance,"' Bette mimicked. 'Well, a fat lot he knows! That's what they said about Fred Astaire. Now where we might've goofed . . .'

But Kim didn't want a rehash, only to put the incident behind her. In a life full of humiliations, that morning's audition had scored a new low.

'Looking for kids who can tap and belt out a tune,' the call had gone out. The Wests had risen to the challenge.

Bette's choice of material was the Ethel Merman show-stopper from *Gypsy*, to which she added a routine that had Kim dancing and romancing a long-stemmed rose in the second chorus.

The audition was a cattle call, open to all comers, with each aspirant allowed a brief exposure. When Kim's turn came, she trotted out on stage, flower in hand, dressed in short shorts and red-white-and-blue spangled bra that made the most of her silicone breasts. She looked luscious.

'"Everything's Coming Up Roses,"' she announced, then cued the pianist. But when she opened her mouth, nothing came out – least of all roses. She cleared her throat and tried again, but the lyrics had gone out of her head. The only words that came to mind were – *what am I doing here*? It was crazy. She was no Merman. From the corner of her eye, she glimpsed her mother in the wings, mouthing the words. 'I forgot!' she wanted to say, but couldn't spit it out. She had gone totally mute.

This rebellion of the vocal cords was inexplicable, unless seen as her body's way of saying that Kim West had no business attempting musical comedy. As if a history of failed auditions hadn't repeatedly made that point.

The pianist continued to vamp, her mother to mouth. Then Bette stage-whispered, 'Dance, for Chrissakes!'

Like a deer caught in the headlights, Kim stumbled into the soft-shoe routine, only to trip over a microphone wire. She picked herself up and faced the director.

'Sorry,' she said and began heading off stage.

In Kim's experience, auditions ended with a 'Thank you, miss. We'll let you know. Next!' They never called back. But today's director departed from protocol.

'Honey,' he said. 'You're a pretty girl, but you can't sing or dance worth a damn. Why don't you give it up and get yourself a husband. Next?'

Kim and Bette didn't exchange a word until they were clear of the theatre. 'He had some gall, that fellow . . .' Bette began when they were safely on the street, but Kim shrugged.

'He was right, Mom. I'm never going to make it in show-biz. I don't have the stuff. Today was my last audition.'

'How can you say that, baby?' Bette pleaded, but Kim held firm. She had given Broadway her best shot, which was not good enough. She suffered from stage fright and nervous indigestion. She would sooner sweep streets than endure such shame again.

'Waitressing yes,' Bette said. 'Lots of actresses wait tables while resting. Especially in places that cater to an up-scale crowd. But street-sweeping? Over my dead body! Keep the faith, cookie. Something will turn up.'

'My Mr Wonderful?' Kim said brightly.

'Don't be smart.'

Despite Bette's sunny premonitions the previous New Year, nothing good had happened since. Almost a year had gone by, and they were still living in a dismal furnished room, pinching pennies, haunting Second Avenue thrift shops for fancy clothes.

Everything had been done by the book: the glossy photos, the composites, the paid listings in talent directories. Kim's face was on file in offices from the Brill Building to NBC to BBDO. On the back of each photo was pasted a résumé, enhanced but still modest, the highlight being her title as the Former Miss West Virginia.

Bette scoured the notices in *Back Stage* and *Show Business*, monitored *Ad Age* and *Broadcast* magazine, keeping an open mind as to where Kim's 'big break' would come, whether on Broadway, in commercials or modeling. Her best hope was to catch the right person's eye.

It therefore followed that Kim had to look 'just so' at all times. She never left the house – not even to take out the garbage – without being immaculately combed, manicured and groomed. In an era of granny glasses and wild hair and faded jeans, in a nation roiled by sex, drugs and rock 'n' roll, Kim was an anachronism, a white-gloved young lady who might have stepped out of a 1950s Doris Day movie.

The Wests managed to make ends meet by baby-sitting and part-time work with, now and then, the odd modeling job. But money was a constant problem. And though Kim had done a television spot for a local car dealer – she opened the door of a used Buick and smiled – her modeling career had stalled.

'Too busty,' Bette was told at a major fashion agency. '*Mademoiselle* and *Glamour* like their gals less voluptuous. In fact, there's an operation for reducing breast size. No? Well, maybe you ought to try the men's magazines.'

Bette was outraged. *Hustler*? *Penthouse*? Her Kim as Playmate of the Month? Was there a more god-awful ambience for a girl who was both a virgin and a teetotaler?

Art, however, was another matter. Particularly fine art. And when a mid-town publisher approached the Wests concerning a set of posters he planned to market, Bette was interested. The fact that the imprint was called *Exotica Press* did not signify. Their goals were purely aesthetic.

'God forbid cheesecake.' Mr Buderian threw up his hands.

'We're a class operation.' Each photograph would be a fresh interpretation of an artistic masterpiece, he assured her, only with some gorgeous American beauty at its center.

There would be Mona Lisa in a black chiffon gown against the Manhattan skyline. Botticelli's 'Venus on the Half Shell' emerging from the Bethesda Fountain in Central Park, her nudity discreetly concealed behind 'great hair.' For Kim, he had in mind a re-creation of Rousseau's Sleeping Gypsy.

'Your girl has such a nice dreamy quality.'

The whole series would be highly educational. Artistic. He had engaged a top Hungarian photographer; they anticipated wide distribution. And though the fee was modest, the exposure – 'I mean it in the best sense of the word' – would be terrific.

At his suggestion, Kim went the next day to the Museum of Modern Art to see Rousseau's painting. She sat before it for a long time, captivated. The painting was indeed dreamy, unreal. A black woman lay asleep on the ground, a guitar beside her. She wore a robe of muted colors. The landscape was desolate. A cold moon lit the sky. Standing over the woman was a lion, tail raised, head lowered.

Kim was puzzled. Was the lion going to ravish the gypsy? Devour her? Protect her? Did the lion exist at all – except in the gypsy's dreams? Who could say? The painting resonated by its very silence. She wanted to crawl inside it. To sleep. To dream.

'Tell Mr Buderian I'd love to do his poster,' she breathed to Bette that evening, still locked in the fantasy. She wondered if the lion in her photo would be live. And why they hadn't picked a black girl. Kim was so blonde. Although they both were gypsies, after all.

The road to fame, Kim later reflected, is paved not only with good intentions but with puffery and humbug and farce. An hour spent in a museum and a half day in a West 10th Street studio had combined to put Kim's face (to say nothing of other anatomical features) in frat rooms and bars across the country.

To begin with there was the matter of the lion.

'We couldn't rent no lion,' explained Laszlo Beresz, while she applied make-up. He was a cheerful middle-aged Hungarian with limping English. 'Or a panser. They're wanting too much money. And the stuffed ones – fake phoney!' He made a moue of distaste. 'We put some silver glitter in your hair.'

His young assistant and a fellow who identified himself as 'Jimmy the handler' soon arrived lugging a huge cardboard box. Kim peeked inside. 'Is it alive?'

'Heavily drugged,' Jimmy assured her. 'His name is Boris.'

'We're getting a long way away from the Rousseau painting,' she said to Laszlo.

'Artistic liberty, darlink,' he said with a smile.

Then there was the matter of the costume. To call the shift diaphanous was to succumb to understatement.

'You can see everything!' Kim exclaimed.

'Don't worry, darlink. We drape Boris about you, here . . . there . . . so tasteful it will be. Nossing indecent.'

Gingerly, Kim touched Boris with her fingertips. He was surprisingly warm. Beautiful. And definitely lethargic.

'Mr Laszlo, sir. Is he . . . umm, a boa constrictor or a python?'

'Do I know?' came the reply. 'Am I in handbags?'

Kim laughed and thanked God her mother wasn't there.

Laszlo had forbidden Bette's attendance at the session, claiming it would interfere with the artistic process. Which was as well to judge by the blow-ups slathered across the studio walls. The photos were of women only, mostly nude, all idealized. When it came to glorifying the female body, Laszlo Beresz was an artist indeed.

However, where Kim was entranced, Bette would have taken one look and yanked her daughter out of there somewhat faster than the speed of sound with an outraged 'Mother knows best.' But on this occasion, daughter knew best. And Laszlo knew more than anyone. She bowed to his superior judgment.

Minutes later, she was stretched out on the blue satin drop, while Laszlo tried out poses, took experimental Polaroids and made decisions concerning hair, snake deployment and technicalities. When he was ready to shoot, he asked Kim to remove the shift.

'Is better without. Will be beautiful pictures.'

Instinct told Kim he was right. She took off the robe, shut her eyes and feeling absurdly languorous, let him make love to her with his camera. The snake kept her warm.

When the session was over, the assistant helped Jimmy pack up Boris, who was beginning to show signs of life, and Kim got dressed. There was a feeling of triumph in the air.

The python poster was – pick your word – outrageous, funny, sexy, indecent, witty, gorgeous, obscene. Juxtaposing the innocent face of a Madonna, trusting and serene, against an overripe body that exuded sexuality, it had been recaptioned 'Virgin's Dream.' The result was as ambiguous as the painting that inspired it, and Kim liked to think that the Douanier Rousseau would have approved.

'It's either a woman fucking a snake or a snake fucking a woman,' said a Mid-West rack jobber in a typical businessman's response. 'I'll take three thousand – and maybe keep a couple for myself.'

Nationwide, Virgin's Dream sold several hundred thousand copies from which Kim derived no royalties. She had signed a release and been paid a set fee. Indirectly, the benefits poured in.

Kim was written up in *People's Magazine*, spoofed in the pages of *Harvard Lampoon*, invited on *Good Morning America*, sometimes recognized on the street. The New York Mets named her their mascot and she threw out the ball on opening day. She appeared at shopping mall openings, auto shows and bottlers' conventions. She was a joke to some, a sex symbol to others. True fame seemed only inches away.

Sometimes she got paid for her efforts, but mostly Kim got free publicity. To what end all this fuss, Kim couldn't fathom.

To be a girl about town? To snag a rich husband? But in the meantime, Bette seemed pacified. Her daughter had become a 'genuine' mini-celebrity.

Because she was quiet, people often wrote Kim off as a classic 'dumb blonde,' and she was smart enough to play that role. Though not an actress in the Actor's Guild sense of the word, she was superb at dissembling. A life with Bette had taught her how to bow the head, placate and soothe. Beauty contests had taught her how to look happy on demand. When dealing with strangers, she was quick to anticipate moods and respond to body language. A moist eye for sob stories, a gasp of delight at their jokes, an 'aren't you wonderful!' smile full of promise. Reporters adored her.

No, she couldn't sing, couldn't dance – but she could please. That was her metier.

Kim even had an official 'escort,' the proverbial eligible bachelor due a mini-celebrity of her rank. The two had met on opening day at Shea Stadium.

His name was Pierre Waxman and his father owned a chain of retail stores. He was moderately rich. He was also shy, pudgy and sexually immature, with a downy upper lip. He was as harmless as sponge cake. Pierre's passion was sports (he had a world-class collection of baseball cards), and he wanted nothing more than to be viewed as a macho man among men.

'You be Marilyn Monroe, I'll be Joe DiMaggio,' Pierre would tell Kim when they went out. Which meant she was to wear her shiniest sexiest dresses and hang on his arm in public.

With this adoring sex-pot beaming love-shafts at him, real men would envy his prowess. Lucky Pierre! He introduced her as his fiancée. In private they never as much as kissed. Kim felt sorry for him.

Pierre took her to the smartest restaurants where she indulged a passion for rich food. She accompanied him to the major sports events (which were mostly boring) and Broadway openings (which were fun) and got her name in the gossip columns. In payment for services Pierre gave Bette a clothes allowance and helped with the rent when they moved to a small but smart apartment on the upper East Side.

As jobs go, being Pierre's 'fiancée' wasn't too onerous. When Kim wanted romance, she read a Barbara Cartland novel. No matter. Her time was sure to come.

FOURTEENTH STREET

If Forty-second Street is the heart of Manhattan, then Fourteenth Street is some nether organ, having to do with the digestive tract.

Once it had been the social hub of the lower East Side: a grand boulevard where tenement dwellers went to revel and laugh and forget their troubles at the Yiddish theaters, Ukrainian friendship clubs, Turkish Baths and busy restaurants where black-suited waiters dispensed *sauerbraten* and Gemütlichkeit amidst old world splendor.

By the 1970s, however, the Europeans had died off or moved away and a new tide of residents arrived. Multi-racial and polyglot, with nothing in common except poverty, this second invasion comprised Latinos, West Indians, East Indians, blacks from Africa and Haiti, blonde flower children fleeing the suburbs in a display of downward mobility, struggling artists in search of low rents and plentiful pot, winos seeking a free flop in Tompkins Square Park.

Shabby and potholed, Fourteenth Street fell upon hard times as the august frontages – those that weren't shuttered – were transformed into bodegas, head shops, Blimpies, discount jobbers, pizza joints that sold by the slice, and, a few steps in from

Third Avenue, the modest law offices of Aaronoff, Martinez and Bryden.

Alix, coming to New York in search of fresh beginnings, liked the neighborhood. It was as distant from the life she had known as she could manage without leaving the planet.

Sam was gone. She might never hear from him again. Meanwhile she couldn't put her life on hold. Not with a career to build, a living to fetch and a child to support.

After law school, Alix had her pick of jobs. The barriers against women were coming down, especially for Harvard grads. She might have joined any one of a dozen blue-chip firms and kissed her financial headaches goodbye. But corporate law, once so attractive, now struck her as absurd. After all she had been through, she couldn't possibly take a job on Wall Street. Sam would despise her. Alix would have despised herself.

To her mind, it was obscene that the best legal minds should be engaged in something so shallow as the further enrichment of the already rich. It was the poor who most needed great lawyering. The poor who plowed the hardest road, faced the direst consequences: eviction, deportation, jail. For them, a top-notch lawyer could spell the difference between life and death. In terms of moral satisfaction, no other branch of law could begin to compare.

Alix's colleagues shared her sentiments.

Like her, Jeff Aaronoff and Eddie Martinez were products of the Sixties: bright, enthusiastic, committed to social justice. Though not a partnership, the three had banded together to share their expenses and savvy. And though they believed that to 'do good' in this world and to 'do well' were not mutually exclusive, doing good received priority.

It was a 'no-frills' operation. The office uniform was blue jeans and tee-shirts, with Jeff claiming he did his best work beneath a Mets cap, worn back to front. In theory, everyone did everything (including the emptying of ashtrays), but before long, each developed a specialty. Jeff Aaronoff was the resident expert on torts. Eddie Martinez, fluent in Spanish, handled immigration. Alix took on the criminal cases.

Of the three, she alone didn't mind dealing with felons. She felt they were victims themselves: of racism, drugs, child abuse. Nor was she fussy about choosing her clients. If, as the adage went, a grand jury would indict a ham sandwich, very well then – Alix would defend a ham sandwich.

That business was brisk, though not particularly profitable, was reflected in the brightly lit reception room. During office hours, there were usually half a dozen people waiting on plastic chairs, thumbing through old copies of *Newsweek* and *Sports Illustrated*, tapping fidgety feet on the worn linoleum and providing all the ambience of a barber shop.

The decor ran to battered desks, second-hand file cabinets and philodendron, packed into three cubicles and a reception area ruled by their secretary Teri Ciccarelli. She was a short bouncy woman with a Bronx accent, a genius for organization and a spare subway token when you were late for court.

'One Columbia grad, one from NYU and one from Harvard,' Teri would cluck. 'But if not for me, you'd all starve.'

'How can you let that slimeball go back on the street?' Jeff Aaronoff asked Alix after she had got the Machete Mugger acquitted on a technicality. 'I know, I know,' he answered his own question. 'Presumption of innocence, every scumbag entitled to a vigorous defense, all that jazz. It's what they taught us in law school and I was wrong to ask. Still . . . !'

Alix grinned. It was the first case of hers to make the papers, though the reporter's tone had been one of outrage. She, however, had no qualms. A cop had cut corners and she had tripped him up on the stand, as was her right and duty. Guilt or innocence didn't enter into it.

As Alix saw it, she was a foot soldier in a lopsided struggle. On the one hand, there was the combined tonnage of the NYPD and the district attorney's office and the judiciary system. On the other hand, her client and herself. A slimeball the Machete Mugger may have been, a man of few redeeming qualities and fewer resources. Nonetheless, a human being, dumb as they come, one more loser about to be buried under the weight of the establishment, with only Alix standing between him and the slammer. Whenever she beat the odds, she felt a David-and-Goliath throb of pleasure.

Like all criminal attorneys, she cut deals when necessary, for plea bargaining was the basic grease of the system. She would sit down with her opposite number, usually an equally youthful ADA and they would haggle, trading off time against crime.

The process was not unlike buying tee-shirts from the Senegalese vendors who set out their stalls on Fourteenth Street – $3.98 marked down from $6.95, give or take a little, or buy two for $7.50. Only at 110 Center Street, the currency was years not dollars.

'I'm offering you a B, six to nine,' the ADA might say.

'Reduce to a C, three to six.'

'Okay, C, but no way under five.'

'Three or we go to trial.'

'Three and a half, just maybe.'

'Three and a half, minus time served,' Alix stipulated. 'Hell, he's been in the can for eight months.'

'Then it's back up to four.'

'Deal.'

And it was often a good one. Yet the bartering disgusted her. It usually meant putting a man behind bars.

Alix hated jails with a passion. Her first trip to Riker's Island had been enough to convince her that no human being, however vile, deserved such a fate. The filth, the stench, the noise – unbearable! The Central Park Zoo treated its denizens better. In her mind, every man in a cage might be Sam Matthews.

As a result she went to trial more often than many other lawyer and won a surprising number of doubtful cases, earning a reputation as a bold and effective adversary with judges and law-breakers alike.

'I send you all my friends, *chica*,' the Machete Mugger told her with a grin as they sailed out of court.

'Gee, thanks, Pancho,' she said. 'Just what I need – more muggers. And don't forget, you still owe me my fee.'

Not that Alix intended to spend her life defending scumbags. She dreamt of becoming a great trial lawyer in the feisty radical tradition – the kind who breathed fire and wrote history and made smug gentlefolk sweat in their club chairs. However, since no ringing civil rights cases had as yet crossed her desk, she plowed along with her pickpockets, grifters, muggers, hippies on drug busts, plus the occasional murder case assigned by the court. If necessary, she could psyche herself to like Dracula.

She never regretted her choice of career any more than she regretted the loss of her fortune. Good riddance.

What was there to miss about being rich? The clothes? All she needed was one decent suit for court appearances. The *chotchkes*, as Mr Rabinowitz might say? They collected dust. The wariness? The suspicion that others were out for her fortune? At least now when people liked her – or disliked her – it was on the basis of what she was, not what she owned.

'I have been poor and I have been rich,' she paraphrased Fanny Brice, 'and while I don't recommend either, believe me, it's better to be poor.'

When Alix started out, she wanted to change her name, putting as much distance as possible between herself and her father. She soon decided against it. A Bryden she was born and would remain. And if her cases figured in the tabloids, if her clients were the 'human trash' Lucius Bryden abhorred, so much the better. The prospect of embarrassing him was irresistible.

'My clients are good clean honest criminals,' she liked to say, 'unlike those creeps in Watergate.'

A week before her twenty-fifth birthday, Alix received a

registered letter from the Park Avenue offices of Trumbull, Haversham, Cadwalader and Phipps.

'One of those ethnic law firms,' Teri said, handing her the envelope. 'They want to meet with you.'

Curiosity piqued, Alix went, to be informed by a senior partner that she was the beneficiary of a trust fund set up when she was a year old.

'I don't want my father's money,' Alix protested, 'and I assure you, he no longer wants me to have it.'

'It's an irrevocable trust,' Mr Haversham noted, 'so neither of you can wish it away.'

'But I can give it away,' Alix said, already charting how the income would be spent. 'I'll set up trusts of my own. The Civil Liberties Union, Amnesty, the NAACP —'

'Don't do anything rash,' the lawyer advised. 'It would provide you with a handsome annual income. There may come a time when you have children of your own . . .' He rattled on about duties, school fees, the risks of signing her offspring's 'heritage' away. Alix heard him out politely, then smiled.

'I have a child,' she said. 'And I don't want her growing up as I did – too much money and too little of everything else.'

She had made her decision, which, like the trust, was irrevocable. Then she took the subway home, in time to give Samantha supper.

Samantha – the light of her heart.

To hear her mother talk about her, Samantha Bryden was only the most beautiful, wonderful, clever, delightful baby since the dawn of time. 'In other words,' Eddie Martinez said – he had two children of his own – 'a perfectly normal kid.'

'Yup,' Alix acknowledged. 'That too.'

The long months of pregnancy had been the worst period of Alix's life. Time and again, Alix agonized over having made the wrong decision. Was it selfish to have Sam's baby – or more selfish not to? Would she have money enough for the hospital? What if the baby were born disfigured as she herself had been? Alix didn't think she could bear it.

A few weeks before her due date, friends at Harvard had pitched in for a layette, moving Alix to tears. If only food and lodging were so easily come by. She had given up the apartment in Cambridge and was scrambling to keep afloat: tutoring, proof-reading, living on four hours' sleep and canned spaghetti. Daily she grew clumsier, wearier, more cumbersome.

Maybe life would have been better had she had an abortion. That it would have been easier went without saying. But she felt an obligation to Sam.

If only—! she tortured herself. If only he were here to hold her hand and help her make tough decisions. Her loneliness was titanic. There were days when she wanted to howl from the pain of it, nights when she cried until her bones ached with grief. She loved him, missed him, craved him, pondered what would have happened had she gone with him.

The hue and cry his exploits had raised soon subsided as yesterday's atrocity was replaced with fresher, bloodier tales. In Greenwich Village, three privileged young terrorists blew up a town house next door to Dustin Hoffman. Body parts were strewn everywhere. In California, a cult murderer killed a family of five. He acted on instruction from his tarot cards. In Kent State, four students were massacred by National Guardsmen. A nation was left stunned and grieving.

Thus though the name of Sam Matthews remained high on the FBI's wanted list, it had vanished from the daily papers.

Even as Alix entered the maternity ward at Cambridge General, she clung to the notion that he would surface at any second, magically arriving before their baby was born.

'Father's name?' asked the intake worker.

Alix gave it.

The woman didn't blink. It rang no bell. 'Can I reach him for you?' she asked.

Alix winced, as much from irony as from labor pains.

'I wish . . . !' she replied.

Yet when the newborn infant was placed at Alix's breast to hold for a moment before the umbilical cord was cut, her doubts vanished. Gone were the pains of childbirth, the wretchedness of her situation. Gone, even, all thought of Sam.

She was awe-stricken.

She counted toes, fingers, marveled at the thatch of black hair. This tiny wrinkled creature, red-faced but unscarred, mewling softly, was a miracle beyond imagining.

I made this, she thought. *I made this perfectly miraculous creature*. She was filled with the purest joy.

'Beautiful, isn't she?' Alix breathed.

'A nice healthy baby,' the doctor said with a smile.

'And all mine!'

She wanted to fling her arms around the obstetrician, kiss the nurses, thank them profusely for having helped her produce this extravagantly marvelous infant. Had she been rich, she would have endowed the hospital with millions. Tens of millions. Instead, she lay there, afloat with happiness.

'Right,' said the doctor. 'Now we're going to cut the umbilical cord and then you'll need a few stitches . . .' but Alix hardly heard, for by then she and her baby had bonded.

As the doctor went about his business, she shut her eyes and smiled. *I will never again be lonely*, Alix thought.

Three years later, she would amend that statement to a mock-plaintive *I never get a minute alone*.

Her office was a madhouse, her apartment a mess, her days overloaded to bursting. She was always dashing from one place to another, usually late, looking harried and a trifle wind-blown in a cotton shirt and blue jeans or an off-the-rack suit. She could balance a toddler in one hand, thumb through a brief with the other, while carrying on three simultaneous conversations. Life was hectic. And – if she stopped to think of it – good.

Alix the Loner was now Alix the Doer. She knew a zillion people: artists, writers, students, lawyers, internes from Bellevue, parents from Samantha's playgroup, to say nothing of those raffish clients of hers who called at all hours of day and night. The Lower East Side (or the East Village as the neighborhood began to redefine itself) was a social dynamo, though no one seemed to have a sou. She even managed a sex-life of sorts, casual affairs that didn't break her stride or take time away from Samantha. No point in living like a nun.

For a while, she considered a dalliance with Jeff Aaronoff, who claimed that nothing would make him happier than waking up one morning to find Alix's sneakers under his bed.

'I never date baseball players or lawyers,' Alix said. The first category didn't know how to talk, she explained; the second didn't know how to shut up.

Undaunted, Jeff went so far as to hint at marriage. 'You and Samantha could make an honest man out of me.'

Alix was touched. He had nearly everything one could ask for in a husband. Or in a lover, for that matter. He was bright, industrious, good-natured, good-looking in his way, with his Clark Kent glasses and teddy-bear smile.

Now and then, when the press of work bore down hard, Alix would feel sorry for herself and fantasize about married life. The Great Escape, she thought of it, picturing herself in an idyllic suburban setting, surrounded by kids and shaggy dogs, puttering in the garden, making gourmet meals for her Mr Right who would be arriving home on the 5:33.

It was a pretty scenario, and maybe Jeff was Mr Right. Certainly, she cared enough about him to consider his offer, but the fantasy never lasted more than a dreamy half hour, after which it was back to work.

For against all logic, she was still waiting for Sam. The ear remained cocked for the late-night phone call, the eye restless for the unexpected sighting. Sometimes Alix would catch a glimpse

174

of his familiar figure walking briskly ahead of her on the street, the shoulders broad and swaggering. *Could be . . . Is . . .!* She would quicken her footsteps, break into a trot, her heart pounding – *Wait for me, Sam! Wait for me!* – only to find she had overtaken a total stranger. Quickly she would turn the next corner and slink away ashamed.

Given those feelings, how could she possibly get tied up with Jeff? Maybe some day, when her heart was free.

'I like you too much to live with you,' she told him truthfully. 'Won't you settle for best friends?'

In the meantime, her daughter Samantha was family enough. And then there was Mr Rabinowitz.

He had been one of her first clients, a fragile old gentleman who had come in off the street to take pot luck with whatever lawyer was available. By chance it was Alix.

His story, tumbling out in a mix of Yiddish, Spanish and English, was filled with pathos.

Twice in his life, he had been driven from his home. First by Hitler. Then by Castro. He had lost his wife. His daughter had moved to Australia. Now it was happening again. He handed Alix an eviction notice. '*Gottenyu*, I die in the streets, *señora*. For thees I come to America?'

She promised to handle it *muy pronto* and *mach schnell*.

In fact, the case proved to be unexpectedly complicated: postponements that ate up hours of precious time, a landlord who deserved to be drawn and quartered, a nitwit of a judge. In the end she rescued Mr Rabinowitz's tenancy – though how such a sweet man could live in such a wretched tenement was beyond her – and even won him a rent reduction.

His gratitude knew no bounds. His finances did, however. The fees were beyond him. Could he make Alix a suit? he asked. A nice winter coat? He was an expert tailor.

Alix's curiosity was piqued. How did a little Polish tailor get on Castro's shit list? Only she phrased it more tactfully.

Mr Rabinowitz's eyes grew rheumy. His crime, he confessed, was that he had once made evening clothes for Castro's predecessor, the notorious Fulgencio Batista.

'He had a thirty-four-inch in-seam,' Mr Rabinowitz recalled, then shook his head. 'Such a difficult man. *Muy hombre*.'

'Because of his in-seam?'

Mr Rabinowitz's nose twitched, as if something smelled bad. 'Dictators!' he said. 'Never get next to a dictator, *kitzele*.'

Alix laughed and promised not to.

Then it was Mr Rabinowitz's turn to ask a question. Why did Alix bring her baby to the office?

Alix almost let the question go unanswered.

'Because I have no one to leave her with,' she said quietly. 'You want to work off your fee?'

And that was how it began.

Within a year, when business picked up, Alix moved to a roomy first-floor apartment on St Marks Place. There was an extra bedroom. Nothing fancy, but better than that rat-trap Mr Rabinowitz had fought so hard to hang on to.

'What do you say, Mr Rabinowitz? Room and board plus whatever salary I can put together.'

He said yes, and after that they were a household.

Samantha adored him. Alix too.

'Is he your baby-sitter?' she was sometimes asked.

'No.' Alix strove to endow him with the respect he deserved. 'He's more like family.'

One summer afternoon, shortly after the Machete Mugger acquittal, Alix was coming from the Tenth Street precinct house in Greenwich Village, headed for the office. While waiting for the light, she noticed a stunning woman on the opposite corner. Despite the heat, the woman was immaculately turned out in a crisp pink linen suit, matching pumps and lots of costume jewelry, platinum hair swirled high in an elaborate coiffure.

She seemed to be staring at Alix. Instinctively Alix tucked in her shirt tails. Elegant women made her feel tacky.

The light changed. The woman bounded toward her, her smile stretching wider and wider.

'Alix!' she shouted. 'It's me!'

Alix blinked. Did a take.

'My God! Kimberly West.'

And so it was, though a much different Kimberly from the fourteen-year-old she remembered. The hair was lighter, the nose more retroussé, the body unexpectedly voluptuous. Alix wondered if her old friend had been back to the plastic surgeon for seconds. Possibly thirds.

A few minutes later, they were immured in the cool depths of the Peacock Café, drinking iced cappuccino, eating cannoli, and catching up on eight years of news.

'A baby!' Kim breathed, admiringly. 'Lucky you! So you found your Prince Charming!'

'Not exactly,' Alix said. 'Samantha's father and I never married. Now he's gone – God knows where.'

'What'll you tell her when she's old enough to ask?' Kim's violet eyes misted with sympathy.

Of course, Alix recalled. *Kim had been there herself.*

'Dunno.' Alix made a face. 'Say that I loved and lost.'

'You can always pretend her daddy was killed in Vietnam,' Kim said. 'Like he's a hero. That's what *my* mom did.' Then seeing how glumly Alix received this proposal, she said cheerfully, 'My bet is he'll come back one of these days, and things'll be fine. Meanwhile I could go for more cannoli. They are scrumptious! That's the curse of my life – my sweet tooth.'

Alix watched fascinated as Kim put away three of the fat creamy pastries, holding them delicately between coral-painted nails, licking the cream off her fingertips, pursuing the last crumbs. After which she excused herself and went to the ladies' room. She was gone a while. When she returned, smiling and freshly lipsticked, Alix eyed her suspiciously.

'Are you okay, Kim?'

'Sure. Why?'

'Well, if I ate like that, I'd either be big as a house or sick as a dog.'

Kim laughed. 'So would I. That's why I barf it all up right away. Don't look shocked. It's an old model's trick.'

The talk turned to happier matters, in particular their burgeoning careers. No, Kim hadn't heard of the Machete Mugger case, she didn't follow crime news. Conversely Alix had never seen Kim's poster.

'"Virgin's Dream," did you say? Sounds terrific. Where would I buy a copy?'

'Yes, well . . .' Kim felt vaguely embarrassed. 'Mom calls it art, but it's kind of gross. However, it's getting me on the cover of the swimsuit issue of *Sports Illustrated*, which is really a milestone. And I'm sure you've heard of *that*!'

Alix had indeed. Eddie Martinez always brought his back copies to the reception room.

The two gossiped over another round of iced coffee, trading war stories. Kim's chatter sparkled with the names of dress designers and chic restaurants and loathsome producers. Alix spun tales of Riker's Island and Center Street and Mr Rabinowitz, all of which Kim declared was 'just riveting.' There was a bit of embellishment on both sides.

Alix checked her watch. She was late for a meeting. They exchanged phone numbers, made a date for dinner the following week. With Bette of course.

'Weird, isn't it?' Kim mused. 'Here we've both been living in New York all these years and never ran into each other until today.'

Alix smiled. 'Not so surprising. After all, we inhabit different worlds.'

The waiter brought the check and set it down before Kim.

'That's because I devoured all the pastries.'

178

Alix laughed. 'That's because you look like a millionaire's daughter, whereas I look like a bum. Let's split it.'

They paid and got ready to leave. But at the door of the restaurant, Kim stopped and seized Alix's arm.

'What you said about our occupying different worlds – if that was true, then we wouldn't have met today.'

'It was chance.' Alix smiled. 'Happy chance.'

'No, Alix. Not chance. It was kismet. Fate. Like our lives are linked. Yours . . . mine . . . and . . .' Her eyes turned inward. 'Do you remember Lady X and that night in Marival?'

'What a question! Of course I remember. Though I haven't thought about it in years.'

'I have,' Kim said. 'I think of her often. I wonder where she is now, if she thanks me or curses me for what I did.'

'Why, Kim!' Alix was staring. 'That was ages ago!'

'Our fates are entwined, Alix. You said so yourself.'

'We were kids then, Kim. Kids talk nonsense.'

'Fate. Destiny.' Kim laughed self-consciously, but her eyes glowed. 'You know I believe that stuff. Truly! One day I'll turn a corner and there she'll be. From out of nowhere. Just like with you and me today. Only it won't be chance. And the really spooky thing is, when it does happen I won't recognize her.' Kim pushed the door open. They stepped out on to the street. 'But she'll know me,' Kim concluded.

The heat was like a blast-furnace, yet Alix felt a chill.

CHICAGO

'What's Miranda doing?'

It was the question on every trader's lips. Was she long on soybeans? Bullish on pork bellies? Cautious on winter wheat? Arnie Baxter caught her reading a copy of *Knitting News*. Did that indicate an interest in Australian sheep futures? Or was she knitting her boyfriend a cardigan?

If she had a boyfriend – yet another matter for guesswork.

It being the nature of speculators to speculate, the life and times of Miranda Vee offered her colleagues ample food for conjecture. How did an unknown woman catapult herself to the top of that most masculine enclave, the Trading Pit? Was she simply bright and 'ballsy' – to use their favorite epithet – or were more sinister factors at work?

The story of her waltzing into the offices of Hershy and Kay with a hundred thousand dollars (in cash, some said) – then waltzing out soon after a million dollars richer – had long since made the rounds, posing more questions than it answered.

What was the source of that hundred thou? Variously, it was posited that Miranda Vee was a front for an Argentinian billionaire, a money launderer for the mafia, the illegitimate daughter of J. Paul Getty, the mistress of an Arab sheik. One fellow at Shearson ventured that her stake came from a hot streak at a gambling casino, though he was pretty much hooted down. Miranda wasn't the Vegas type.

Just as the origins of her fortune remained obscure, her private life was also wrapped in secrecy. To those traders with an eye for women, this dearth of information was frustrating. *Did She or Didn't She*? And if she did, then with whom?

Not with her peers, that much was certain. Beyond that was anybody's guess. For all they knew, Miranda might be a respectably married woman with four kids or the raunchiest broad in Chicago. Hard evidence was limited to the fact that she lived in an apartment on Lake Shore and presumably liked animals, since she'd once brought a stray cat on to the trading floor.

Often, these guessing games took place at the Bored Room Café, a popular hangout where traders gathered to drink and swop war stories after hours. On occasion Miranda herself turned up at the bar for a weak Scotch and water. She would stick around for an hour, nursing her drink, ostensibly friendly, picking up on market tips and trends, but she always left early and alone. Which led to a fresh round of speculation.

'The Ice Queen,' Richie Alpert dubbed her, after she rebuffed his overtures. A self-styled lady killer, Richie took rejection hard. The woman was a lesbian; no other explanation made sense. To prove his contention, he bet a thousand dollars that no man could bed Miranda Vee.

The Bet started as a joke at the Bored Room, but it soon became a challenge. Rules developed. Refinements were added. Word of it spread across town. There were many takers. Losers made out their checks to the Bored Room Club.

With luck, an attractive bachelor might get to buy Miranda a drink, even dinner at Le Perroquet, but none had ever gotten past her front door. The penalty for failure was one thousand dollars to be added to the pot for the next contestant.

Roger King heard about the Bet from Larry Walters in the locker room at the Chicago Athletic Club. A hot-shot lawyer who specialized in mergers and acquisitions, King was blessed with good looks, a Robert Redford smile and a way with women.

'I tried everything – flowers, perfume, the works.' Larry was bewailing his failure. 'Couldn't get to first base.'

Roger was intrigued. Fiercely competitive, he determined to score a home run where others had batted zero.

'Is she attractive?'

'Gorgeous. But eyes like ice.'

'She takes in strays, you say?'

'Only cats. But try your luck. Want an introduction?'

Roger smiled. 'Just tell me where she lives and what she looks like.'

The next day, Roger went to the SPCA and picked out the saddest, scruffiest, shaggiest, goofiest mutt he could find. The dog had HOMELESS written all over him. He was ready to set his plan in motion.

Thus one crisp March morning, Miranda walked out of her building to be bowled over by a large shaggy dog. She landed in a snow bank.

'Oh, God! I'm so sorry!' The young man helped her to her feet, all apologies. 'He just slipped off the leash. Are you okay? I feel terrible.'

Miranda brushed herself off. The blue eyes blazed.

'You really ought to discipline . . .' she began to scold, but the poor fellow was crest-fallen. It was hard not to feel sorry for him.

'He's just a stray,' Roger said, with a shake of his head. 'Some poor dopey mutt I picked up off the street. I suppose I ought to turn him into the pound' – he smiled his movie-star smile – 'but I'm a sucker for animals.'

Miranda scratched the dopey mutt behind his ears.

'What's his name?' she asked.

'He doesn't have one yet. I'm open to suggestion.'

The ice-blue eyes melted and a gentle conversation began.

The following night Roger took Miranda to dinner. They dated steadily over the next few weeks, sometimes dinner and the theater, sometimes long walks in the park, accompanied by the shaggy dog whom she had christened Ole Shep. The three of them got along famously. Up to a point. For to Roger's chagrin, Miranda always said goodnight at the door. She seemed content to have found a man who shared her love for animals.

Yet clearly she liked him, appearing to be awed by his professional prowess, with the result that he talked shop rather more than he meant to.

'You're quite the wheeler-dealer!' she said admiringly.

Roger found her charming but elusive. She was a superb listener: smart, discreet, eating up his every word. He enjoyed her company. However, at the end of a month he knew little more about her than on that first morning, whereas she had learned a good deal about him. Worse yet, he was no closer to winning his wager. Despite time and effort, his sole reward had thus far been a couple of swift pecks on the cheek.

One night, Roger took her to a charity ball at the Palmer House. It was a gala affair. She wore an exquisite velvet gown the color of pomegranates, the chestnut hair swept up high and held in place with a diamond clip. She looked ravishing.

They danced till midnight, close as paint, then listened to jazz over on Rush Street. She liked jazz. Knew all the tunes. In the cab home, she sang in that low throaty voice of hers, an old Billie Holiday number. It was past two when they arrived at her building and Roger was geared for action. Tonight, he vowed, would be the night.

'It's been a lovely evening,' Miranda offered her hand, but he didn't take it. He was weary of the chase, just as he was sick and tired of putting up with Ole Shep. Even more than he wanted to win the Bet, he wanted to make love to Miranda.

'Won't you invite me in for coffee?' he asked. 'And I've never seen those famous cats of yours.'

'They're just cats. Nothing special.'

'Still, I'd like to see 'em. You know me with animals.' It wasn't working. He switched tactics. 'Besides, I have a couple of business problems I'd like to discuss.'

'Oh yes?'

'The Blake–Halsey merger I told you about? It's going through, after all. Would you like to hear how I did it?'

Miranda hesitated. 'Of course, Roger. Do come in.'

The living room was spacious and magnificently furnished with art deco *objets*: Lalique vases, Erté lithographs, hand-loomed rugs from Heal's of London. A lop-eared cat was snoozing atop the piano. Another lounged on a priceless Gaudí armchair. It was blind in one eye. Why the hell would a woman live with maimed animals? Roger wondered. She had to be the ultimate soft touch. Which boded well.

He settled on the couch, while Miranda went into the kitchen. When she returned, he patted the seat next him. She sat down at the far end of the sofa and poured coffee.

'You look lovely,' he said, edging over. 'But don't you ever take down your hair?'

She smiled and looked away.

'Do you mean that literally or metaphorically?' she said.

'And that perfume you're wearing . . . it's enough to drive a man wild. Oh, my beautiful Miranda!' He plucked the diamond clip from her topknot. Her hair cascaded over bare shoulders. 'Such lovely hair,' he murmured. 'I want to bury my face in it.'

'No! Please!'

She pulled away. The cat on the piano hissed.

'Lovely hair . . . lovely woman . . .' he crooned, his hands caressing her throat.

'I mean it, Roger. I thought you wanted to talk about the Blake–Halsey merger.' She tried to wriggle out of his grasp.

But the only merger Roger King desired at that moment was that of himself and Miranda Vee. Not for a minute did he believe in her protests. A woman gives out signals and she'd been transmitting all evening. Roger's instinct never erred in such matters. He knew when No meant Yes. Only a wimp would wait upon a formal invitation.

'Miranda . . . darling . . . you know I'm crazy about you.' He swooped. She reared back. He plunged a hand down the cleavage groping for one of those luscious breasts.

'Don't touch me!' she screamed.

'Come on, Mir. Lighten up. It's been a great night. Let's make it greater. You want it as much as I do.'

The next thing he knew, Roger King was picking himself up off the floor.

'My God!' he said. 'You didn't have to use a karate chop.'

'It appears I did,' she said frostily. 'Now will you leave or do I call the police?'

The following day, on his way to work, Roger returned Ole Shep to the pound. Good riddance. He loathed the furry bastard with a vengeance.

'What happened to you?' his secretary asked when he limped into the office. 'You get hit by a truck?'

'It's a shaggy dog story,' he growled. Then he sat down and wrote out a check for a thousand dollars.

Don't touch me!'

You want it. You know you want it . . .'

She screams. Help! Au secours!

Screams at the top of her voice. In English. In French. Until her throat is raw. Until she has no more breath in her body. And still she screams. But there is no one to hear. No one to see. Not even the moon. The only light comes from the headlights of the car. She is on a lonely stretch of country road. It is late. Dark. She is terrified.

Don't touch me!'

But he has no heart. No mercy. He shoves her to the ground. Pinions her with his body. The pebbles bruise her flesh. She can smell the funky odor of dank autumn leaves. Poplars. The famous poplars of the Loire. His breath comes fast and hard like an animal. His arms are steel clamps.

She struggles, but she cannot break free. He forces her legs apart. She writhes beneath his weight. Lost. Powerless. Yet she will not succumb. She fights for air, adrenaline infuses every pore. God damn! No man can force himself on her. She has her pride. Her honor.

She thrashes in vain. Her struggle excites him. He is ripping off her clothes. Forcing himself inside her. She has one weapon left. An animal's weapon.

She is an animal, fighting for survival. She twists her head to the side and with all the might left in her body she sinks her teeth into his earlobe. Her jaws snap shut.

'Bitch!' He jumps up. Howls in pain.

Blood spurts from the wound. Drips on to her face, hot and viscous.

'Bitch!' His fist crashes into her cheek. The pain is excruciating.

He has a knife! He takes it. Lays it flat against her cheek.

'I'll teach you some manners.'

The steel is cold. The point gouges her flesh.

'And when I'm done, no man will ever want you again.'

'Nooooo!' She screams but who will hear? Her eyes shut in pain. She is being dragged into oblivion. She sees nothing, feels nothing but terror. She is going to die, here on this godforsaken road far from home.

The knife streaks across her throat.

'Nooooo!' she cries. 'Nooooooooooooooooo . . .'

'Nooooooo!'

Miranda woke up, bathed in sweat, the cry echoing in her ears. Everything was black. She was confused. Where was she?

For one vivid moment, she was back in France. Young. Eager. Biking through the ancient towns of the Loire Valley. Biking down a country road after dark.

The château country is lovely in autumn, friends had told her. *One mustn't leave France without seeing the châteaux. Blois, Tours, Chinon, Chambord.* Chambord was the last. The most magnificent.

Chambord! Miranda shivered.

She was near Chambord, then. In a ditch. Slashed. Mutilated. Left to die. But where was the blood? The pain?

Her heart was racing like a jackhammer. She touched first her face, then her throat.

Nothing! No blood. No raw flesh. She shook her head cautiously as the realization dawned. She had been dreaming.

Gradually, her eyes adjusted to the dark. The bedside clock read 3:18. She was safe, thank God! Safe in her own bed, four thousand miles away. She wanted to weep with relief.

What a nightmare!

Miranda sat up and switched on the light. She was still trembling, drenched in sweat.

Because the worst of it was, it wasn't a nightmare at all. It was a fragment of memory that had lain buried for years, only to surface this very night. A flashback – unwanted, unbidden – of pain and horror.

Already the images were fading, leaving murky outlines. The poplar trees. The flash of steel. The taste of flesh. Even vaguer, the image of the man. He was strong. And young. She sensed that she had known him. Beyond that – nothing!

Which was as well. Miranda didn't want to learn the details. No good would come of it. Such memories would only taint her waking hours. Meanwhile, she had a life to live.

With an effort of will, she pushed the dream away, then went to make tea and ponder more pleasant matters.

The Blake–Halsey merger, for instance. Now there was food for thought. Tomorrow when the market opened, she would buy five thousand shares of Blake Instruments. She figured the price to soar within a week. A nice piece of change, as her pals on the trading floor were wont to say.

What a fool Roger King was! Trumpeting his professional triumphs as if they held the key to her heart.

He had thought to use her, but she had managed to use *him*. She had enjoyed excellent meals, received stock-market tips, even coaxed him into a large donation to the Humane Society. Perhaps she should write him a thank-you note.

Yet she felt disappointed too. She had wanted to like him more than she did. If only he hadn't lunged! So crude. To say that men behaved like animals was unfair. Animals were nicer.

'Isn't that so, OJ?' She stroked the cat on her lap. He licked her hand with a sand-paper tongue.

One thing was clear to Miranda: Roger's aggression had brought on the flashback. From now on, she would have to be on her guard to prevent any recurrence.

No more dates or flirtations, she vowed. She must finally

relinquish all hope of romantic love. That happiness was closed to her, especially now that Peter Mainwaring was married.

Ah Peter! She still couldn't think of him without sighing. But sighs were better than tears.

Miranda had been devastated when the detective informed her that Peter was married. She had locked herself in her apartment and cried for a week. Later, when her depression had lifted, she kept the detective on, requesting that he make brief monthly reports. Not that Peter's life was any of her business, yet she felt it hard to break the link a second time. He still mattered. And what harm could it do for her to know where he was, how he was?

The entertainment business was risky, she rationalized. A man could be famous one day, forgotten the next. There might come a time when Peter needed help, in which case she would come to his aid as he had once come to hers. All she asked was the opportunity to look after his welfare, anonymously, and from a great distance.

Beyond that, she would try to rid herself of all intense emotions – the good *and* the painful. God forbid she should spend the rest of her life racked by love for a man she could never possess. Or – she remembered her nightmare with a shudder – by her hatred for another.

That monster!

Suddenly she could taste his flesh on her tongue. Feel its texture. The sensation was vivid. From a distant past, an ugly memory had been summoned; she feared it would never die.

But he too, her unknown assailant, had cause to remember that night. For she had swallowed a piece of his ear.

MANHATTAN

'If you ask me, she's just plain nuts.'

Bette West had just come from dinner at Alix's apartment in St Mark's Place, and, stunned by the change of circumstances, was letting Kim have the benefit of her judgment.

'Squalor! It's the only word for how she lives. The street! The neighborhood! Yecch! Her furniture looks like it came from the Salvation Army. Plus she does zilch for her appearance. I wanted to hand her my comb. At least she used to dress well – not to my taste, I admit, but classy if you liked that Boston blue-blood look. To think I used to envy her back in Marival. Whatever she wanted, charge it up to Daddy, no questions asked! Clothes, limos, swanky restaurants. Remember that scrumptious pheasant in Glovier? From that to meat loaf and mashed potatoes! And this Rabinowitz person who looks after the baby . . . fella doesn't even speak decent English. Frankly, I was shocked.'

'She seems happy, though,' Kim ventured.

'Happy! Crazy's more like it. Imagine throwing away a fortune for *love*?' Bette didn't try to disguise the sneer in her voice. 'The guy didn't even have the decency to marry her. And notice how she clammed up when I asked for details? Ashamed, is my bet. Some people!' Bette grunted. 'Some people oughta have their head examined!'

But Kim was entranced. To have surrendered everything for love struck her as splendid.

Kim believed in grand passion. So did her astrologer. The day she had run into Alix on Tenth Street, she had come from a reading and it had been a knockout. The next time Venus was in harmony with both Mars and the moon, Madame Allegra promised, Kim would be swept away on a tidal wave of love.

'You are destined for a remarkable fate,' Madame said.

However, since Kim had yet to star in a drama of her own, she was all the more respectful of Alix's. Such courage. Such self-sacrifice. How Alix must have suffered!

True, Alix didn't seem to be suffering now. When Kim asked her if she was happy, the question brought Alix up short.

'I don't know,' she replied. 'I guess I've been too busy to think about it.'

Which Kim interpreted as a Yes, if being happy was the opposite of being bored. For though Bette had cooled on Alix, Kim had not. She admired Alix's energy, her drive, her baby.

Lately, Kim had grown disappointed with her lot. The days were given over to shopping and beauty care; the odd evenings spent with Pierre. The Virgin Dream poster had been superseded by newer and sassier displays. And on those increasingly rare occasions when Kim was interviewed or made a PR appearance, Bette spirited her off the moment it was over. Most nights, the Wests stayed home, watching television or playing honeymoon bridge. You wouldn't think a 'glamor girl's' life could be such a yawn.

But what she envied Alix most was her casual lifestyle, Kim herself being, as Bette constantly reminded her, a 'public figure' and therefore constrained from kicking her shoes off or cussing or doing anything other than look vacuous. As a result, she had few friends and no intimates. Sometimes she felt a million years old.

Whereas Alix! Alix may have tossed away her father's fortune, but – Kim felt – she had gained twice what she had lost, though Kim's mother could hardly be expected to agree.

'She's not what *I'd* call a lady,' Bette sniffed. 'I wouldn't be surprised if she smokes pot. You don't want to waste time in that madhouse.'

'But all I want is to hang out with people my own age.'

Alix, who understood this, took pity.

'Come over tonight' – she would ring Kim up – 'nothing fancy but you'll meet some interesting people.'

When Kim went, it was with the relish of a kid playing hookey. To be young and free. That was the ticket. To dress down and be easy.

But once inside Alix's noisy living room, Kim was tongue-tied. It was all very well to sit cross-legged on the floor and drink lager and not worry about your hair, but Kim's liberation went no further. What could she possibly say that might be of interest to these witty young artists and journalists and lawyers? They sounded like guests on a PBS talk-show. This one had written a novel, that one had returned from a fact-finding trip to the Middle East. Of what could she boast? That she had posed in the nude with a snake?

Mostly she sat and smiled.

'Good grief!' Kim said at the end of one such evening. She had stayed behind to help clear away. 'I felt like a total dummy tonight. I mean, everybody's got opinions on everything, whereas I don't even know how I feel about Nixon, let alone Samuel Beckett or the situation in Chad. They didn't teach that stuff at Mechanicsville High.'

But instead of laughing and comforting Kim, telling her that it was quite enough to be sweet and look decorative, Alix frowned.

'You ought to do something useful with your life,' she said. 'Get involved with real issues. Find out what's going on in the world. Only connect, as they say. For instance, why not take a couple of courses at the New School? I've got the catalog here somewhere. And read some good books for a change instead of that Barbara Cartland drivel. I'll make you a list.'

'I'm no great brain —' Kim began to apologize.

'That's a cop-out!' Alix broke in. She took both of Kim's hands in hers. 'Now listen to me, Kimberly West. Don't try to hide behind that little girl mask. I know you better. So when I tell you that you've got as much native intelligence as anyone who was here tonight, I'm only speaking the truth. You're quick, intuitive. You have a gift for languages. I remember how you picked up French at Marival. You know how to listen. Why waste your talents? For that matter, why waste your time on a guy like Pierre Waxman? Unless you love him, of course.'

'Pierre's a creep.'

'Well, then! All the more reason to declare your independence. You're a twenty-two-year-old woman with a world of possibilities on every hand, yet you behave like a telephone on HOLD. What are you waiting for?'

'Prince Charming?' Kim said tentatively.

Alix rolled her eyes in despair.

'There ain't no such animal, believe me.'

'But my horoscope says —'

'Fuck your horoscope, Kim. We have to make our own happiness, and we can only do it if we live in the now. Otherwise I'd still be rotting in Cambridge, waiting for Sam. God, I hate to see you dream your life away.'

Kim brushed back a tear. 'You're right,' she said.

Alix went into the bedroom and returned with a stack of books. '*Grapes of Wrath* . . . *Lucky Jim* . . . the latest Malamud . . . and think about what I've said.'

Kim nodded. She would certainly read Alix's books. And she would definitely think about going to college. Studying history, literature . . . She'd always been interested in art and design.

Yes indeed, maybe she should sign up for something. Next week. If not next week, then one of these days. But in the taxi home, her resolve vanished.

She'd probably flunk everything anyhow. Besides, she'd have to check the idea out with Bette.

Already she could hear her mother's comments: 'Education is grand, but what about your beauty regimen, your aerobics, your afternoon nap? Honey, you can't spare the time.'

*

One morning, Kim went to Manhattan Criminal Court to watch Alix perform.

'You're in show-biz,' Alix said. 'Catch my act.'

The crime was sensational, even for New York. A prostitute, one Nancy Graves, had been charged with murdering a client in the heat of passion. Miss Graves had stabbed the gentleman forty-seven times with an ice pick.

The press picked up on the case, dubbing it the Swiss Cheese Murder in deference to the victim's wounds, and turned out in force for the trial.

But to hear Alix plead in her final argument, you wondered – who *was* the victim? Kim listened spellbound as her friend chronicled a life of unrelieved misery.

'This child,' as Alix referred to the hooker, a skinny black woman who kept gazing off into space. 'This child' had been the victim of incest, neglect, beatings, rape, assault, lead poisoning . . .

Alix punctuated each point by thwacking the rail with her fist. As she spoke, she showed photos: the street corners, slums, rats, schools, the environment that had nurtured Nancy Graves or failed to.

'Society dealt this poor kid far more than forty-seven blows, from the day she was born. Forty-seven blows? (THWACK THWACK!) Four thousand blows! Her whole life has been a crime. A crime against childhood!'

Kim wanted to leap up and applaud.

The jury brought in a verdict of manslaughter.

'Not bad,' Alix said afterward, swallowing a salami sandwich as they crossed Foley Square, already late for an appointment. 'Though I was hoping for acquittal.'

'Well, you were terrific, anyway, ' Kim said sincerely. 'So eloquent. And I loved the way you kept thumping your fist. Just like in the movies.'

Alix grinned. 'You know what they say. If the law's on your side, hammer on the law. If the facts are on your side, hammer on the facts. And if you don't have either the law or the facts, hammer on the table. God, I hate losing.'

In fact, Alix was pleased with herself.

Ever since that day she had jumped on the platform alongside Sam Matthews in Boston and discovered a gift for oratory, she had cultivated her 'acting' skills. And though happy to win on technicalities, it was absolute bliss to sway a jury by her eloquence.

On demand, she could be sarcastic, angry, passionate, tearful, though like most good actors, Alix had her favorite 'bits.' One was a talent for arriving in the courtroom at the very last moment, breathless. 'Sorry!' she would say within earshot of the jury, 'but my baby-sitter was late.' Sometimes, when things were going badly, she would 'accidentally' drop her briefcase and send papers flying. Then, with an embarrassed grin, be all thumbs when it came to picking them up. She took care never to dress so smartly as to distance herself from the jurors, appearing both modest and vulnerable. How could jurors not empathize with this struggling young lawyer? And – by association – with her client?

But the real key to Alix's success was her ability to put herself in her clients' shoes. The first questions she asked herself were *why* and *how*. How would I be if I lived as they lived, why would I feel what they felt? By focusing not on the crime but on the person, she could argue from the heart. She never forgot that this fallible human being might, but for the luck of the draw, have been herself. Or Sam!

One afternoon, Alix took Kim to the office and introduced her around. Jeff Aaronoff's eyes popped out of their sockets.

'You're the girl with the boa constrictor!' he gasped.

'It was a python, actually.'

'God, Alix. You never told me you knew celebrities.'

They chatted for a bit, then Jeff had to leave. He did it with obvious reluctance.

*

That Jeff should be bewitched by Kim West was not surprising. Kim was everybody's fantasy girl. In fact, he only got to take her out once. It was a traumatic experience.

'She's sweet as they come,' Jeff said to Alix afterward, 'though you wonder who she gets it from. The mother makes Dragon Lady look like Mother Teresa. She came along as part of the package, to grill me I think. Anyhow, I took 'em both to dinner at Quo Vadis. My God, those two can eat! Though all Mrs West did was bitch about the food and the service. How unsatisfactory everything was, me included. She kept yattering on about this glorious future she has in mind for Kim, and made it clear I didn't figure in it. Poor Kim. She just sat there like a lamb, while the old hag is wiping the floor with me. Then dinner was over, she has the nerve to ask for a doggie bag. Can you beat that?'

Alix nodded. 'At least she didn't swipe the tip.'

'I paid with plastic. It was half a month's rent. Jesus!' He shuddered. 'Imagine having Bette West for your mother-in-law! Now there's a scenario! I guess I'm well out of it.'

Mother-in-law? Alix did a take, startled that Jeff had even been thinking along those lines.

'So Bette scared you off.'

'I can't even get through on the phone,' he said.

Alix was troubled. She liked to flatter herself that Jeff's highest affections were reserved for her. In the back of her mind, he remained the man whom, when all else failed, she might eventually marry. Her rock and anchor.

Instead of which he mooned about for weeks, victim of a king-sized crush, rehashing his big night with Kim West.

'She's not stupid, you know. People think so because she's so lovely. She's just, what I guess you'd call untrained. By the way, Alix, did you see the picture of her in this month's *Sports Illustrated*?'

'Only on every newsstand.'

'Yeah . . .' Jeff sighed. He had perched himself on a corner of

Alix's desk, lost to reality. 'In that bitsy white bathing suit. What a lovely girl . . .'

'You're sitting on my correspondence,' Alix said sharply.

'Sorry!' He jumped off and began straightening out the papers. Then he saw something that made his jaw drop.

'Jesus, Alix! What the fuck is this?'

'What the fuck does it look like?'

'It looks like a letter of retainer from Vince Mazzetti. Big Vince, as I believe he's known in the cement-overcoat trade. Since when do you represent Mafia?'

'Since I spent a bloody fortune on the Graves case. Background investigation, expert witnesses, shrinks. That stuff doesn't come cheap. I wound up seven thousand bucks out of pocket. Listen, pal, if I based my courtroom strategy on my clients' ability to pay, I'd have to plead them all guilty.' Suddenly, Alix laughed. 'God! That Swiss Cheese defense had as many holes in it as the dear departed. However, it sure is bringing in business. Not just Mazzetti. I'm representing Mike Roamans as well.'

'The Wall Street swindler?'

'The *alleged* Wall Street swindler. ' Alix smirked.

'Terrific!' Jeff said. 'And I suppose those goons are also just poor misunderstood kids?'

Alix laughed and leaned back in her chair, content within herself. 'You're funny, Jeff. You want it both ways. You want to champion the little guy, but not get your nails dirty in the process. Roamans is giving me a thirty-thou retainer up front. Mazzetti's down for twenty. Well, fifty grand does a lot of championing.'

'Miss Robin Hood,' he said airily. 'You know those kind of clients don't win you popularity awards.'

'Nope. They win me more top-paying clients. And it's not all Robin Hood either. I happen to have a household to support. You know Eddie Martinez is moving up to the Bronx and I'm taking over his space. Then I'm going to hire some nice bright kid out of law school to work for me.'

Jeff smiled. 'If you're not careful, you're gonna wind up rich and famous. Just like your old man.'

'Rich I've been,' Alix said. 'I'll settle for famous.'

One Monday morning, Kim returned home from her aerobics class to find Bette in a state of exaltation.

'Look!' she commanded.

How could Kim not! for the apartment was inundated with orchids. They flowered in pots, in bowls, in planters suspended from the ceiling. The fragrance numbed.

Kim moved gingerly from blossom to blossom, doubting the evidence of her senses. The room looked like a tropical jungle ablaze in colors. Deep lavender, lustrous emerald, brilliant yellow with feverish spots, luminous pink. The flowers ranged from the elegant to the grotesque. Some were delicate as tea roses. Others gaudy as Christmas decorations. A few were faintly obscene, but the massed effect was boundless beauty.

'Fabulous!'

Her mind reeled. Who could have sent them? Not Pierre, who had hay fever, poor slob. Jeff? She had given him up for dead.

'Is there a card?' she asked Bette in a shaky voice.

Her mother handed her a note on creamy white paper. It contained a handwritten message in a forceful script.

For the most beautiful woman in the world, a few of the most beautiful flowers from my garden. There was no signature.

They had been delivered by a chauffeur at nine that morning. It had taken three trips to bring them all up.

'A mystery admirer!' Bette's eyes glittered.

They spent the rest of the morning speculating who it might be – with prospects running the gamut from Howard Hughes to Elvis Presley. A man of great wealth, obviously. Perhaps he had been smitten by her photo in *Sports Illustrated*.

The special issue had generated a brief flurry of fan letters, duly forwarded by the magazine. They included, among other

197

more colorful suggestions, a couple of dozen offers of marriage. Kim laughed, and threw them away.

But this . . . ! It was so romantic!

'He's probably a hundred years old,' Kim said to spare herself disillusion. 'And we'll never hear from him again.'

'Old is a relative term,' Bette reasoned. 'You mustn't be prejudiced.' Had Kim looked in her eyes at that moment, she would have seen dollar signs.

On Tuesday, a Vuitton trunk arrived, packed with confectionery. Candied violets, Belgian truffles, pralines from New Orleans, French almond dragées, Godiva chocolates, nougats from Montelimar, Harrogate toffees, boxes of fragrant Turkish delight. The mysterious admirer had looted the confectionery shops of the world.

Sweets to the sweet – the note said.

Kim rushed to the phone and called Madame Allegra.

'I have to know, is Venus in conjunction with Mars and the moon this week?'

'Could be,' the wise woman said.

The suspense was agonizing.

Wednesday was perfumes in a crocodile case. Shalimar, Arpège, Joy, L'heure bleu, Bellodgia, scents by Chanel and Dior, each packaged in precious gift bottles, none smaller than an ounce. Enough fragrances to last a lifetime.

Soon – the note read. That was all.

Kim couldn't sleep that night. She was up at dawn, waiting for the next installment. 'Assuming there *is* a next installment, knock on wood.'

Around ten, a messenger came with a box from Revillon. Kim buried her face in the honey-colored fur. Never had she felt such softness, such unabashed luxury.

'Is that mink?' Bette asked. 'Looks like it. Full length, too. Here, honey, let me look at it.'

But Kim was foraging through the tissue for a note.

'Ah! Here we are, Mom. Read what it says!'

To keep you warm until we meet. Tomorrow evening at 9:00.

'Wow!' said Bette, who had already slipped the coat on. 'It's Russian sable. I wonder what he does for an encore.'

Early Friday morning, a small package arrived in a Tiffany box. Kim tore it open. Inside was a cardboard egg carton.

'An egg carton?' Kim and Bette said in unison.

Kim opened it, half afraid of finding eggs inside and discovering that she had been the object of a massive practical joke. What she found took her breath away.

Nestled in each hollow was a gemstone, perfect but unset. Twelve glittering jewels, each different, all beautiful.

'I don't get it . . .' she began, but Bette was studying them intensely, lips pursed.

'This one's a garnet, that's amethyst, and this yellow jobbie I think is a topaz. A diamond . . . I guess it's genuine. And will you look at the fire in that opal. Why, that's your birthstone, Kimmy! That's what they all are. Birthstones. One for each month. What does the note say? Quick!'

She snatched it from Kim.

I didn't know which gem was yours, so I bought them all.
I will call for you tonight at nine.

Within the hour, Kim had embarked on a frantic round of activity. She must be flawless tonight. More beautiful than ever, a love goddess worthy of a tycoon's dream.

The morning was spent at Georgette Klinger, getting a facial and having her legs waxed. Not the tiniest blemish must mar the perfection of her skin. Then on to Michel Kazan's to have her hair streaked and styled. Eyebrows newly plucked, nails freshly manicured, she went home to face the day's hardest decision: what to wear.

'Well, the sable, of course!' Bette said. But beneath it?

The discussion lasted an hour – long dress or short? Cocktail length would be safest. Was there time to make a quick trip to Martha's for something ravishing? What the hell, Bette said. They could charge it up to Pierre.

'Oh, my God!' Kim turned pale. 'I forgot! Pierre's supposed to take me to the Knicks game tonight. What'll I do?' She began wringing her hands. 'I've never stood him up before.'

'Don't worry, hon. I've already canceled. I told him you were home with the mumps. Now, what do you think about the green chiffon . . . ?'

By seven that evening, every garment Kim possessed had been dragged out of the closet, discarded, reconsidered, discarded again before they settled on a simple pale yellow satin cocktail frock. It made Kim look both girlish and sexy.

While Bette pressed her dress, there was just time enough for Kim, coiffure protected by a plastic mobcap, to relax in a bubble bath and contemplate her future.

After the date with Jeff Aaronoff – the first proper date Kim ever had – her mother had begun trumpeting the virtues of Pierre. Pierre was pliable, undemanding, comfortably off.

'Very comfortably! And if he isn't much in the manhood department, Kim, count yourself lucky. You won't have to be peeling him off you every night. Besides, who else will support me in my old age?' At that moment, Bette looked as solemn as though someone had died. Kim's heart flip-flopped.

'You know, darling, I've devoted my entire life to your welfare. Every waking moment. I've scrimped, I've saved, I've done without basics so you could have lovely things and grand opportunities. You owe me a little something in return.'

What could Kim say without sounding like an ingrate? She lowered her eyes, and Bette took it for assent.

A week ago, Bette had sent off an engagement notice to *The New York Times*. And in his own vapid way, Pierre was willing.

At the memory, Kim sank down deeper amid the bubbles.

Well, she supposed, if she had to marry for money, it might as well be one man as another. And her mystery admirer must be infinitely rich. Certainly richer than Pierre.

The logic troubled her, however. For if Pierre were moderately wealthy and moderately obnoxious, what would this unknown Midas be like?

Bald, ugly, dwarfish, hunched – Kim prepared herself for the worst – with yellowing teeth and hair sprouting from his nostrils. Her stomach churned.

Still . . . !

Kim thought of the doctor in that hotel in Atlantic City. However awful it was, she consoled herself, it was hardly worse than plastic surgery. And if you were lying face down with your head in a pillow, you didn't even have to look.

By quarter of nine, she was dressed and nervous as a bride. Bette kept peering out of the window.

'Kim! Quick! Look! But don't muss your hair!'

A Cadillac had pulled up in front of their building, black and ceremonial. A block long. The kind of car you saw at the United Nations and in gangster movies. But at this distance you couldn't see the occupant. Kim crossed her fingers and prayed.

A minute later the doorbell rang.

Bette went to open it. Kim tried to keep from throwing up.

'Mrs West?' he said with faintest of French accents. 'And this must be Kimberly! Ah . . . but your picture doesn't begin to do you justice. That photographer should be shot for understatement. If you will permit me to introduce myself . . . I am Tonio DuMesne of San Miguel.'

For a moment Kim thought she was going to faint.

For a few feet away – tall, slim, immaculately clad in a white Palm Beach suit – was Prince Charming.

HOLLAND PARK

Five years of marriage hadn't dulled the glow. The Mainwarings remained as blissful as newlyweds, as comfy as Darby and Joan.

From a man who had rarely been seen without a glass in his hand, Peter was now a thoroughly domesticated animal.

Soon after the wedding, the Mainwarings bought a flat in Holland Park of the type known as 'handyman's special.' No more pub crawls for Peter, or rowdy nights out with the boys. These days, he and Anne spent their free time sanding floors, stripping wainscotting, restoring Victorian plasterwork to its former grandeur, painting, polishing, haunting antique shops in the quest for the perfect Suffolk corner cupboard or a set of William Morris screens. Anne proved to be a vigorous gardener while Peter cultivated his culinary skills. His specialty was creating elaborate pâtés and terrines, with attendant results to his waistline.

Yet all who knew him agreed he had never looked better. His writing, once so caustic, acquired a mellower edge. He talked about taking a sabbatical from *Off the Wall* to develop a situation comedy.

Anne's career too looked rosy. The adventures of Morgan the Mandrill were selling crisply in British bookstores, with the perky simian threatening to push Paddington Bear off the shelves. There was *Morgan Goes to Paris*, *Morgan Goes on Safari*, *Morgan Flies to the Moon*, *Morgan Meets Sherlock Holmes*. Kids adored him, and a goodly number of adults enjoyed the sly humor that slipped into each tale.

If there was a flaw in their happiness, it was that they were childless. They had a sunlit room that would make a wonderful nursery, names picked out. Each month brought a new curve of hope, a fresh dip of disappointment.

A week after their fifth anniversary, Anne learned that she was pregnant. It was a dream come true. The following morning, she received a call from New York. A top children's book publisher wanted her name on a contract. She was on the telephone for over an hour. 'What do you think, Peter?' she said as he made coffee. She sounded dazed.

'I'm overjoyed, darling. How could I not be?'

'I mean about my going to America next month. My new editor is awfully keen on meeting me personally. It seems they'd like me to do some publicity, tape a few interviews, that sort of thing, before I get too big and pregnant. You know how the Yanks are about promotion.'

'Do you want to go?'

Anne scratched her ear.

'I've never been to the States and, yes, I'd love to go for a week or two. New York, Broadway, all that jazz, as they say. It sounds like so much fun. Besides, once the baby arrives, I don't know if I'll be so mobile . . .'

'You don't have to rationalize, love. Go by all means. I'm sure they'll wine and dine you in grand style. May as well get it while it's hot. I only wish I could keep you company. But we're short-staffed on the show as it happens.'

Anne grinned, then kissed him on the forehead.

'You must promise to be very good while I'm gone. No dancing girls or orgies. If you do, then be sure to clean up after them. I don't want to come home to find lipstick on the sheets.'

'Spoil sport.'

But three weeks later, having a pre-flight coffee in the lounge at Heathrow, Anne was in a more somber mood.

'We've never spent a night apart before,' she observed. 'Are you sure you'll be all right?'

'It's only for a couple of weeks. Good lord, darling, I'm not an utter incompetent.'

'Of course not,' she said. 'You won't forget to water the asparagus fern every three days . . .'

Freda Bright

'. . . the asparagus fern.'

'Or pick up your gray suit from Sketchley's . . .'

'. . . Sketchley's.'

'And be sure to ring up your mother on Sunday . . .'

'. . . mother, Sunday. They're announcing your flight, Anne.'

'So they are! Would you believe I have butterflies in my stomach? Peter?' She was suddenly wary. 'Do you ever get the feeling life is too good?'

'Why, Annie, what a question!'

'I mean, we've got so much. Everything really. Success. Each other. And now a baby coming. It's sort of spooky, so many good things happening in conjunction.'

She looked about for some wood to knock on, but there was only chrome and plastic. 'Well, I would knock on wood if I could find it. Damn synthetic world we live in.'

'Knock wood, indeed! Of all the rubbishy superstitions. Now go catch your plane so I can get on with my orgies.'

He kissed her vigorously, then held her close.

'I love you, Annie. I'll count the days.' To his surprise, he was choked up.

'I love you too, darling. Sorry I sounded like an idiot.'

She shouldered her flight bag, winked, and headed for the departure gate. At the gate, she turned. Waved. 'I'll call you from New York.' He watched her slight brisk figure until it was lost from view.

'She's only been gone two minutes,' he thought descending the escalator, 'and already I miss her dreadfully.'

CHICAGO

One morning, Miranda called her staff together and announced her retirement from commodity trading. She planned to sell her seat and move to New York.

'Any business in which a kid can make a million bucks overnight,' she said, 'doesn't deserve the attention of a full-grown adult.'

The previous day, she had taken Jim Bisseau to lunch at Chez Paul and told him her plans. He was the closest thing Miranda had to a confidante.

Soft-spoken, pale-haired, whistle-thin, with the drawl and courtliness of a Southern gentleman, Jim had come to Chicago fresh from Tulane University, hot for a career in commodities. Miranda took him on as a trainee, then quickly promoted him to personal assistant. Both loyal and discreet, he served on the trading floor as her eyes, ears and good right hand, for which he was handsomely rewarded.

Miranda was fond of Jim. Fond enough to set tongues wagging. But she knew what the gossips did not, that Jim was gay. With no question of romantic complications, Miranda was able to relax in his company.

He escorted her to trade banquets and fed her cats when she was away. In return she provided him with a 'date' on those occasions when his ultra-respectable family came to town. 'We're each other's beards,' she said. Though unfamiliar with the term, he got the gist.

It was Jim who told her about the Bored-Room Bet. Miranda was saddened but not surprised.

'Just what you'd expect from those slobs. Every one of 'em is a case of arrested development. I used to think there could be nothing grander than to be allowed to trade on the floor. The

Pit,' she sneered. 'The pits is more like it. I'm fed up with their antics. Grown men throwing spit balls and paper airplanes, tossing order cards about like they were Frisbees. The fist fights. The language! My old man worked in the stock yards and now that you know, please forget it. But when it comes to profanity, your average foul-mouthed meat-packer can't hold a candle to our brethren on the trading floor.'

After five years, Miranda was restless. She had always been restless, even as a child, running from the present to the future. Having proved herself in Chicago, she saw no reason to stay on. Money hadn't made her as happy as she had hoped and the work, once so exciting, now palled.

Worst of all, the bad dreams persisted. Fragments of the past kept sneaking up on her in the dead of night. It was getting so she hated going to bed. Perhaps if she could keep on the move, she could leave the dreams behind. And nothing so concentrated the mind as a change of venue and a fresh challenge.

'I watch my cats,' she told Jim the day they lunched at Chez Paul, eating *moules marinière*. 'It's very instructive. You'd never guess they'd once been alley cats, fighting for survival. They've gone soft, lazy. Shuffling between the bowl and the box, then back again. The only break in this whirl of activity is when they settle down for a twelve-hour snooze. They wouldn't know what to do with a mouse if one came and tweaked their whiskers. Probably roll over and go back to sleep. They've lost their edge, you see.'

'They're still good for scratching on furniture,' Jim said, but Miranda shook her head.

'Then I look at my own life and I wonder if it's all that different. Shuttling between home and office, then back again. Buy a little, sell a little. Such a narrow world. You know, Bryden Electronics has developed a computerized trading program. The day will come when you won't even have to go out your front door. You could do it all in one room. Your whole life. Bowl and box. Box and bowl.'

She waved her fork for emphasis while Jim attended to his *moules* with gusto.

'As bowls go,' he said mildly, dipping bread into the broth, 'this one isn't bad. Maybe a little more garlic.'

Miranda pushed her plate away.

'Life needs a little more garlic. I want to sample a lot of different bowls and boxes, Jim. In places like New York and Mombasa and Bangkok. I've been ripe for change for a long time and when you told me about the Bet, that clinched it. I want to start a new business. Something with garlic, so to speak. How do you feel about barter?'

'Barter?' Jim abandoned his *moules*. 'As in beads and wampum? Where they give you Manhattan in return?'

'Not quite, though that's a nice idea, too. I meant international barter, in goods and currency. I'll spell it out.'

With the Vietnam war over, opportunities were springing up everywhere, especially for the flexible entrepreneur.

In recent years, American companies had accumulated a great deal of wealth in third world nations. We sold, they bought, often paying for American goods in local currencies. In *escudos* and *dirhams* and *bahts* and *guaranis*. The problem lay in getting the money out. Many of those countries had currency restrictions. Which meant you had to convert the money into local products, bringing it back in the form of imports.

But what happened if those countries didn't produce any goods that our country wanted?

'In that case, the American company is stuck. So the money just sits there, in *bahts* and *dirhams*, doing zip.'

Miranda's idea was to buy up those foreign credits cheap, then use the capital to finance intricate deals.

'For instance, Jim. Say a US corporation has piled up ten million bucks' worth of *kwanzas* in Angola, whose major national product is bat guano. I'm talking totally theoretical examples, you understand. Well, we Americans don't have much call for bat guano, but the Koreans prize it as fertilizer. And the

Angolans could sure use a few million pairs of Korean sneakers. The plan is, I buy up the *kwanzas* from the American firm at a discount, and use it to finance the swop. The US company gets some of its money back, the Angolans get their sneakers, the Koreans are up to their ears in bat guano. That's the plan and everybody winds up happy, especially me, because I get to keep what money's left over. I could be up a couple of million dollars on a deal like that.'

'Or down the same,' Jim observed with a smile.

'That's the risk. Look, Jim, neither of us would be playing the market if we were averse to risk. If you're as much like me as I think you are, that's part of the attraction. That, plus the chance to travel all over the world. Now there's a choice. If you want to stay here and buy my seat on the exchange, I'll finance you. But if you're in the mood for something adventurous, throw in your lot with me. We'd be great together, Jim. We're both free spirits. Ready to hop a plane on a moment's notice. I plan to set up an office in the World Trade Center for openers. Eventually, I can see branches in London, Rio, Hong Kong. One on every continent . . .'

By the time the waiter cleared away, Jim had signed on.

'Have you thought up a name for this baby?' he asked. 'You can't just keep calling it the Plan.'

'Been too busy. Any suggestions?'

'How about Miranda Corporation? MiraCo, for short.'

'MiraCo.' Miranda laughed. 'MiraCo! Well, why not?'

Once committed, Miranda felt exuberant. She was starting a new life – yet again.

The night before leaving Chicago, she went to the Bored Room Café and stood everyone drinks. The men were lined up three deep at the bar.

'So what are you guys going to do with all that money?' she asked.

'What money?' Alarmed glances were exchanged.

'Why, the money from the Bet.'

A half dozen customers headed for the door. Miranda called them back by name. She was grinning.

'I hear there's approximately eighty thou in that account. Now don't bother to deny or look dumb or prevaricate. As usual my sources are excellent. I'm shocked. Truly shocked, as I'm sure your wives and girlfriends would be if they knew the details. I'd hate to be the one who disillusioned them. Why, they'd probably think you were a bunch of horny adolescent retards instead of the mature and compassionate gentlemen I know you to be. And to prove my contention, you wonderful folks are going to draw up a check tonight to the benefit of – let me see – I think the Northside Home for Unmarried Mothers would be a suitable charity. Let's make it eighty thousand even, shall we? And if there's a little left over, you can drink my health on Christmas Eve. Okay, guys. Cough up.'

Kennedy was a mob scene, hot and noisy. Especially for Miranda waiting in line for a taxi, while juggling an oversized briefcase and a brood of unhappy felines. There were fifty people ahead of her in line. It moved slowly.

When Miranda's turn finally came, the cabbie was no help, content to sit there, arms folded, and watch her struggle with the cases. What they said about New York manners was true.

'Here!' said the woman in line behind her. 'Let me give you a hand.'

She was a small, trim woman with curly black hair and a crisp English accent. She held the door open and helped Miranda load the cats into the taxi.

'Thank you. I can't imagine how I would have managed.'

'Not at all.' They exchanged smiles.

'Your first visit to the States?' Miranda inquired.

'Yes, it is.'

'Well, I do hope you enjoy it.'

'Thank *you*,' Anne Mainwaring said pleasantly. 'I'm sure I shall.'

SAN MIGUEL

In the 1975 *Statesman's Yearbook*, the Republic of San Miguel ranked as the second most populous country in the Caribbean and second from the bottom in literacy.

Its primary exports are bauxite, ebony, indigo, sugar and the famous Mère Marie black rum. Though not particularized in the *Yearbook*, drugs also play a vital role in the economy, with San Miguel serving as a way station between the *fincas* of Colombia and the streets of Harlem.

The official language is French, with English spoken by the upper classes. The language of the people, however, is the colorful *patois* – an amalgam of Spanish, French, Portuguese and West African dialects from the days of the slavers. The official religion is Catholicism, but primitive cults flourish among the ignorant.

With its mix of blacks, Creoles, Caribs and mestizos (as well as Syrian traders, Indian shopkeepers, and the US and European contingent who have come to exploit its resources and run its casinos) San Miguel might purport to be the world in micro-cosm. In fact, there are but two classes of inhabitants: the rich and the poor.

Shaped roughly like a bowler hat, the main island (San Miguel Majeur) boasts many interesting features: the volcanic mountains of the interior, the primeval hardwood forests (now giving way to sand and scrub), the sugar plantations, and, along the brim of the bowler, mile after mile of exquisite palm-fringed coral beaches unequalled in the Caribbean. Here at sea-level, the tropical heat is tempered by cooling trade winds nine months of the year, though during the rainy season (June through August), the temperature frequently rises above 100°F.

The capital city, with its deep-water port, is named Benedicta, after the Spanish monks who founded an abbey there in 1548. Though the monks perished within a decade, the abbey survived and now houses the National Museum. Today, Benedicta is a metropolis of over a million people.

Discovered by Columbus on his second voyage (he disembarked just long enough to give the island its name and remark upon the docility of the now-extinct Arawaks), San Miguel has a long and tortured history. It was, variously, colonized by Spain, France, England, then France again, before achieving independence. One of the major naval battles in the Napoleonic Wars took place in the Straits of Cerbère, with Nelson commanding the British West Indies fleet from nearby Antigua.

In the early nineteenth century, San Miguel boasted the Caribbean's most vibrant economy. This prosperity was based on a constant infusion of slave labor to work the mines and plantations, though the French Colonial Office preferred the term *volontiers*, implying that the labor was willingly given.

During that period, vast fortunes were made in sugar, mining, forestry, and from the highly prized sponges plucked from the coral reefs and shipped the world over. By mid-century, wealthy Creoles (the term denotes native-born islanders of European ancestry) were sending their wives to France for the latest fashions and their children to England for public-school educations.

In the 1860s, San Miguel embarked on a building spree. The vision was heroic: broad mansion-lined boulevards, spacious parks, zoological gardens, public works of sybaritic splendor. The Grand Palais de Musique was expected to surpass the Opéra, then under construction in Paris. With its shops and theaters and plazas, Benedicta would soon rival the most splendid cities in Europe. Money was no object. It was everywhere, infinitely renewable, pouring out in an unbroken stream from the rich black earth, from the ancient forests, from the sea.

In August of 1869, a blight of unknown origin destroyed the

sponge beds. The following year the sugar crop failed. Hobbled by this dual blow, the economy collapsed.

Work on the opera house was halted, palaces remained half built. Gradually, the jungle reclaimed the grand boulevards. Hunger, always a familiar in slave households, now stalked the dining rooms of the bourgeoisie. In 1870, the government in Paris emancipated the *volontiers*.

The first great uprising (*La Révolte des Grandées*) took place in 1871. It was a conspiracy of wealthy Creoles who hoped to rid themselves of French rule and bring back slavery. The timing was perfect, for France, embroiled in war with Prussia, had no troops to spare for its wayward colony.

Thus was born the First Republic. It lasted three turbulent years and ushered in the longest, bloodiest chapter in San Miguel's history.

In 1874, slaves in the Benoix sugar plantation rebelled, setting off a firestorm. Hates and rivalries that had simmered silently for centuries now burst into the open. Slave against owner, farmer against shopkeeper, Frenchman against Spaniard, mulatto against octoroon.

Thus began the *Temps' Fou*, the Time of Madness. Crops rotted in the fields, mines were flooded, corpses hung in the wind at every crossroad. The civilized world watched in horror as the wealth of San Miguel hemorrhaged back into the ground. Not even the landing of Teddy Roosevelt's marines in 1903 could stanch the bleeding.

All told, the civil wars raged for over sixty years, by which time San Miguel was a synonym for chaos and cruelty. As coup followed coup, the former Jewel of the Caribbean became the Land Without Hope – *tierre sin expeira* in the patois. By 1936, its destruction seemed complete.

Say what one will about Tito DuMesne, and only history can render full judgment, he brought order out of chaos.

An army sergeant of Corsican parentage, El Tigre, as DuMesne subsequently came to be known, was scarcely thirty when he engineered a palace coup and declared himself president. He spent the next two decades consolidating his position with a blend of political skills and terror tactics. His model was Mussolini. Like Il Duce who made the trains run on time, El Tigre believed that the masses preferred stability to freedom. He ran the country like a private fiefdom.

Under the new regime, strikes were forbidden, taxes collected with a vengeance, the press brought to heel. Civil peace was maintained by the dreaded *Lou-lous*. This ubiquitous police force, recognizable by their black shirts, cockade hats and smoked glasses, had sworn a personal loyalty oath to El Tigre and were privileged to dispense summary justice with billy-clubs and gun butts. To some, it appeared that the new regime had reinstituted slavery, but few were so unwise as to say so. Dissenters had a way of disappearing in San Miguel. There were rumors of mass graves.

In 1954, oil was discovered offshore. In 1956, the Hilton chain opened the island to tourism. In 1960, El Tigre named himself Benefactor for Life and designated his son Tonio as sole heir.

According to a recent article in *Forbes*, the family's personal wealth was estimated as between two and six billion dollars, most of it resting safely in foreign banks.

Such were the fruits of Bette West's research, gleaned during an afternoon in the public library. She came away mightily pleased.

As to the disparity between the haves and have-nots of San Miguel, who was Bette to sit in judgment? Some people were lucky in this life, some were not. Tonio DuMesne, who had been lavishly blessed by fortune, might be Kim's last chance.

The girl was getting on in years, Bette fretted. Pushing twenty-five, and no knowing how long her looks would hold out. Worse yet, she had been growing restless. Bette worried that her influence was slipping. She blamed this state of affairs on Alix Bryden and her circle.

'You begin by sitting around on floors,' she carped, 'swilling beer with hippies, smoking pot, and before you know it, you've put on weight and your skin goes bad. Then what!'

To which Kim had groaned, 'Oh, Mom! Get real.'

But it was Kim, Bette feared, who was ducking reality. The python poster was old hat, the *Sports Illustrated* cover had come and gone, and true celebrity was as elusive as ever. Bette had to face the fact that Kim was not star material. Just a curvy body that looked good in a swimsuit, and as such, subject to the ravages of time. Marriage was the sole option left.

The engagement to Pierre had been a desperate measure. Bette saw it as an adequate *first* marriage, to be followed swiftly by a lucrative divorce. After which, Kim might remarry even more profitably. With luck, she could be another Slim Keith or Pamela Harriman. Which made for a career of sorts.

And then – like a gift from heaven – along came Tonio DuMesne, with his good looks, silky voice and vast fortune. God had tuned in to Bette's prayers.

For this was big! Bigger than Broadway, bigger than Hollywood, bigger even than the Miss America pageant.

What a bridegroom Tonio would make! What a son-in-law! You had to look to Princess Grace and the Duchess of Windsor for a parallel. If only Kim could land him!

'Be sweet,' Bette urged, 'and be beautiful. And remember to smile when you look in his eyes. And let him know that you're a decent girl. The type who holds out for marriage.'

Kim needed no prompting. For once, her own desires and her mother's coincided.

'I'm in love,' Kim gushed on the phone to Alix. 'I can't believe this is happening to me! It's like a fairy tale. Every night I keep waiting for the limo to turn into a pumpkin on the stroke of twelve. I'm blue from pinching myself that this is real. Tonio is – oh, Alix! – everything I ever dreamed of. Handsome, romantic, sophisticated. He plays polo, just like Prince Charles. He has his own string of ponies.' She giggled self-consciously. 'That's what it's called, a string – like they were pearls. He's a terrific all-round sportsman – big-game hunting, that sort of thing. And he collects antique armor.'

'Sounds about right,' Alix observed.

'Plus he breeds greyhounds. In fact, he reminds me of a greyhound himself, so elegant and aristocratic. My bet is that Tonio could've been a movie star if he wanted, except of course that he's in line to be the next Benefactor of San Miguel. That's their word for president, though the way he describes it, it sounds more like being king or emperor.'

'I think dictator is the proper term,' Alix said wryly, but Kim, lost in happiness, hardly heard.

'You've gotta meet him, Alix. We'll have dinner together. I told him you were Lucius Bryden's daughter.'

'Ex-daughter,' Alix said, though she understood Kim's need to impress her suitor by showing she had connections of her own. 'But I promise to be on good behavior. What about your fiancé? I thought you were engaged.'

There was a pause at the other end, and Alix wondered if Kim had forgotten the name.

'You mean Pierre? Oh, that's over. Mom gave him his walking papers. And I'm sorry about your pal Jeff, but that wasn't in the cards. This is, though. Because I'm really . . .' – she sighed – 'really really really in love.'

Though how anything so magical *could* also be real was beyond Kim's comprehension. Not even those romantic novels she adored could do justice to Tonio's courtship. Three weeks of being 'rushed' had intensified her awe. They danced and dined in splendor, and since they both loved to shop, spent many a delirious afternoon in Bergdorf's and Bulgari's, buying on impulse whatever struck Tonio's mood.

'We're like two kids in a toy shop,' Kim said, which made him laugh. They were together daily from noon till night.

He was bruisingly handsome, her Tonio, with smooth olive

skin, dark glittering eyes and black hair. The elegant bone structure was inherited from his mother, a former French fashion model. In other respects, he resembled his father, which is to say that he was dynamic, willful and given to quick changes of mood.

Tonio could be imperious when crossed. The second time they dined out, he tried to have a waiter fired for the crime of bringing luke-warm food. Kim made a note of his temper, then put it behind her, unable to imagine ever having any cause to contradict him. Tonio was so worldly, so masterful.

Of average height, he had, at thirty-three, the body of a runner, taut and muscular. He worked out every morning for two hours and scrupulously watched his diet. In New York, he stayed at the San Miguel Consulate, a limestone mansion in the East 70s, where he kept a private suite furnished in French Empire antiques. Technically, he was a member of the diplomatic corps.

'Appearances matter,' he told Kim.

His own was flawless, from the well-cut hair styled long in the continental fashion to the Italian suits to the tips of his alligator shoes. He worshipped physical beauty. It was what first attracted him to Kim.

'Not that beauty is enough, my angel,' he told her one luminous evening as they cruised the East River in a chartered yacht. 'For I have possessed many beautiful women, you may believe me. But I enjoyed them only briefly. I found them to be hard, grasping creatures. Brittle as glass. They lacked – how shall I say it? – innocence. Then I saw your photograph in the magazine. I was enchanted. Such sweetness in your face, such purity. I decided I must look into those violet eyes and see for myself if you were everything I read into that picture.'

'And . . . ?' Kim turned those violet eyes upon him, radiant with love. With Tonio, she had no need to fake emotion.

'And!' He kissed her softly on the lips. 'And more!'

He liked her best in white and delicate pastels, colors that

216

spoke of youth and virginity. He called her 'my angel,' 'my princess,' 'my pearl.'

'Look at us,' he murmured one night as they danced in a ballroom glittering with mirrors. With his dark smooth elegance and her pale-gold beauty, they were figures that might have stepped out of a fashion magazine or a fairy tale.

The trait that surprised Kim most was Tonio's respect for her mother. The two got along swimmingly, enjoying long intimate chats while Kim was changing for dinner.

'I like the fact that you and your mother are close,' he said one night at Lutèce. 'Respect for your elders, for properly constituted authority – that's so rare these days. Too many girls your age try to live like men. All this talk of being liberated, independent. Hardly better than whores.' The black eyes flashed. 'Feminists, they call themselves. The word makes me cringe. But what can be more feminine, I ask you, than sweetness and compliance? I sometimes think that I should look for my future wife in a convent, but convent-bred girls are so provincial. And none are so exquisite as you.'

Kim blushed and lowered her eyes. It was the first time he had mentioned marriage.

'What do you think, Mom?' She crawled into Bette's bed that night, a-tremble with hope. 'Is he going to propose?'

Bette was sure of it. But when the offer came, a few days later, there were stipulations.

Kim had been out shopping that morning and returned to find Tonio huddled with her mother in the living room. They both looked grave. Kim was shunted off to her room until further notice. She tried listening at the door but to no avail. The loudest sound was the pounding of her heart.

Some time later, Bette came in, aglow with excitement.

'Tonio left,' she announced. 'If all goes well, he'll be back tonight with an engagement ring. He's already discussed the situation with his father. Now here's where we stand.'

Freda Bright

Tonio demanded of his bride two assurances. First, that they be married in the Catholic faith.

'Oh, lord!' Kim groaned. 'That means I'll have to take instruction. It'll take forever.'

'No problem, sweetheart. We've always been Catholics.'

Kim stared at her.

'Not observant ones, I admit,' Bette continued. 'But I can assure you that you were baptized when you were three months old at the – well, I forget the name of the church, St Something or Other's, but it was in San Diego, California. The priest's name was O'Donnell, that I'm sure.'

'Really!' Kim was agape.

'Cross my heart. Religion's no problem. Now the second item—' Bette narrowed her eyes. 'All I can say, toots, is that I hope you've been as good a girl as you should have been. Everything is riding on it.'

An appointment had been made for that afternoon with the Consulate's official physician. If, upon examination, Kim proved to be a virgin and capable of child-bearing, Tonio would marry her in the Cathedral of Benedicta. The wedding would take place on the first of May, the anniversary of his father's accession to power. If Kim failed the physical, she was to keep Tonio's gifts with his compliments, but she would never see him again.

Kim mopped her brow, sweaty with relief. Those years of fidelity to an ideal had finally paid off. Yet she also felt dismayed. What kind of love was this, she wondered, that came with conditions? Love that could be granted or withdrawn at will? On her part, she would have married Tonio this very minute no matter what he'd done. Even if he had slept with a thousand women. The past was the past.

That evening Tonio returned, bearing an eighteen-carat marquise-cut diamond ring that had once been the property of the Empress Eugénie. Kneeling before her, he slid it on her finger and, in that moment, Kim's doubts were resolved.

As they kissed and cuddled and exchanged sweet nothings, Bette was busy writing up the press release.

'Of course,' Kim rationalized to Alix, who was outraged by the doctor story, 'it's not as if he were free to choose for himself. After all he is heir to—'

'The throne?' Alix snorted. 'We're talking serious male chauvinist here. However, you love him and that's what counts.'

'When you meet him—' Kim sounded wary. 'Well, I hope you'll like him. It would mean a lot to me. I know what you're thinking, about his dad and all that. I remember that study group you had on the political situation in San Miguel. It got pretty heated, I recall. But I'm not marrying the country. I'm marrying the man. And I want you to be my maid of honor. So — tonight for dinner! And I know you'll look lovely.'

Alix laughed at the cautionary note.

'Does that mean best jeans? Don't worry, Kim. I won't disgrace you.'

As Alix had expected and Kim had feared, the dinner was a disaster. She disliked him instantly. From the start, the air crackled with antagonism.

Tonio opened the conversation with the remark that the San Miguel Defense Ministry did a great deal of business with her father's firm. He admired Lucius Bryden enormously and looked forward to meeting him one day soon.

Alix smiled coolly. 'I'm afraid I can't help you there. My father and I haven't spoken in years.'

'May I ask why not?'

'Because my father is a fascist and a tyrant.'

Tonio's eyes flashed with anger.

Alarmed, Kim steered the talk into neutral channels and the evening was gotten through with a show of surface politeness. Yet underneath was a deeper level full of hidden barbs and jabs and loaded silences. Alix took her leave as soon as was decently possible.

'That scruffy left-wing lawyer!' Tonio exploded as soon as she had gone. 'I don't want her at our wedding! I don't want her in your life.'

'But, darling!' Kim's eyes brimmed. 'I've already invited her.'

'Then you can un-invite her and make your farewells. That's final. You'll do it first thing tomorrow!'

When Kim called the next morning at an ungodly hour, Alix smelled trouble. She sent Samantha and Mr Rabinowitz to the park. Now, from her front window, she watched as the driver maneuvered the Mercedes into a parking space sufficient for three normal cars. The long black limo reminded her of Lucius.

It was a grim but determined Kim who knocked on her door a moment later. Her eyes were puffy.

'Who died?' Alix asked as she let Kim in.

'Why, what do you mean?'

'Well, you came in a hearse.'

'That's not funny, Alix. Not funny at all.'

Then Kim flung herself on to the sofa and burst into tears. She had had a wretched night, her conscience ached. 'I'm such a coward, Alix,' she said between sobs. 'I don't know how to tell you this but . . .'

Fists clenched, she blurted out Tonio's message.

'I feel sick about it. After all, you're my oldest and dearest friend. Damn! You're my *only* friend, except for Mom. I pleaded and pleaded, but Tonio won't budge. He can be very stubborn sometimes! And you know me – I hate confrontations. Besides, what could I do? I gave in and here I am. But you've been crazy in love, Alix. You understand how I feel.'

'No problem,' Alix soothed. 'Believe me, I know the things we do for our Mr Wonderfuls. And I'm not surprised. Tonio and I didn't exactly hit it off, and after all, it's his wedding too. I don't want to cast a shadow on your happiness.'

'I was up all last night, thinking how to tell you.'

'I was up all night too,' Alix said. 'Thinking about you, your future. Listen, Kim, for this is important.'

She took Kim's manicured hand and covered it with her own.

'You've been granted a great opportunity,' she began. 'Not only to be happy, which I hope you will be, but more than that. You have the chance to play a role in history. You're marrying a man of awesome power, and I know that's intimidating. But remember, you have power too. You have the power that comes of being loved. Just as Tonio influences your actions, you can influence him in turn. You can steer him toward the better, the kinder action. He has a monster of a father. Well, so have I, for that matter. But it doesn't follow that we children are clones. We're free to choose. And Tonio chose you, which is certainly an excellent sign. One of these days, Kim, you will become the First Lady of San Miguel—'

Kim mustered a smile. 'The Benefactress, it's called.'

Alix nodded. 'The Benefactress. I like that. And I hope you'll *be* one, Kim. A doer of good. A woman of strength and compassion and heart. As Tonio's wife, you're in a position to set a moral standard. To make a difference in the lives of thousands of people. The other day you said that you weren't marrying a country, you were marrying a man. But you can't separate the two, really. And I don't think you should try.'

'Oh, Alix,' Kim choked up. 'If only you could be there to give me courage!'

In the street, the chauffeur honked the horn. Kim started at the sound.

'I have to go. I'm late for a fitting. My wedding gown. It weighs a ton. Tonio's family is paying for everything, thank God.' Impulsively she flung her arms around Alix and held her close. 'I wish . . . I wish . . .'

'. . . that I could come to the wedding? I'll be there in my thoughts. I wish you joy, Kim. Great happiness.'

Kim pulled out a silver compact and dabbed at her eyes.

'I mustn't cry any more. I don't want to look like a wreck for Tonio. Goodbyes are so miserable, I don't think I can bring myself to . . . say it.' She swallowed hard. 'So I won't say it. I'll just pray we'll meet again in this life.'

Then she turned and ran out the door.

Crazy in love, Alix thought. You had to be crazy if you were in love. And if you weren't crazy already, love made you so. What else but love fucked up life so completely?

Well, Alix too had once been crazy in love, for all the good it had done her.

True, she had gone on with her life, borne a child, built a career, had affairs. Too many perhaps, some better than others, but none had touched her heart. Sex was not her hang-up. Love was. Impossible indefinable love. The most treacherous four-letter word in the language.

Alix had loved, it turned out, neither wisely nor well. But had she been loved in return? For she had never forgotten her father's charge that Sam Matthews had pursued her only because of the Bryden name. If Lucius was right, then the great love of Alix's life was a swindle.

She refused to believe it. The notion was too humiliating. After all these years, she missed him still. Despite her contempt for Tonio DuMesne, Alix envied Kim her happiness.

To be in love again! To be swept away in a tide of passion! Did life hold any greater bliss?

Alix sighed, changed her shoes and went into the office.

HEATHROW

Peter had got up at dawn to drive to the airport though Anne's flight wasn't due in until eight fifteen. Still, no telling what the traffic might be like at that time of day. Rush hour going into London. Probably almost as crowded going out. To be on the safe side, he'd allow an extra ninety minutes.

He shaved. Dressed. Left the house by six fifteen. It was a fine April morning.

'Now I don't want you dragging out to Heathrow to meet me,' Anne had said on the phone, and he promised he wouldn't. Which meant his presence would come as a total surprise.

Serve the woman right. She was always pulling surprises herself. Like the time he came home from work to find she'd booked them into a hotel for the weekend. A hotel in Marrakesh. Or when she slipped a pair of silk knickers into his briefcase. Which naturally fell out in the middle of a staff meeting.

Sweet irrepressible Annie. Hard to believe she had only been gone a couple of weeks. 'Every hour is a lifetime,' he'd told her. It was not quite hyperbole.

By her own report, Anne had been having a glorious time in New York, feted by publishers, shopping, catching Broadway shows. But she missed him too, and sounded eager to get home.

'I'm bringing you the most marvelous present,' she said. 'Something supremely goofy and very very New York.'

'A baseball bat? Radio City? A Central Park mugger?'

'No good guessing. You'll have to wait and see.'

She made smacking noises on the other end of the line. He kissed the mouthpiece back.

'I love you, Annie.'

'I love you too. See you tomorrow.'

Then tomorrow became today.

Traffic was light on the M4 and he arrived at Heathrow well before seven. So early, her flight hadn't been posted. He looked around for a shop to buy flowers, but nothing was open. He picked up the *Guardian*, got coffee and a roll, then settled down at a bright red table within view of the bulletin board.

At least another hour to kill. He felt foolish being so eager. Like a schoolboy really. Every few minutes he checked the board to see if Trans-Atlantic Flight 106 from New York would be arriving on time.

JFK

'It doesn't bother you flying?' the driver said. He was a husky young Israeli sent by the livery service. He had driven her to Kennedy before. His name was Zev.

'Not at all,' Miranda said. 'I enjoy flying. New faces, new places, like the travel agent says.'

'Where you off to this time?'

'Nairobi.'

'Well, be careful. All these hi-jackings – Cubans, crazy Arabs. Ay ay ay.' Zev scowled. 'And that business last month.'

But Miranda wasn't listening. Her attention was riveted by a publication lying atop the dashboard.

'Your *Celebrity* magazine,' she said. 'May I see it?'

He handed it back. 'Enjoy. I'm done with it.'

Miranda grabbed it, then sucked in her breath. Incredible!

There on the cover, resplendent in bridal white, was that girl from Marival. The very one who had pulled her out of the lake ten years ago. Kimberly West.

She had grown up, of course. Not a child any longer, but a lovely woman, tall and graceful. The photo showed her dancing in the arms of a darkly handsome man, also in white. A uniform, perhaps, for his chest gleamed with medals.

SAN MIGUEL'S PRINCE AND PRINCESS CHARM-

ING was bannered across the top, while a cover-line promised: *Inside! Wedding of the Year! A Suzi Exclusive!*

Her one-time rescuer had done well for herself, Miranda thought. She waited until she was settled in the first class lounge to read the article in full.

The story, a mix of gee-whiz reportage and tongue-in-cheek prose, featured an interview with the bride, in which the former beauty queen declared that her hobbies were patchwork and reading to the blind, that her greatest wish was for world peace, and that marriage into the DuMesne family was 'a thrill and an honor and a privilege.'

The article was lavishly illustrated, with photos of the wedding party, fireworks displays, cheering crowds, celebrities by the gross. The text was packed with figures, a kind of outrageous *Can You Top This?*

As the newlyweds made their way out of the cathedral, three helicopters bombarded the cortège with 100,000 pink and white rose petals to match the bridesmaids' gowns. An estimated one million people lined the streets.

The reception took place in the grounds of the presidential mansion, where forty tents had been erected of pink-and-white silk shot with gold. The twenty-course banquet had been flown in from La Tour d'Argent in Paris aboard two jumbo jets. A separate plane was required for the two hundred cases of fine wines and vintage Remy Krug champagne. Another had delivered a hundred kilos of Beluga caviar, a gift from the Shah of Iran.

The guest list was as imposing as the menu: heads of state, movie stars, sportsmen, international glitterati, Euro-trash. Among the nine hundred invited guests: Liz Taylor, Henry Kissinger, Pele, Imelda Marcos, the Maharajah of Hyderabad, Mick Jagger. The American ambassador had given the bride away. Luciano Pavarotti sang 'Ave Maria.'

The wedding gown, designed by Oscar de La Renta, was made of antique lace from a convent in Bruges renowned for its needlework. Six thousand seed pearls were sewn into the bodice.

Eighty meters of Milanese silk satin had gone into the train which weighed over fifty pounds and required four pages to carry it. The bride's tiara, composed of eighty-seven white diamonds and four pigeon's blood rubies, had belonged to the Empress Josephine, with whom the groom's family claimed a kinship.

And still the assessment went on.

One thousand white doves . . . thirteen orchestras . . . two bishops and a cardinal . . . two tons of confetti . . . $300,000 worth of Grucci fireworks . . . six people trampled underfoot . . . Rolex watches for the ushers . . .

To complete the numeric roundup, the newlyweds had set off on a three-month honeymoon: fourteen countries . . . eighty pieces of Vuitton luggage . . . a personal entourage consisting of —

Miranda's flight was called. She put down the magazine with a shrug. Such excess! More like a Hollywood spectacular than a proper wedding. *Cast of thousands, cost of millions,* as the ads used to say. In Technicolor and Cinemascope.

Which was amusing to read about, but a ridiculous outlay for one of the poorest, most backward nations in the hemisphere.

Yet as Miranda boarded the plane, she supposed she was glad for Kimberly West. The girl had made a brilliant marriage, and looked radiant in the photos.

She wondered if the new Madame DuMesne ever thought back to that night at Lac Leman. Or had she, like Miranda, done her best to put it behind her?

Miranda thought of the debt owed Kimberly West, nothing less than her life. She considered sending an anonymous wedding present, costly and beautiful, then decided against it. Judging by the article, it was unlikely Miranda could ever grant the new bride anything she didn't already have — in triplicate! Best to let sleeping ghosts lie.

Her flight was a red-eye special. Miranda pushed her seat back and shut her eyes.

226

Although she had left the magazine behind, it refused to stay put. The pictures kept dancing before her closed eyelids. Especially the cover photo of the bride and groom.

Perhaps it was the memory of Marival, perhaps it was the caption – 'Prince and Princess Charming.' The phrase set her teeth on edge, though she couldn't think why.

A feeling left over from childhood, most likely. Maybe from a book of fairy tales. Yet as far as she could recall, Miranda had never believed in that Prince Charming nonsense. Nor in ogres either. She had been a most pragmatic girl.

A little before dawn Miranda dozed off. In sleep, dream mingled with memory.

Seamlessly, the hum of the plane had become transmuted into the rhythm of a jukebox.

There was music playing. Billie Holiday. She was in a dark room. A bar. A small smoky bar. She couldn't make out faces. Only moods. And words. And the acrid smell of Gauloises.

She was sitting at a table, drinking red wine out of a tumbler. Smiling to herself.

Imagine, she said. Imagine finding Billie Holiday records in a small café in France. And the tune. 'Travelin' Light.' One of her favorites.

She sang along with the jukebox, feeling sexy and free. A little drunk, maybe, but happy. There was a cat on the bar. A huge gray tabby. He looked contented too.

'You have a lovely voice,' said the man. He was sitting at the next table. He spoke English. She was pleased.

Pleased too, when they danced, the way he crushed up against her. He had taken off his jacket, put it on a chair. As they danced, the room grew hot. Their sweat mingled.

'What's your name?' he asked.

'You tell me yours first.'

He smiled. White even teeth. 'Prince Charming.'

She laughed. Very happy. It was good to be here tonight. In France. She adored France. Dancing with a beautiful man.

'And mine is Little Red Riding Hood.'

They talked. He had a place nearby. A house? No. A room. A huge room in a luxury hotel. Would she come with him?

'I'm very good in bed,' he said.

Pourquoi pas? she thought. Why not? He pressed against her. She felt her body respond.

'My Ferrari is outside.'

'What will I do with my bike?'

'Leave it. I'll buy you another. Shall we go?'

Then – the dream grew murky. She could still hear the music of the jukebox, but it had turned sour. Jangly. Something had happened to spoil the mood. What?

The cat! Yes. The big fat tabby. It had settled on his coat to take a snooze.

'Goddamn fucking beast!' The man picked it up by the tail and hurled it across the room. The cat screeched in pain.

Bastard! she thought. You bastard!

What kind of man would do a thing like that?

He brushed the cat hairs off his coat with a meticulous gesture. 'Are you ready to go now?' he asked.

She wasn't feeling romantic any more. By God, no.

'Fuck you,' she said. 'I wouldn't sleep with you if you were the last man on earth.'

She stalked out and climbed on her bike. Pedaled away fast as she could. Down a gravel road lined with poplars.

The night was dark. Cycling was hard. She had lost all sense of direction. She stopped at a crossroad to make out the signs. She felt frightened. It was so dark. Dark but no longer silent. Behind her, the roar of a motor, the crunch of wheels on gravel, the screech of gears.

She whipped around, blinded by the headlights, too astonished to cry out.

*

228

'Are you all right, ma'am?' The steward was shaking her.

'Yes . . . fine.' Miranda blinked herself awake.

'You were having a bad dream.'

He leaned over and pulled up the shade. Day had dawned over the new continent.

'We'll be landing in twenty-five minutes.'

Miranda freshened up and had coffee. She felt better, though still shaken. And as breathless as if she'd run a four-minute mile. She could feel her heart thump.

Run fast as you can, she thought, go as far as you will. You can never outrun your shadows.

FOURTEENTH STREET

On April 19th, at precisely 5 a.m. Greenwich Mean Time (midnight in New York) Trans-Atlantic Flight 106 from JFK to Heathrow exploded off the Irish coast, killing all aboard – the second worst tragedy in aviation history. The weather had been fine. There was no indication of mechanical failure.

Like most people, Alix Bryden's first thought was – *terrorists*.

Her second thought was – *Sam Matthews*.

Her third – *I'm being ridiculous*.

The bomb, if it was a bomb, could have been planted by any terrorist group: the PLO, Irish Provos, the Baader-Meinhof gang, Iranian fundamentalists. So why jump to conclusions?

Sam Matthews indeed! Alix reprimanded herself. By now, he had to be either dead or in jail or totally tamed. The last most likely. The once dashing young firebrand was now pushing forty – too old to sustain white heat.

Alix tried to picture him in middle age. Thinning hair and a pot belly. Living quietly in Sweden, like as not, with a wife and kids (she suppressed a twinge of jealousy), smoking a pipe and tuning pianos for a living. Hardly a picture consistent with the blowing up of jumbo jets. The fact that Alix had even suspected Sam of such an act seemed to say more about her than about him.

She went to bed depressed that night. Seven years down the road, and the man was still under her skin.

Damn you, Sam Matthews! she muttered into the pillow. *When are you going to get out of my life?*

Not until August did the authorities make an arrest and when they did it was a stunner. The 'terrorist' turned out to be a teenager from Riverdale, a high-school student with no criminal record.

Alix breathed a sigh of relief (*See? It wasn't Sam at all, nitwit!*), then gobbled up the details.

The term 'nerd' might have been invented with Rodney James Gilchrist in mind.

The son of a prosperous cardiologist, he looked both older and younger than his seventeen years, with a pale round face and plump hands. Shy, awkward, with a 170 IQ packed away behind thick bifocals, Rodney was a loner, living only for chess.

He played every chance he got and dreamt of becoming the next Bobby Fischer, dazzling the chess world in such places as Reykjavik and Moscow. Meanwhile, he was flunking out of school.

Then Dr Gilchrist cracked down. No more chess, he ordained, until the boy shaped up academically. Soon after, Rodney solved his problems, both personal and financial, by packing a home-made bomb in his father's suitcase when Dr Gilchrist and his wife left on a trip to London.

That others should die was part of the plan. He assumed the explosion would be blamed on terrorists, while he himself inherited a comfortable sum and could resume his chess career.

Such might have been the case had not the Gilchrist house-keeper peeked into his diary and run to the FBI. When questioned, Rodney made a full confession.

'They were always nagging,' he said by way of explanation.

For weeks the story dominated the media. Not since Charles Manson had a miscreant so aroused public wrath. On the day of his arraignment, thousands gathered in Foley Square, screaming for blood. For if ever a crime called out for a return to capital punishment, it was Rodney Gilchrist's.

Alix hadn't gone looking for the Gilchrist case, she insisted. It had come looking for her.

'You could have said no, ' Jeff Aaronoff argued.

He had ambled into her office 'to ask a favor,' he said, but instead started schmoozing about the forthcoming trial.

'I couldn't.' Alix shook her head. 'No one else would take him on.'

'Alix Bryden, the St Jude of Fourteenth Street.'

'The patron saint of lost causes?' Alix laughed. 'Is that a step down or up from Robin Hood? As it happens, I believe the case is winnable. After all, he's just a kid.'

'Give me a break!'

'OK, he's a crazy kid, but he belongs in an asylum, not jail. I'm not minimizing the tragedy, Jeff, but turning Rodney over to a media lynch mob won't bring back the dead. The boy is demonstrably wacko. And since it's a federal case, the prosecution has the burden of proving him sane. Mind you,' she said with relish, 'they have one hell of an argument. The bomb took planning. Plus Rodney's attempt to shift guilt on to innocent terrorists, if that isn't an oxymoron, is tough to explain as a momentary aberration. I was hoping to cut a deal, but the US Attorney wants a trial. The case is too high-profile to bury.'

'You're actually licking your chops,' Jeff observed.

'Well, it's a terrific chance for me to make waves. And the beauty part is – I'll be taking on Bill Cairns.' Alix grinned at the prospect. 'In case you didn't know, he's the fair-haired boy of Number One Saint Andrews Plaza, with a ninety-six per cent conviction rate. Very smart and sassy. We went head to head once before and he clobbered me, so I'm due for a rematch. Now the way I see it, my strategy will be . . .'

She rattled on a few minutes more before she realized that Jeff was studying his knuckles. Poor bastard, she thought, still mooning over Kim's marriage. Alix had just the cure. It was her belief – what better example than her own life? – that the best remedy for a broken heart was hard work and long hours. That said, nothing could beat a nice juicy murder case.

'Help me out on this one, Jeff. We could make music together. I'm trying to get the confession suppressed on the basis that Rodney was too young to realize his rights. No parent there to guide him, so to speak. Once the confession is out, I can contest the legal grounds for the search, maybe get the physical evidence excluded as fruit of the poisoned tree. It's a long shot, but intriguing. What do you think, Jeff?'

'I think that it's a defense only a lawyer could love.'

'Well, we're all lawyers here, though I doubt Judge Braverman will buy it.' She snorted. 'Not unless he wants his own sanity questioned. Still, it's worth a try. How about it?'

'How about what?'

'How about coming in on it with me?'

Jeff drew a finger across his throat.

'I guess that means no,' Alix said. 'At least I tried. Anyhow, you said you had a favor to ask.'

'Can you lend me a few bucks till tomorrow?'

Alix dug out her wallet. 'Help yourself.'

He counted out fifty dollars, then handed it back.

'Aren't you curious why I'm short?' he asked.

'We don't have to give each other reasons.'

'I'll tell you why, anyhow. A dainty vignette of New York. I'm leaving rent court this morning, where I'd been doing what, in my youthful folly, I used to call fighting the good fight, when

I discovered my billfold was gone. I think my client took it – the little fucker. Jesus, nothing like getting ripped off by the people you bust your butt defending.'

Alix sighed. 'Yeah, it sucks, but these things happen.'

'Sucks!' Jeff winced. 'That is such a disgusting term! Does it ever strike you, Alix, that we're starting to resemble the bums we represent? The day may be coming when we can't distinguish them from us. Look at this!'

With thumb and forefinger, he picked up a slice of cold pizza from her desk as though it were a dead rat. 'Revolting!' He plopped it into the wastebasket.

'Hey!' Alix protested. 'That was my lunch!' But Jeff was unrepentant. The corners of his mouth were turned down, his nostrils quivered in disdain.

'Garbage!' he said. 'We eat garbage. We talk garbage. We listen to garbage. We dress like garbage.'

'Maybe you should have got yourself a three-piece suit and gone into corporate law,' Alix said.

'Maybe I should have.' He leaned back and peered at her, as though seeing her for the first time. 'You amaze me, Alix. The way you manage to combine those lofty Ivy-League ideals with gutter tactics. The garbage factor never fazes you. Well, it does me. I guess I'm hopelessly bourgeois.'

'So am I,' Alix said, eyebrows arched.

'Un-unh!' Jeff shook his head. 'You grew up rich. To you anything that is *not* rich is wildly romantic. You don't feel threatened by this life the way I do. I hate my clients for being poor and scruffy and foul-mouthed and ignorant. I even hate 'em for reeking of garlic. Somewhere along the line, I ran out of compassion. Today was the last straw. You know what I treasured about Kim West? She was a joy to look at. Now isn't that a profoundly shallow thing to say? You seem surprised.'

'I am!' Disappointed too, she might have added, there being more to Kim than tidy hair. But Jeff went on without apologies.

'It was the contrast with my clients, I suppose. She was

always immaculate, beautifully turned out. Like a good deed in a dirty world. As simple as that. Oh, well . . .'

He got up. 'Thanks for the fifty. And good luck with Gilchrist. If anyone can get that nut-boy off, it's you.'

A few days later, Jeff announced that he was moving to Binghamton to work for his father in the catering business.

'It's a pleasant town. A nine-to-five job. And maybe I'll find a girl to really care for me. Third time lucky, they say. Sorry to leave you in the lurch, Alix – about the lease, I mean. You want me to find you another tenant?'

'No problem, Jeff. I'll take the space myself, though I hate to see you go. First Eddie Martinez leaving, now you. The old gang breaking up.' She choked down a lump in her throat. Jeff had been a major part of her life. 'You know, I always hoped some day you and I would make it—'

'Our toothbrushes sharing a tumbler?' he mocked.

'Something like that. I guess I blew my chances. What'll I do without you? I need your company, Jeff. Your friendship.'

'You never need anyone,' he said with a tight smile. 'It's your strength and your weakness.'

After his departure, Alix hired two young lawyers, plus a clerk-typist and a paralegal. Then she called in a sign-painter to change the lettering on the door.

Aaronoff, Martinez and Bryden had become Alix Bryden & Associates.

If she couldn't like Rodney Gilchrist, she ought at least to understand him. Climb inside his skull and view the world through his eyes. Yet despite her best efforts, he baffled her.

The boy had about as much life in him as a two-hundred-pound rutabaga and gave her nothing to go on. Sometimes, when pressed, he would shut his eyes and feign sleep. Alix followed the movement of his eyeballs under the lids and suspected he was playing chess in his head.

'Wake up, Rodney.' She poked him in the ribs as the trial date drew near. 'This is important.'

Rodney opened his eyes.

'Tell me,' Alix asked for the twentieth time. 'What were your feelings at the time?'

'About what?' He didn't seem to grasp the question.

Jesus! Like the dormouse in *Alice in Wonderland*.

'About your *parents*, Rodney. Mom and Dad. Did you love them? Hate them? Do you miss them? Give me something I can understand. Concentrate!'

Rodney grappled with the problem. Words were not his forte.

'You play chess?' he asked.

'I used to.'

'Well, my father was the king, my mother was the queen.'

'And you were a pawn?'

The dull eyes gleamed fitfully. 'But a pawn can become a queen. Potentially, it's the most powerful piece on the board.'

'Exactly so,' Alix said. She was beginning to understand.

He asked if she could get him a new chess board next time she came. Also a Big Mac with fries.

Alix walked back to her office, whistling. She had found her strategy. It was novel, granted, but one never knew. Given a battery of expert witnesses, a decent jury and a rousing performance on her part, she just might pull it off.

And wouldn't that frost Bill Cairns.

Alix was at her desk one afternoon, when Teri buzzed to say a Mr Mainwaring was in reception. It took a moment for the name to register, then Alix flew into the waiting room.

'For heaven's sakes!' She seized his hands. 'It is you, isn't it! What a pleasure after all these years!'

In fact, his appearance shocked her. The high color and English freshness had vanished. His face was haggard. His clothes looked as though they had been slept in. Hard to believe that he had once been a figure of authority.

'And what brings you to New York? Checking up on old patients? I know this place doesn't look like much but . . .'

As she led him into her office, she wondered how he had found her and why.

'Would you like some coffee, Doctor? Teri!' Alix buzzed the intercom. 'Make us some espresso, sweetie, and hold my calls. Well, well, Dr Main—'

'I don't practice any more. Please call me Peter.' He sounded woefully ill-at-ease.

In trouble with the law, she supposed, which made for an odd sensation – her former shrink coming to her for advice.

Looking lawyerly, she folded her hands and waited.

Peter sat erect, apparently calm, though his foot beat a tattoo on the linoleum.

'I understand you're acting on behalf of the man who killed my wife,' he said after a pause. 'Can you tell me why?'

Alix's heart wheeled to a stop.

'What are you talking about?'

'My wife,' Peter clarified. 'Anne Golovin. She was on TA Flight 106. We were expecting a child in September.'

'Oh, God!' Alix's fingers fluttered helplessly. 'I didn't realize.'

She squeezed her eyes shut, trying to remember.

Rodney Gilchrist was charged with 271 counts of murder. Naturally, Alix had seen the list of victims but she had never studied it in detail, preferring not to know who these people were or imagine how they had suffered.

What could she say now to Peter? That she was sorry? What could she *do* – except pray that the floor might open and swallow her up?

In all her pre-trial planning, she had never imagined such a confrontation. How Peter must hate her!

Just then, Teri arrived with coffee. Grateful for the diversion, Alix busied herself setting cups out, fussing with the sugar.

'Would you like something stronger?' she asked. 'I know I would. I've got some brandy here somewhere.'

She retrieved a bottle from the filing cabinet, spiked both coffees, then gulped hers down in a single swallow.

'Do you want to talk about it?' she asked, feeling like an idiot. *Why else was he here?*

'First, you have to understand,' Peter began.

In a restrained yet eloquent voice, he told of leaving Marival, starting a new career, meeting Anne, falling in love. Marrying. As he spoke, he twisted his wedding band round and round on his finger. Alix couldn't keep her eyes off it.

'We had great joy in each other,' Peter told her. Now that joy was shattered forever amidst the wreckage of Trans-A 106. 'We talked on the phone the day before she died. She was bringing me something from New York.' He choked up. 'A surprise. Annie was full of surprises. Now I'll never know what it was. Perhaps it sounds trivial, but it's yet another unfinished story. Like our marriage. Like Annie's life.'

It horrified him to learn that Rodney Gilchrist's champion should be one of his old patients. This was a hurt that went deep. He remembered Alix fondly from Marival. She had been so full of hopes and dreams. He was glad she had met with success.

The smartest woman in the criminal bar, the papers said. If any lawyer could get this monster off, they implied, it was she. To Peter, this was the final twist of the knife.

'What exactly do you want me to do?' Alix asked.

'Drop the case.'

Alix was stunned. After months of arduous preparation, she couldn't possibly back out. Nor did she want to. How could he ask her to make such a sacrifice? Yet as she framed her answer, her conscience twitched. She felt for Peter in his grief. 'I've often thought about you,' she began cautiously. 'You helped me at a critical juncture in my life. I've thought about you and Marival and Dr Frankl. And the woman who used to sit by the lake.

Lady X, Kim and I called her. Do you remember that night at the lake? But of course you do. I think it was a seminal moment in all our lives.'

She leaned across the desk toward him, hoping to draw him into her logic.

'After it was over, Kim told me what Lady X's face had looked like. How she had begged Kim to let her die. But she didn't die, did she?'

Peter was staring at her.

'No,' he said slowly. 'In fact, she made a remarkable recovery. Though how could you be so sure?'

Alix felt a flicker of triumph.

'Because I knew you would save her, Peter. I knew you'd keep her alive with your skills, your dedication. I can still picture you kneeling beside her, offering hope and comfort. That scene is engraved in my memory. You did what you were bound to do, as a psychiatrist —'

'As a human being too, I hope.'

'Well, of course,' Alix echoed. 'That too. Now put yourself in my shoes. In this . . . this unfortunate case, I too am doing what I'm bound to do. As a lawyer — and a human being. It's not for me to sit in judgment. You of all people ought to understand. You've dealt with the aberrant, the mentally ill, the Rodney Gilchrists of this world. In our professions, Peter, there are no pariahs. Only clients needing help.'

'*Your* profession. I no longer practice.'

'But you still have the knowledge,' she stressed. 'The art.' She went on to speak of principles, of ethics and codes of conduct, but Peter cut through the verbiage.

'In other words, you're committed to Gilchrist's defense.'

'I am.'

'And will do all you can to get him acquitted.'

Alix fidgeted. She hated being cross-examined. Out of reflex, she checked the phones on her desk. Every button was lit up. Peter followed her glance. She flushed and looked away.

'I'm sorry. And I'm particularly sorry that we should meet again under such circumstances. It's a bitter irony. What Kim would call destiny, I suppose. But that doesn't alter the situation. I have a duty that transcends my personal feelings.'

She had meant to be sincere but had wound up sounding sanctimonious. There being nothing to add, she offered her hand. 'May I hope that we might yet be friends?'

'You're amazing,' Peter drawled. 'I could never do what you're doing. I couldn't keep the emotional distance. You're full of principles. I say that with awe and respect. But my wife, you see, was not an abstract principle. She was a woman I loved very much.' He got up, ignoring her outstretched hand. 'I can see you're busy, Alix. Thank you for your time.'

By the time his words registered, Peter had left.

Alix was devastated. She was *amazing*? An object of *awe*? What were those words except euphemisms for coldness and lack of humanity? His farewell contained no trace of affection. Yet Peter had been fond of her once.

Suddenly, it was intolerable that he should carry away a picture of her as some kind of automaton. She was human too, goddamnit! Tender. Vulnerable. Could no one see past the façade? The 'tough guy' exterior?

Not even Peter?

Carve your mask, Marcus Aurelius had written. Perhaps she had carved hers too well.

Alix grabbed her coat and tore out of the office after him. 'Wait!' she hollered, running down Fourteenth Street dodging pedestrians and pushcarts. 'Wait for me!'

She caught up with him two blocks away.

'You can't' – she gasped – 'you can't just pop into my life and vanish as suddenly. You think I'm some kind of Ice Queen, all head and no heart. But it's not true. I'm woefully fallible. Please, Peter. I know a nice quiet bar where we can talk. There's so much I have to tell you. I mean – we both have loved and lost.'

They spent the rest of the afternoon at a cocktail lounge in

University Place, downing malt whiskey and nibbling Cheezits. The booze that dulled Peter's pain loosened Alix's tongue.

She found herself blurting out ancient secrets. Her affair with Sam, the bombing on Route 128, the break with her father, her role in Sam's escape. It was like being back in Marival: she was the patient, he the shrink.

'I can't believe I'm telling you all this,' she wept at one point. 'I'm at your mercy. You could have me disbarred. Except you wouldn't. You're too much of a *mensch*.'

'I think we need another drink,' was Peter's comment.

'I think so too. I hardly ever drink, you know. And I never get drunk. I lead such a sober responsible life you wouldn't believe.' Her voice quavered. 'But I'm lonely. There. I've said it. Would you believe it, Peter? I live surrounded by people but I get lonely.'

She sniffled into a cocktail napkin. Such a relief, getting all this misery off her chest.

'I know Sam was probably a shit, Peter, and I'm ready to move on. I want to fall in love – honest! Get married, wake up with the same warm body in bed with me every morning. I want more kids, all that jazz, like normal people. But I never meet a guy I can care for. I have had – would you believe? – seventeen lovers since then, and I haven't come within yards of falling in love. What is it with me, that I can't commit? It's because of Sam, isn't it?'

Peter, in his wisdom, ordered another round.

'What do you want from me, Alix? Absolution?'

'Explanations. Why why why?'

'Again, I'm not a shrink any more. What can I tell you?'

'Then tell me as – fellow human being.'

'As an observer,' he said, hoisting his drink. He had an astonishing capacity for alcohol. 'As a trained observer.'

It was the legacy of her twisted childhood, he told her. It had imbued her with a sense of worthlessness. First, rejection by her father, later abandonment by Sam. Twice victimized by cruel and domineering men, she had grown wary.

Before she could truly love, she must learn how to trust. And the only way one learned to trust was by trusting, he said.

'But first, you'll have to dispose of that unfinished business with your father. They sound disturbingly similar, by the way,' he remarked. 'Your father and Sam.'

'How can you say that?' Alix shot back with drunken indignation. 'They despised each other.'

Peter managed an expression halfway between a grin and a grimace. 'Very well. Have it your way. Another whiskey?'

'Oh, God! It's half past six. And I didn't even call. Sober responsible me! I have to go home and give Samantha dinner.' Alix wobbled to her feet. Her head was starting to pound. 'We will see each other again, Peter, won't we?'

'Absolutely,' he said softly.

She beamed. They were friends, her drunken logic told her. Confidants. All difficulties smoothed over.

But Peter's face was sad.

'Yes indeed, Alix. I'll be in court every day for as long as it takes. I'll be there when they bring in the guilty verdict. I'll be on hand when your monster is sentenced. I won't rest until justice is done.'

AU PARADIS

Well before the young couple were to return from their honeymoon, the goodies began to arrive. Scarcely a day went by without a delivery: cartons, packing cases, entire container cars stuffed with the treasures plucked from their travels.

There were designer clothes from Paris and Milan, English antiques, Bohemian glassware, trunks bulging with upholstery fabrics, a Hamburg Model D Steinway, a gold-lipped Rosenthal dinner service, a red Lamborghini Miura SV with leopard-skin upholstery, a wrought-iron Tunisian bird cage stocked with rare specimens, seventeenth-century Mogul paintings, Benin masks, Ashanti gold weights, Javanese shadow puppets. From the workshops of Asia and Africa came enough sculpture, pottery, candelabra, ethnic jewelry to open up a shop on Fifth Avenue.

The shipments were addressed to: *Chez Paradis, ATTENTION Mme Bette West*. It was the ultimate shopping spree.

Bette had hoped to make the trip with them. Why not? she implored. Since the entourage already included a valet, maid, secretary and driver, one more body hardly mattered. But on that score Tonio, though charming, was adamant.

'Take a mother-in-law along on one's honeymoon? No, *ma chère*.' He pecked her cheek. 'It's simply not done, except in French farce.'

He thanked Bette for having reared Kim so splendidly, then went on to praise her organizational gifts. He had important work for her right here in San Miguel.

As a wedding present, El Tigre had made over to Tonio a spacious villa in the grounds. An airy white-washed confection, Le Paradis had been built in the 1880s to house the then prime minister's English mistress. It stood in its own shady park, exquisitely private yet only a few minutes' drive from Le Castel, where El Tigre resided.

That the villa had been designed for amorous pursuits could be surmised at a glance. From the carved cupids above the doorways to the mirrored ceilings in the bedrooms to the wrought-iron jalousies with their theme of interwoven hearts and phallic arrows, Le Paradis was a temple of love.

Kim adored it as it was, but Tonio had other plans. 'Victorian kitsch,' he teased. 'Although I may keep the mirrored ceilings.'

Not that Tonio had anything against sybaritic splendor; he

merely wished to combine it with modern technology and taste. Nothing less than a total overhaul would suffice: central air-conditioning, a solarium, a gym, jacuzzis, a media room, a cinema, a soda fountain for his bride. (For his own amusement, he decided to install hidden TV cameras in the guest bedrooms, though of this he said nothing to Kim.) And for good measure, he planned a private zoo filled with exotic birds and beasts. Le Paradis would be worthy of its name.

An international team had been assembled. From Mexico, an architect who specialized in luxury resorts. From New York, a decorating firm whose rooms were a staple of *Architectural Digest*. From Milan, the Bardinis, a stylish husband-and-wife duo in charge of interior design. The plans were all set.

'And you, Bette, are to supervise the lot.'

'*Moi?*' Bette exercised her one word of French.

'*Toi!* Of course, you'll have your own wing which you're free to decorate in any style you choose. For the rest, just see my instructions are carried out.'

Bette's charter was broad. She could hire and fire, ride herd on his consultants, do whatever was necessary to ensure that the work was completed by the time the honeymooners returned.

'I'm thrilled to bits!' Bette exclaimed. 'To think you'd trust me with such responsibilities!'

'But you're *family*!' Tonio replied. 'Whom can one trust if not family?'

By now Bette had observed that the DuMesnes trusted *only* family. Outsiders were excluded from the ruling cabal.

For just as Tonio was currently Minister of Culture (he had previously been an ambassador and a four-star general), his uncle was Secretary of Defense, his mother ran the national lottery, a cousin in Switzerland handled European investments and another performed a similar function in New York. Key posts in government and the diplomatic corps were filled almost exclusively by family, extending to second and third cousins and their spouses.

243

Such loyalty, Bette thought. It was downright touching. She herself, as befitted her rank as First Mother-in-Law, was given an office, a salary, a personal staff, a car and driver, and even a title: *Directrice* of National Monuments.

Which meant, in addition to overseeing the work at Le Paradis, she lunched twice a week with the well-placed ladies of Benedicta society. This delightful ritual was usually followed by a rousing afternoon of gossip and a bridge game from which she invariably walked away a winner.

With leisure, money, and a full-time maid to pick up after her, Bette West was in her element. For once in her life, people treated her with *respect*. She had Tonio DuMesne's ear, and few qualms about letting others know it. It was heady stuff.

Bette was thankful that her new-found clout was based upon a Catholic marriage. Otherwise, it might be *Easy come, easy go*. She soon hit her stride.

As it turned out, the work at the villa was hardly arduous, consisting mostly of accepting consignments and okaying payments. Initially, Bette had had trouble with one of the decorators, a sleek young person named Laura Vincent who had been assigned to furnish her quarters. Laura had queried Bette's choice of bedroom wallpaper.

'Gold flocked velvet?' she echoed in disbelief.

'I like it,' Bette said. 'Any objections?'

The young woman flushed. 'It looks – um, a bit tacky!'

Laura was shipped out on the first plane next morning and Bette got her wallpaper without further cavil.

The incident was instructive. Nothing so validates personal taste, Bette realized, as the power of the checkbook.

The only other run-in she had with the staff concerned a plane shipment from Ruanda. The small frightened creature inside was alive, though a trifle dehydrated. The bill of lading described it as a chimpanzee.

Simone Bardini's eyes popped when she saw the creature.

'That is a mountain gorilla,' she said.

Bette grinned. 'Isn't he adorable?'

'But that is an endangered species, Mrs West.' The designer was very upset. 'Illegal to buy . . . to sell . . . to ship.'

'Maybe for ordinary people,' Bette smirked. 'But not for my son-in-law. He enjoys diplomatic status. He can do as he likes.'

Signora Bardini, perhaps remembering the fate of Laura Vincent, said no more.

My son-in-law!

How Bette loved to wrap her chops around the phrase. 'My son-in-law Tonio DuMesne.'

Almost as good as 'my daughter's father-in-law, El Tigre.'

Now there was a name to strike fear! She used it sparingly.

He was a pip, the old man. As ugly as Tonio was handsome. Looked every bit the murderer he was reputed to be. Bette gave him a wide berth. Not that she was invited to Le Castel that often, though she did, upon request, play gin rummy with Tonio's mother, Albertine. Bette always went when summoned, and was smart enough to lose, though the stakes were uncomfortably high. Extortionate, in fact. Bette knew she was being hustled, but what could she do?

Still, Madame Albertine was always gracious. An elegant woman, with the sharp precise bones of a bird, she had been a model in her youth and was the source of her son's good looks.

'You must miss your precious Kim,' she commiserated.

'Oh, I do!' Bette said. 'We've never been apart before.'

'Mother love. So sweet. You didn't want that eight of hearts, did you? Yes, I can hardly wait till our darlings come home.'

Bette had hardly slept at all on Kim's wedding night. She only wished she could have gone along to give advice.

Poor Kim! So naive, so carefully nurtured. What would she make of that first taste of marriage? Of sex! The very word left a bad taste in Bette's mouth. She only hoped Kim wouldn't suffer too much.

'Don't expect what pleases him will please you,' Bette had

warned. 'Men, even nice ones like Tonio, are basically animals. However, you gotta make him happy. That's your job.'

She recommended that Kim shut her eyes and think of it as a necessary procedure. 'Like an operation, you know.'

But when Kim called from Bermuda, where they were spending the first leg of the honeymoon, the girl sounded euphoric. Tonio was wonderful, she raved. So strong. So virile. Marriage was bliss bliss bliss. They hadn't left the suite in three days.

Bette was simultaneously disappointed and relieved. Did the young couple ever get out of the sack? she wondered. When would they find time to eat? to shop? to lead normal lives?

'I'm glad he's so perfect,' Bette said wryly.

'Well, not absolutely perfect.' Kim giggled. 'Not quite. He has one teentsy secret flaw . . .'

'Oh yes?' Bette asked. 'Something I should know about?'

The giggle turned into a full-throated laugh. 'Don't worry, Mom. It's nothing that affects his . . . our . . . Well, you know what I mean! Gotta dash now. Our plane leaves in an hour.'

Throughout the journey, Kim and Tonio phoned her often, to tell her what shipments to expect and get reports on the progress of the house. Tonio, particularly, insisted on detailed rundowns. He was a man who liked things 'just so.'

They phoned from Palm Springs one September afternoon to say they would be home in two weeks.

'Is everything ready?' Tonio wanted to know.

'We're in the home stretch. The decorators are hanging the pictures right now. I think you'll be thrilled with the results.'

What was there not to like? The house had everything that a ten-million-dollar budget could buy.

That afternoon, Bette went into her quarters, stretched out on a pale yellow velvet chaise and ordered a Planter's Punch with a sprig of fresh mint. While she sipped the rum and nibbled Macadamia nuts, her maid Maria massaged her toes with a fragrant unguent from Floris of London.

'Not so rough on my corns,' Bette murmured. Actually, it felt divine, but you didn't want to spoil the help.

Then she loosed a long slow sigh of satisfaction.

It had taken her a while to learn the art of being pampered, of living rich, but she was finally getting the hang of it.

Catching sight of herself in a mirror, the maid at her feet, Bette winked at her reflection.

No more stealing tips off the table for you, my dear. From here on, it's first class all the way.

Bette was at the airport to see the honeymooners arrive, but then so was half of Benedicta.

It was an exquisite day, breezy and bright now that the summer heat had broken. On the tarmac, the *San Miguel One* shimmered in the sun. As the ground crew wheeled the staircase up to the cabin door of the jumbo jet, a brass band struck 'Mi boom Patri.' It was the national anthem of San Miguel. On the second chorus, the bystanders joined in. Bette sang along with them, loud and clear, in a flush of patriotism. *Mi boom patri*, 'My beloved homeland' in the patois.

Then the door of the plane opened, and down the staircase they strode. Tonio and Kim. Two tanned and magnificent specimens, tall and proud, dressed in matching white silk suits. Immaculate. Radiant as royalty at a ball.

Tonio carried an ivory walking stick. Kim's throat gleamed with diamonds. They were holding hands. The band stopped. The crowd caught its breath.

Even Bette, who considered herself such a woman of the world – even Bette had to gasp. She was beholding a God and a Goddess.

FOLEY SQUARE

'You know the classic definition of *chutzpah*?'

Bill Cairns clapped Alix on the back as they were leaving the courthouse. 'A boy who murders his father and mother, then throws himself upon the mercy of the court claiming he's an orphan.' He laughed. 'That motion of yours was off the wall. Even Judge Birnbaum was stunned. You're amazing, Alix. You truly are.'

At the bottom of the steps, both lawyers halted momentarily. A light snow had fallen, dusting the streets with a layer of lace. In that dusky moment, Foley Square was serene in shades of gray and white, like the nostalgic New York of pre-war movies.

'Calm before the storm, eh, Alix?'

She nodded, then buttoned up her coat.

'See you in court, counselor,' Bill said and turned the corner at a clip. Always running. The Gingerbread Man, the tabloids called him. Just as she was Amazing Alix.

She strolled home in the gathering twilight. It had been a day of pre-trial motions, most of which she had lost. She had never expected the 'orphan' ploy to succeed, but she had hopes on one other score. She had wanted the families of the bereaved to be excluded from the courtroom.

'Their presence would be inflammatory,' she argued. 'What jury will have the guts, let alone the heart, to acquit, after seeing these people sitting there day after day?'

But Judge Birnbaum had ruled against her.

'If you're telling me that folks who've lost their nearest and dearest are not entitled to see justice done on the grounds that it might upset the jury . . .' He sighed. 'This trial is bound to be upsetting, whether relatives are present or not.'

Which meant that Peter Mainwaring would be on hand every day with his *j'accuse* eyes. The prospect made her shiver.

Alix walked slowly, playing scenarios in her head. Crossing Houston Street, she switched off. Work was work, family was family, and if you didn't segregate the two, you went nuts. The Gilchrist trial was consigned to mental limbo, at least till Samantha was in bed.

Alix picked up the dry-cleaning, then stopped at Win Lee's for a take-out. They usually ate Chinese on Friday night in a ritual that made for easy housekeeping. Mr Rabinowitz would have already set the table, his final chore for the week.

'You should see my little girl handle chopsticks,' she told Mrs Lee, then hoped it didn't sound like a racist remark. But Mrs Lee grinned and threw in some extra fortune cookies.

By the time Alix reached home, her mood was upbeat.

At six, Samantha Bryden was the image of her father. She had his black curly hair, flashing eyes and high cheekbones. One-eighth Choctaw Indian, assuming Sam Matthews had told the truth. It made for a good story anyhow.

She also had inherited her father's volubility, chattering non-stop through dinner with news from the front: a fire drill at school, the antics of Bert and Ernie, the life expectancy of gerbils, and how Nancy Marsh's mother was a streaker.

'A streaker?' Alix said, trying to picture Ellen Marsh sprinting naked down Eighth Street with a briefcase. 'Are you sure you've got that right, sweetie?'

'Yes,' Samantha said. 'She puts streaks in her hair.'

'I see,' Alix said gravely. They finished their meal and opened their cookies.

'Read my fortune, Mommy,' Samantha asked.

Alix squinted at the thread of paper. *'When fleet come in, beware of wolf in ship's clothing.'*

Alix groaned. Who wrote this smart-ass stuff anyway? she wondered. Whatever happened to the old-fashioned fortune cookies, the kind that said you were going to make a long journey or meet a handsome dark-haired stranger? For that matter, whatever happened to handsome dark-haired strangers?

'It means it's high tide and time to go to bed.'

'Does not, does it, *zayde*?' Samantha appealed to a higher court.

'Your mother is always right,' Mr Rabinowitz confirmed.

'Yeah,' Alix said. 'I'm just amazing.'

At seven thirty she tucked Samantha in bed, read an install-ment of *Sylvester and the Magic Pebble* and kissed her goodnight.

Then Alix washed her hair, threw on a terrycloth robe and worked in her room for a couple of hours. The glamorous life of a hot-shot attorney, she thought, rubbing red eyes.

At ten, she went into the living room where Mr Rabinowitz was watching the news on TV.

'Come look!' he said. 'They're talking about your case.'

On the screen, a coat swaggered across his shoulders, was Bill Cairns in his public persona. Mr Clean. He was playing to the cameras – '*fair trial . . . outrageous crime . . .*' – managing to sound simultaneously energetic and lofty, hot and cool. Which was, Alix decided, a neat trick.

'That's my opposite number,' she remarked. 'They call him Send-'em-to-the-Slammer Cairns.'

'A nice looking fella,' Mr Rabinowitz opined.

'You think . . . ?' Alix peered dubiously at the TV set.

Well, she supposed so, if you liked that Celtic type. Sharp features, pale freckled skin, ginger hair which, though the camera didn't show it, was getting thin on top. He reminded her of a greyhound, not tall but limber and built for speed. Her bet was he jogged every morning.

'Are you nervous about the trial, *kitzele*?' Mr Rabinowitz asked.

'I could say no, but I'd be lying. Edgy, excited, all that stuff. Yeah, I'm nervous but in a nice kind of way – like a bride on the night before the wedding.'

Then she gave a self-conscious laugh. How the hell would Alix know how a bride felt before the big event?

It was a circus, complete with spotlights and sideshows. As much action outside the courtroom as in.

Day after day, they jammed Foley Square. Not a crowd, she thought, for crowds were benign. Crowds went to ball games and cheered themselves hoarse. This was a mob. Mobs rioted. Mobs lynched.

By eight thirty every morning, the demonstrators were in place: noisy, volatile, diverse. Friends of the victims, members of the Flight Attendants Union, of the British–American Friendship Association, students from Cornell (whose fencing team had been wiped out), a contingent from the Staten Island Post of the American Legion, pilots, air-safety proponents, activists crusading for a return to capital punishment, plus the usual assortment of ghouls and curiosity seekers who liked to identify themselves as 'John Q. Public.' Also present were camera crews, working the scene in hopes of action footage for the evening news, plus the odd entrepreneur selling GET GILCHRIST! tee-shirts with an electric chair embossed on the back.

Alix's appearance inevitably drew jeers and abuse. 'You'd think I was the defendant,' she griped.

Inside, the atmosphere, though quieter, was equally tense, the benches crammed with hostile spectators, Peter Mainwaring among them. A pity they couldn't have been excluded.

A pity Rodney Gilchrist couldn't have been excluded as well. He was the kind of defendant you loved to loathe.

Prison routine had done nothing for Rodney's appearance; he had grown fatter, his skin was the color of library paste. Throughout the trial, he sat there like landfill, staring into space. Now and again, he picked his nose.

Usually, when defending the indefensible, Alix would remind herself that even the most despicable felon was someone's son, someone's daughter. In Rodney's case, that tactic didn't work.

Mostly, Alix fixed her gaze on the jury, the witnesses and the prosecutor's table – most particularly, on Assistant US Attorney William F. Cairns.

Early in the trial she and Bill had made a wager: Loser buys the winner lunch.

'At the restaurant of the winner's choice,' Bill added.

'I'll be kind, then. Wah Kee's in Chinatown. I know how poorly you guys are paid.'

Bill was a worthy adversary. Like Alix, he was fiercely competitive, a glutton for work, a merciless cross-examiner. Each time they clashed, sparks flew.

Everything was tactics, even clothing. Where the prosecution team favored dark suits and white shirts, Alix switched to warm colors and pretty fabrics. 'Friendly' clothes, that might appeal to a jury and take the curse off Rodney Gilchrist.

'Don't you look nice!' Bill commented one morning when she turned up in a peach-colored dress. Alix flushed with pleasure, though she wasn't sure if that was a genuine compliment or simply a stratagem meant to disarm.

She bitched constantly: the trial was wrecking her home life, the pressure was killing her, the forces against her were too powerful. All of which was true. That said, when it came to thrills, nothing compared with the excitement of a trial. It was a duel of wits, full of parries and thrusts, adversarial yet also collegial. At its best, it was as good as sex. In some ways, better. For if, by chance, you had fucked up your private life irreparably, you could still prove yourself a winner in court.

Peter Mainwaring waylaid her in the hall one day, his face pale with undischarged anger.

'This trial isn't about Gilchrist or Annie or what happened on that flight. It's about winning and losing. That's all.'

Alix felt a momentary pinch of shame.

At first Rodney had balked at an insanity defense. 'People will think I'm crazy.' But Alix talked him around, assuring him he'd be better off in a mental institution. 'The doctors can help you. Perhaps in a few years, if you've made progress . . .'

Rodney looked dubious. Alix was too, for that matter. Yet who could say? The day might come when Rodney would be cured and emerge a new person. She suggested as much to Bill Cairns during a break one morning, as they sipped coffee out of styrofoam cups.

'You gotta be kidding,' he said.

'Absolutely not!' Alix said. Everyone alive was capable of change. She believed that profoundly. Besides, she pointed out, Rodney was not likely to repeat his crime.

'After all, how many sets of parents does a boy have?'

It was an atrocious joke, yet both lawyers laughed. Given the stress of the trial, gallows humor brought welcome relief.

The expert witnesses too provided an occasional break in the tension, though much of the testimony was mired in jargon. Bill's pet peeve was a Dr Weintraub, a psychiatrist of top credentials and murky syntax who testified for the defense. After three hours of rigorous questioning, Bill got the doctor to concede that blowing up a 747 with all aboard was 'inappropriate behavior.'

'Inappropriate behavior?' Bill rolled his eyes, eliciting a wave of titters.

Alix sprang to her feet. 'I object, your honor. For Mr Cairns to roll his eyes in court is – inappropriate behavior.'

Alix's strategy was simple.

Rodney Gilchrist was so obsessed with chess, she set out to show that he was unable to distinguish between the game and reality. Indeed, the game was more real than real life.

Ergo, there had to be a grave deficiency in his make-up – neurological or chemical or otherwise. For just as some people are tone deaf or color blind, Rodney Gilchrist also lacked an essential component. He was incapable of empathy.

His world was the chessboard, populated by inanimate pieces

to be moved about and sacrificed as necessary. His parents were but pieces in play. In removing them from the 'board,' there had been neither malice nor qualms nor a grasp of the suffering involved. There was only the game. And if that wasn't insanity – Alix would like to know – then what was?

Alix called her strategy the 'Chess Defense.'

In her closing argument, she planned to play directly to the jury's finest feelings. Pity the emptiness and horror of such a life! she would implore, thus appealing to those same moral sensibilities her client lacked.

As the trial proceeded, Alix studied the jurors. All it took was one hold-out. If the prosecution thought they faced a hung jury, they might cave in and do a deal. Which would be a legal triumph for Alix, a genuine tour de force.

And best of all, that Bill Cairns would be buying her a Chinese dinner. At which she lushed up on Szechuan beef and crystal prawns and ginger-fried crabs. While he ate crow.

PARK AVENUE

The most recent report was not satisfactory. Miranda insisted upon a personal interview.

Accordingly, early one morning Mr Joel Baker of Surveilla-Systems presented himself at her Park Avenue duplex. A man in his forties, he had a low-key manner and a forgettable face.

'Please clarify.' Miranda read from the report. '"The subject checked out of the Hilton and now resides at the Olcott Arms on Eighth Avenue." I couldn't find any Olcott Arms in the phone book. What kind of place is it?'

'It's what's known as an SRO. Single Room Occupancy

hotel, though in this case "hotel" is a euphemism. I'd say it's between a flophouse and a fleabag.' The detective talked of shabby rooms, peeling paint, the stench of urine in the hall. Most of the residents were on welfare. Some were on drugs.

'To sum up—' Baker looked at a sleek tabby sleeping on a watered-silk sofa. 'Your cats live better.'

Miranda betrayed no emotion. 'In your report, you note that Mr Mainwaring has been drinking. Is that your own observation? How often? How heavily?'

'The subject spends the day in court. Then when it breaks, he heads for a bar on Eighth Avenue. It's called Smitty's . . .'

More details followed. By the time Baker finished, Miranda had formed a picture of a man at the end of his resources, emotional *and* financial.

'From now on,' she said, 'I want daily reports. Where Mr Mainwaring goes, what he does, how he's coping. But he mustn't know he's being watched.'

'In other words, round-the-clock surveillance?'

Miranda bit her lip. *Surveillance* had a nasty ring. 'I don't want to *spy* on him in any sense of the word. I merely want to ensure his safety. Should Mr Mainwaring appear to be – ' she grimaced – 'suicidal or in physical danger, I expect your people to take suitable action. But discreetly,' she added. 'Without giving the game away.'

'A bodyguard?'

'An invisible bodyguard.'

'It'll cost,' Baker said.

'I have money.'

Just as she had once charted Peter's rise, now she watched his decline. He was hurtling into an abyss, unstoppable.

After the crash, he had sold his London home, quit his job, cut himself off from his friends, abandoned his writing. He lived only for the trial, which Miranda found morbid. Did he think that Gilchrist's conviction would numb his misery?

Put the past behind you, he had advised Miranda. *Make a new life*. But the doctor had failed to take his own prescription.

As the trial drew to a close, the reports grew more alarming. Peter was drinking. Drowning. Dying, for all she knew.

The situation screamed for action. But what?

One half of her ached to be by his side. To offer him everything she had: wealth and compassion and loyalty. The other half cautioned prudence.

Peter was a widower now. What would he think if she surfaced at this juncture? What *could* he think – except that she was still besotted by him? That she was one of those ghouls who preyed off the dead.

Nor was it lost upon Miranda that their situations were reversed. Once she had been weak and he strong. But now it was Miranda who wielded power and influence; Peter who was bereaved and in pain. She had everything. He had only grief.

Even if she induced him to accept her help, she would have purchased his gratitude. It was too humiliating – for both of them!

No. Better that she and Peter not meet at this juncture. To do so would cheapen everything she had once felt for him. If Peter were to be saved it must be done anonymously.

The question was – how?

Miranda being Miranda, she devised a plan. It was both complex and expensive. While it was being executed, she would go abroad. Manhattan wasn't big enough for the two of them, she felt, not as long as there was the risk of a chance encounter.

One morning, she called Jim Bisseau into her office.

'As you know,' she told her assistant, 'I'm going to be away for a while. Ouagadougou, Seoul. That sneakers-for-groundnuts deal came through, by the way. Then Jakarta, Brazzaville. After which I want to squeeze in a trip to London. Christie's is auctioning off a collection of Puiforcat silver next month, and you know what a sucker I am for that Art Deco stuff. My housekeeper will take care of the cats, and I'll be in touch with you every day. While I'm gone, I'd like you to look into something for me. It's a whole new area for investment.'

She handed him a half dozen pages of notes.

Jim scanned them, then tented his eyebrows.

'That's an odd business for you to be getting into, Miranda. A long way from groundnuts and sneakers.'

'I like odd businesses,' she said with a smile. 'Remember?'

SAN MIGUEL

'I got the basic idea from Joan Crawford,' Bette gushed, 'and took it from there.'

'Very nice,' Kim said. 'Just like at the dry cleaner's.'

'It holds seven hundred and fifty outfits – sportswear, ballgowns, dresses, suits, and so on, with every item tagged, coordinated, cross-indexed. It's a marvel of organization, if I say so myself. In my next life, I'm coming back as a wardrobe mistress. You don't seem excited, Kimbo.'

'It's terrific, Mom.'

'Anyhow . . . each rack is mechanized to hold fifty outfits. And every outfit has a file card so your maid can enter the last time you wore any particular number, and who was present. That way people never see you in the same thing twice.'

Kim sighed. 'It seems an awful lot of trouble . . .'

'Easy-peasy. Look! Say you want a short red cocktail dress for a reception.' She consulted her directory, then pushed a button on an electronic keyboard. 'Rack seven.'

The designated rack slid down a metal rail, stopping a few feet from where they sat on wooden gilt chairs.

'Okay. Now I enter number thirty-five.' As she did so, the rack rotated until a padded hanger bearing that number popped into view. On the overhead shelf was a transparent plastic box, also numbered thirty-five.

'Coming up!' Bette crowed. 'One red bouffant Dior cocktail dress, never worn, plus matching shoes and gloves and bag. Everything in one swell foop. Ain't that a kick?'

Bette was justifiably proud of her brainchild. It was a dream dressing room: twelve hundred square feet of storage space, cedar paneling, with a refrigerated vault for furs.

Certainly not like any dry cleaner's *she'd* ever seen! Bette sniffed at the implication. More like having your own private Bergdorf's. And everything in it altered to fit.

Such clothes! The most exquisite creations of Paris and Milan and New York and Rome had been assembled in this space. Luscious silk crepes and brocades and baratheas; cashmere suits, vicuña coats, hand-woven Irish tweeds; ballgowns by the dozen, some heavy with sequins and crystal beading, others light as butterfly wings.

One portion of the room was given over to elaborate costumes in pristine white, gleaming like a snowfield under the halogen lights. They constituted Kim's 'official' wardrobe, to be trotted out on state occasions.

'If you ask me,' Bette commented, 'those clothes are asking for trouble. I mean, one blob of spaghetti sauce and you can throw 'em away. Personally, I like you better in colors.'

Kim scarcely raised her eyes. Her voice was flat.

'"In public wear white," that's what Tonio says.'

'And in private, wear sexy lingerie?'

But Bette's teasing provoked no response.

Kim's behavior had changed, her mother observed. Nothing seemed to please or excite her any more. The dark circles under her eyes hinted of illness or secret grief. Whatever the source of trouble, and Bette made a shrewd guess, it must not be permitted to fester. Too much depended on Kim. Perhaps a little 'mother–daughter talk' would do the trick.

'You musta spent every minute in Paris shopping,' Bette began. 'Did your hubby go with you to the salons?'

'He had other things to do,' Kim murmured.

Bette caught the undertone of resentment.

'Is something wrong, pussycat? Some little problem with Tonio? You've been looking peaky since you came back.'

'Jet lag,' Kim said.

'But you've been home ten days already. No, tootsie. I don't buy that explanation.' She lowered her voice, not that anyone was there to hear. 'You can confide in your mom, sweetheart. I'm the best friend you have in the world. It *is* Tonio, isn't it? Has he done something stinko?'

The violet eyes suddenly brimmed with tears. 'Oh Mom,' Kim cried. 'I never knew love could hurt so damn much!'

The first week of their honeymoon surpassed Kim's dreams. To say she was content did scant justice to her feelings: she was enraptured, enthralled. Tonio was by turns tender, playful, passionate, loving, sensual, sweet, virile. She didn't think she'd ever get enough of him. He had a magnificent body, strong and tautly muscled, the product of long hours in the gym. Even watching him in repose was aphrodisiac.

'I could spend the rest of my life in bed with you,' she said their last morning in Bermuda.

Tonio laughed and threw her a robe. If all they were going to do was lie in bed and make love, he pointed out, they might as well have stayed in San Miguel.

Not that he himself wouldn't be delighted with such a scenario, but they were public people, he stressed. And *noblesse oblige*. Their duty was to see and be seen.

Kim was perplexed.

'Is this our honeymoon or a goodwill tour?'

'A bit of both, *mon ange*. Now ring for your maid and get decent.'

Kim soon came to accept the days filled with luxury and pomp. She actually enjoyed the protocol. It was what she had been trained for: a life in the limelight, ever gracious and serene. And when, as often happened, Kim found herself in unfamiliar surroundings, she remembered the guidance of her tutor Lally Goodwin and proceeded to behave with aplomb. *Bust Out, Belly In, Butt Under* still came in handy. And always remove your gloves when being introduced to a head of state.

The neat thing about being rich and famous, Kim decided, was that it gave you instant access to other rich and famous people.

Wherever they went, wedged in between the days of shopping and nights of sex, there were receptions, parties, dinners and teas. Life was one dressy occasion after another with those glamorous folk whom Tonio dubbed *The Few Who*.

In Haiti, Baby Doc declared a national holiday in honor of his fellow dynast. In Miami they stayed with Sinatra. Then on to London, where the young couple had tea with Princess Anne, were photographed by Snowdon, and night-clubbed with Joan and Jackie Collins. After which it was off for a shooting party in Scotland as guests of a Kuwaiti prince. Tonio was a crackerjack shot, his wife noted with pride, totting up the biggest kills. At his urging, Kim tried her hand too and though she didn't wing a single bird, Tonio assured her she had an excellent eye. Plus she looked just terrific in Harris tweeds!

By the time they reached Paris, the young couple had hit their stride. Kim had made a list of all the great restaurants.

'But Paris is for clothes, darling,' Tonio said. 'Magnificent clothes. I want you to get a wardrobe fit for a queen. Indulge yourself. It's your patriotic duty.'

San Miguel was a small country, he explained, but this was one way to make a splash. With Kim's name on the Best Dressed lists, San Miguel would be a synonym for wealth and style.

'You'll be like Jackie Kennedy or Princess Grace,' he said, eyes twinkling. 'A credit to your country and to me.'

His secretary had made appointments at the great couture houses: Dior, Chanel, Givenchy, St Laurent, Ungaro. A former *Vogue* editor was hired to help in the selection. Kim's days would be taken up with fittings.

'Think of it as a job, darling. And a favor to me.'

'But what will you do while I'm busy?' Kim asked.

'Don't worry, lamb. I'll find ways to amuse myself. Paris is full of diversions.'

She left for her 'job' every morning at ten thirty. Sometimes Tonio picked her up in the late afternoon. Otherwise, they met at their hotel in time to bathe and dress for dinner.

'How was your day?' she would ask, and Tonio would chatter cheerfully about picking ties at Sulka or horses at Longchamp.

One afternoon, he came back smelling of sex.

Kim tried to convince herself she imagined it. No man cheats on his bride of three weeks – especially since they had made love that very morning.

Another time she noticed scratch marks on his back and was certain they weren't hers. But what could she say?

Then one evening he didn't come back to the hotel at all.

Kim was frantic. She rang up his secretary, a cool sleek Englishman who had been with him for years.

'Something's happened to my husband, Simon. Please call the police.'

'I don't think that's advisable, Mrs DuMesne. Just leave things to me.'

A few minutes later, Simon knocked at her door. By then, Kim was in tears.

'Please, Mrs DuMesne!' Simon sat her down and took her hands in his. 'I assure you your husband is perfectly safe. I just spoke to him. He'll be here in half an hour.'

'But where is he? I tried the embassy, the Ritz Bar, the Jockey Club, every place I could think of—'

'Paris is a city of *many* attractions, not all of them quite reputable,' Simon enunciated with special emphasis.

'I don't understand!' Kim cried.

'I think you do.' He was watching her carefully.

Her stomach lurched.

'Then I don't think I *want* to understand!' she whispered.

'What a very wise young lady you are.'

She ran into the bathroom and vomited.

Neither that night nor on any of his subsequent disappearances did Kim confront Tonio. She was terrified lest he should accuse her of a gutter mind. After all, she was sweet Kimberly, his virgin bride. An innocent to be guided by him in sexual matters.

Yet as they continued their royal progress, she agonized constantly. What had she done to offend him? Where had she failed? The thought that her husband should seek satisfaction elsewhere – in brothels, if what Simon hinted was true – tormented her beyond endurance.

And yet . . . !

And yet Tonio continued to treat her with warmth and affection. And yet they made love every night. He still had the power to make her cry out in ecstasy, though now she suspected that his joy was less rapturous than her own.

By the time they left Paris, Kim was convinced that the trouble lay not in the frequency of their encounters, but in their quality. Their sex life was too conventional. Kim's fault, clearly. She lacked a worldly repertoire.

In Rome one day, when Tonio was off God-knew-where, she ventured into a Via Veneto bookstore famous for its collection of erotica. She emerged with a number of illustrated 'guides.' In her spare moments, she studied the pictures as solemnly as she had once studied the guitar. She was determined to master the various arts of love and please her husband.

Some of the illustrations were unspeakable. Group sex,

couplings with animals, golden showers, aberrations too gross to contemplate. Kim flipped past those pages in a state of shock, unable to link her husband mentally with such acts. Yet even in the classic combination of one man and one woman, there was an infinity of experience to be explored.

There was one book in particular, printed in India, that showed three hundred and sixty-five different positions, one for every night in the year. In the drawings, the man's eyes were wide with bliss.

Kim also found the pictures erotic. Some of the couplings required an athleticism beyond her abilities. Others, however, looked feasible. Bondage intrigued her, as did oral sex. She also noted variations on the theme taught her by that 'doctor' in Atlantic City. Not so unusual an act, apparently, yet Tonio had never done it with her.

Sometimes when Tonio was in his bath or shaving, Kim would lie in bed naked, nipples taut, silken skinned, thinking of the pictures in the book. By the time he emerged, she was aroar with desire.

'Darling!' She would pull him down on the bed. 'Take me every way you want. Every inch of me . . . every way possible!'

Yet though Tonio dutifully responded with an erection and deftly brought her to orgasm, he never explored new techniques. The sole request he had ever made of her was on the night of their wedding, when he asked that she shave her pubic hair.

'I want you sweet and smooth,' he had said. 'Like an angel.' She was happy to oblige.

Yet though she kept her body in a perpetual state of readiness, clean and soft and perfumed, nothing changed. Neither Tonio's love-making technique nor his unexplained disappearances. He never discussed sex with her, and the few times when Kim had whispered vague suggestions in his ear, Tonio had cut her off. 'Where does a lovely girl like you learn such things?' She didn't dare be more explicit.

By the time they reached Bangkok, Kim was in a state of alarm. The city's brothels and massage parlors were notorious. Tonio was certain to sample their wares.

True to form, their first two days in the Thai capital, Kim and her maid Celeste were shunted off on shopping expeditions, while Tonio followed other pursuits. By the third afternoon, Kim was devastated. What could the whores of Bangkok offer that she, his loving wife, was unwilling or unable to provide? Why some of them were mere children of nine and ten!

Instead of dressing to go out, Kim sent for her maid.

'I want you to do me a favor, Celeste.'

'Of course, milady.' Celeste smiled her wise smile.

A sprightly mulatto with a warm smile and blackberry eyes, Celeste Guinot was proving indispensable to her mistress. Her command of English was excellent, and she could work wonders with hair. Sometimes she told Kim's fortune with tarot cards. In Bette's absence, Kim turned to her for comfort and advice.

'I would like,' Kim said shyly, 'to surprise my husband. But I'll need your help.'

Kim explained what she wanted done. Celeste never arched an eyebrow.

'Of course it's a joke, you understand, Celeste.'

'Of course, milady.'

The bonds chafed when she moved, but Kim gave them no thought. What did pain matter, when the prize was pleasure?

From time to time, as she lay naked on the silken sheets, Kim twisted her head to catch a glimpse of herself in the mirror. Even by her own exacting standards, she had never appeared lovelier. More seductive.

Her skin glistened with aromatic oils and unguents. Her golden hair was fanned across the pillow to catch the sunlight. Her delicate wrists and ankles were tied to the bedposts with brilliant lengths of Thai silk, sculpting her form into a lascivious X. In the absolute silence, Kim was aware of every inch of her body. She could hear her heart beat, feel the throb of her clitoris. Every orifice ached for fulfillment.

Soon Tonio would arrive. One look and he would do what any man worthy of the designation would do upon being greeted by such a sight. He would fling himself upon her with unbridled passion, ravishing her, devouring her flesh, while she trembled beneath him in abject surrender. Helpless, yet happy.

For a long while, Kim lay there, eyes half shut, picturing what was to come. In her mind, she lived a hundred orgasms.

Then toward dusk – Kim's pulse quickened at the sound – the bedroom door opened, and there was Tonio, silhouetted against the dying light. Kim moistened her lips.

'My lover!' she whispered, and felt her body flood.

Tonio paused at the threshold, looked at her for a moment, then burst out laughing.

'What on earth do you think you're doing?' He placed his hands on his hips.

Kim's heart stopped. Her body, that luscious body so scrupulously readied for love, turned pink with humiliation.

'Don't you want me?' she cried. 'Don't you want me like this? I did this for you, Tonio! To please you!'

'What a silly creature you are sometimes.' He sounded faintly annoyed. Then he marched over and untied her bonds. 'Now I want you to wash off all that muck and put some clothes on. I swear to God, you smell like a whorehouse.'

Suddenly the months of pent-up rage and misery exploded, sending her out of control.

'Like a whorehouse?' she screamed. 'What would I know about whorehouses?' She began beating her fists against his chest. She wanted to wound him, bloody him, to do to his flesh what he had done to her spirit.

'But you—!' she wept as her arms flailed wildly. 'You're the expert on whores, aren't you, Tonio? You must be, since you spend so much time in brothels.'

'That's enough!' Tonio roared. 'Come to your senses.'

With the deftness of a wrestler, he seized her wrists and held them in a hammerlock. Even as she thrashed, she knew that struggle was useless. He had an athlete's body and strength.

In his grip, Kim was helpless. Not the helplessness of sexual surrender that she had craved only moments ago, but a helplessness born of failure and frustration. She had no weapons left except words and tears.

'Sneak! Cheat! Liar!' she wailed. 'To treat me like that. You bastard!'

Tonio reared back and slapped her. It was only a slap, crisp and sharp, but enough to send Kim's head slamming into the padded headboard with a thud. The action sobered them both.

'I'm sorry, darling!' He looked genuinely shocked. 'Are you all right?'

Kim sat up and rubbed her neck gingerly. Nothing was broken. Nothing even hurt. Tonio was kissing her fingertips, all care and concern. Yet for the first time in her marriage, she knew physical fear. She began to tremble.

'How *could* you . . . ?' she wept.

He meditated for a moment, as if she had asked some exotic conundrum, then kissed her gently on the brow.

'How could I slap you? Believe me, angel, I'm sorry. It's that hair-trigger temper, I'm afraid.'

But Kim shook her head as tears coursed down her cheeks.

'How could you sleep with whores on our honeymoon?'

'Ah, that!' Tonio sighed.

He picked up a coverlet and threw it over her, then pulled up a chair, like a doctor sitting at a patient's bedside.

'There's something you must understand, my precious Kim. Men are different from women. We have more and different needs and no one female can ever satisfy them all. To your ears that may sound a bit macho, but it happens to be a biological fact. We men have animal sides to our nature, and that can't be changed. Understand, my angel, that I love you very much. You are my bride, my wife and, if God is good, you will be the mother of my children. And because I love you, I would never dream of subjecting you to the kind of sexual acts that take place in a brothel. You're too pure, too precious for that.'

'But I would do anything to please you,' Kim burst out. 'Everything! You're my husband.'

'Precisely. I'm your husband. And you are my angel – just as they are my sluts. No, darling, it demeans you to get yourself up like a whore. It demeans *you* and disgusts *me*. What I treasure most about you is your innocence. You look splendid in white, by the way. Like a virgin bride. When we return to San Miguel, it would please me if you wear white in public. And always remember – you are my sweet little angel.'

'But I'm a married woman,' she pleaded, 'not an angel. And I'm entitled to marital love.'

Tonio looked amused.

'Tell me, Kim, have I ever neglected you in bed? Do we not make love often enough to suit you? How many times have I heard you cry out in pleasure, cries that cannot be faked, and then I knew that I had satisfied you as a husband should satisfy a wife. That is my joy—'

'But—'

He raised his finger, commanding silence.

'—and my pride as your loving husband. Don't degrade my feelings for you. As for my 'pastimes', as I prefer to think of them, you could not really expect that a man would travel to Bangkok and not quench his curiosity concerning the finest brothels in the world? He would be less than a man if he did. In the future, however, I will try to be more discreet. And you will learn to live with it.'

He poured her a glass of water from the pitcher.

'Now that we have had this little conversation, we will never discuss such matters again. It would only provoke me. Do you understand?'

She was too frightened to do anything but nod.

'Good,' Tonio said with a smile. 'Now shower and get ready

for dinner. We're dining at the American ambassador's tonight and we want to look our best.'

It was this tale, much truncated, that Kim related to her mother as they huddled in the dressing room at Le Paradis. Kim had omitted the precise sexual details, knowing Bette's distaste for the topic. Besides, what would her mother know of such matters as bondage or pornography?

Sometimes, Kim wondered if her mother even remembered what sex was like. As far as she could tell, Bette's own experience was limited. There was Kim's father, of course, but after that? Except for Uncle Ed, the periodontist in Tulsa (and he was twenty years Bette's senior), Kim could not recall a single instance where her mother had spent a night with a man. *Mama knows best* had been the family motto, but now Kim wondered if she was looking to the wrong person for guidance.

Still, Kim reasoned, one didn't need to be an Ann Landers to know that a man who cheated on his wife within a month of the marriage was guilty of atrocious behavior.

'So there you are, Mom. The story of my honeymoon, and the thing is, I don't know what to do.' Kim raised her brimming eyes. 'I'm not sure I can go on living with him.'

'Kimberly West!' Bette had sprung to her feet. 'What *are* you talking about? Of course you'll go on living with him! You're a married woman. You were married in church with holy vows. I'm not saying Tonio has been the perfect gentleman, but to be fair —'

'My God! You're taking his side!'

'I'm not taking anyone's side, sweetie. I'm just saying that Tonio was right in one respect. All men have these animal instincts and you're silly to make a fuss about it. In fact, if anything, you should be grateful —'

'Grateful!' Kim screamed.

'— that he's been so up-front with you. I'm sure he'll keep his fly zipped in public. He promised, you said. Give him credit for some common sense. Why, any idiot can see Tonio worships the ground you walk on.'

'Well, he has a helluva way of showing it!' Kim cried.

'You betcha! And if you want proof, look around you.' Bette flung wide her arms in a gesture that encompassed a universe. 'Look at these fabulous clothes, your furs. Look at the rock on your finger – big enough to choke a horse. And that's just for starters. How can you even contemplate giving up all this? You have wealth, Kim. Position. The things people kill for, so let's not talk glibly about tossing it away. And if you don't think of yourself, then think of me. All the sacrifices I've made over the years—'

But Bette had gone too far. Kim, who had been staring at her, let loose a howl.

'What an extraordinary thing to say! We weren't talking about you, Mom. This has nothing to do with you. We were talking about Tonio's infidelities.'

'Which are really trivial,' Bette hastened to smooth over the breach. 'Of course your feelings are hurt, pet, but taken by and large, your husband is a prince of a fellow—'

'Who cheats on his wife.'

'Who is as human as the next guy,' Bette said. 'And I speak from experience. Believe you me, Tonio's no worse than the rest of them. They're all sex-crazed. But that's the way God made him. The important thing is, you love him, don't you?'

'I don't know any more.'

Bette put her arms around her daughter. 'Of course you do, sweets. Otherwise you wouldn't be so upset. And Tonio loves you too. Now you just go on being the good affectionate wife he expects you to be. Everything will work out fine. You'll see.'

For the next few weeks, Kim moped around the villa while Tonio exerted himself to be the model of gallantry, all compliments and kisses and gifts. Kim suspected that Bette had spoken to him. In fact, the two were thick as thieves.

The friendship between Tonio and her mother, which Kim had once found pleasing, now struck her as a kind of conspiracy. She would be a little less trusting in the future.

Still – her mother was right. Kim *did* love Tonio. Men *were*, doubtless, all the same. And in any case, she had nowhere to go.

But before long the question of staying or leaving resolved itself in a definite fashion.

She was pregnant, the doctor told her. With twins.

Tonio was overjoyed. Impossible to imagine a future father more tender, more loving. Kim would have been a monster not to forgive him.

Bette, too, nearly burst with relief.

'These little storms, darling. They blow, they pass. Nothing like an adorable baby to put things right.'

'Twins,' Kim said, quietly. 'I was so surprised. You never told me that twins ran in our family.'

THE PLAZA

The night before she was to make her closing argument, Alix worked straight through, fine-tuning every word. At daybreak, she showered, dressed, checked her appearance in the mirror and groaned.

She looked awful. Alley-cat skinny, as though she had lost a pound for every one that Rodney Gilchrist had gained. Her eyes were ringed with dark circles. Her brain felt as though it had gone ten rounds with Muhammad Ali. She couldn't recall the last time she had sat down to a decent meal or seen a movie.

That goddamn trial! It had taken over her life. For months she had eaten, drunk, dreamt the case. She was euphoric when it went well, suicidal when it didn't. By now she had invested so much emotional stock she didn't dare think about losing.

And as if the strain of the trial itself weren't enough of a steam-roller, there were the death threats. Not many, but they made her nervous. Hardly a day passed without the menacing phone call, the anonymous letter.

'Don't worry,' the police assured her. 'They'll stop once the jury brings in a guilty verdict.'

Her private life was no better. First Jeff's defection. Then her current lover opted out.

'I hate quickies,' Bob Jacobs groused at a mid-day rendezvous in a downtown hotel.

'We have forty-five whole minutes,' Alix pleaded.

'Plus I'm tired of getting in bed with Rodney Gilchrist.'

Alix was devastated. Or would have been, if she'd had the time. 'I'll call you when it's over,' she said.

'It's over now.' He kissed her and left.

But the biggest blow was the one closest to home.

Poor Samantha! Even the kids in first grade had seen the publicity. Far from being proud of her famous mom, Samantha felt like a pariah. Why couldn't Alix be 'like normal people'?

One day, when court broke early, Alix tore uptown to collect her at school and was jumped on by the other mothers. 'How could you defend that monster?' Phyllis Langley asked, with bitterness. 'It's outrageous,' added Evvie Brooks.

'Please!' Alix whispered. 'Not in front of my daughter.' Samantha promptly burst into tears.

Alix comforted her with a double-decker ice-cream at Angelica's, while trying to explain abstract principles of fairness and justice. But the little girl couldn't care less. All she wanted was for her friends to stop teasing.

Soon, soon, Alix promised.

Samantha didn't believe a word of it. Six years old, Alix brooded, and already a seasoned cynic.

*

At nine o'clock, Alix arrived at the courthouse, as keyed up as a finalist at Wimbledon. The usual vultures had gathered in Foley Square, but she didn't flinch. Today was the day.

As she strode down the corridor toward Courtroom 506, the bailiff intercepted her.

'Judge Birnbaum would like to see you right away.'

Alix's heart did a somersault. Maybe the US Attorney was finally willing to do a deal! Already she could taste that victory dinner.

She patted down her hair and swallowed a grin as the bailiff conducted her into the judge's chambers.

Bill Cairns and Judge Birnbaum were already there, as well as an older woman with cropped gray hair. Everyone looked grim. The judge didn't wait for Alix to sit down.

'Last night,' he announced in a shaky voice, 'between the hours of three and four, Rodney Gilchrist died in his cell of cardiac arrest.'

'I don't believe it!' Alix burst out.

It was impossible. Outrageous. Some kind of cover-up.

Suicide, yes. That she could understand. Or the kid's being murdered by a fellow-prisoner. But a heart attack?

'Dr Kendall is here to give you the details.'

Alix listened slack-jawed as the physician went through her paces, stressing the boy's weight, his poor condition, the stress he had been under, dispelling any possibility of foul play. 'The tragedy,' as Dr Kendall called it, 'was unforeseen, but not unimaginable. 'These things happen,' she concluded, 'sometimes without warning. However, in view of the young man's future, perhaps it's for the best.'

'For the best?' Alix and Bill shouted in unison.

For *whose* best? Alix was seething with rage. Not hers! She had been cheated. Robbed. On top of which she felt guilty for not having liked the kid more.

'How could he do this to me?' she cried. She wanted to hit

somebody – ideally, Rodney Gilchrist. 'How could he leave me high and dry? Jesus! I could kill him!'

'Not if I got my mitts on him first.' Bill Cairns brandished his fists in frustration. 'Six months' work down the drain.'

'That's enough!' Birnbaum raised his hand. 'If you two want to take it out on each other, fine. But you'll have to wait until I've dismissed the jury. Okay. In we go.'

'That's it?' Alix was incredulous.

After all she had been through – the drudgery, the sacrifices. And what about her closing argument? she wanted to scream. Huh? What about that, you goddamn kid? She'd sweated over every word till it was a fucking work of art. Now it would go forever undelivered.

'It's not fair!' she wailed. Bill grunted in agreement.

'Life isn't fair,' said the judge. 'Look, you've both done superb jobs these past four months. Never seen better lawyering. But it's over. Get that through your skulls.'

Eyes downcast, the two lawyers trailed Birnbaum into the courtroom. It was packed. The judge made a brief statement announcing Rodney Gilchrist's 'natural death.' No details, no more than two sentences in fact. He thanked the jury, then pounded his gavel. 'Case dismissed.'

In the few seconds before the shock fully registered, Alix and Bill exchanged glances, then tore out of the room like twin tornadoes. There was an ominous silence, followed by a sonic boom.

'Run!' Bill yelled, his voice almost drowned out by a fury of shouts and screams. The courtroom door burst open and out they poured: jurors, spectators, reporters waving notebooks and running for the phones.

'There they are!' a woman yelled. 'The lawyers!'

The human tide wheeled and came after them.

Alix panicked. 'Oh God! Bill – get me out of here.'

'This way!' He grabbed her hand and ran, propelling her this way and that, down a corridor, up a staircase, down another, the galloping herd behind them in hot pursuit. Bill turned a corner.

'In here!' He opened a door, shoved her in, then slammed it shut behind them. It was pitch dark, except for a sliver of light from the hall. A few feet away the stampede was thundering by, wave upon wave.

'Where are we?' Alix panted.

'Dunno!' He banged against something metallic. 'Ouch! I think it's a broom closet.'

She felt his breath on her neck. He was panting too. His breath made her hot.

'A broom closet! You're supposed to know your way around this place. We could be trapped here forever.'

The accumulated pain and shock swept over her. She started to weep out of sheer frustration.

The next thing she knew she was in Bill Cairns's arms and they were chewing each other's mouths in hot sloppy kisses.

'This is crazy!' He reached for her breast.

'You're telling me!' She grabbed at his fly.

'Shall we?' He had her up against the wall that vibrated with the trampling of feet.

'God yes!' She pulled him to her.

Never before had sex seemed so urgent. So logical. From anti-climax to climax. There was no other way this long ordeal could end. No other partner but William F. Cairns.

Ten minutes later, panting but sated, they untangled and began groping in the dark for clothes and combs.

'Listen!' Bill whispered.

Alix cocked her head. 'They've gone.'

Bill exhaled, then laughed that brisk sharp laugh of his. 'I've been thinking about this moment for months.'

'You have?' Alix was staggered.

'Since that day you showed up in that orangy dress with the lace collar.'

'Peach,' she said. 'It was a peach-colored dress.'

'God, you looked sexy. I could have devoured you then and there. How about you?'

Alix fumbled with her buttons. 'How about me what?'

'Did you ever think of me romantically?'

'This is *romantic*?'

'You know what I mean.'

'No ... yes ... maybe. Not in a broom closet, though. Definitely not in a broom closet.'

He kissed her. 'Yeah. It was good, though. Let's do it again.'

'Almost immediately. But not here.'

'Right! Blow the jailhouse stink off of us.'

'Yeah! The smell gets into your pores.'

'Well then – out of the closet . . .'

'And into the streets?'

'. . . and into the Plaza. A room with a view.'

'. . . with a bathtub built for two.'

'. . . and champagne . . .'

'. . . and smoked salmon sandwiches.'

'No television . . .'

'No newspapers . . .'

'Nothing but each other.'

'And tons of smoked salmon sandwiches.'

'Cost a fortune.'

'The smoked salmon?'

'The whole schmeer.'

'Fifty–fifty?'

'What else!'

Alix cracked open the door. The corridor was deserted.

'Let's make a dash for it.'

Bill laced up his shoes. 'Now!'

Like a pair of thieves, they scurried down a back staircase, through passageways Alix didn't know existed, and out a service entrance. Around the corner, Foley Square was packed with demonstrators. Sirens sounded every few seconds. For the swooners, was Alix's guess.

Bill hustled her into a cab.

'The Plaza,' he told the driver. 'It's an emergency.'

Safe inside, they fell upon each other like starvelings.

'Listen,' Alix breathed between kisses. 'There's something you should know.'

'Ummmmh . . .' he was nibbling her ear.

'I never date baseball players or lawyers.'

'Very sensible,' he murmured. They kissed some more. He fondled her thigh.

'My God,' he said. 'You're skinny as a pretzel.'

'What a thing to say!'

'I'm crazy about pretzels.'

'You're not married, are you, Bill?'

'Certainly not. Why, you interested?'

'I never date baseball players, lawyers or married men.'

She ran her fingers through his hair, happy to be here, not there, then kissed him some more.

'I would have won, you know,' she said when they came up for air.

'No way. I had you on the run.'

'I had this great closing statement . . .'

'Mine was an absolute doozy . . .'

Alix gazed out the window. It was a little past ten by the IBM clock on Madison Avenue. They had the whole lovely day ahead of them. The city looked chaste and pretty.

'Not that it matters.' She rubbed her cheek against his.

'Not that what matters?'

'Who would have come out on top. Because we'll never know now. Will we?'

'No, my sweet. We'll never know.'

SMITTY'S

Less than a mile from the Plaza Hotel where Alix Bryden and Bill Cairns were making love, Peter Mainwaring was in Smitty's Bar and Grill on Eighth Avenue. He had come with a mission. He planned to disappear completely into a bottle of Scotch and no one would ever find him again.

AU PARADIS

The twins were named Richard and Laura, each the image of the other, except in basic anatomical details. And gorgeous. As handsome as their handsome parents.

Tonio was over the moon. To show his gratitude, he bought his wife an emerald necklace from Cartier's and didn't go *near* the local brothels for another three weeks.

CLARIDGE'S

Miranda unpacked her suitcase, ordered lunch, then settled down with the British papers. What she saw made her grab for the phone.

She checked her watch. It was only seven in the morning in New York, but matters couldn't wait. Her first call was to Joel Baker of Surveilla-Systems. They spoke for twenty minutes, after which Miranda phoned her assistant at his home.

'Sorry to get you out of bed, Jim, but that new business venture you've been developing for me? The time has come. Got a pen handy?' She gave him a name, an address and a handful of instructions. 'Now I want his signature on the bottom of that contract before the week is out.'

'How high should I go?'

'Money's no object, though I don't think it will be much. He's not a greedy type. Talk about his unique talents, his professional pride, what a challenge this is, etcetera. And if all else fails' – she gave a nostalgic sigh – 'then appeal to his better nature. That ought to do it.'

PART THREE

The Eighties

SAN MIGUEL

The masses called her *Ladorita* and kissed her hems.

In the patois, the word had dual meanings. *La dorita* – The Golden Woman. *L'adorita* – She Who Is Adored.

Both definitions applied.

Her glorious blonde hair, her radiant face, the sweetness of her smile were on view at state occasions. Tall, gracious yet lovable, an icon of perfect posture and voluptuous curves, a-dazzle in white, gliding in and out of her bubble-topped Mercedes, Ladorita launched ships, opened charity drives, laid cornerstones, cut ribbons, visited hospitals, was on hand to see and be seen. Schools were named after her, as were soccer teams and toll roads and girl babies. To the populace, she occupied a place in the female hierarchy second only to the Queen of Heaven, before whose shrine, in the national cathedral, Ladorita placed fresh lilies during Holy Week.

It was a perfect piece of theater.

Thus it came about that Bette West's little girl – the actress who couldn't act, the singer who couldn't belt out a tune, the not-quite Miss America – at last found the role for which she was born: to be adored.

Ladorita, a.k.a. Kimberly West DuMesne.

'All I have to do,' she marveled, 'is to *be*!'

But while her public persona projected a virginal innocence, in private life she was opulent. Wherever they traveled (and the young couple traveled constantly to ski, to shop, to party), they entertained on a scale that evoked the Renaissance. To see Kim enter a ballroom, brilliantly gowned in Dior's latest, the milky arms and throat and ears weighted down with the DuMesne emeralds (or diamonds or pigeon's blood rubies), was a sight to make the most jaded jet-setters fall silent.

Still, as Kim was the first to admit, being a model of purity for the downtrodden masses while doubling as a model of style for the jet-set elite involved lots of hard work.

She was always up early to breakfast with the children before beginning her daily regimen. First an hour of aerobics, followed by another of massage, then it was time to wash, dress, get manicured and appropriately coiffed for such functions as were on her calendar that day.

Ever conscientious, Kim had finally attained the flawless grooming of her role models: Princess Grace and Evita Peron. She never complained about the effort it took, even though she had numerous other calls on her time. She was, in addition to Ladorita, Tonio's wife, Bette's daughter, and the mother of those two adorable children whose likenesses graced a special issue of postage stamps.

From the start, Kim relished her position and wealth. Now, five years on, living any other way was inconceivable. Yet though the novelty wore off, the thrill remained.

Sometimes, striding into an exclusive salon or three-star restaurant, seeing the staff grovel in their eagerness to serve, she would recall the thrift shops and dollar-a-slice pizza parlors of her youth. How times had changed! These days it was always *Yes, madame. Right away, madame. Madame has such exquisite taste.* When you were Ladorita with a billion-dollar fortune behind you, it was very hard to put a foot wrong.

Her life with Tonio had settled into a pattern. Kim remained the ideal wife, loyal, compliant, while Tonio continued in what she thought of as his 'compulsions.'

No matter. What couldn't be cured must be endured, and Kim consoled herself with the knowledge that her husband would never leave her as long as she continued to fulfill her role.

Over the years, she learned to rationalize his exploits. They involved his ego, not his heart. She was his wife, his true love, and though she abandoned all hope of recovering the innocent joy of her wedding night, she cared for him deeply. Tonio still had the capacity to charm. When his mood was sunny, he spoiled her as Napoleon had once spoiled Josephine.

On their first anniversary, Tonio had presented her with the deed to a luxurious mansion on Long Island's Gold Coast. 'In case you get homesick for the States.'

Every summer, when the rainy season arrived in San Miguel, the DuMesnes departed. They began their summer 'holiday' by spending a month apart.

The children went to France with their paternal grand-mother, Albertine, while Tonio took off for a hunting expedition in some exotic locale. He had a passion for blood sports that his wife did not share. Presumably the hunting party included female companions, but Kim asked no questions, preferring not to know. While he was pursuing jaguars in Brazil or rhino in Uganda, she returned to Marival with her mother.

Kim looked upon the clinic as a second home, a place to rest and loaf and repair the ravages of the previous year. There was always work to be done. Hormone treatments. Liposuction, for the twins' birth had wreaked havoc with Kim's figure, as had her love of rich food. And no one matched Dr Frankl's virtuosity in excising the signs of age with his scalpel.

Over the years, Kim had her buttocks lifted, tummy tucked, belly-button resculpted, the jawline firmed, the luscious mouth made more luscious with collagen.

The work was ongoing, with eternal youth as the goal. It was, after all, her meal ticket.

At the beginning of August, the family rendezvoused at the Villa Fiorentina, such being the name of the Long Island retreat.

With its swimming pools and formal gardens and a ballroom that held five hundred guests, the Old Brookville mansion, once the property of a railroad tycoon, was designed for entertaining. And entertain the DuMesnes did. Every August the villa's guest rooms and gardens were packed with movie stars and famous writers and Wall Street tycoons and what Tonio liked to call 'the plain old idle rich.' This was, after all, Gatsby country.

The DuMesnes enjoyed their month in America to the hilt, taking time off now and then, a holiday within a holiday, to visit Manhattan for theaters and shopping.

The last weekend in August, they threw what *Women's Wear Daily* defined as the 'glitziest' party of the season. A wallow of extravagance, each celebration (so Tonio decreed) had to surpass the ball of the previous summer.

To prepare for the event, a staff was retained all year round. Based in New York, this group consisted of a public relations expert whose duty was to draw up the guest list in keeping with who was hot and who was not; a famous restaurateur to plan the elaborate menus; and a theatrical producer to stage each entertainment as though it were a Broadway spectacular.

Each ball revolved around a theme, invariably lavish, be it the Last Days of Pompeii or the Court of Louis XIV or Chicago in the Roaring Twenties. Invitations were sent out two months in advance, to give the lucky recipients sufficient time to plan their most magnificent outfits, the most splendiferous gems, as befit the party's theme.

For Bette, the gala was the high point of her life. What bliss it was to entertain the celebrities and show-biz folk she couldn't get in to *see* a few years earlier. 'And the chow!' she exclaimed. 'My son-in-law must have bought out Petrossians.'

Kim's maid Celeste put it differently. 'So much food,' she remarked softly, while dressing 'milady' for the most recent ball. 'The cost of the caviar alone would be enough to feed all the children in Benedicta for a month.'

'Is that true?' Kim felt a twinge of anxiety.

'Yes, milady. It is.'

Sometimes when doing her mistress's hair, Celeste would volunteer such insights, terse but provocative, making Kim think

of Alix Bryden's admonishments. 'Be a force for the better,' Alix
had urged.

Kim liked to believe that she had made a difference. That by
setting an example of grace and serenity, she had brightened the
lot of the poor. At heart, she knew better.

She knew the masses lived in squalor. She had eyes, but her
effectiveness was limited. With no skills, no expertise, what could
she do other than fulfill her ceremonial role? Bette constantly
warned her to steer clear of politics.

Sometimes her conscience nagged. It tweaked that night,
triggered by Celeste's remark, as she watched mountains of caviar
and lakes of Dom Perignon disappear down the gullets of the
rich. While in the slums of Benedicta, children starved.

That year's ball was, the columnists agreed, the best yet, and
Tonio was delighted. A few days later, the DuMesnes flew home
in their private jet for another winter of pomp and ceremony.

'Some cushy job, huh, kid?' Bette jabbed Kim in the ribs as
their plane made its descent. Below them, the red carpet was out,
the brass band was striking up, the school children were waving
flags. Even the palm trees seemed to sway with the beat. 'Who
would've thunk it when we were back in Mechanicsville!'

Kim smiled, and checked her make-up. Who indeed! And
yet . . .

And yet some aspects of her life were unchanged.

Bette, for instance.

Though Kim had now been married five years, her mother
still stage-managed her life. She supervised Kim's wardrobe,
vetted her speeches, told her which invitations to accept and
which to turn down.

'My staff can handle all that,' Kim complained, but Bette
loved to let it be known that she was indispensable and that she
operated with Tonio's approval.

Her mother and her husband! Kim used to joke that it was a

'conspiracy,' but recently the joke had gone flat. Though nearing thirty, Kim had no autonomy. She yearned to be something more than a wind-up doll. She thought of Alix and felt shame.

Shortly after her return, Kim visited one of the great sugar plantations. She was horrified to discover that the men who worked them were yoked together, like oxen, in the burning sun.

She mentioned it to Tonio that evening over dinner. No business of his, he said. The plantation was US-owned.

'The thing is, Tonio, it's not a pretty sight for the tourists. Couldn't you issue some kind of official regulation forbidding it?'

Tonio found the notion humorous.

'What a tender-hearted creature you are,' he said. 'But the workers don't mind. They're bred to it, my dear. They have slave mentalities. They don't even speak our language, you know.'

Our language: French and English. By now, Kim was equally at home in both. But later, thinking about Tonio's remark, she realized it was he who didn't speak *their* language. The patois. The language of the poor. Tonio had never bothered to learn it.

The more she thought about it, the more remarkable it seemed. Here she was living in her adopted country, beloved, almost worshipped, yet cut off from the very folk who adored her. She could smile and bow and christen ships and make little speeches in French. Yet there was no real communication.

That morning, while Celeste was brushing her hair, Kim sounded her out.

'Tell me, Celeste, do you speak the patois?'

'Why of course, milady.'

'I would like to learn. Would you teach it to me?'

'Oh, milady.' Celeste's eyes were bright and wide. 'I am not capable of such a job. I can hardly read and write. But I have a cousin . . . my cousin Maxim.'

'Yes?'

'He is brilliant, my cousin. A university student. A wonderful teacher. Maxim will be happy to instruct you.'

Kim brooded for a minute.

'Very good,' she said. 'But I don't want to trouble my husband with petty details. Perhaps Maxim could come in the mornings while you do my hair, and tutor me for an hour or so.'

'Very good, milady. He will be here tomorrow.'

Kim was pleased that she had managed to arrange this without help from Tonio or Bette. It made her feel quite independent.

HOLLYWOOD

'Scriptwriting,' S. J. Perelman once said, 'is no worse than playing piano in a whorehouse.' A sentiment with which Peter Mainwaring happily concurred.

For all the clichés of his situation – Peter was overpaid, underworked and did his heaviest thinking by the swimming pool – he found the life enjoyable. He liked the climate, the cuisine and much of the company, though he generally avoided the 'British colony' as being a tad too English for his tastes.

And, oh yes, he liked the pay. Amazing how much heavy money could be derived from writing lightweight screenplays. The BBC – bless 'em – had never been so lavish with funds. And though he had lived comfortably in London, his present circumstances were, by comparison, positively sybaritic. A house in the hills. A swimming pool in the shape of a swimming pool. A Porsche. And an Oscar. Who could ask for anything more?

Other people could, of course, and did, this being a town of creative consumption, but Peter's attitude was 'let them.' Enough was even better than a feast.

After the emotional assaults that had begun with Annie's death, he was content to live on the surface of things. Not to feel, but to be. The secret of happiness surely lay in forgetting the past and not taking the present seriously. This profundity came to him as he unfurled his long legs on the striped yellow chaise, a piña colada within easy reach, and availed himself of the California sunshine.

The day was sublime, the air sweet with the scent of camellias. He shut his eyes. The sun lapped his skin in a gentle tide, while on the stereo Miles Davis was doing nice things to a Cole Porter tune. Above his head a dragonfly was buzzing, but Peter didn't bother to brush it away. Live it up and let live was his motto.

Drowsing in the afternoon heat, he was at peace. How benign the world could be! And to think it almost didn't happen!

Even years later, he couldn't reflect on that fateful evening without a retrospective sense of awe.

He was in Smitty's that night. In fact he was always at Smitty's, where he had staked out a corner of the bar as his private turf. It was the only place to be on those wintry New York nights when the weather was foul and all you wanted was to crawl inside a nice warm bottle of booze.

What a winter it had been! Sleet and snow, howling winds and sub-freezing temperatures. The ice outside had matched the ice within his soul. Looking back, he knew it for the low point of his life, a non-stop inebriated blur. The wonder was that he'd survived – let alone flourished.

There was the night he had left Smitty's falling-down drunk, then proceeded to pass out in a lonely alley. He could have frozen to death. But damned if some unknown samaritan didn't spot him and get him safe home. Piece of luck. Almost enough to make a man believe in fairy godmothers. Which of course Peter didn't, being a rational person.

Then there was that horrendous moment when Peter stumbled into the path of a moving taxi. He would have been killed, probably should have been, except that some total stranger managed to pull him out of harm's way.

And they say New Yorkers are a hard-hearted lot!

However, to go back to the night in question—

Peter was in Smitty's as usual, getting drunk, as usual, feeling very sorry for himself when a blond-haired young man in a Brooks Brothers suit sat down on the adjacent stool. He looked absurdly out of place.

'You're Peter Mainwaring, aren't you?'

Peter acknowledged he was.

'Thank God! I had a hell of a time finding you. I'm on a deadline, you see.'

The newcomer appeared nervous, like a college kid first time out of the box. He spoke in a polite drawl, introducing himself as Jim Bisseau of MiraCo. It was an international investment firm.

'Never heard of it,' Peter grumbled. He wished the fellow would shut up and leave him alone, but instead the young man ordered a round of drinks.

Over bourbon and water, Bisseau informed Peter that his company had recently expanded into film financing. They had put up money for a screwball comedy starring Judi Syme.

'Are you familiar with her work?' the young man asked, anxiously.

Peter shrugged. 'I haven't been living on Mars.'

As it happened, Syme was the brightest new comedienne since Goldie Hawn, but how that concerned Peter, he couldn't fathom.

'Splendid! We ... I ... by *we* I mean my boss, who is the world's toughest customer and a huge fan of yours. Anyhow, my boss wants you to do the screenplay and that's that.'

'Zat so?' Peter mumbled and returned to his drink.

Bisseau confessed that he was new on the job and finding it hard sledding. 'Anyhow, I'm supposed to have you signed, sealed and delivered to Los Angeles on the morning plane in time for a two p.m. story meeting.'

'Why me? I've never written for the cinema.' In fact, he

hadn't written anything in nearly a year. By now, he must have lost the knack. 'I'm flattered of course, Mr Bisseau —'

'Please call me Jim.'

'But I'm afraid the answer is no.'

Jim didn't give up. For the next hour, he pleaded, reasoned and cajoled. There were references to money and contracts and something called 'points.' Mention was made of artistic challenge and professional pride, which made Peter smile.

He seemed a nice enough young fellow, if verbose, and though Peter was sorry to hurt his feelings, he had no intention of going to Hollywood, thank you very much. He had made other plans for his life: mainly booze.

'Don't you understand the word *no*?' Peter asked wearily, signalling the bartender for fresh drinks.

The young man looked crestfallen. 'You really meant that?'

'Yes! I mean, yes I mean *no*.'

'Oh, God!' Jim buried his head in his hands.

'Cheer up, my boy. It's not the end of the world.'

'It is for me. What'll I tell Amy?' he moaned.

'Who's Amy?'

'My girl, my fiancée, actually. Most wunnerful girl in the world. She'll be crushed when she hears. What is it about me, Mr Mainwaring —'

'Peter.'

'What is it, Peter? I fail at everything. I'm a total flop on the career front . . . a rotten salesman . . . can't hang on to a job. This will be the third time I've struck out since Amy and I got engaged. Sorry.' He blew his nose on a cocktail napkin. 'I didn't mean to drag up my personal problems . . . don't usually drink much. Except that it's just hell having to disappoint her – yet again! God, why on earth should she want to marry such a loser?' He looked ready to burst into tears.

'You're not a loser.' Peter tried to comfort him. 'You made an excellent presentation. The fault's not yours, it's mine, for giving you such a hard time.'

But Jim was inconsolable.

'The thing is, Peter, I'm crazy about her. I mean if you've ever been nuts about someone,' he said, 'if you've ever really put your heart on the line . . .'

Despite himself Peter was touched. Such a nice lad, Peter thought. And so very much in love. It made him nostalgic.

'And hanging on to your job will make the difference?'

'All the difference in the world.'

'In other words, my name on a contract.'

Jim nodded ordered another round of drinks.

'I'd like to oblige, Jimbo, but I don't think I can be funny any more,' Peter said. 'The world's a very serious place. I mean, how can you make other people laugh if you can't laugh yourself?'

'Dunno!'

Jim reached for a pretzel and took a Groucho Marx dive off the bar stool.

Laughing, Peter picked him up off the floor.

Quite how it happened after that Peter couldn't swear – they were both terribly drunk. Well, Peter certainly was, though after the fact he had had his doubts about Jim Bisseau. Who stuck around just long enough to pour Peter on to an early morning flight to Los Angeles and was never heard from again.

In fact, the whole thing smacked of a set-up, but no matter. The challenge turned out to be just what he needed.

By the next afternoon Peter Mainwaring was back in business, his brain champing at the bit after its enforced vacation.

With the success of *Smart Money*, his first feature film, Peter's life had turned around. These days he had all the work he could handle. And all the sunshine and flowers too.

The past was, though not forgotten, at least laid to rest, and the future was immeasurably pleasant.

As Peter dozed off, he thought for the hundredth time how

lucky he was that Jim Bisseau had found him that night and shipped him here. It was a fate better than death.

'Hey, lazybones.' She kissed him on the ear. She smelled of perfume and spice.

Peter rolled over and gazed into that sunny face.

'Hello, darling.' He smiled up at Judi Syme. 'I'm glad you're home.'

OLD WESTBURY

Money, Miranda knew, could work wonders.

Already her fortune had saved Peter from himself, endowed animal shelters in New York and Chicago, assisted unwed mothers, provided scholarships in the arts and sciences. The one thing money couldn't do was control the subconscious.

The dream – for it was really just the one, unchanging, recurrent – might begin at any point in the sequence: in the café, on the gravel path, at the crossroads, but the ending was always the same. Pure terror. The knife at her throat. *And the man.* Sometimes she could feel the heat of his breath.

Lately, the images had grown sharper, clearer, like a camera gradually being pulled into focus. Sometimes, she thought she could make out his features, though they faded by the time she awoke. Not his eyes, though. Black, glowing, deepset. Nor the sleek hair. Those impressions managed to survive the dawn.

She never knew what would trigger off the dream: a face in the crowd, a snatch of music, the pungent smell of French cigarettes. Sometimes it vanished for weeks on end; at other times it visited her night after night.

What disturbed Miranda was that the dream led a life of its own over which she had no control. She tried to think of it as an insidious poison that was working its way out of her system. Once it did, she would be cured.

For the rest, Miranda had no complaints. Business was excellent. She traveled, dressed well, patronized the best restaurants, saw all the new shows. She was never lonely, for her cats and dogs were a source of infinite companionship. Coming home from a day at the office, all she had to do was put her key in the door and her 'fan club' tumbled out to greet her, tails wagging, noses wet with excitement. Bless 'em! They knew how to make one feel cherished.

Not that Miranda had anything against people, but animals were better companions: loyal, playful, patient, affectionate. They kept you warm on chilly nights, didn't haggle and never welshed on a deal.

Miranda loved them all.

Her neighbors, however, often complained, and she had trouble keeping staff. The menagerie was outgrowing her apartment. Miranda decided to buy a country retreat.

'I want a place for my pets as well as myself,' she informed the realtor. 'Somewhere they can run free.'

Mrs Connor knew just the house. A Frank Lloyd Wright jewel from the 1920s. Clean, sleek, modern, three acres of privacy.

'Stables, kennels, a dog run,' the agent crooned as she showed the property. For Miranda it was love at first sight. As they walked, she began furnishing the rooms in her head.

'And you'll have very fashionable neighbors,' the realtor added as a clincher. 'The young DuMesne family. They own that enormous mansion on the hill. Villa Fiorentina, it's called.'

Miranda wheeled around.

'Do you mean Tonio and Kimberly DuMesne of San Miguel?'

'The same. Do you know them?'

Did she know them? The blood rushed to Miranda's ears. *Did she know the woman who had saved her life?*

The real estate agent was smiling blithely, unaware that her client was in the midst of an anxiety attack. The years in business had trained Miranda to conceal her emotions behind a bland façade. Her mastery of body language was complete, but her mind was in turmoil.

How could it be, after all this time, that she arrived at this very spot? Coincidence? Impossible. Miranda didn't believe in random chance. Such juxtaposition had to be more than just the luck of the draw. It was fate – an inexorable destiny that had brought her to this place. The past was demanding its due.

Her memory sped back to Marival. What if, in a chance encounter, Kimberly West should recognize her? She would be exposed, unveiled. All her secrets thrown to the wind.

Then suddenly – it was like a weight being lifted from her heart – she realized that Kimberly had never learned her name. Besides, their encounter had taken place early in her stay at Marival. Before Miranda had a face. A voice.

Miranda Vee was safe! Safe behind her mask. Safe as houses, as the expression went. Safe enough to meet her new neighbors.

If there was a providence in all this, it lay not in the exposure of her past, but along some other line. Perhaps, she speculated, there was some service she might render. Some opportunity to repay the ancient debt.

Miranda's heartbeat calmed.

Why not? she thought. It would be fascinating to see her savior in this milieu. To meet her husband. Observe their lives. To move among them. To know – and not be known.

Miranda turned to the realtor with a cryptic expression.

'I'm sorry,' she said in a casual voice, 'but I'm afraid I've never had the pleasure of their acquaintance. Now as for this house –'

'Perhaps we can get the owner to come down on the price a bit,' Mrs Connor broke in, sensing difficulties.

But for once, Miranda was in no mood to haggle.

'Sold as is!' she said with a smile.

COBBLE HILL

Marrying Bill Cairns was the right move at the right time. Alix never regretted proposing.

'A man with political ambitions needs a wife and child and someone to scratch his back at the end of the day,' she argued. 'Besides, we're so fond of each other.'

'That's one way of putting it.' They were lounging in bed at the time, doing what Bill called 'fondly fondling.' 'But you have to promise not to do the "little woman" number.'

'And what exactly does a "little woman" do?'

'They cook and play bridge and crochet antimacassars.'

'I don't even know what antimacassars are.'

'Well, that's a step in the right direction.'

They explored the proposition thoroughly, like the two smart people they were, came to terms, agreed on the place (City Hall) and the date (a month away), and decided upon a small reception at Windows on the World, to be financed fifty–fifty.

'Though it's not quite fair,' Alix mused. 'You have this humongous family and I only have Saman—'

'That's crap!' Bill broke in. 'You have a father, brothers, a step-mother. Invite the lot. In fact, it would be a nice gesture if you asked your old man to give you away.'

'My father gave me away ages ago,' she said bitterly.

In the end, Mr Rabinowitz did the honors.

Of necessity, Alix had confided bits and pieces of her life: her childhood disfigurement, Marival, the break with Lucius Bryden, the fact that Samantha was born out of wedlock. She skimped on details, however, and never mentioned Sam Matthews by name. Bill was a public prosecutor, she reminded herself, and Sam was still a fugitive.

Bill himself came from a large, close family. 'More of a clan, actually – like the Kennedys. Only poorer.'

Like the Kennedys too, Bill nurtured ambitions. Upon graduating from Columbia, he had clerked for a Supreme Court justice, and maintained connections in both Washington and New York. His current position was intended to serve as a launching pad for elected office, hence his pursuit of high-profile cases. He had his eye on the State House or the Senate, whichever opened up first. Meanwhile, he waited and planned.

His parents ran a marina in City Island and lived nearby in a rambling frame house large enough to serve as a meeting place for Bill's brothers, sisters, nieces and nephews, as well as visiting friends and local pols from the Democratic party.

There was always beer in the fridge, cold-cuts on a sideboard, stacks of magazines, a no-breed dog or two underfoot and, spread out on a table in the den, a thousand-piece jigsaw puzzle to which any passerby could add the odd piece. Alix supposed there was method in this messiness and Bill himself was very organized. He organized desk drawers, basketball games (he was a nut for sports), law dockets and theater parties. He organized Alix as well.

The first time he visited her office on Fourteenth Street, he threw his hands up in mock horror. The place was a rabbit warren, he declared, crowded and crummy. Why did she put up with such squalor? She was making a fortune.

'I am not,' she protested, which merely confirmed his suspicion that she had no financial judgment.

He himself was keenly conscious of the cost of things, having come from a family with a surplus of everything except money.

296

Bill had worked his way through law school playing saxophone in a dance band and kidded that if he ever lost his job, he could always scrounge a living doing bar-mitzvahs. He was appalled at Alix's mismanagement.

Once the idea entered his head, nothing would do but that Alix leave Fourteenth Street and rent a smart set of offices in a glass-and-steel skyscraper in Hanover Square. 'You'll attract a better class of criminal,' he said. 'It's good business sense.'

After they married, they bought a turn-of-the-century brownstone in Brooklyn's Cobble Hill. It was a pleasant neighborhood, in the process of being 'gentrified' (which was also good business sense) and convenient to the courts, if you weren't too proud to ride the subway.

Everyone should live in a house, Bill felt, particularly families bringing up kids. Which was Alix's cue to do what she'd been thinking about for years: have another baby.

The child was christened Thomas Jefferson Cairns, which Alix thought had a lovely ring and Bill said would be a good name if the boy ever decided to run for office.

Soon after, she was back at work full throttle. Marriage hadn't dampened her professional drive; being a lawyer was how she defined herself. Though some adjustments were necessary – never again could she appear in court opposite Bill – her career continued to thrive. Bill was right. She was getting a better class of criminal these days.

After hours too, they led a crowded life: he loved sports, she loved opera, he learned to play chess, she learned to swim. On most matters they compromised, though they wrangled merrily at dinner parties for the sheer joy of debate.

To their friends, Alix and Bill came across as an updated version of the Tracy/Hepburn legend: smart, sassy, competitive, yet crazy in love beneath it all. The model of what a two-career marriage should be.

In fact, there was both more and less to their relationship than the image conveyed. Despite the bickering, they shared similar taste and values. They were both honorable people. They made each other laugh. Their union was marked by affection, kindness, loyalty and respect. What it lacked was grand passion.

Alix had wanted a home. Bill had wanted a family. They were at that time of life when romantic illusions had waned.

As a marriage of convenience, it succeeded very well. She liked Bill. Enormously. Loved him even. They got along fine. The trouble was, she wasn't *in* love with him, not head over heels. Not in that great savage, searing way that left cleat marks on your heart. Not the way it had been with Sam.

The feeling – or lack of it – was mutual, she presumed, for Bill, despite his eloquence in court, was not given to romantic effusions. Still – he was a good companion, a doting father and a faithful husband. What more could one ask?

Samantha was delighted with this turn of events. The former first-grade pariah was now fitted out with a proper father, a house, a baby brother – to say nothing of a wealth of cousins and aunts and uncles, courtesy of the City Island clan. Returning from a Sunday dinner at the Cairns', Samantha squeezed her mother's hand and giggled. 'It's nice being normal people.'

Bill and Alix both laughed.

Alix had toned down over recent years, but the times had changed too. The nation's mood had moved away from the passions and upheavals of the Vietnam era. The rhetoric had faded, and along with it the notion of saving the world. Goals had become more private, pragmatic.

Whether it was marriage or the house or the second baby, or simply that she was over thirty, her life had entered an era of smooth sailing.

Sometimes, she would glimpse herself in the mirror – nicely turned out in a Harve Benard suit, hair in a neat blunt cut (Bill liked it that way), shoes polished, fingernails too – would size herself up and say, 'Ye gawd, Alix Bryden. You've become a member of the establishment.'

Not that Alix was rich, though she ought to have been in light of the fees she commanded, but to Bill's dismay, money continued to stream out of the office as fast as it came in. Much of it was spent on what he called her 'extended family,' meaning those luckless clients for whom she remained a soft touch.

More of a political animal himself, Bill rarely got caught up in lost causes, his normal stance being a certain cautious irony. Mostly he kept his troubles to himself, though sometimes when the mood was upon him, he would disappear into the attic to noodle on his saxophone in a bluesy isolation. It was better, he said, than beating his wife.

Just as Bill dreamed of office, Alix too enjoyed her fantasies. One of her favorites was an image of herself as lady of leisure. On occasion, particularly if she had had a drink too many or been suckered in by a house-and-garden spread in the *Sunday Times*, Alix would declare she was fed up with the law.

'Who needs it? The responsibility, the grind, the *agita*. I think I'll pack it all in, stay home, grow roses, run up curtains, all that jazz. Have more babies. Learn to bake bread. That's supposed to be very satisfying. Ryes, pumpernickel, Alaskan sourdoughs. Those wonderful smells coming out of the oven . . .'

'Right,' Bill said. He was too good-natured to squelch her Earth Mother fantasies, too polite to point out that she was a disaster in the kitchen. He also knew the mood would pass.

The next morning, Alix would rise at the usual hour, dress, grab her briefcase and be raring to go.

And though she never did get around to baking bread or running up curtains, she was nonetheless a woman to be envied. Her career was thriving. Her children were adorable. Her husband a prince. What more could any reasonable woman ask for?

One day in early spring, Alix returned from lunch to check her phone messages. She was feeling great, basking in the glory of the recently concluded Choirboy Murder trial. Not only had the outcome been all she desired and the publicity phenomenal, she had even got a congratulatory note from the Vatican.

'Now you really have friends in high places,' Bill had teased that morning.

Still smiling at the memory, Alix thumbed through the pink slips on her desk. Mostly old clients, nothing urgent. She looked forward to a quiet afternoon.

'Who's this?' she asked Teri. 'A Mr Hap Mendelssohn?'

'He phoned three times this morning,' Teri said. 'Said it was urgent, but he didn't leave a number. I think he was calling from a phone booth. In trouble with the law is my bet.'

Alix shrugged. 'So what else is new? Did he say what kind of trouble?'

'Only that it's heavy stuff. He sounded real panicky. I asked, did he want an appointment but he's afraid to come to the office. He says it's life and death. Could you meet him at' – she checked her note pad – 'the Acropolis Café on West Twenty-first? He says he'll wait for you for however long it takes.'

'Jesus!' Alix sighed. 'Clients. The next thing you know they'll be wanting room service.'

She had had requests like that before. It could be some kid shouting wolf, or it could be some person at the end of his tether. Either way, she felt an obligation.

'Yeah . . . okay.' She flipped through the rest of her messages: nothing that couldn't wait. May as well put Mr Mendelssohn out of his misery. She freshened her lipstick.

'Right,' Alix said. 'If he calls again, tell him I'm on my way. By the way, how will I recognize him?'

'He said he'll recognize you.'

But the question turned out to be academic. For when Alix walked into the Acropolis Café, there he was. Big as life and twice as dangerous.

Sam Houston Matthews.

AU PARADIS

Every morning at ten, Maxim Brunel came to tutor Kim in the patois.

At Celeste's suggestion, the young man was listed on his visitor's pass as a t'ai chi instructor, that being the kind of personal service least likely to attract attention. He looked the part well enough.

Slender and tall, with soft hazel eyes and softer brown hair that tumbled over his forehead, Maxim had the freshness of the student about him. When he spoke he gestured with graceful hands which Kim came to think of as 'artist's hands.' She found him gentle and attractive.

He began by instructing Kim in the patois – its vocabulary and grammar and idiom – and ended by teaching her about her adopted home. As Kim's mastery of the patois grew apace, so did her knowledge of San Miguel. Seen through Maxim's eyes it was another country.

His was a San Miguel that never appeared in the press or the travel brochures, a place that Kim had only glimpsed from behind the smoked glass of a limousine. An island magical and frightening, where poverty dwelt in the midst of plenty, a land of primitive beliefs and political ferment. Maxim was eloquent, able to evoke a culture in powerful vignettes.

They read poetry together, the throbbing folk poetry of the plantations. He sang her the plaintive music of the mountain tribes, the shanties of the fishermen. He spoke of things seen in his travels: weavers plying ancient skills, unlettered peasants hoeing the land with wooden sticks, mud-hut villages where women suckled farm animals, and urban slums where children died of rickets. He told her tales of hardship and bravery among the simple that made her weep.

301

As they came to know each other better, Maxim related more intimate stories, his voice thick with emotion: how many of his closest friends – students, writers, poets – had vanished without warning, never to be heard from again.

'But why?' Kim wanted to know.

Because they wrote, they tried to publish, they spoke their minds freely, 'even as I now speak to you.'

If one morning Maxim should fail to appear, Kim would understand and, for her own sake, make no inquiries. To do so was to ask for trouble. Why, his presence here today might be construed as an act of treason.

'I can't believe that,' Kim said. Yet once Maxim had opened her eyes, she looked about her with new clarity.

One day, he told her about the old religion.

'In Haiti, the faith is known as voodoo. In the West Indies, it is obeah. In Brazil, macumba . . . santaria. These are the old African beliefs that reach back farther and deeper than your Catholicism, milady. Practices and rituals that came here with the first slaves and took root. Everything else is an overlay. Here in San Miguel we have our own version, *chichanga*, which is similar to voodoo but with one significant difference.'

To the faithful, chichanga (the word originated in the savannahs of Dahomey) presented a world ruled by spirits, some evil, some benign. There was Wangal, the Master of the Earth; Ogoun, the God of Fire; Damballa, the Serpent-Deity; Uxman, the Pig-God; Baron Samedi who guarded the spirits of the dead – and dozens more. These old gods, more potent than the saints of the Christian calendar, dwelled intimately among the people of San Miguel, inhabiting each hearth, home and soul. They governed one's destiny.

To appease these spirits and channel their powers for the good, there were elaborate rituals involving music, dance, animal sacrifice and the drinking of potent herbal concoctions. Such ceremonies might go on for days, under the guidance of the *hougans* or sorcerers, until the celebrants, in a state of physical and emotional exhaustion, fell into a trance, thence into a paroxysm of religious ecstasy. In this frenzied state, the spirits were invoked and entered the bodies of the worshippers. Then wondrous things happened: simple people could speak in tongues, walk on coals, commune with the dead, become one with all nature. It was the very culmination of chichanga.

Kim was fascinated. 'Do *you* believe in chichanga, Maxim?'

He smiled. 'They say that San Miguel is only ninety per cent Catholic but one hundred per cent chichanga. It's true. It is the national religion.'

At that, Kim had to smile.

'You're in error there, my friend. My in-laws are devoutly Catholic. In fact, when my husband and I were in Rome on our honeymoon, we had an audience with the pope. What could be more Catholic than that?'

It was Maxim's turn to smile, as though privy to some fine secret. Kim fretted. Was he saying her husband's family practiced chichanga? She tried to picture El Tigre slitting the throat of a sacrificial animal. It was an image too easily arrived at. She tried to picture Tonio – and shuddered.

'You said,' she pursued, 'that there was one significant difference between chichanga and voodoo. What is it, Maxim?'

'It is the myth of the Golden Goddess.'

A blade of fear pierced her heart.

'The Golden Goddess?'

'In the religion of chichanga, she will come from the north, from the land of snow and ice and bring happiness to the land. There is a chant that is sung in her honor.'

He sang in his haunting baritone. It was a strange melody.

> 'She is fair of face as she is fair of heart.
> Her hair is made of the sun,
> Her skin is of snow.
> Her eyes are the blossoms of the massala tree.
> Her feet are the feathers of the white dove.

She will bring you peace and wealth and many sons.
Blessings drip from her golden hands.'

Maxim stopped singing and the room fell quiet.

Kim was stunned.

'The massala tree – what color are its blossoms?'

'They are violet, milady.'

Like her eyes!

This goddess — She wanted to ask, but did not dare. *Does she have a name?* Though in her heart, Kim knew the answer.

The goddess was Ladorita. The Golden One. She Who Is Adored.

That night, Kim couldn't sleep.

Was it possible that Tonio had selected her from a host of swimsuit beauties, had wooed and won her – not out of romantic passion but as part of a calculated plan? Could it be that she had been cast as carefully as any Hollywood star to fill a leading role in the drama of his family's reign?

Pretty blondes were plentiful, but few had violet eyes.

If so, then this harsh truth explained a great deal. Certain oddities fell into place. Why Tonio insisted she wear white in public. Why he emphasized her beauty and youth. Why he put her on a pedestal while he himself cavorted with whores.

Upon his father's death, Tonio would be the Benefactor, and she would sit by his side. Not just a wife, but a kind of insurance policy, a guarantee of virtue, to be trotted out in public when the natives got restless.

She was, after all, a divine being. Ladorita. Loved by the multitude, as the DuMesnes themselves were feared. And that they were feared, Kim had no doubt.

But a few weeks earlier, on Army Day, there had been an attempt on the life of El Tigre during the course of a parade. The assassination, mercifully, had gone awry, but since then Tonio had taken to wearing a revolver.

'We live in dangerous times, my pet,' he told Kim.

The gun accompanied him everywhere: to church, to parties, sporting events, on country drives. Upon retiring, he unholstered it and placed it, cocked and ready, on the night table.

Kim hated it, as she hated everything that had to do with violence.

One night, when Tonio came to her bed, he placed the dark dead thing across her belly. There it rested, black and evil against the white of her flesh. 'Get it off me,' she cried. 'Please . . . put it away!'

Tonio smiled. 'It won't hurt unless fired.'

Then he did a curious thing. He picked up the gun and gently slid the barrel between her legs. She felt the shock of cold steel playing against her clitoris. Then slowly slowly, Tonio edged the shaft into her vagina.

It was thrilling. Loathsome. Terrifying. Kim was paralyzed. She lay there frozen for what seemed like an eternity, while the gun slithered in and out like an enormous black viper. To her horror, her body flooded in orgasm.

Then Tonio laughed and withdrew the weapon. It came out glistening with her juices.

'My God!' She was trembling uncontrollably. 'Is it loaded?'

'Of course it's loaded, darling.'

Then he put the barrel in his mouth. For a wild instant Kim thought he was going to kill himself out of shame for what he had done, but instead he licked it off as though it were a candy cane, the tongue darting to lap up the last drop of fluid. Then he replaced it on the night table.

'Were you afraid?' he asked softly, but with a lethal smile. 'How foolish! Why should I even think of hurting my loving . . . loyal . . . faithful wife. Provided she *remains* my faithful wife.'

From that night on, Kim walked with fear.

*

For weeks after, Kim brooded about leaving Tonio. She would take her children and her jewels and go some place where her husband could not reach her.

But where could she hide? What would she do? And what about Bette? The more she thought about it, the more absurd the notion became. She doubted if she could get as far as the airport. Her marriage was, as Bette once said in her execrable French, a *fate accompli*. And Kim still believed in the sanctity of her vows.

Yet the incident with the gun made Kim look outward in a way she hadn't done before. Whatever her feelings toward Tonio, to the populace of San Miguel, Kim was still Ladorita – the Golden One – with all the obligations that entailed.

Knowledge was power. And now that she had the knowledge of the patois, Kim had a direct line to her people. Now she began cautiously to use that power. To discover for herself the real San Miguel Maxim had told her about.

With Celeste by her side, she visited tenements and mines and rural cottages, listening to grievances, offering sympathy and understanding, bringing gifts of food and money and toys.

The next day, in a flush of enthusiasm, she would confide her impressions of what she had seen to Maxim, eager to win his approbation. Indeed, she was halfway to falling in love with the dashing young poet if for no other reason than that he was everything Tonio was not: sweet and warm and sympathetic.

For the first time since her marriage, Kim was exercising some independence, deciding for herself where she would go, whom she would see. Tonio knew of her wanderings, but didn't take them seriously. On the contrary, he appeared pleased.

'That trip to the mines was a stroke of genius, my darling.' He pecked her on the cheek. 'Public relations at its finest.'

Kim lowered her eyes and thought of the gun thrust between her legs. Private relations. The shock was still fresh.

*

Kim never told Bette of the gun incident, knowing in advance what her mother's position would be: *Don't rock the boat unless you're wearing a life-saver.*

To Kim, it was a perpetual source of disappointment that Bette never backed her in any conflict with Tonio, but persisted in treating her like a child, though the child was now thirty.

As a form of minor revenge, Kim liked to bait her mother by carrying on conversations in patois right under her nose. It drove her mother wild; Bette loathed being shut out of anything.

'I don't understand a word of that gibberish,' she would say crossly. 'Why can't you speak English like everyone else?'

And Kim would smile her one-up smile.

Before long, however, the zest went out of the game. Bette had not been well. First she complained of headaches, then of pains in her joints. Always thin and wiry, she had begun to lose weight, though she loved quoting Babe Paley to the effect that one could never be too rich or too slim. Yet she was worried.

'I don't know what it is, popsie,' she said to Kim, 'but I don't seem to have my old vim and vigor.'

'Well, what do the doctors say?'

'Pah!' Bette waved the notion away contemptuously. 'I don't want to badmouth San Miguel, but this is not exactly the medical center of the universe. If you ask me, these jokers don't know their ass from their elbow macaronis.'

Kim wondered if perhaps the doctors had told Bette something she preferred not to hear.

'Maybe you should see the hougan, Mom.'

'The who-whats?'

'The hougan . . . the *curandero*. You know, the witch doctors. I understand they can do fabulous things with herbal cures, often better than Park Avenue MDs.'

Maxim had told her of their powers, how they worked upon the mind as well as the body, and instituted miraculous cures.

Bette, however, remained skeptical.

'I understand they cover you in all kinds of disgusting stuff and make you drink cat piss. No, toots. Let's hope it's all in the head, menopause or whatever. If I ignore it, it'll go away. Mind over matter.'

But Tonio too was alarmed, insisting that his own physician give Bette a thorough examination and report to him.

'Your mother has a rare form of leukemia,' Tonio told Kim. 'Regrettably, our hospitals can't handle it. I want you to take her to the Carnegie Clinic in New York for treatment. It's the best in the world.'

But Bette refused to budge. She had a bridge tournament scheduled, a charity ball, this or that important dinner party. The Duchess of Kent was coming to San Miguel, as were Mick Jagger and Roxanne Pulitzer in what promised to be the most brilliant social season in a decade.

'Leave now?' Bette said. 'Not on your life!'

Nor on hers.

With a zeal bordering upon the superhuman, she flung herself into every social item on the calendar, determined to milk every last drop out of life. Frustrated, Kim watched her mother wasting away, turning grayer, dryer, more shriveled every day, even as she danced and partied. But not until the last of the notables had departed did Bette agree to go to New York.

They would travel without fuss or fanfare, as Mrs and Miss West, illness being a private affair. While Bette was in the clinic, Kim was to stay a few blocks away at the consulate, where Tonio maintained a flat.

No, Tonio said firmly, in answer to his wife's request, the children were not to accompany her. 'What would they do in New York, darling, except get under your feet?'

The night before she left, he took all her jewels and placed them in his safe.

'What would you want with jewels in New York, lamb? It's a city of thieves.'

Even had Kim still been planning to make her 'escape,' Tonio effectively insured against it.

The morning she left, Kim felt a pang of regret. She would miss her darling children, though she promised to call every day. She would miss the life of ease and splendor at Le Paradis. She would miss Maxim, she thought with a catch of the heart. Young gallant Maxim, whose passion for her shone out from behind those soulful brown eyes. Twice she had had to stop him from declaring himself, which would have been the height of recklessness, though she fantasized about him more often than she should. Yes, she would miss her morning sessions with Maxim.

Nonetheless she yearned to be away. To break free from Tonio's grip and the marriage that was crushing her soul.

Perhaps she might call Alix when she was in New York, if it could be done discreetly, and seek her old friend's advice.

Wise wise Alix. Even wiser than Maxim.

CHELSEA

Idiot!

That one sight of Sam Matthews should turn her knees to rubber and her head to mush. And she had given him up for dead. But not in her heart. In her heart, she had known that this must happen. And there he was – vibrant. Rugged. Even more real than she remembered.

Inevitable! Incredible! Disaster in a blue denim shirt.

Alix collapsed into the red plastic booth, amazed at her vulnerability. He still had that power over her. The power to attract. To dominate.

Alix Bryden, you idiot! Get away from this man!

'I need a drink,' she gasped.

'Here you go, babe.' Sam handed her his glass. 'Scotch and water straight up, the way you like it.'

Alix gulped it down in a single swallow. The whiskey went to her head like a bullet. She thought she would faint.

Sam leaned forward and covered her hand with his giant paw as though to give her strength.

Alix trembled. How many times had she dreamt about this moment? And how long had it taken to squelch that dream? But at his touch, at the sound of his voice, the years fell away. She was young again. He was ardent. Nothing had changed.

Sam leaned toward her, his voice low and intense.

'I was afraid if you knew who it was, you wouldn't come.'

'You're right, Sam. I wouldn't have. Ten years!' The tears coursed down her cheeks. 'Ten years without a word.'

'Ten years on the run,' he said. 'I've been all over the world, Alix, had incredible adventures, slept with hundreds of women and yet I've missed you every living minute. Ten years! Yes, ten years of wondering – were you well? were you happy? did you ever think of me? Oh, Alix, I never stopped loving you!'

'Oh, Sam!' As he spoke, she drank him in afresh. Amazing how few changes the years had wrought. At forty, he still exuded virility and youth. No matter that the black hair was shot through with steel filings of gray; the eyes were magnetic as ever, the voice as seductive. If anything the passage of time had given him a kind of seasoned glamor, like burnished leather.

She heard his alibis without troubling to ask herself whether she believed them or not.

He hadn't written, he declared, or phoned in the months that followed his escape, precisely because of his love for Alix.

'I wouldn't risk even a postcard. Not with the FBI waiting to pounce. Too dangerous! One word out of me and the Feds would have been all over you. It would have been your ruination. I couldn't do it, Alix. You had your career at Harvard, your whole life ahead of you. I couldn't take that chance. How many times I'd pick up a phone, my fingers just aching to dial your number, hear your voice once more – but I couldn't, for your sake. Then you moved away, and I didn't know where to find you. It was as if we were lost to each other forever. Until last week –'

He had been sitting in a café in Istanbul, when he came across her name in the *International Herald Tribune*.

'It leaped off the page at me. *Alix Bryden, the famous defense attorney*, the paper said. My own Alix. As soon as I saw it, I knew I couldn't stay away any longer. I had to come back. The hell with the consequences. I had to see you . . . touch you . . .' He smiled. 'Remember the first time we made love? I came to your apartment for my lighter – that little orange Cricket I had . . .'

'Please! Don't do this!'

'Don't do what? Don't remember? I can't forget. You're the only reason I came back!'

Alix was in agony. Tears streamed down her face. She wanted . . . she didn't want . . . she was crazy to stay here . . . would be crazy to leave. This was Sam, for God's sakes! The one man she had really loved. Ever could love. The father of her child. The possessor of her soul.

'You shouldn't have!' she burst out. 'You'll cause us nothing but misery.'

'Don't tell me "shouldn't".' He leaned forward to cradle her face in his hands. Beneath the table, their thighs brushed. It was like an electrical charge. 'I had to, Alix. I had to see you, to be with you once more. I've never stopped loving you, I never shall. I want to make love to you, today, this afternoon. Even if it's for the very last time. If I'm arrested tomorrow, it'll have been worth it. Don't say no, Alix. I've risked my freedom just to see you.'

Say no? How could she say no? Not when she was intoxicated with love and desire. One last time, he had begged. One last chance at fulfillment. Perhaps it was her last chance as well.

Sam was a part of her life, part of her blood. He could never be exorcised. She would tell him about Samantha, of course.

311

What a surprise that would be. Sam never even knew he was a father. Yes, she would tell him. But afterwards . . . ! After they had sated their needs.

In a trance, lacking all will of her own, she permitted Sam to lead her out of the café and into a cheap hotel around the corner. She had no memory of checking in, of going up to the hotel room – only that at last they were alone. That a decade of deprivation was about to end.

Afterwards . . . !

But what could she say? He was a magnificent lover. He knew which buttons to push, which words to murmur, when to be tender, when to be passionate, how to bring her to paradise. In his arms, the years of longing were put to rest. The pain. The anguish.

But afterwards . . . she thought of Bill.

Idiot! How could she have done such a thing? With Sam Houston Matthews, of all people! Correction: Sam *Harold* Matthews. The ancient lie stuck in her craw.

Lying in bed in a scruffy hotel room, Sam's hand flung across her belly, she felt frightened and ashamed, yet for the first time that day, oddly clear-headed. Something in Sam's story hadn't rung true. She had been a lawyer too long.

Of course she intended to tell him about Samantha. He had a right to know. But not until she satisfied her curiosity.

He stretched, and reached a lazy hand to the night table.

'Alix?' He offered her a Gauloise Bleu.

She shook her head. 'I don't smoke any more.' *My husband doesn't like it.*

She watched as he lit the cigarette. His mood was happy and relaxed. He inhaled slowly, drawing the smoke deep into his lungs, consuming that cigarette as thoroughly as he had consumed her minutes earlier.

Sam Matthews was, she sensed, extremely pleased with

himself. Happy – because he felt he was in control. Happy – because she was 'good old Alix,' well-fucked and malleable, just like in the old days.

The love-making was merely a prelude – the insight came with the force of revelation. Sam wanted something from her that she had yet to give. He believed she would be bound to him by sex.

'Tell me, Sam,' she said softly. 'All those years we were apart, where were you living? What did you do?'

He kissed her on the nose. 'Do you love me, babe?'

'I'm here, aren't I?' she replied with a reassuring smile.

Sam lay back and blew a smoke ring. It was perfect. Round as a wedding band. Alix followed its lazy progress upward till it flattened out and dissipated against the ceiling. The plaster was peeling – but not as rapidly as her illusions.

'You didn't answer my question,' she prompted.

Sam smiled and his eyes grew distant. When he spoke, a note of braggadocio crept into his voice.

Such a life he had led! Such a crazy existence since the night they had parted! Alix wouldn't believe the half of it. It was sufficient to fill a dozen books.

'What happened to my car?' she asked.

'The Jag? I ditched it outside of Bangor, then hitched my way to the Canadian border.'

'And my pearls?'

'Pawned 'em for two hundred bucks.'

'They were worth a hundred thousand,' she murmured.

'Yeah, well – you couldn't expect me to stroll into Cartier's and ask top dollar.'

In Toronto, he followed James Earl Ray's example, obtaining a Canadian passport under false pretenses as Ray himself had done after the assassination of Martin Luther King. 'It's amazing the people you can learn from,' Sam said with a laugh.

'And then . . . ?'

'Ah then! You name it, babe. I've been there. In the heart of the action. Iraq. Chile. Algeria. Northern Ireland ... spent a terrific winter in Belfast.'

Alix listened in mounting horror. Indeed, he had not been peacefully tuning pianos in Sweden, as she had wished to believe. Every place he mentioned was a scene of political turmoil, of terrorist activity. In a flash, her eyes opened on the truth.

When she entered this room, she had willed herself to push the clock back, to recapture the passion of the past. But now she knew: this hour with Sam had been a fantasy. And the reality was ugly as sin.

But not for Sam, she realized. He prattled on, talking about Reagan's Amerika the way he had once talked about Nixon's Amerika and Vietnam. For him, it was still the late sixties. A revolutionary era. A time of bombs and barricades.

Essentially, nothing in his life had changed over the years – except his aliases. Suddenly, everything fell into place for Alix. Why should Sam not be as youthful, as reckless as ever? He had managed to grow older without ever growing up.

Mellow in the afterglow, he confided in her that he was known in the underground as the Chameleon, switching passports and identities the way other men changed clothes. Today, for instance, he was Hap Mendelssohn.

'Joke,' he announced with impish glee.

'I don't get it,' Alix said, though she was beginning to.

'Well, you know what a music freak I am. So I pay homage to my favorite composers by using pseudonyms. Usually with a twist. As you know, *felix* is Latin for happy. Ergo: Hap Mendelssohn. Amazing how few people catch on. Just a mark of our uncultured times, babe. But I find it amusing. When I was running guns for the IRA, the Brits had a warrant out for Frankie Schubert. And no one tumbled.'

In Lebanon, he used the alias Joe Green which was how Giuseppe Verdi translated to English. The Mossad knew him as John Brooks, in honor of J. S. Bach. He boasted of other exploits, claiming he was wanted by the authorities in eight different countries.

Alix listened, aghast. As he rambled on, it struck her that Sam was mad. Certainly, he sounded crazier than most of the murderers she represented, but cleverer too. Had he always been mad, and Alix merely blind? Was it his madness she had found so exciting?

She let him rave, trying to sift fact from fiction, bombast from bombs. Then without warning, he turned the spotlight on her.

'And what about you, Alix?' Sam gave her a playful punch. 'I understand you're married to a US Attorney. Any kids?'

Alix's heart stopped. She was poised above a minefield. God forbid Sam should find out about Samantha! Even the name would be a giveaway. All her protective instincts rose to the fore. She stalled for time.

'How did you know my husband is a federal attorney? Was that in the *Herald Tribune* too?'

'Word gets around, babe.'

'We have no children.'

'That's good. Kids are a pain in the ass.'

Alix got out of bed. 'God, I feel grubby, I simply have to take a shower. Besides, it's getting late.'

'We'll shower together,' he offered lazily. 'You used to like that.'

'No . . . no . . . Sam. You enjoy your cigarette. I'll be out in a couple of minutes.'

The water was scalding hot – at least one amenity this fleapit enjoyed! Alix scrubbed until her flesh was raw. Scrubbed until all trace of their sexual encounter was washed away. Scrubbed as though she could scrub Sam Matthews out of her system.

Then she got dressed.

'I have to leave,' she said quietly, but there was no romance in her voice. She spoke like a lawyer conducting a deposition. 'But before I do, I want the truth from you. Why *did* you come

315

back, Sam? It wasn't out of love for me, so let's cut the pretense. If you really cared for me, you would have been in touch long ago. You want something. Isn't that right? My legal savvy, is it? Or something connected with my husband's position? Don't bother buttering me up, Sam. It won't wash any more.'

He hesitated just for a moment. She saw the endearment die on his lips, then his expression adjust to the new set of circumstances. There was no romance in his voice, either.

'In part I came for you, Alix. That much is true. But I also came for other things.'

He pulled on his shorts, then sat up in bed, crisp and businesslike.

He was weary of being a fugitive, he told her, always on the run, never safe in his bed, never remembering from one day to the next which passport, which name he was supposed to be holding.

With all its faults, America was still the most exciting country in the world. Sam wanted to return, to travel freely in his native land.

He realized the problems involved, and that he needed legal expertise. He wanted Alix to use her influence, or more particularly her husband's, and get the charges against him dropped.

'It was years ago, Alix. Another lifetime. Isn't there a statute of limitations?'

'Not for murder,' she said. 'You killed a man, remember?'

'People get away with murder every day in the week,' he said irritably. 'I don't have to tell you that, Alix. You're the one who gets them off. Besides, this guy was a nobody – some little Puerto Rican janitor.' He mashed out his cigarette as though squashing a bug. 'For that I have to pay all my life?'

In that moment, any vestige of her love for him died. *Ten years of romancing a ghost!* Alix sighed. There was a bitter taste in her mouth.

'I suggest you turn yourself in, though I know you won't. As an officer of the court, I should do the job for you. Well I won't do that either, because I'm not in the habit of handing people over to the fuzz. That's my gift to you, Sam. And now I suggest you get out of the country the same way you got in. And fast! As for this afternoon, it never happened.'

His eyes flashed.

'Well, nobody can accuse you of not laying it on the line. You've turned out to be a very hard lady. Well, that's your privilege. I used to think you cared for me. The thing is, Alix, I'm broke. I don't have enough money to pay the hotel bill let alone an airline ticket. I counted on you, babe. Please, for old times' sake.'

She opened her bag. 'Here's two hundred and sixty dollars and a couple of subway tokens. It's all I have on me.'

He didn't reach for it.

'I meant *real* money. A bit of the Bryden millions.'

'I forfeited them,' she articulated. 'All those big beautiful bucks. Because of you, Sam. The more fool I.'

He appeared surprised.

'Your old man threw you out?'

'I threw him out is more like it.' She permitted herself a low harsh laugh. 'And now I'm throwing you out. Funny – a shrink I know once told me you and my father were exactly alike – two sides of the same coin. I daresay he was right.'

'Spare me the analysis, Alix. I'm not in the mood for discount Freud.' He picked up the money and tucked it into his shirt, like a waiter pocketing a tip. 'I don't think we have a helluva lot more to say to each other.'

'There is one more thing I have to hear from you, Sam. Now that there's nothing to lose, you may as well level with me. Tell me – did you ever really love me?'

Sam smiled.

'You want value for your two hundred bucks, eh? Fair enough.' He rolled the proposition over in his mind. 'Put it this way, I liked you, Alix. Very very much. But the truth is, it gave me a terrific high to know I was fucking a Bryden. To have all

317

that wealth and privilege beneath me, crying for more. Money is very sexy stuff, you know. But don't take it personally, Alix. I've never loved anyone. And that's a fact. I don't know what people mean when they start bleating about love and sacrifice. No one human being is worth living for, let alone dying for. As for me, I'll go on as I always have – living for my beliefs. I have my work, you see.'

Planting bombs and killing janitors? Alix shuddered.

'Where will you go from here?' she asked.

'Who knows?' Sam pulled on his pants, buttoned his shirt. 'Wherever there's oppression, injustice. Wherever there's action going on. South Africa, the Philippines, Haiti. Maybe San Miguel. I understand there's a nice little civil war hotting up there.'

MANHATTAN

For decades, the revolutionary movement in San Miguel had been confined to the *montagneros*, who dwelt in the interior. The descendants of runaway slaves, these mountain folk nibbled at the heels of the regime in a low-grade guerilla war. They stole supplies, cut power lines, hi-jacked the unescorted truck.

When they were caught, retribution was swift and terrible. Torture was a fine art with Tito DuMesne's black-shirted Loulous, who liked to make the air 'sing' with bull whips and electric prods. A few hours of such 'singing' were followed by summary execution, and the outside world was none the wiser.

As the old dictator said in private, a little bloodshed is the price of governance. If the rebels were troublesome, it was as a gnat troubled an elephant.

In the winter of '81, the violence began to spread from the

mountains to the farms and urban slums, even to the resorts along the coast. Ironically, the source of this rebellion was one of Home Secretary Tonio DuMesne's most progressive policies.

Swine fever was endemic in San Miguel. Upon expert advice from the World Health Organization, Tonio decreed that all the indigenous black pigs be destroyed. They would be replaced by pink-and-white Durocs, to be paid for by a tax hike. The international firm contracted to provide the new porkers had agreed to kick back a dollar per head to Tonio, adding sweetness to the deal. Who said you couldn't do good and do well simultaneously, Tonio quipped. Until the changeover, the masses must learn to do without pork.

Had he been closer to his people, Tonio might have recalled that the black pig was a household icon, embodying the spirit of Uxman, protector of the harvest. Each Easter, in an ancient ritual, the pig was ceremonially slaughtered, providing not only a feast for the family but assurance that the gods had been appeased.

This year, however, the ritual would not take place. At a stroke Tonio had deprived his subjects of their favorite food and their religion.

Daily the violence escalated. Every night the air crackled with gunfire, every morning the sweepers came to clear away the dead. Yet though the regime matched terror with counter-terror, the rebel ranks continued to swell. The guerilla army embraced priests, peasants, intellectuals and artisans, mercenaries and, lately, foreign agitators who swarmed to Benedicta in hopes of a full-scale revolution.

Even in Le Paradis, high above the city, one could hear the chanting of the mob, the random burst of Molotov cocktails.

It was enough, Tonio remarked wryly, to spoil one's siesta.

No such sounds invaded the quiet suite in the Carnegie Clinic where Bette West lay dying.

Thus far every treatment had failed. Her disease had been

too long neglected, Dr Osborne said. He was a short stocky man with a businesslike manner that reminded Kim of Dr Frankl. He could be disturbingly direct. Bette was going rapidly downhill.

'She should have entered treatment months ago,' he grumbled.

'I know,' Kim replied, 'but she wanted one last fling.'

The doctor shrugged. 'She can't have enjoyed it much. She must have been in agony most of the time.'

'My mother is a strong-willed woman. So what now?'

One therapy remained to be tried, the doctor said. It was possible that a bone marrow transplant, combined with radiation, might arrest the progress of the disease. The best hope lay in a syngeneic graft, only possible with marrow from an identical twin, which was not the case here.

'Ironically,' Kim said, 'I'm the mother of twins myself.'

The next best chance was an allogeneic graft, from a parent, brother or sister. He leafed through Bette's admission form.

'Your mother indicates she has no siblings. Is that correct, to your knowledge?'

To her knowledge, yes, though Kim couldn't swear it. In fact, she knew very little about her mother's background. Almost as little as she knew of her father's.

She looked Dr Osborne in the eye.

'I'm afraid I'm all the family my mother has.'

'Then you're it, young lady. Let's hope it works.'

It was a complex procedure, the doctor warned. Kim would be given a spinal anesthetic, then marrow would be drawn from her pelvic bone. The operation lasted approximately three hours and Kim might feel pain for several days.

'Doctor,' Kim said, 'I've probably had more surgery than you've had hot meals. This one will be a breeze.'

He looked at her with a quizzical expression.

'You understand, Miss West, that there's no guarantee . . .'

'I know. It's a long shot.'

He nodded. 'But a long shot is better than no shot at all.'

*

The operation was scheduled for the following morning, but first Kim was sent to the lab for blood tests, tissue typing and a general check-up. Routine procedure, Dr Osborne said, to make sure the donor herself was in good health.

After taking the tests, Kim visited her mother.

Since arriving in New York, she had been spending most of each day with Bette. She would comb what was left of her hair, bring flowers and sweets, relay the latest gossip from San Miguel.

Usually, Bette soldiered on like a trouper. Today, however, she was agitated. Dr Osborne had informed her of the transplant.

'I don't want them sticking other people's bodily fluids into me,' she croaked in her failing voice. 'It's not natural.'

'But, Mom!' Kim reasoned. 'I'm not other people.'

'I don't care,' Bette whispered. 'I don't want it.'

Kim knew better than to argue. The procedure had to be done, and that was that. Though it was paradoxical, to say the least, that Bette – so quick to ship Kim off to Marival to be nipped and tucked – should herself have a morbid fear of doctors.

'Why should I see a quack?' she used to say in happier days. 'I'm the picture of health. And I hate it when they poke around down there.' *Down there*, in Bette's lexicon, referred to anything more invasive than a tongue depressor.

Kim stayed all afternoon, relentlessly cheerful. When it was time to leave, she leaned over to kiss her mother goodbye. As she did so, she couldn't help noticing that Bette's pores exuded a faint acrid odor. It was the smell of death.

Sick at heart, she returned to the consulate and had supper on a tray, too depressed to call home.

That night, she succumbed to a bout of panic.

What if the graft failed? What if – Kim clenched her teeth – Bette died? Dr Osborne had done his best to prepare Kim for that eventuality, yet she couldn't picture life without her mother.

For good or ill, Bette had always been by her side: strong, assured, the ultimate authority – making decisions, passing judgments, guiding Kim's course.

The only time the two had been separated had been during Kim's honeymoon. And what a disaster that had turned out to be!

'Don't abandon me now, Mom!' Kim wept into her pillow.

Granted, Bette's helping hand had often lain heavily on Kim's shoulders. Bette could be testy, stubborn, unsympathetic. But even at her most outrageous, Kim believed, Bette had always acted with her daughter's welfare in mind.

Who but Bette had ever loved Kim sincerely? Selflessly? Who would fill the emptiness once she was gone? Not Tonio, that much was certain. As Bette often said when the chips were down, 'Who do we have, toots, if we don't have each other?'

Who indeed?

Kim was up early the next morning. She washed, dressed in a simple sweater and skirt. No breakfast, the doctor had told her. She dismissed the limo and walked across East 60th Street to the clinic. The cherry trees had blossomed overnight, and the city looked lovely. That augured well, Kim thought.

At a little before nine she presented herself to the front-desk receptionist.

'I'm here for my graft,' she said. 'Where do I go?'

The receptionist dipped her head. 'Dr Osborne wants to see you in his office.'

'Right.' Kim nodded. 'I know the way.'

She went into his office, waited twenty minutes. Thumbed through a copy of *New York Magazine*, then waited some more, wondering what had caused the delay.

At nine thirty, Dr Osborne came in, looking very grave.

Kim's heart flipped.

'What's wrong?'

He sat down at his desk and folded his hands, like a school teacher about to deliver a failing grade.

'Why didn't you tell me?' he said, taut with anger.

Tell him what? Something awful must have turned up in her blood test. Had Tonio given her some loathsome social disease? Was she an unfit donor?

'Why didn't you tell me straight off,' he repeated, 'and spare us this farce?'

'I don't understand,' Kim cried out in confusion. 'What was I supposed to tell you?'

'Why didn't you tell me she's not your mother?'

The breath went out of Kim.

'You're crazy,' she gasped. 'Not my mother? You're out of your mind! What in God's name are you trying to do?'

There was a deathly silence. Dr Osborne was staring at her, incredulity writ large across his face. Then he softened.

'You didn't know you were adopted?'

'No!' Kim cried. 'There must be some mistake. Please! Tell me it's an error . . . a joke.'

'No mistake, I'm afraid. I double-checked the blood tests, the tissue types. No doubt about it. It isn't even remotely possible that Mrs West is your mother. You're completely unrelated types. In fact, we were all amazed . . .'

But no one was more amazed than Kim, who had fainted dead away.

On the bedroom dresser in the consulate stood an ormolu mirror that Tonio had acquired in his youth, when he had been ambassador to France. The mirror had come from the boudoir of the Empress Josephine. Its lyre-shaped contours framed the face to produce a portrait effect and Kim liked to think that if she came upon it unawares, she might glimpse in its depths reflections of an earlier era.

Kim had long felt an affinity with Josephine Bonaparte, collecting her hair ornaments, perfume bottles and jewels. The empress had herself been born a Creole in Martinique, and Kim had read that she was an adept in the black magic of the islands. Perhaps some of that magic still resided in this looking-glass.

The morning after Dr Osborne's revelations, Kim sat herself down before the mirror with a desperate intensity. She was in search of nothing less than herself.

Who was this Kimberly West, so called, who stared back at her with puzzled eyes? Where did she come from? Who were her parents? What was her heritage? The mirror image offered no answers. It was as close-mouthed as Bette West herself.

'I have to know,' Kim had pleaded relentlessly. 'I can't go on living in ignorance. I beg you – tell me the truth!'

Bette turned her face to the wall, refusing to answer. By now, the deception was deep in her bones, second nature, and neither Kim's tears nor entreaties could prevail.

'I'm sick,' she rasped in a barely audible voice. 'Have pity and let me be.'

Kim was torn between rage and grief. She felt heartless badgering someone she loved so much, yet she was terrified that Bette might slip away with her secrets intact. There were moments when Kim ached to pick her up by the shoulders and shake the truth out of her – quick! before the spirit left the body.

As the end drew near, Kim never left Bette's side. She passed her nights in a cot beside the sickbed, in a state of perpetual readiness, waiting either for Bette's death or her revelations. Whichever came first.

Perhaps Bette might talk in her sleep, utter something in delirium. Perhaps she would take pity on Kim and relent. *One word* – Kim prayed. *A name. A place. A clue.* But it must be soon, for Bette's speech was growing faint and unintelligible. She slipped in and out of consciousness a dozen times an hour. Her grasp of reality grew more tenuous. Kim was frantic.

Her only companions were the nurses. One in particular, the night nurse, soon became her confidante.

Lily Maddox was a motherly Jamaican whose island speech sat sweetly on Kim's ears. Lily called her 'milady,' which reminded Kim of Celeste, and fussed over her.

'I've got me two patients here,' she would say. 'Why, you poor child, you're wasting away to a shadow. You must rest, milady. If anything happens, I promise to wake you right away.'

But Kim couldn't sleep, couldn't eat, couldn't think of anything except the imminence of death. In the silence of the room she became attuned to every change in her mother's breathing. Daily it grew shallower, weaker as life ebbed.

'Not long now, I'm afraid,' Dr Osborne said one morning in early May. 'A few days at most. All we can do is minimize the pain. The nurses will see that she's made comfortable.'

That night, when Lily came on duty, she motioned Kim into a corner. A few feet away, Bette dozed fitfully.

'When your mam wakes,' Lily whispered, 'I'll give her a shot.'

'Yes . . . the doctor told me. Morphine, is it?'

'I'm going to give her sodium pentathol. Do you know what that is, milady?'

Kim started. 'It's truth serum, isn't it?'

Lily nodded. 'Then I leave the room, and you and your mam can say your goodbyes in private.'

Kim flung her arms around the nurse. 'Bless you, Lily!'

It was nearly midnight. The drug had begun to take effect.

Kim sat with her face inches away from her mother's lips. Briefly, she had a moment of bizarre recall, of leaning over a half-drowned body on the shores of Lake Leman and striving to make out another whispered message.

But Bette hadn't the strength to project anything beyond a stream of gurgles. Her movements were febrile, uncontrolled. One eye wandered as though loose from its socket; the other was fixed on Kim.

'I love you, Mom,' Kim whispered into Bette's ear, 'and I know you love me, but we may never get a chance to talk again.

You are dying, you know that.' A tear trickled down Bette's leather cheeks. 'So now I'm going to ask and you will tell me. That will be your legacy to me – the truth. Whatever you say, whatever you've done, it will be forgiven and you'll be at peace with yourself and God. You want to tell me, don't you? I can see it in your eyes. So say it. Who am I? What is my name?'

Bette opened her mouth.

'K . . . K . . .'

'Yes, my name is Kimberly. But what is my last name?'

'K . . . K . . .' The lips worked and twisted as Bette grappled to communicate, but already she was passing beyond speech. The only sound to issue from her throat was a low dry rattle.

'Oh, God!' Kim was in a race with death. And death was galloping toward the finish line.

With all the will in the world, Bette would soon be unable to make the simplest statement. She would die, and leave Kim forever in the dark.

Kim took Bette's hand, so shriveled and ringless. It was like the paw of a small helpless animal.

'I know it's hard to speak, but try to answer my questions any way you can. With a nod of the head, a squeeze of the hand . . . anything! I'll understand. Squeeze once for yes. Is what you told me true – that I was born in California?'

Kim was rewarded with a faint pressure on her palm.

One step forward. Next, Kim tried to dredge up earliest memories. They had lived in so many places! Yet Bette once mentioned that Kim had been baptized in San Diego.

'In San Diego?'

The second squeeze was so faint, Kim wondered if she had imagined it, but the agitation in her mother's eyes seemed to spell Yes. Repeatedly, Bette gasped for breath, like a fish out of water. Kim could feel the inner agony, the drug-induced struggle to communicate. But how much could one say without words?

Kim had a swift insight.

'I am a twin, aren't I?'

Bette's eyes flashed, and Kim's insight became a certainty.

Suddenly, Bette tore loose from Kim's clasp and tried to sit up. In a massive effort, she was galvanizing all the energy left in her frail body, forcing it up through her throat, into her mouth, formulating it into a few final words.

'What is it, Mom? What do you want to say?'

Bette opened her mouth. A gob of spit dribbled down her chin. Her lips contorted into a painful grimace.

'I . . . took . . . the . . . girl!' she croaked.

'My God!' Kim reared in astonishment. 'I have a brother. Tell me, I beg you, before it's too late.'

But it already was, for Bette fell back exhausted, her eyes rolling as wildly as though she had seen the angel of death.

'Please, Momma!' Kim shrieked. 'Don't die without telling me! What is his name?'

But even as Bette collapsed into Kim's arms, the only word that issued from those cracked lips was *'you . . . you . . . you!'*

Bette West died an hour before dawn, without ever recovering consciousness. Kim was by her side. She felt strangely calm, almost transported. And though the grief was too fresh and unreal to accommodate, yet she was aware that a chapter in her life had come to a close.

A little after eight, Kim called Tonio to break the news.

'I want to bury her in San Miguel,' Kim said. 'She loved the island so very much.'

'Of course, *chérie*. I'll send a plane for you this evening.'

'Tomorrow will be soon enough,' Kim said. 'I have things to do here. Forms to fill out, that sort of thing.'

'As you wish, *mon ange*.'

She changed into street clothes and left the hospital. As always, the official limousine was waiting, egregiously parked in a No Standing zone, its diplomatic plates ensuring immunity from anything so mundane as a parking ticket.

Spies! Spies everywhere. Kim waved the driver away.

'I'll walk,' she said, and began making her way across Second Avenue, then Third, aware that the Cadillac was following a few feet behind. Kim quivered with resentment. Even in her most private moment of grief, Tonio's agents kept her in sight, restricting her freedom. But where she was going – and why – was no one's business but her own.

In back of Bloomingdales, the limousine became wedged in a line of trucks making deliveries. Suddenly Kim quickened her pace, turned a corner, and darted into the subway to disappear into the rush-hour crowd.

Twenty minutes later, she was at Alix Bryden's office.

COBBLE HILL

'Some incredible story, wouldn't you say?'

Bill grunted what sounded like assent, though his nose remained buried in the sports page of *The New York Times*.

Typical, she thought, that on one of their rare evenings alone, Bill should take advantage of the breather to catch up, not on his wife's activities, but on the Mets and the Yankees.

Over the years, their house in Cobble Hill had come to resemble the Cairns family home in City Island, an endless site of comings and goings. In addition to Alix, Bill, the children, Mr Rabinowitz (now semi-retired but still a family member), a housekeeper, a live-in law student from NYU who earned his room and board by baby-sitting, and a floppy-eared mutt named Moses (whom Bill had trained to sink to the floor at the sound of *Go Down Moses*), the Cairns kept a virtual open house.

Scarcely a night went by, at least those nights when Bill was home, without the living room being surrendered to a committee meeting or a strategy conference or a fund-raiser.

The occasion for this burst of activity was the announcement that New York's junior senator would not seek re-election the following year. It was the opportunity Bill had been waiting for. He quit his job and threw his hat in the ring.

The timing was perfect, Bill having scored a coup with a string of high-profile Mafioso convictions. The public adored him, the press was hot to trot. He was everybody's 'Mr Clean.'

He lived now amidst a cloud of people: speech writers, ward heelers, PR consultants. He had hired a campaign manager, a street-smart politico named Harry McAfee, with whom he conferred a dozen times a day. And though Alix helped out, particularly on policy questions, she refused to be type-cast as a candidate's wife, all smiles and simpers and sweetness. She had her own career to run. His biggest problem was finance.

'So,' he told Alix, 'all I've gotta do between now and next year is raise a few million dollars in campaign money. Three and a half should do nicely. Any suggestions?'

She wondered if this were a round-about hint that she ought to mend the rift with Lucius Bryden, a matter he brought up every Christmas, Easter and Father's Day, with the suggestion that Alix send him a card. Alix resented the pressure.

'Why should I make the overtures?' Alix would bristle. 'He's the one who was in the wrong.' To which Bill would reply, 'Because he's the only father you'll ever have.'

Now, with the prospect of spending most of his waking hours hustling for contributions, the Bryden millions must look attractive indeed. Why bust your ass criss-crossing New York state, begging bowl in hand, eating rubber chicken, making promises you didn't want to keep, when all your wife had to do was sit down and write a check?

To do Bill justice, Alix conceded, he never mentioned her father in that context, but the unsaid always hovered in the air between them. Alix could, if she would, pave the way.

She wouldn't budge. Better that Bill should beg money from strangers, she felt, than that Alix beg forgiveness from her father.

The years had not softened the memory of that last meeting with Lucius. The fact that he was right about Sam only made it worse. She had her pride to consider.

She felt sorry for Bill, though. He had a tough slog ahead.

Tonight, the first time in weeks there had been nothing on the campaign calendar, Alix had looked forward to his company.

She repeated her question.

'I said, it's incredible, isn't it?'

'What is?' He didn't look up from *The Times*.

'What I was telling you over dinner, about Kim. Honestly, Bill. I sometimes wonder if you listen when I talk?'

'Of course I listen, Alix,' he said absently. 'I take in your every word. You want to cross-examine me on the details, go right ahead. Poor Kim . . . mother not her mother . . . husband a no-goodnik . . . missing twin . . . Oh, God!' He shook his head. 'I just can't believe this!'

'It sounded incredible to me too, Bill, but . . .'

'You bet it's incredible. They sound serious! I still can't believe they'll actually go ahead and do it.'

It took Alix a moment to realize they were talking at cross purposes.

'Who's going to do what?' she asked.

He gazed at her with a curious expression. 'My God, Alix, don't you live on this planet with us earth folks? The baseball players! They're threatening to go out on strike next month. Nothing like it has ever happened before in the history of the majors.'

Baseball! Alix flushed with annoyance. She wanted to talk about real people, real problems and he was worried about a bunch of overpriced prima donnas in archaic uniforms.

'Can't you get an injunction?' she said drily. 'Call out the federal marshals and goddamn make them play? Isn't that what the politics is all about?'

Bill folded the paper carefully and put it down.

'Okay,' he said with a sigh. 'You can let up on the sarcasm. Just get whatever it is off your chest.'

'There's nothing to get off my chest. As you pointed out, I told you the story over dinner and you absorbed my every word, so what can I add?'

He looked at her, perplexed.

'Then what are you so sore about, Alix?'

'I'm not sore. I just thought we might discuss the situation in a little more depth.'

'We discussed it for an hour, honey – the ins and outs, all the wrinkles. What do you want – my endorsement? Yeah, I think you gave her sound legal advice. No, I don't think you could do anything more. She's a grown woman. She'll make her own decisions. Maybe she doesn't want to be rescued. Maybe she likes living the fantasy.'

'What's that supposed to mean?'

'Let's face it, your friend Kim has the world by the nuts: health, youth, all the clothes you can eat. Most women would give their eye teeth to be in those gold-lined Ferragamo shoes. And if her husband's such a rat, she can dump him, no harm done, and still wind up with a fortune. This is bad? I wonder sometimes' – he shrugged and picked up his paper – 'what do women want?'

'You and Freud,' Alix muttered.

When Alix had entered her office that morning, she'd walked right past the blonde woman sitting in the waiting room.

'Alix?' The voice sounded querulous. 'It's me. Kim West?' More of a question than a statement.

'My God!' Alix did a take, then crunched her old friend in a bear hug. 'What a surprise. It's good to see you!'

It had been what – four years? five? – since that night she had dined with Kim and Tonio. Long, but not a lifetime. Not so long that Alix shouldn't have recognized her straight off.

Maybe the difference was that Kim wasn't wearing make-up. Or maybe the face had been back to the plastic surgeon's too many times. She looked unfamiliar and faintly unreal.

But one thing Alix did recognize was Kim's expression. She'd seen it on a thousand clients. Panic. Despair. This was a volcano ready to blow.

Alix ushered Kim into her office. 'We're alone now. I can see you're in trouble. Tell me about it. You'll feel better.'

That invitation was all Kim needed. Numbly, in a voice that conveyed her own sense of disbelief, Kim told her story.

'She died a few hours ago, and I don't know what to feel any more. I don't even know if I'm sorry she's dead.'

'You're still in shock,' Alix observed.

'Shock! Shock doesn't begin to explain it! I feel as if I have been violated. Betrayed. All those years she ran my life – *do this, do that, Mama knows best, you gotta listen to your mom.*' Kim sucked in her breath. 'She had no right, Alix. No right at all! I grew up hearing how much she "sacrificed" for me, how she had gone without this and that so I could have my big break. And mutt that I was, I believed her! But all I was was an instrument. I was going to be her passport to fame, to big bucks. I was going to live the life she'd wanted for herself. Sacrifice? *I* was the one who made the sacrifices, Alix, only I didn't know it. She robbed me of my identity . . . of my family, my own flesh and blood. She lied right up to the end. You know what her last words to me were? *You . . . You.* Like it was all my fault. Even on her death bed, with truth serum in her veins, she couldn't be honest. *Me . . . me . . .*' Kim mocked bitterly. 'As if I even knew who *me* is. My whole life I thought I was one person, and now I find out I'm somebody else. I feel exploited, emotionally raped. Well, I'm glad she's dead.'

Suddenly Kim burst into a paroxysm of tears. 'No! No! Forgive me, Mom. Forgive me for saying such a thing. I loved you all my life.'

Alix waited with a supply of Kleenex and coffee until Kim regained her composure.

'I know this has been a terrible blow, Kim,' she consoled, 'but still – you have your husband, your children, a fabulous life . . .' Alix paused. 'Have you mentioned any of this to Tonio?'

'Tonio!' Kim cried out bitterly. 'My prize package Tonio. No. I didn't tell him. What's the point?'

But you're telling me, Alix thought, sensing there was more to come. 'I'm your friend,' she prodded, 'but remember – I'm also a lawyer. I can help, but only if you tell me everything. Trust me, Kim. I have your welfare at heart.'

'I wonder if I can trust anyone,' Kim said, but the need to confide overcame her scruples. Suddenly, her pain spilled out: the years with Tonio, his infidelities, the psychological torture she had endured. The threat of physical torture behind it.

'There's a room in the presidential palace called the Black Chamber. It's where political dissidents are taken to be "interrogated" by the Lou-lous, the official goons. Bunch of sadists, if you ask me. Tonio takes part in the actual torture.'

'Do you know this for a fact?' Alix asked.

'I speak the patois,' Kim said. 'I heard this from a guard. The common people worship me, you see.'

Kim told her about the legend of Ladorita.

'It's why Tonio married me. It's why I go to Marival each year to be remade. God forbid I lose my youth, my looks.' Kim touched her hand to her cheek in a tentative gesture. 'My face is my fortune – literally.'

Even Alix – no stranger to tales of domestic horror – was stunned. The man sounded like a psychopath.

'And you're going back to him? Why, for God's sakes?'

'My children are there.'

'Then grab them and take the next plane back to New York. Don't even pack a suitcase. Just get the hell out of there. And once you're safe, we'll file for divorce.'

But Kim was shaking her head. No no, it couldn't be done. 'If Tonio even knew I was telling you all this, he'd kill me.'

'All the more reason to get the hell out,' Alix urged, but Kim grew agitated at the thought.

Tonio would never let her have the children. He was powerful, stubborn. Anyhow, what was the point of going to law in America when the DuMesne family *was* the law in San Miguel? She had a life down there, a position, obligations. She couldn't just walk away.

'Besides . . .' Kim's voice faded.

Besides what? Alix wondered. Was she so much in love with the role of Ladorita? Or did she still love Tonio? The latter, Alix decided, reflecting on her own obsession with Sam.

'Listen, Kim. I know what it's like to be into that kind of relationship. I was trapped in one myself for years. The man – Samantha's father – was not so different from Tonio. Cruel, violent. We're talking criminal types, but there was something about him—' As Alix spoke, she grasped the truth about herself more clearly than ever before. 'He appealed to my dark side. He abused me – not physically, but emotionally. He abused my trust, my love. Yet destructive as it was, some part of me kept coming back for more. In a way I wanted to be a victim. When he flayed me, at least I knew I was alive, or so I told myself. Well, that kind of stuff may be sexually exciting, but it's unhealthy. A no-win situation. Believe me, Kim, I've been there. I know the attraction. And the risks. At best, you wind up leading his life, not yours. At worst, you could wind up dead. Benefit from my experience.'

Alix softened her tone, for Kim was weeping again.

'I'm not saying that cutting the tie is easy, but you must do it – for your children's sake, if not for yourself. You don't want them growing up in that atmosphere. Let them grow up in the light. Think about what I'm saying when you get home and I know you'll do the right thing first chance you get. Will you be coming back to the States any time soon?'

'We spend August in Long Island. We give our annual ball.'

'Do the children come with you?'

Kim nodded, glassy-eyed.

'Great! Then all you have to do is, once you land at JFK, you grab the kids and come straight to my office. You're still a US citizen, Kim. You have rights. And remember, I'll be behind you all the way. My husband too, and he's an influential man. There won't be a damn thing Tonio can do. You'll get a divorce, custody of the children. Then you can start living your own life for a change. Freedom, Kim! Think of it – the freedom to live your own life!'

'My own life,' Kim echoed, then shook her head. 'How can I live my own life, live any sort of life, when I don't even know who I am? I'll consider your advice, Alix, but I need breathing time. I have to learn about myself. Who I am. See how I function without my mother. That's why I came here.' She drew a deep breath. 'I have a twin brother somewhere. My flesh and blood, the family I've been deprived of. I see my own twins, how close they are, and it's everything I missed in my childhood. I want you to find my brother, Alix, the other half of me. It's the only way I can ever be whole.'

Alix understood.

It was a job for private investigators, she explained. She had an excellent firm. But first, she would need such data as Kim could supply.

Alix handed her a pad. 'Write down whatever's pertinent.'

Kim's scribbles amounted to nothing more than her presumed birth date in San Diego and the fact that she had been baptized at a 'St Something or Other's' shortly after by a priest named O'Donnell.

'Not a lot to go on,' Alix conceded, 'but it'll do, I expect. Twin births are fairly uncommon. I'll start on it today. Meanwhile, how do I get in touch with you? Is it safe to phone you at home?'

'No . . . no!' Kim's eyes widened in alarm. Then she scribbled another couple of lines. 'This is the address of a personal friend. You can enclose any message in an envelope to him.'

'Maxim Brunel,' Alix read. The name meant nothing.

Bill and Alix watched the ten o'clock news, had tea, checked the kids, after which he went up to bed. Alix returned to the kitchen. It was where she did her best thinking.

The day's events had disturbed her. Not just Kim's revelations, but the unwelcome insight into her own behavior with Sam. She thought of Bill's question. Freud's question.

What *did* women want? What did Alix herself want? She didn't know. She wasn't even sure what she wanted of her husband.

Ever since that afternoon with Sam, Alix had been guilt-stricken. Why had she done such a thing? Why had she jeopardized her marriage to hop into bed with that creep?

Alix blamed herself. Had she loved Bill more, she never would have cheated on him. But then (she couldn't help thinking) if Bill had loved *her* more, if he had adored her, worshipped her, made her feel like a princess, she wouldn't have been tempted to cheat.

Shit though Sam Matthews was, hypocrite and tyrant, he had filled one need that her husband had not. He had made her feel beloved.

True, Sam had accomplished this magic through lies. Whereas Bill Cairns, on the other hand, was hopelessly honest. He never cheated on his taxes, stole towels from hotels, or embroidered the truth – even in court.

He was the most prudent of husbands, though Alix sometimes felt this awesome rectitude had as much to do with the fear of compromising his political future as it did with personal morality. Bill didn't fuck around with either.

In short, he was not the romantic hero she had yearned for all her life. Not a Galahad, not even a Heathcliff.

Far be it from Bill to profess ardent love, undying passion, to lay the world's embroidered cloths at her feet. Alix was a fool to hunger after them. Bill had his own agenda and style.

In the throes of passion, he might express some enthusiasm, with 'God, you're terrific!' at the top of the scale. Otherwise, his endearments rarely ranged beyond the occasional 'honey.' She tried unsuccessfully to recall if he had ever once stated that he loved her in exactly those words. Three little words. *I love you.* So why the big deal!

He had never spoken them because he'd never felt them.

That said, he was physically affectionate, a good husband and father who didn't deserve to be betrayed by his wife.

So what *did* women want? Alix would be damned if she knew.

She put the teacups in the sink and went up to bed.

Bill was still awake, reading Gore Vidal. Well, at least it wasn't the goddamn baseball.

She got undressed, aware that he was watching her out of the corner of his eye. Then he set down his book and put his glasses on the night table.

'I hate it when we bicker,' he said. 'It's a waste of energy. Let's snuggle and hug and do nice things.'

Feeling guilty for her thoughts of a few minutes past, Alix slid into his embrace with practiced familiarity and soon they were going at it hammer and tongs.

What the hell – they both enjoyed the act of love. At least that pleasure hadn't palled.

But later, as he lay back in bed, arms clasped behind his head, Alix thought he looked troubled.

About her, was her bet. He was a decent man, considerate at heart. He knew how anxious she was over this business with Kim. Okay, he wasn't prone to expostulations, but that was his style. Alix had really been too hard on him.

A cloud seemed to pass above his brow.

'A penny for your thoughts, Bill.'

He flushed, as though caught in the act.

'Nothing important . . .'

''Fess up, or I'll give you my Nazi torture treatment.' She began tickling him under the arms, which always drove him crazy. 'Ve heff vays of making you talk,' she giggled. 'So talk.'

'Well, actually,' he dragged. At least he had the grace to be embarrassed. 'Actually, I was wondering if the Mets ought to bench Espinosa.'

Alix sighed and reached for the light.

'Good night, Bill.'

'Good night, Alix.'

HOLLYWOOD

'Good morning, sweetheart.'

'Good morning, darling.'

'And how's my great big lambikins this morning?' She planted a wet smoochy kiss in his ear. 'How's my luvvy-wuvvy teddy bear whom I adore beyond anything on earth?'

'Woof woof!' Peter growled amiably. 'Feeling luvvier all the time.'

He fumbled sleepily under the duvet until he encountered the firm, perfectly shaped breast of Judi Syme. One touch was enough to make him horny. 'What do you say we fool around for a little while, Judi?'

'Wish I could, my sweet love. Believe me, there's nothing I'd like more, but I have to be on the set by eight.'

'It's only quarter to six.'

'Good lord!' She jumped out of bed. 'Quarter of six already? I'd better get a move on.'

Peter rolled over and went back to sleep.

*

When he and Judy first started living together, he had been fascinated by her morning regime. From needle shower to aerobic workout to organic breakfast to massage table to jacuzzi to make-up table to front door, the routine took a minimum of one and a half hours.

She reminded Peter of the milkmaid in the nursery rhyme: 'My face is my fortune, sir, she said' – though in Judi's case, that fortune extended to body, nails and hair. He understood the momentum behind the push-ups and placenta creams. Fitness was a professional burden, good looks being to movie stars what good plots were to writers. Judi was protecting her turf. Happy, as she gleefully informed Peter, that she was still 'bankable' and determined to stay that way for years to come.

In California, Peter once remarked at a dinner party, youth was the national religion and aging was the ultimate crime. His hostess, the skinny sixty-ish editor of a popular woman's magazine, had hurled a bread roll at him.

Yet after so many years of residency, the narcissism of the culture still fascinated and repelled him. Los Angeles in particular was a plastic surgeon's paradise, proof positive of Peter's assertion.

Back in the sixties, when Peter was at Marival, a woman of a certain age and eminence would sooner confess to infanticide than admit that 'those lips, those eyes' were anything other than what nature had intended. No more. Such matters now were table talk, and Peter never ceased to be astonished by the explicitness with which the procedures were discussed. At lunches and dinner parties, seemingly well-bred people swapped names, traded tips and recommendations. Over the apricot soufflé, one might find out where to go to purchase the poutiest lips, the firmest breasts, the flattest tummy. Obtain a veritable shopping list of body parts.

Nor was the pursuit of the ideal limited to those who, like Judi, earned a living on camera. Peter knew a seventy-five-year-old shoe tycoon who had had his buttocks lifted, a ten-year-old girl who was saving her pennies for a nose job. Even Mrs Gomez who came in twice a week to do the ironing was trying to get her insurance company to pay for 'the works.'

'But why do you want a face lift?' Peter asked in consternation. 'You're a nice looking woman.'

'Thees eez America, señor!'

Which was about as much of an explanation, he thought, as Sir Edmund Hillary's 'Because it is there!'

These reflections were by way of Peter's acknowledgment that he was getting gray. But if he had chosen to ignore that fact, Judi Syme certainly had not.

'Poor darling,' she remarked one afternoon when he was reading by the pool. 'You're getting gray as a grizzly!'

He smiled. 'Runs in the family, I'm afraid. At my age, my mother was gray and my father was bald. Take your pick.'

Judi was not amused. He wasn't that old, she insisted, but he should start working on himself *now*, 'working' being Judi's favorite verb.

'I'll send you to my colorist on Rodeo Drive. Elena works marvels, and she loves doing men.'

Peter laughed. 'I don't think my nerves could stand it.'

Judi Syme had been his close friend and only lover since they made their first movie together. She was bright, charming, blonde oftener than not, played a great game of tennis and was wonderful in bed, though he sometimes wearied of her mania for keeping in shape.

Like most actors, she couldn't pass a mirror. She lived by her image. Many a time, Peter would catch Judi scrutinizing herself with the seriousness of a general inspecting the troops in wartime. Admittedly, the results warranted the effort.

At thirty-five, Judi looked ten years younger. It bothered her that Peter looked forty.

'Forty-three,' he corrected.

'Forty's bad enough.'

They had been together five years, and his affection for her was wide, if not deep, as (despite the extravagance of her endearments) was her feeling for him. Nonetheless, having never been married, she made matrimonial noises from time to time. For though she *looked* twenty-five both off screen and on, her biological clock wasn't so easily fooled.

Only the previous night, she had brought up the subject of marriage – again.

'Not a good idea, I'm afraid,' Peter responded.

'Why not, sugar lamb?' She was examining her face for blackheads with a magnifying glass. 'You won't find anyone nicer. Or nicer looking, either, I might add.'

'True,' he said amiably. 'The problem is when I'm fifty, you'll be thirty. When I'm sixty, you'll be thirty-one.'

She turned around with a curious expression.

'Would you prefer it if I grew old and fat?'

Which was an interesting question. Would he? Perhaps, considering the alternatives. An incident that had taken place the previous winter came to mind. The memory still jarred.

One of the perks of Peter's success was the opportunity to travel. Movies were shot all over the world, and Peter, a fast, facile writer, enjoyed a reputation as a 'script doctor,' the man who solved problems on the spot. His agent, amused by the fact that Peter really *was* a doctor, invariably mentioned it when touting his talents, with the result that he became known in the industry as the 'Doctor Doctor' – the specialist most likely to be called in for emergency operations on sick scripts.

Since, as they say in Hollywood, good movies aren't written, they're re-written, Peter had his pick of assignments. The ones he liked best were short and sweet and far away.

New places, new faces – the more exotic the better. Join the film colony and see the world. Already special projects had taken him to Tahiti, Kenya, Patagonia, the Philippines. Then along came a job in San Miguel. He was in the mood for a change of scenery.

The name of the film was *Karnival King*, a comedy about a Brooklyn boy with dreams of a fast-food franchise on a remote tropical island. It sounded like it might be fun.

Once settled into a suite at the Benedicta Hilton, Peter decided to send Kimberly DuMesne a note. Nothing pushy, just a reminder that they had met in Marival. In fact, he was devoured by curiosity, but thought it best to leave any overtures up to her since Kim might prefer to forget those bad old days.

To Peter's delight, she responded immediately with a phone call and an invitation to dinner.

'I'll send the car for you at six, so we can watch the sunset. It'll be just the four of us. You, me, Tonio and Mom. *En famille*, as they say, so don't dress. It'll be just great seeing you again!'

On the way over in the Rolls, Peter speculated about what he would find. Kim had been fourteen when he had last seen her, cute as a button and just as artless. He remembered that night by the lake when she had risked her own life to save another's. A sweet, spirited, courageous girl. Of course, she had grown up since then, filled out, matured, but he hoped she hadn't lost that youthful exuberance.

The limousine passed a series of checkpoints, with Peter being twice asked to produce his ID by armed men with smoked glasses and cockade hats, after which they saluted smartly. The grounds were magnificent. Peacocks dotted the grass, parrots jabbered in the trees. What looked suspiciously like a highland gorilla loped across the road causing the Rolls to stop and let it pass. All Peter could think was – what a movie set!

At last, the car slid down an avenue of royal palms to pull up at the entry of a white marble villa. Peter stepped out.

The woman who ran down the steps to greet him confounded his expectations.

'Peter!' She kissed on both cheeks, three times in the French fashion. 'It was so good of you to come!' Then she took his hands and stepped back. 'Welcome to paradise.'

Peter was abashed. Her 'don't dress,' he realized, was not to be taken literally for she herself was turned out head to toe. She was wearing a fuchsia silk gauze dress with a plunging neckline and a handkerchief hem (he took careful mental notes, since he was expected to report these details back to Judi), fuchsia high-heeled sandals, fuchsia manicure, and enough diamonds hanging from her ears to anchor a medium-sized ship.

She was still holding his hands.

'Let me look at you. You look wonderful. Gosh! How many years has it been? No, don't you dare remind me.'

'And you look marvelous too,' he declared. 'Lovelier than ever.' In fact, he thought she looked – bizarre.

Beautiful *yes*, but synthetic, unnatural, like a Barbie doll. Both older and younger than her years. She might have been fifteen – or fifty.

The features were greatly altered. The body was as pneumatic as a mannequin's. Peter had the odd notion that were she to make some sudden gesture, the entire construct would be blown to smithereens.

She led him up a flight of stairs and on to a patio with a breath-taking view of the harbor. A white-coated waiter served drinks and canapés.

'Thank you for laying out such a fantastic sunset,' Peter said. In fact, he found it lurid. The dying sun had slashed the sky with furious colors: gold and hot pink and burnt orange. The ocean had turned to liquid fire.

Kim sighed. 'This is a very beautiful country.'

A small dog pattered on to the terrace and jumped on to Kim's lap. She fed it a scoop of caviar.

'This is Ding-ling, my Lhasa apso. Isn't he cute? He's a gift from the Dalai Lama. Tonio will be along any second,' she said. 'Unfortunately my mom can't come. She has a dance at the beach club tonight and wanted to rest up first. She's turned into a real party animal, my mom. How do you like our native rum, Peter? Have you ever had a better planter's punch?'

'It's wonderful,' Peter said.

'One of our biggest exports.' For the next minute or so, Kim expounded on the glories of San Miguel, like a one-woman Chamber of Commerce, and he wondered if this display was for his benefit or for the waiter who continued to hover within earshot. Beneath the chatter, she seemed edgy.

'Ah Tonio, there you are!' Reflexively, her hand flew to check her hair, though the coiffure was perfect, and Peter intuitively knew the source of her anxiety. She was afraid of offending her lord and master.

The man who entered was trim and handsome as a movie star, yet Peter found him repellent: the whip-hard body, the glittering eyes that spoke of cocaine. He wore a gun at his hip, which had to be an affectation, considering the tight security around the estate. Peter wondered if he beat his wife.

However, once introductions were effected, Tonio behaved with exquisite courtesy.

They sipped rum punches, watched the sunset and discussed the movie business. Peter found him intelligent and articulate.

Tonio announced his desire to promote his island to the American film industry. He hoped to lure a major studio into building sound-stages here.

'We can offer natural beauty, excellent weather, and cheap labor. Tell me, how have you found San Miguel as a location?'

'We've had problems,' Peter admitted. Twice, filming had to be shut down due to bomb scares. On another occasion, the sound of gunfire had disrupted a shot and scared the hell out of the cast. American investors, Peter noted, tended to be wary about filming in areas of civil unrest.

'Civil unrest!' Tonio's nostrils quivered. 'A few half-baked communists with home-made bazookas. Vermin. We know how to take care of those types here.' He patted his gun and smiled.

'Swiftly and surely. However, if you like, we can double the guards on the set. My Lou-lous are very efficient, as you doubtless have noticed.'

There seemed little point in remarking that American actors would not find working in an armed camp conducive to happiness.

After sundown, they went in to dinner. *En famille* – as Kim had said. Which meant a formal dining room furnished in Louis Quinze, and four elaborate courses served on gold Meissen. Behind each chair a footman in blue-and-silver knee breeches saw to it that no wine glass was left unfilled.

Though the food was superb, Peter had no appetite. He was too busy observing his host and hostess, especially the former, whom he viewed with a psychiatrist's eye.

The talk was general: sports, travel, recent movies, the best places to dine in Paris, the new American president of whom Tonio approved heartily. 'He understands the communist menace.'

Halfway through dinner, Kim's little dog shuffled into the room, sniffing for goodies. Tonio's eyes flashed fire. For one crazy moment, Peter thought he was going to pull out his gun and shoot the poor pup. Kim must have thought so as well, for she sprang to her feet.

'I'll get him out of here,' she said, panic in her voice.

'No need, *mon ange*.' Tonio snapped his fingers and a footman removed the tiny offender without a word.

'I adore animals,' Tonio said with a smile. 'But not in the dining room, where their presence is both unsightly and insanitary.'

The meal was got through somehow, a crystal decanter was brought in. 'Cockburn '23,' Tonio said. 'I know how you English love fine port.' But Peter begged off, claiming he had to be on the set early next morning.

He only regretted that he hadn't had a chance to speak with Kim privately, to take her aside and warn her that her husband was, quite possibly, a psychopath and in any case a dangerous man – but in this household no such opportunity was likely to arise.

'It was so nice of you to come, Peter,' she said in her good-little-girl voice.

'Wonderful seeing you, Kimberly.' He kissed her hand.

Tonio escorted him to the door.

'How do you think my wife looks?' he asked. 'Do you find her appearance greatly changed?'

Peter wondered what he was expected to say. 'Kimberly was a beautiful child and now she's a beautiful woman.'

'A beautiful *girl*,' Tonio said softly. 'So young and fresh-looking, you'd hardly think she was out of her teens. You see' – he smiled revealing sharp white teeth – 'my lovely wife has found the secret of eternal youth.'

Now, remembering that night in the warmth of a Los Angeles summer morning, Peter felt a chill. He thought of Kim, the eternal Galatea, resculpted anew year after year, fearful of age. He thought of Judi Syme, also fearful, searching her face in a thousand-watt mirror. Hunting for the start of a wrinkle, the birth of a mole, dreading the inexorable march of time.

But time wasn't the enemy. Time was a friend. It mellowed the heart, enriched the soul, added lustre to each day. Time coated over ancient hurts as a pearl builds upon the abrasive sand beneath to create something precious and beautiful.

No, he wouldn't marry Judi, dear though she was. True love was absent. He could never feel for her as he had once cared for his cherished 'Lady X' of Marival, as he had adored his darling Annie. He had loved twice and lost. That was enough. He had his memories.

And if ever he should chance to marry again (a highly iffy proposition), it would be to a woman who would grow old along with him.

LONG ISLAND

Having run a business for so many years – and made a fortune in the process – Miranda Vee now turned her energies to running her new life. The time had come to put down roots.

Before long, she had made herself a prestigious force in nearby institutions, endowing a chair in Business at C.W. Post College, sponsoring ballet at the Westbury Theater, active in numerous charities. Though not a flashy presence on the social scene (she never permitted herself to be photographed), she was nonetheless considered a mover and a shaker.

As a director of the Historical Society, Miranda had wide entrée and enjoyed escorting distinguished visitors on a tour of the local landmarks from Gatsby-esque mansions to wild-life reserves to the historic homes of Oyster Bay. That her own glass-and-cedar Frank Lloyd Wright residence ranked high among the area's architectural gems was a fact she never mentioned. Miranda valued her privacy. Except for a housekeeper and her animal companions, she lived alone. Casual guests were not welcome.

Yet her own home might have doubled as a private museum, small but of the finest quality.

Over the years, Miranda had assembled a superb collection of art deco, an interest first cultivated at Marival. She loved the shapes – the dazzling geometrics and streamlined curves of that period between the wars, whether expressed in a LaCloche diamond brooch or a Bauhaus sofa.

The walls were hung with the bold paintings of Foujita and Balthus. Her shelves were graced with Lalique glassware and the jazzy ceramics of Clarice Cliff and smoky *pâte-de-verre* vases by Decorchement. Now and then a rambunctious cat would mistake one of these treasures for a plaything with disastrous results, but Miranda always forgave her pets. What was love if not absolute

347

forgiveness? Yet on the whole her animals were well behaved. Perhaps they knew they were in the presence of art.

Her unlisted number was prized by auctioneers and gallery owners the world over, who knew her for a tough, shrewd bargainer; and when she traveled abroad these days, it was largely to buy for the collection. Even so, she traveled only rarely, preferring the ambience of home.

She continued to oversee MiraCo, but from an office in her home packed to the walls with new technology. With the recent advances in computer software (especially the superb Bryden Businessware line) and a bank of sophisticated phones, one could run a multi-million-dollar empire without stirring from the house. Miranda worked only a few hours a day.

In fact, commercial success was no longer the lure it had been a dozen years earlier. Familiarity had bred, not contempt, but ennui. She preferred to leave the day-to-day decisions to a hand-picked management team, all of whom, with the exception of Jim Bisseau, were female, for Miranda was eager to give ambitious young women the breaks she herself had been denied.

These days, she found it far more pleasant to stroll in the woods with her dogs or garden or sculpt or lunch with friends. She was busy, healthy, in control of her life and would have been happy. Except for the dream.

It had always been worst at the beginning of summer, as if commemorating the anniversary of her pain. Always the same. The dark man. The assault. The taste of flesh. This year was the most vivid yet.

One night in June she woke up from the dream, heart pounding, fists clenched in rage.

'I know you!' she cried out. 'I know your face. I have seen you. I know your name.'

She shuddered at the thought that her suspicion might be valid. It was almost beyond the bounds of credulity. And in that moment, she was Miranda Vee. Not for Victim. But for Vengeance.

But could she be mistaken? It was possible. Dreams, after all, are only dreams.

Peter Mainwaring had warned her against being obsessed with the past. Look forward, he had told her. Look to the future.

God knew she had tried. Had struggled mightily to put the horror behind her, yet it lay lodged deep in her soul.

What future could there be, what kind of life could she lead, when her nights were ruled by dreams that grew more graphic with each repetition? When she felt she had found the key?

Before she could go forward she would have to exorcise the past. A bill had fallen due and must be paid.

At dawn, she called her dogs and took them for a run on the beach. The air was brisk, invigorating and the animals in high spirits. As they came to the road, Miranda paused to catch her breath.

On a rise was the Villa Fiorentina, proud as an ocean liner.

She shivered.

Before the summer was out, she would renew her acquaintance with Kimberly West. And meet the infamous Tonio DuMesne.

SAN MIGUEL

Bette West's funeral was a state occasion.

El Tigre had seized upon it as a political opportunity. He would show himself in public after a year-long lapse, simultaneously scotching rumors of his own demise while exploiting the widespread sympathy felt for Ladorita in her grief.

A national day of mourning was declared. Schools were closed, work halted, purple palls placed on every public building.

Across the land, flags flew at half-mast, while in the capital of Benedicta, hushed crowds lined the streets as the funeral cortege wound its way to the cathedral where, atop a marble catafalque, Bette West's body lay in state.

Though the weather was humid, the rains were mercifully late that year, and, the solemnity of the occasion notwithstanding, there was a sense of fiesta in the air. Among the simple folk of San Miguel, the rituals of life and death have always cohabited.

In the square before the cathedral, the first of the long line of Daimlers stopped to disgorge a grieving Kim DuMesne, her husband on one arm, her father-in-law on the other.

At the sight of Ladorita, a gasp of sympathy rose from a thousand throats. For the first time in public, the Golden One was dressed in black, the radiant face was veiled.

The crowd pulled back as the funeral party, flanked by a crust of armed guards, mounted the steps. Kim staggered. For a moment, it appeared she might faint. Then, propped by her husband and father-in-law, she resumed her progress up the worn marble steps of the cathedral. Within, the cardinal who had, years earlier, bound Kimberly West to Tonio DuMesne in matrimony was waiting to conduct the requiem mass. The mood in the square was hushed, expectant, like a first-night audience. All eyes were on Ladorita.

Suddenly, from the depths of the crowd came a ripple of noise. Someone was screaming, 'Down with the DuMesnes! *A bas les DuMesnes!*' at the top of his lungs in English and French.

It was a crazy man. Necessarily crazy, for who but a madman would voice such thoughts in public? He had broken through the police line – a tall, powerfully built fellow wearing blue jeans – and lurched into the square, shouting curses.

It was Tonio who fired first. His reflexes faster than the bodyguards', he began shooting at the zig-zagging figure. Then, following suit, the Lou-lous opened fire into the crowd.

Within seconds, a half dozen people lay dead or dying, including the madman. It was chaos. Onlookers began running in crazy quilt patterns, screaming in panic, diving behind trees, under cars.

Tonio holstered his gun and cursed.

'The funeral will proceed on schedule,' he announced. Then, clutching Kim's elbow, he dragged her up the steps.

'Omigod . . . omigod . . .' she intoned, numb with horror.

'That's enough,' Tonio said firmly. 'I'm sorry you had to see that, but it was a necessary measure. Now come along. The cardinal is waiting.'

That evening Tonio went to police headquarters in Benedicta to view the bodies. They were laid out without ceremony on the floor of the cellar. Two women, a child, three men.

'This one.' Contemptuously, he nudged the corpse with the pointed toe of his Gucci alligators. 'This is the trouble-maker, is it not?'

'Yes, Your Excellency,' the police chief confirmed.

'He died instantly?'

'Yes, Excellency.'

'Too bad. I would have enjoyed entertaining him in the Black Chamber. An unfamiliar physical type, it strikes me. Not one of ours, I don't think.'

'Your Excellency is most astute. The man is a foreigner.'

'Do we know who he is?'

'No, Your Excellency. The only identification he had was an Algerian passport, which appears to be fake. Presumably, the name is false as well. W. A. Trazom.'

'Trazom?' Tonio shrugged. 'What kind of stupid alias is that? Well, my dear Mr Trazom or whoever – you've come a long way to meet your death. What did you think – you terrorist scum – that you could unseat the DuMesnes with a few ill-chosen words? That we don't know how to deal with types like you? With revolutionaries and agitators? Ah but we do, sir. And before I throw your body to my pit bulls for them to play with, I shall give you something to remember me by.'

With that, Tonio DuMesne opened his fly and pissed on the corpse of Sam Matthews.

In the bloody landscape of San Miguel, the unfortunate 'incident' on the cathedral steps was considered too inflammatory to make the newspapers. But the word spread from household to household. As did the rebellion.

After the funeral, Kim was taken to her quarters in a state of collapse. She told Celeste to admit no one, then fell on her bed and slept for sixteen hours in a heavy dreamless slumber.

A little before dawn, her eyes swollen with grief, Kim awoke and tried to sort out her thoughts.

The events of the last few weeks had been so swift, so devastating. First her mother's bizarre secret, then her death, now the horror of watching her husband gun down innocent bystanders. Why? Because some harmless lunatic had disrupted his parade.

Maxim had warned her that such violence was common in Benedicta, but she had wanted to believe he exaggerated.

No more. Not having witnessed the supreme ease with which her husband had committed mass murder. Without a flicker of hesitation or a hint of remorse.

Could she continue to live with such a man? To share his bed on those nights when he wearied of whores?

The conversation with Alix came back to haunt her. Leave everything, Alix had urged. Just grab the kids and run. *Freedom!*

But would Kim ever be free of Tonio? He would never grant her a divorce. They had children together – children they both loved. Tonio would never give them up. Neither would she.

And if she left, what would she live on? Tonio controlled every penny. Presuming she would be permitted to live at all!

Tonio was fearsome when crossed, as he had proved on the steps of the cathedral.

So what was this freedom Alix had spoken of? The freedom to be a fugitive? To hide in cheap lodgings under false names? To jump at every sudden noise and flee from every shadow, for the DuMesnes had agents everywhere? The freedom to die a violent death? Freedom! The word made her shudder.

And what of her children? Could she deprive her darlings of their heritage? At the thought of them, Kim began to weep.

She regretted having confided in detail to Alix, especially since she felt guilty about not following her advice. She was so alone in the world. If only she had someone to turn to. Someone to hold her hand and tell her what to do. Even Bette was better than the void.

Huddled under the covers, her pillow dank with tears, Kim felt overwhelmed by a sense of helplessness.

She must stay with Tonio, for she had no choice. Stay — because change was too hard. Because children need two parents. Because — though Kim tried to suppress the notion as unworthy — she had grown used to a life of wealth and beauty and luxury. Because she had become Ladorita. Because her fate was sealed.

In this heightened emotional state, she rang for Celeste.

'Yes, milady?'

'Please would you bring me ice for my eyes and some coffee.'

'Of course, milady.'

The Creole returned a few minutes later with breakfast on a silver tray. Then she went to the window to let in the morning.

'You may open the drapes,' Kim said, 'but leave the shutters drawn. I can't face the light of day.'

'Very good, milady.' While Kim sat in bed sipping coffee in the slatted shadows, Celeste moved about the room, doing chores. She plumped up the pillows, drew Kim's bath, arranged fresh flowers on the night table.

'That will be all, Celeste. Thank you. I shall spend the rest of the day in my room.'

'Very good, milady. I shall inform the staff that you are not to be disturbed.' Yet Celeste seemed reluctant to leave. 'It is terrible what happened yesterday, milady, at the cathedral. But life goes on.'

'So they say.'

Celeste looked about her nervously, though they were alone. Then – 'Maxim is here, milady. He has been waiting since dawn to pay his respects. He begs you to see him if only for a moment.'

'Maxim!'

At the sound of his name, Kim's heart surged.

She had not seen her tutor since her return from New York, grief having pushed all else from her mind. Now she knew with the force of revelation that here was a friend. An ally.

Maxim! Suddenly, the name rang with magic.

For Maxim was everything her husband was not: warm-hearted, impassioned, romantic. And though he had never declared his inmost feelings, Kim had read them a thousand times in his eyes, in the music of his voice. He loved her, as she loved –

Maxim!

In a world full of strangers and schemers, he stood apart.

'Milady is trembling!' Celeste placed a lacy shawl across Kim's shoulders.

Kim turned to her with brimming eyes.

'You may tell Maxim,' she murmured, 'that I will receive him at the usual hour. That is all.'

After Celeste left, Kim buried her face in the bowl of ice shavings till the swelling in her eyes had gone down. Then she bathed, made up her face, dabbed her throat with Opium, and put on a loose négligée of black Alençon lace.

In the silence she could feel her pulse race.

When Maxim entered, she was reclining against the pillows, classic and lovely as a statue in the shuttered light. A Venus in mourning.

'Milady!' He sprang across the room and knelt before her.

Gently, she stroked his cheek. 'Not Milady,' she whispered. 'No, my dear Maxim. You may call me anything but that.'

'My love!'

He was at her feet, then in her arms, then in her bed, raining kisses on her eyes, her lips, her hair, the smooth soft flesh beneath the open négligée. Kim shut her eyes in blissful surrender. For even sweeter than his caresses were the words she had ached to hear. Passionate, tender, ecstatic invocations – not to the goddess, but to the woman within.

'If I die for loving you,' he murmured, 'I will die happier than any man has ever lived.'

As she opened herself to him, she felt no guilt. To whom should she be faithful? To her mother, who raised her on a diet of lies? To her husband, who had betrayed her with every whore from Benedicta to Bangkok? This once, she would be faithful to herself.

Maxim made love with the full ardor of youth. And even as she wound her legs around him, even at the moment of surrender, she thought of – freedom. Not Alix's freedom, but the sexual freedom that she had been denied all her life. This once, she would love as she chose.

Afterwards they lay together for a long while, arms and legs entwined in perfect felicity.

'We are being very reckless, my darling,' he said with a tender smile. 'You as well as I.'

'I know,' she said, and played in his ear with her tongue. 'But please – can we be reckless again?'

She let him stay until mid-afternoon, knowing Tonio would expect to see her at dinner.

'Tomorrow.' She kissed him. 'The same time.'

Every morning at ten, he came to her room for three hours of explosive love-making behind drawn shutters while Celeste guarded the door. Every afternoon Kim went about her official functions. Every evening she dined with her husband in a seamless display of wifely duty.

She felt no guilt. Fair was fair. She was entitled to conduct her own life in the same manner as Tonio: performing her duties in public, enjoying her private pleasures after hours.

Moreover, casual affairs, many quite blatant, were common in their circle. Indeed – more than common. Universal! Everybody slept with everybody. Was Kim DuMesne expected to be the last faithful wife in the world? How totally naive! And unfair!

Yet though the notion ought to have made her breathe easier, she knew that such sauce-for-the-goose logic would not sit well with Tonio. She made her lover swear to be discreet.

The weeks sped by. May became June and the rainy season drew near. In a few days the DuMesnes would be leaving: Tonio to hunt rhino in Zambia, Kim to Marival, for what she described to Maxim as a 'rest cure' at a quiet spa. The children, as usual, would spend July in France with their paternal grandmother. Then Long Island in August. In September, she would be back with her Maxim.

The last morning with her lover, Kim felt a pang at the prospect of separation.

'Oh, sweetheart, I wish I could slip you into my steamer trunk and smuggle you out with me,' she said. 'Will you be true to me while I'm away? Promise me – no sweet young things.'

'Kim!' He was chagrined. 'How can you think such thoughts! Every minute we're apart will be an eternity. What if –' His eyes blazed with passion. 'What if, while your husband is off hunting, I meet you at this spa of yours? Think of it, darling. We could be together a whole month, make love morning noon and night. What bliss!'

'No! No!' Kim protested in alarm. 'You mustn't come after me. It's too dangerous.' Though in truth she was afraid not of being discovered by her husband, but by Maxim, at a time when his 'golden girl' would be a dozen shades of black and blue. God forbid he see her so soon after surgery! It would be the end of illusion.

They would only be separated for two months, she consoled him, after which they would be together again.

He accepted her fiat – 'What choice do I have?' – and made love to her again, the sex all the sweeter since it must last them the summer, then it was time to go. Reluctantly Maxim got up and pulled on his khaki trousers over thin boyish flanks. How serious he looked, she thought. How young and vulnerable.

Outside, the rain beat against the shutters, descending in marble sheets. The dry season had ended. Tomorrow she would leave San Miguel and go to Marival. Her Fountain of Youth.

'How old are you, Maxim?'

'Twenty-three, my darling Kim.'

She kissed him again. 'As old as that!'

After he left, she lay back in bed, reliving each embrace. Twenty-three, her Maxim. Almost a decade her junior. So young and fresh while she herself felt ancient and world-weary! She was grateful that the shutters had been drawn. These days, darkness served her better than daylight.

She thought of the teenage beauties of Benedicta, with their sparkling eyes and sensuous lips, quick to laugh, eager to please, to find young husbands. God – they were as delicious as ice-cream sodas. For San Miguel was a youthful country, where girls 'came out' at fifteen, married at sixteen, became grandmothers when scarcely older than Kim. Now that she had found Maxim, how dreadful it would be to lose him to some beauty half her age. And Maxim was so handsome!

She rang for Celeste.

'I have decided not to take you with me to Marival this year. I want you to stay here and look after—' she started to say, 'my wardrobe,' but there was no point in lying – 'to look after Maxim and see that he is well. I will be in touch with you from Switzerland.'

'Very good, milady.' Celeste dipped her head. 'And may I say, I have never seen milady more radiant.'

Liar! Kim thought. How radiant could a woman be at her age?

The following Monday, in his brilliantly lit examining room, she conferred with Dr Frankl. 'I'm in a radical mood this year,' she told him.

He smiled. 'What does this mean – radical?'

It meant, Kim explained, that he must exercise his highest skills, his finest art on her behalf. He must banish every portent of age, no matter how minute, pull the skin till it was as taut as a newborn's, no matter how much misery it entailed.

For the surgeon's scalpel could accomplish what the calendar could not. It could stop time in its tracks.

'Make me young,' Kim begged of the Great Rejuvenator with a despair born of passion. 'Make me younger than my lover.'

LONG ISLAND

To Alix's bafflement, Kim never got in touch.

Two months had passed without an update on her relations with Tonio, without a single inquiry concerning the search for her twin. The latter silence was particularly puzzling, in light of Kim's urgent appeal on the day Bette died. 'Find him!' she had pleaded. 'Find my other half.'

And Alix had done it – well, almost.

Though the man's whereabouts were still unknown, her investigators were hot on his trail. Daily new facts were unearthed, new leads raised to be swiftly quashed or confirmed.

Already, there was a name, an identity. It was but a matter of time till Kim's twin brother was in hand. Even Alix, so inured to high drama, found the chase exciting.

Weekly, she sent a written report to the accommodation address that Kim had given, but received no acknowledgment. Whether this Maxim Brunel ever got the letters, let alone passed them along, she couldn't tell.

August arrived, and presumably Kim DuMesne along with it, and still no word. Did Kim regret having confided in her, Alix wondered? Or had Tonio so terrorized her that she dare not risk even a phone call? Alix teetered between anxiety and vexation.

Yet though Kim appeared to be alive and well, according to the cover of *People* magazine (and astonishingly youthful, to boot), hard news was difficult to come by, and Alix was reduced to culling the popular press for information.

According to Suzy, the DuMesnes had arrived at their Long Island estate by private jet from Paris. According to Liz, they were planning the most fashionable ball since Truman Capote's Black and White extravaganza of '66. According to Regis, everybody who was anybody had been invited. The theme was Saints and Sinners and it promised to be an exercise in excess.

Yet the news pages of *The New York Times* told a more somber story, and it appeared that there might be no San Miguel for the partying DuMesnes to return to. The guerilla war had burst into a full-scale revolt, lawlessness reigned in the streets, communications had broken down. Yet even as the regime lashed back with unmitigated fury, the system threatened to collapse.

El Tigre himself had not been seen in public since the spring, giving rise to rumors that he had fled – to Mexico, to Spain, to Uruguay, to any of the dozen countries where he had stashed the plundered wealth of San Miguel.

Even a lesser student of history than Alix might have seen in this great ball the last Wagnerian gasp of a moribund regime, a veritable *Twilight of the Gods* in fancy dress.

If ever the time was ripe for Kim to break away and be her

own woman, this was the moment. Perhaps, Alix speculated, Kim was unaware of the gravity of these developments. Perhaps she just needed a push.

A few days before the ball was to take place, Alix drove out to Old Brookville on the off-chance of getting in to see Kim.

The house sat on a hill, surrounded by acres of lawn, as serene in its setting as San Miguel was turbulent. Alix pulled up at the gate. A uniformed guard approached the car. He had a jaw like a Southern sheriff.

'I trust you have a permit for that thing,' Alix said cheerfully. 'One doesn't often come across an Uzi semi-automatic in the suburbs.'

'May I help you, miss?'

'I certainly hope so. I'm a childhood friend of Mrs DuMesne and since I was passing through the neighborhood . . .'

He eyed her dusty Volvo with a faint disdain. 'Your name please?'

'Mrs Cairns,' she said blandly. 'Just say Mrs William Cairns is calling.'

He scanned a computer printout, then began speaking into a two-way radio. Calling Central Intelligence, she supposed.

While he checked her out, Alix studied the house. It was built in the Italian Renaissance style so favored by turn-of-the-century millionaires. A big house pretending to be a palace. Behind that grandiose façade, there must be fifty rooms at least, she ventured. By comparison, her father's home in Pride's Crossing was a country cottage.

Alix gazed at the upper stories, hoping to see a woman's face peeping out. The princess imprisoned in her castle.

'Maybe your friend doesn't *want* to be rescued,' Bill had suggested that morning. 'Maybe she's happy as she is. People get hooked on having big money.'

'I didn't,' Alix said tartly, but now she wondered if Bill's reading was correct.

The front lawn buzzed with activity. Under the direction of

a man on a cherry-picker, an army of gardeners was digging up and replanting hundreds of rose bushes in some arcane pattern. Busy busy busy. Like the gardeners in *Alice in Wonderland* who painted the white roses red to placate the Queen of Hearts while the old gal kept yelling, 'Off with their heads.'

It was all fake. Make-believe. The house, the grounds, the works. *Alix* in Wonderland. The notion made her smile. But there was no rabbit hole for her to slip through, for just then the guard thrust his jaw through the car window.

'Sorry, ma'am. We have no Mrs Cairns on the visitors' list and I am not permitted to admit strangers.'

'But I'm an old school chum . . .' Alix began, then gave it up as a hopeless cause. 'Fuck you, buddy!' She gunned the car and drove off.

'The bitch of it is,' she complained to Bill at dinner time, 'everybody who's anybody has been invited to this goddamn ball except us. Society people, rock stars, celebrities, publicity freaks, from Don King to Donald Trump to —'

'Donald Duck?' He had taken over the dining-room table, and was alternately wolfing down lamb chops and roughing out a speech on a yellow legal pad.

'Yeah. Him too,' she said. 'Though not, I'm sorry to say, the attractive and brilliant candidate for the US Senate, the Honorable William F. Cairns and frau.'

'Just as well,' Bill muttered, scribbling away. 'Because if we were invited, I couldn't accept. It'd be political suicide for me to break bread with the DuMesnes. About as tasteful as visiting Hitler and admiring the lampshades.'

'Honestly, Bill!'

'Honestly, Alix! They're tyrants and assassins.'

'He is. She isn't,' Alix protested. 'Anyhow it's a moot point, since I haven't a thing to wear. What say we take the kids to City Island and go sailing instead?'

'Sure. Great.' He was chewing on a pencil. 'If I can get away.

Gotta be in White Plains at six. Fund-raiser. Which phrase sounds better, Alix? *A political platform only a mugger could love* or *a license to steal*?'

'The latter,' she said, and finished her meal in silence.

Alix sighed. Come Saturday night and Bill would be out beating the bushes while she stayed home and did zilch. Silly though it seemed, she would love to have gone to the DuMesnes' ball, if for no other reason than the novelty of seeing Kim in that exotic habitat.

Especially since everybody who was anybody had been invited.

Peter Mainwaring was invited.

'How can you *not* go?' Judi Syme wanted to know. 'It's the party of the year, and I'm dying to dress up in my Cleopatra number with an honest-to-God live asp on my breastplate.'

'Was Cleo a saint or a sinner?'

'A bit of both, I expect. And you could come as Mark Antony, bony knees and all.'

But Peter could scarcely conceal his distaste. He had had enough of the DuMesnes for one lifetime, thank you very much. *Peter Mainwaring regretfully declines.*

Miranda Vee was invited.

The invitation itself was an extraordinary affair. Handwritten by a master calligrapher on a sheet of gold foil, it was set into a kilo slab of Swiss chocolate. The chocolate had been carved to resemble an open book, the left hand leaf made of white chocolate, the right hand of dark, thus reflecting the theme of Saints and Sinners.

Their Excellencies
Tonio and Kimberly DuMesne
request the pleasure of your company
at a Masque

on the first Saturday of August
Come as a Saint
Come as a Sinner
But Come!

Miranda studied the wording carefully. *A Masque*. Not a ball, mind you, but a 'masque.' What exactly did that mean? She reached for her dictionary.

Masque: 1. A dramatic entertainment based upon allegory. 2. A masquerade. 3. A masked ball.

'A dramatic entertainment,' Miranda murmured thoughtfully.

She would go, of course. Nothing could keep her away.

PARIS

At the end of July, Tonio went to Paris to collect his wife at the Ritz Hotel. She was sitting for a photographer from *People* magazine when he arrived, presenting her new face for the world to see. After the photographer left, Tonio congratulated Kim on her appearance, albeit archly.

'My lord, but the good Dr Frankl has excelled himself this time. I swear, you could pass for a teenager. Ah, how I envy you the bloom of youth and innocence. Remarkable what modern science can do. Now about your costume for the ball, has M. St Laurent completed it yet?'

Kim nodded.

'And will you be a saint or a sinner, my love?'

But Kim didn't want to talk about the ball. It hurt to move her jaw; her face throbbed from the last operation. Perhaps she had pushed Dr Frankl too hard. But Kim had another reason to be anxious. Since leaving San Miguel, she had heard from neither Celeste nor Maxim.

'What's going on at home?' she cried. 'All I know are these

363

dreadful reports I read in the paper. Shootings, riots – it sounds like everything is in total chaos.'

'Don't believe half of it,' Tonio said. 'I was there a few days ago and I assure you, the situation will soon be in hand.'

'But, Tonio!' She tried to quell the panic. 'For the last month, I haven't been able to get my maid on the phone. The switchboard won't put me through.'

He gazed at her cooly. He was playing a game.

'What do you want with your maid, *mon ange?*'

Kim picked her words cautiously. 'I wanted to speak to her before she left for Long Island, to tell her what clothes to bring, what jewels I'll need for the ball.'

Tonio smiled. 'As to your jewels, that's taken care of already. I thought, since at present things are a bit troubled down there, it would be prudent to remove all your valuables from Le Paradis. Your lovely baubles are perfectly safe in a bank vault in Manhattan. So you have no need of Celeste.'

'But Celeste . . . she does my hair so beautifully.'

'There are hairdressers in New York,' he said. 'T'ai chi instructors too.'

T'ai chi? For a moment, Kim had forgotten the pretext that covered Maxim's daily visits. She felt sick with horror.

'No one does my hair like Celeste,' she managed to say.

'I disagree. In fact, I haven't cared at all for her work lately,' he said carefully, 'which is why I have had her removed.'

'Removed?' Her stomach tightened at the word even before her brain had grasped it.

'Removed' – Tonio's eyes had a reptilian glitter – 'from the payroll, my dear. Permanently. Her so-called cousin as well, if that's what he told you he was. Cousin indeed! The fellow was nothing but a trouble-maker. No matter. You shan't be bothered by them again. I have given them – what is that quaint American expression? – I have given the pair their walking papers.'

It took all Kim's strength to keep from crying out, *What have you done with them, you monster? With him?* But the words died in her throat. One untoward movement, one reckless tear would be tantamount to an admission of adultery.

He suspected something clearly, but what did he *know*? That Maxim was a rebel? Or that Maxim was her lover?

And what if Tonio's innuendoes were true? What if Maxim was not Celeste's cousin, as she had been led to believe, but had played her like a puppeteer, exploiting Kim's affections for political ends. It made a horrid kind of sense, for who was closer to power, who could wield greater influence than the man who slept with the woman who slept with the leader?

Kim thought her heart would break. She loved Maxim. This past month in Marival, she had undergone agonies, endured the greatest suffering only to please him. She loved Maxim. More than that! She had trusted him to the depths of her being. As she had trusted Celeste. If the poison Tonio was spreading were true . . . But no! She refused categorically to believe such filth. Why, Maxim and Celeste were her only true friends in San Miguel. Her sole confidants. Without them, she had no one.

Where were they now? Rotting in the *oubliettes* of San Miguel. Hiding in the mountains with the guerillas. Or dead – strangled by Tonio's own hands. But whatever the fate of Maxim and Celeste, she knew better than to ask, terrified that she might share it.

'So, my love.' Tonio was observing her every motion as though she were a specimen on a slide. 'Will you be ready to leave in the morning?'

Mutely, Kim bowed her head.

Pleased by this proof of her submission, Tonio grinned and had champagne sent up.

The next day on the plane, he spoke only of the ball.

'It will be our best yet. Our most significant. A notice to the world that despite the recent unpleasantness, San Miguel remains a land of wealth and stability. The arrangements are complete. Of five hundred twenty invitations, we have had five hundred thirteen acceptances. Which is not bad, considering all the racket in the left wing press.' He laughed. 'The editorial writers of the *New Republic* may label us social pariahs, but I suspect that's only because they didn't receive an invitation. Did I tell you Malcolm Forbes is coming . . . ?'

As he chattered on, Kim stared out the window. She felt bludgeoned, numb. The codeine didn't help. The pain in her face was excruciating. But not as great as the pain in her heart.

VILLA FIORENTINA

In her thin shimmery dress and silver sandals, Miranda walked the quarter mile from her house, past the slow-moving flotilla of limousines that jammed the road leading to the gates of the mansion.

At the entrance way, guests had lined up like theater-goers at a hit Broadway show. The security was fierce, precluding any possibility of gate-crashers. Yet the formalities were handled with style and aplomb.

In keeping with the theme of the evening, the guards were in costume: some dressed as cinematic Keystone Kops with swirling mustaches; others got up as period 'gangsters,' flamboyant in double-breasted white suits and fedora hats. As a graceful excuse for having the staff pack weapons, the silent-movie bit was inspired.

When her turn came, Miranda presented her invitation to have it double-checked against the list. Then, passing between a pair of metal detectors, she made her way up the circular path to the house. A few steps ahead of her, Count Dracula walked arm-in-arm with Joan of Arc. An odd couple indeed.

For her own costume, Miranda had drawn upon the mythology of Camelot, with a nod to her favorite decorative style.

Tonight, she was King Arthur's wicked sister, the fairy Morgan le Fay. She found it intriguing that Morgan le Fay was also known as Fata Morgana, which is to say a dream, a mirage, an illusion.

As inspiration for her costume, she had drawn upon a 1920s children's story book, illustrated by the art deco master, N. C. Wyeth. Working with a New York costumier, she had concocted the sheerest slip of a gown in a metallic gauze that shimmered and gleamed as mysteriously as the mists of Avalon. The fabric had to be specially woven and was fragile as smoke. Her only ornament was a pendant of platinum, onyx and pavé diamonds suspended on a fine silver chain. It was her favorite piece of jewelry. It depicted a lorelei, the billowing diamanté hair lightly veiling the naked bosom beneath. The eyes were of lapis lazuli, blue as Miranda's own. An exquisite piece, designed by Alphonse Mucha for the House of Fouquet, Miranda had acquired it at auction the year before.

Like the lorelei, Miranda too had let down her chestnut hair so that it flowed about her shoulders like molten fire.

'Do I look wicked enough?' she had asked her housekeeper before leaving home. Mrs Andeson was stunned. She was used to seeing her employer in softly tailored clothes: Armani suits or Ralph Lauren sportswear.

'It's not like you, Miss Vee. It's so very . . . very . . .'

'Very what, Millie? Revealing? Sexy? Indecent? What?'

But Millie Andeson's vocabulary failed to rise to the occasion. 'Very *very!*' she exclaimed.

Very provocative, Miranda thought. It had been years since she had dressed to entice.

Light blazed from every window. Music filled the air. As Miranda neared the house, it struck her that the DuMesnes had arranged everything to perfection – even the weather.

Wherever one turned there was something to delight the eye, the ear, from the elaborate plantings of dwarf rose bushes in the shape of a salamander (the national emblem of San Miguel) to the ripe sound of big-band music emanating from the ballroom within. Though it was only ten thirty, the party was in full swing.

Miranda passed into the hall where two stentorian figures, one in white, one in black, announced the arriving guest.

'The Prince and Princess Von Hochberg!' the one in white sang out, identifying the Dracula and Joan.

'Miss Miranda Vee,' announced the page in black.

Miranda smiled and stepped into an enormous ballroom. She had expected an official reception line, but there was nothing so formal. Merely merry-makers by the hundreds, outrageously dressed and bejeweled, drinking, dancing, swirling, whirling, filling the ornately decorated chamber with their laughter.

It was a maze of bodies, a daze of color, a miasma of costly perfumes. If the costumes were fabulous, even more so were the faces that leapt out from the mass. Movie stars, opera singers, the new heavyweight champ (togged out in white as Sir Gala-had), merchant princes, politicos, corporate raiders and traders, titans and trash. All dressed to amuse, to confuse, to delight, to deceive, to trick the eye and lure the senses.

The waiters were kitted out as Swiss Guards, presumably on the side of the angels, while the bar was staffed with Chinese demons in red satin. Yet as Miranda scanned the sea of faces, the ones she looked for eluded her.

Where were the DuMesnes?

Remembering the teenage girl who had rescued her that night by the lake – not a vision one was likely to forget – she was puzzled by the invisibility of Kimberly West DuMesne. Had the passage of time altered her savior beyond all recognition or was she hiding behind an exotic disguise? Impersonating a man, Miranda speculated. Or a monster.

Some of the guests wore masks in a playful attempt at concealment. Miranda did not. Why don a mask when her disguise was complete? When her face itself was a deception?

Miranda Vee wore the mask given her at Marival. She needed nothing more.

As she passed through the room, Miranda was greeted by numerous acquaintances: socialites, Wall Street bankers, notables from the diplomatic community. But not a glimpse of her host or hostess.

She began circulating, exchanging greetings, dancing in succession with Genghis Khan, Al Capone and Professor Moriarty, whom she knew better as the respected chairman of a British merchant bank.

'Why is it, Nigel,' she asked, 'that most of the guests chose to dress up as sinners rather than saints? I've counted three Lucrezia Borgias already, and God knows how many Draculas.'

'Because, my dear Miranda, the devil has all the good lines. You look, by the way, absolutely smashing.' His free hand began wandering down the back of her dress. She disengaged herself lightly from his embrace.

'Thank you, Nigel,' she said.

The old goat!

Yet there was something erotic in the air. Perhaps it was the sense of anonymity. *That's not me making love to a total stranger –* a respectably married woman might say – *it's Mme Dubarry or Lola Montez.*

Even Miranda felt herself falling prey to the mood. For the first time in years, she felt sexual, seductive. Betsy Gimpel, a veteran of these extravaganzas, declared that the DuMesnes had fed an aphrodisiac scent into the ventilation system and that before long the twenty guest bedrooms would be bulging with sweaty bodies coupling and recoupling in the most bizarre configurations.

'Why, Betsy!' Miranda teased the ancient dowager. 'You make the Villa Fiorentina sound like a hot-sheets hotel.'

'Don't mock, my dear.' The old lady chastised her with a jeweled fan. 'I already have my eye on that adorable Swiss Guard in charge of the gravlax.'

369

The rooms grew hotter. The music louder, more intense. A scattershot of white lights exploded here and there among the dancing couples, illuminating some, thrusting others into darkness.

Miranda danced, chatted, picked up flutes of champagne only to set them down untasted. The program called for supper at midnight, breakfast at dawn, followed by a morning swim in the pool. Yet as the evening progressed there was still no sign of the DuMesnes.

'Have we been abandoned?' she asked around.

Their host was indeed here in the ballroom, several guests assured her, though rumors abounded as to his absent wife.

One woman, claiming to be a family intimate, announced that Kim was sulking in her quarters, furious at her husband's affair with a Brazilian porno star. Another was convinced their hostess was zonked out on coke, while the editor of a slick fashion magazine speculated that Kim DuMesne's costume was so weighted down with precious stones that she was incapable of locomotion. It soon became apparent that no one had actually set eyes on Kimberly since her arrival from the Continent the previous week.

'But if you want to meet the husband, he's over there.'

'Where?' Miranda was on instant alert.

'Over by the bar. With what's-her-name.'

She whipped around. And there he was. No mistaking the man. Even in costume, she recognized him. Was it because he resembled his photos – or her dreams?

Not tall, but slim and handsome. A line had been drawn down the middle of his face; one half was painted black, the other white. He was dressed in evening clothes, a long formal tailcoat, one half black, one half white, like a cubist painting. Dark hair combed long in the European fashion. He wore a gun at his hip. Black gun, white pearl handle.

Miranda moistened her lips and headed in his direction. He

was flirting with a raunchy sit-com star, whispering something that made the woman laugh and then move on.

Miranda pasted on a smile and stepped forward.

'I cannot spend another moment at this charming party without thanking my host,' she said, holding out her hand. 'You are, I believe, Tonio DuMesne.'

'At your service.'

He bent to kiss her hand with a continental flourish, then straightened up. Their eyes met.

It was he! He was smiling, as he had smiled at her before. White teeth, sharp and feral.

'And you, my beautiful stranger, your name is . . . ?'

In his gaze she read unfeigned admiration.

'My name?' To her own ears, her voice came from a very great distance as if in a dream. It was all happening – here and now!

But what if she were wrong? What if she confused the face that plagued her in sleep with the image seen so often in the press? There was a resemblance, certainly. But beyond that? Was she doing anything more than inventing a memory? If ever Miranda had needed to exert consummate mastery over every facet of her body – her voice, her expression, even the sweat glands on her palms – that moment was now. She had to learn the truth.

Without moving a muscle, she gazed at the painted face.

'I am Morgan le Fay.'

DuMesne locked his eyebrows, and very eloquent eyebrows they were. 'I'm afraid I'm not familiar with any woman named Morgan,' he said. 'Does it come from a book?'

'From the Arthurian legends. In old English, the word fey means – charmed. Supernatural.'

'I see. And is our Morgan a good fairy or a wicked one?'

'Wicked.'

'I'm so glad! For as you can see, my enchantress, I am already under your spell.'

He leaned forward to examine the Fouquet pendant that lay between her breasts. He held the piece in his palm for a moment, examining it with a lapidarian eye, then returned it to its resting place. As he did, his thumb brushed her nipple. Accident or design?

Design, she had no doubt, for his black eyes danced with sexual fervor.

'Very beautiful,' he said.

'The pendant?'

'I meant the wearer, Miss Vee.'

With a rush of adrenaline, she realized he had addressed her by name. Was it possible that he knew who she was? Why she had come?

'I don't believe we've met,' she said softly.

'Ah but we have' – Miranda's heart stopped – 'at least vicariously.' He laughed. 'At Sotheby's in London. You outbid my agent for that pendant which I had quite set my heart on. However, I'm glad to see it found such an exquisite home.'

She drew closer to him, unable to rid herself of that last smidgen of doubt. Was he the man? The braggadocio was the same. The arrogant tone, the extravagant compliments, the way he stripped her with his eyes. The gun, too, was in character. Yet the painted face played tricks, defied certainty. Her memory was of smooth olive skin. Of short crisp hair and high cheekbones.

To be sure, dead sure, she must get closer to him. Dance with him. Feel the thrust of his body, inhale his scent.

She glanced down at the pendant, then up at him.

'If I outbid you, Your Excellency,' she answered smoothly, 'then I must have overpaid wildly.'

'One can never overpay for the objects of one's desire. That much I have learned. I find it interesting, though, that we both covet the same things.'

'I find it fascinating,' she replied honestly.

The band had struck up a soft smoky ballad. 'Do you dance with your guests?' she asked.

'I do everything,' he said, 'everything that can make a woman happy, but only if you call me Tonio.'

'And I am Miranda.'

'I know.'

He held out his hand to lead her across the parquet, but she hesitated, then adopted the teasing tone he seemed to prefer.

'I've never danced with a man who wore a gun. It makes me feel – at a disadvantage.'

'You have weapons too, my dear.' As he spoke, the traveling spotlights singled them out. In its glare, her gown was almost transparent. As for Tonio, he was regarding her breasts with naked sensuality. 'Weapons only barely concealed,' he said with a laugh. 'And far more potent than mine, *ma belle chérie*.'

Miranda's mouth went dry. Why had he addressed her in French? Was he playing games? Remembering that bar near Chambord? The spotlight moved on.

'I'm sorry. I don't speak – was that French?' She smiled innocently. 'And what is your costume meant to convey?'

He paused at the edge of the dance floor. 'I am the Baron Samedi, who stands watch between the living and the dead. Like your Morgan le Fay, my character is also a figure endowed with unearthly powers.'

'Is he a saint or sinner?'

'Ah, very much a sinner, I'm afraid, my delicious Miranda.'

He pulled her to him and they began dancing skin to skin. It was hot. Their sweat mingled. She felt his lips in her ear. 'A thoroughly bad character,' he whispered, 'but he can be very very good in bed.'

The exact words! Now memory was keen. Yes, this was the man! Who had danced with her at a café near Chambord. Who had gone on to murder her soul. In her neck, a pulse beat wildly. Miranda Vee she had styled herself. But she would be a victim no longer. Miranda Vee – for Vengeance.

She had to get him away, alone. Induce him to take the gun

off. She was well aware that she was contemplating a capital crime, but first, she had to be certain.

She moved up against him as though to crawl inside his body. She felt the urgent press of his penis against her stomach. Good! It was exactly as she desired.

Seductively she twined her arms around him, caressed his face. His lips, the curve of his cheek. Then slowly, she slid her hand into his hair and pushed it back gently. Her finger came to rest on his ear lobe.

'What happened to the tip of your ear?' Miranda asked.

He shrugged, suddenly annoyed.

'It was bitten off years ago . . . by a wild animal. A hunting accident, so to speak.'

'In Africa?' she asked, with seeming awe in her voice.

He gave a sardonic laugh. 'In a small town in France.'

'And what happened to the animal?'

'I destroyed it.'

She kissed him full on the mouth.

'God, you excite me,' she murmured. She tasted his teeth, chewed on his mouth.

The music stopped. He released her from his embrace.

'Lovely Miranda,' he crooned. His lips were bruised. 'What a hungry little mouth you have.'

'The better to eat you with, my darling.'

They exchanged a quick fervid glance. Then he said the words she ached to hear.

'Let's go.'

'Where?'

'Where we can be private and fuck each other blind.'

She moaned as though with longing. 'Oh, yes! I want it too. But won't your absence be noticed? And where's your wife?'

Already he was steering her through the crush of dancers to the sweeping staircase that led to the upper floors. The music seemed to follow them, faster, more rhythmic.

'My wife' – his voice grew playful – 'is both here and not

here, you might say. A conundrum.' He led her up the stairs, down a long corridor hung with tapestries to a pair of oaken doors.

'You needn't worry about my wife, Miranda, for this is the one place she never ventures.' He flung open the doors. 'My bedroom.'

It was a huge room, designed for fantasies. The walls were frescoed with opulent Renaissance nudes and lecherous satyrs. He led her to a huge circular bed beneath a canopy of Florentine velvet. Inside Miranda's head, voices screamed.

'Now,' he smiled, falling back on a cloud of pillows, 'take that absurd garment off and let me enjoy those lovely breasts that have been driving me wild all evening. They are genuine, aren't they? One gets so weary of silicone.'

'Absolutely genuine.' She leaned over, as though to straddle him, then placed her hand across his holster.

'Does that thing come off?' she asked softly. 'It makes me feel inhibited.'

Tonio laughed. 'For you, everything comes off.'

She watched as he unstrapped the gun and placed it on a marble table a foot away.

'And now, my wicked fairy,' he said, 'I'm at your mercy.'

No one heard the shot. The walls were too thick, the crowd downstairs too raucous, the band was playing full blast.

Just as no one observed when – a few minutes past midnight – Miranda descended the stairs and walked down the corridor in the direction of the ballroom.

Nigel Carpenter was heading for the men's room when he saw her. The first thing he noticed (he was later to testify) was an astonishing gray streak in the chestnut hair. The second thing he noticed was the gun.

'Miranda!' he called out. She didn't hear him.

She moved past him slow and purposefully until she came to a security guard.

'Call the police,' she said in a well-controlled voice. 'I have just killed Tonio DuMesne.'

Then she sat down in an armchair and waited.

IN LIMBO

Bill had left the house before dawn, waking Alix in the process. She couldn't remember the last time they'd had breakfast together. And it was Sunday morning, to boot.

Beneath half-closed eyes, she watched him check his itinerary, then rummage through his dresser for appropriate gear. What would it be today: yarmulke, kente cloth cap, mortar-board, metal hard hat, Shriner's fez? Which speech would it be: foreign relations, race relations, chaos in the classroom, crime in the streets? He had an issue for every audience, a platform to match each change of gear.

Bill had budgeted a year for the pursuit of a seat on Capitol Hill. Like everything else in politics, the time allotment seemed excessive, but he was up against a mass of entrenched interests. And while Alix applauded his grit, she resented the fact that he was spending more time with his campaign manager, Harry McAfee, than he did with his family.

Periodically, Bill groused about the circus aspects of office-seeking, the 'funny hats' as he called them or those photo ops that required him to eat hot dogs at ball games or march in Polish parades, but he was willing to undergo minor humiliations if he could get his message across.

'At least when I'm talking to voters,' he confided, 'I'm standing on my own two feet. Whereas when I'm grubbing for campaign finance, I have to get down on all fours.'

Money money money. Alix sighed. That's what running for

office came down to: chasing after enough bucks to pay for the ads, the posters, the mailings, the telemarketers, the buttons – even the shopping bags to match his opposition's expenditures. His opponent had a war chest that topped two million dollars. His opponent had had the good sense to inherit a supermarket chain.

These days Bill was spending as much time in fund-raising as spreading the word, which was regrettable. However, he had known the rules of the game before he started. He was a big boy, the choice was his. Though that driven quality she had admired so much when they were adversaries was beginning to pall on the personal level.

Not that she didn't believe Bill would make a splendid senator. She would have voted for him even if he weren't her husband. She liked to think she had helped him shape his platform, thrash out issues. But Alix would be damned if she was going to tread the beaten path as behoved a politico's wife. She refused (a) to have 'teas', (b) to kiss children (other than her own, of course) or (c) to sit behind him on a platform wearing white gloves and a worshipful smile. Nancy Reagan she was not.

'You're not helping Bill any,' Harry McAfee complained. 'It's almost like you don't want him to win the nomination.'

Maybe she didn't. If nominated, he might get elected which would be even worse. Because then Bill would be in Washington, she would be in New York – and what kind of marriage would they have? A day here, a few hours there, snippets of time snatched from two major careers.

She could move with him, of course (and it was always the wife who moved, never the husband). She could pick up the kids, abandon her practice, settle in Washington and start a new life. Except it wouldn't be her life; it would be Bill's.

Just as she might have gone with him this morning to whatever stops were on his campaign trail. Kissed the babies. Smiled the smiles. And blended neatly into the background.

Other women followed their husbands, putting their own careers on hold in deference to his (presumably) more important one. But Alix wasn't other women.

It was not as if Alix were incapable of sacrifice. Had she not forfeited a fortune for Sam Matthews? But Sam had loved her – at least she had believed so at the time – whereas Bill! She felt that Bill had married her for the most unromantic reasons: because she was bright, self-sufficient. Because it was time he got married anyhow. And it was hard not to suspect, given the scope of his dreams, that the possibility of one day plugging into the Bryden millions had also been a factor.

With that notion lodged in the back of her brain, she could hardly consider giving up her career or her way of life just to satisfy her husband's ambitions. Why should she? Where was the quid pro quo in all this?

If Bill Cairns truly required the warming presence of a female at a rally or a fund-raiser, Alix felt, he could always call on his mother or one of his sisters. Let *them* wear white gloves and look worshipful.

Not her, thank you very much! She had spent years building up the best criminal practice in New York and she wasn't about to kiss it off lightly. Least of all now, with a remarkable case about to come to trial.

It had been Bill's turn to grouse that Sunday morning six weeks earlier when the bedside phone had blasted them awake before sun-up.

'Goddamn,' he said handing her the phone, 'don't your clients ever take a night off? Whatever happened to the sanctity of the home?' Then he burrowed back down under the covers. (Though when he learned the nature of the call, he felt differently. 'They ought to give the woman a medal,' he said.)

That morning, however, it had been Alix who slipped out of the house before dawn in hot pursuit of a career, although it wasn't until she arrived at the Nassau County jail an hour later that she realized the full dimensions of the case.

'We've met before,' Miranda Vee said.

'I think not.' Alix was puzzled.

'Perhaps not *met* in the social sense, but our paths crossed at Marival. I'm the woman who sat by the lake.'

Alix, who liked to boast that nothing surprised her, was flabbergasted.

'Lady X!' she gasped.

Miranda smiled. 'It's a small world, isn't it?'

Considering the gravity of the charge, Alix's new client appeared calm, almost serene.

'However,' she said in a throaty voice, 'I didn't wake you at dawn to discuss old times. You're reputed to be the sharpest criminal lawyer in the East and I suspect I'll need the best. It was premeditated murder. I saw him at the ball. Lured him into a situation where we could be alone. Then I shot and killed Tonio DuMesne. Simple as that.'

Alix shook her head. 'Nothing's ever that simple. Let's have it all.'

Miranda's recital of the events that had led up to the murder was compelling: the initial assault, the trauma, the years of amnesia, the recurring dreams, the growing suspicion, the shock of recognition at the ball.

Concerning the crime itself, however, she was loath to go into details. 'What is there to say? There was a gun on the table. I picked it up. I shot and killed him.'

At the moment, Alix had only one question.

'There's no doubt in your mind that he was the man who attacked you in Chambord?'

'None whatever.'

'I should be surprised, but I'm not. I met him once years ago – not exactly your Mr Nice Guy. Poor Kim!' She sighed, then

379

turned to the matter at hand. 'You realize that everything will come out now. Your past will be dredged up, your real identity, the fact that you were the victim of a vicious crime. You'll have no secrets left.'

'I don't need my secrets any more,' Miranda said. 'I did what I had to and have no regrets. Prison doesn't scare me, Alix. I've been through bigger hells already.'

'Whoa there, Miranda! Let's not get romantic about jail time.'

'I'm not being romantic, just practical. I've been in prison for years, Alix. The prison of my mind, which is worse than anything the state of New York has to offer. At least I'll be able to sleep without dreams now, which is a pretty fair trade-off. I'm resigned to paying whatever price the law exacts.'

'Well, I'm not!' Alix broke in. 'My whole career has been devoted to keeping people out of the slammer. It's a holy cause with me, so don't start throwing away your future so lightly. I won't have it. And don't kid yourself, the penalties can be stiff. Look at Jean Harris – the woman who killed the Scarsdale Diet doctor. She got fifteen to life. That's hard time, Miranda. We could be talking about the rest of your life.'

'But I've lived my life already,' Miranda said. For a moment the cool aplomb wavered, the voice shook. 'This may sound crazy, Alix, but looking back on Chambord, I realize that my survival was a kind of aberration. I should have died the night Tonio attacked me. I nearly did. If not then, I should certainly have drowned in Lac Leman. And would have, if not for Kimberly West. You see, my number had already come up—'

'That's bullshit!' Alix protested.

'Is it? I can only tell you what I feel. Which is that I was never entitled to all the time between then and now. Don't get me wrong. I'm not complaining. The interim years have been very good to me, but they were a mistake, a kind of a cosmic book-keeping error. I'd cheated Fate, you see. And now Fate is calling in her due bills. It's as if she was saying, "Okay, my friend. You've had a free ride all those years and now it's time to pay up."'

Alix was appalled. 'Fuck fate,' she said crisply. 'I don't want to hear another word of gloom or doom or numbers coming up. Only on how to present the best defense possible.' Then she laughed. 'Look, Miranda, if you were really such a fatalist, you wouldn't have sent for *me*, because I make it my business to win. So you can just tell Fate to take a flying jump. Meanwhile, let's go see about getting you out of here. Bail should be no problem. You're an upstanding citizen with a fine reputation. Plus you've got lots of money, which never hurts.'

A few hours later, Miranda was free on bond. The two women walked out of the courthouse into a blaze of TV crews, then Alix made her escape and started the drive back to the city.

In the car she switched on the radio. The murder was headline news on all the wire services, although details remained sparse. *Notorious playboy . . . female tycoon . . . Long Island mansion . . . masked ball . . .* She switched it off.

What a case! There were almost too many ironies to absorb. Small world, Miranda had commented. That it was. Not fate, though. Never fate, Alix scowled as she battled Sunday traffic. It drove her nuts when clients nattered on about fate with a capital F. The ultimate four-letter word.

Had Alix Bryden believed in fate rather than reason, she would never have become a lawyer, which was all about taking so-called 'fate' by the scruff of the neck and giving it a thorough trouncing. Fate was a fraud. A sham.

Alix did, however, believe in justice – and there was a kind of justice in Miranda's act. What goes around sometimes comes around, and killers do on occasion get killed. But that had less to do with fate than with character.

Sooner or later, someone was bound to have murdered Tonio DuMesne. His disgruntled countrymen were probably standing in line for the privilege. As they say down south, the man wanted killing. Miranda just happened to be the first one to have a clear shot. Not fate. Merely chance, which was another matter.

Although to his widow it must have appeared a divine retribution, for Kimberly West believed in Fate with a capital F.

As Alix pulled on to the parkway, she recalled a long-ago conversation with Kim over iced coffee and cannoli about fate, inexorable destiny. The memory made Alix uneasy.

How was Kim bearing up, she wondered. Was she devastated by Tonio's death? Shocked? Grief-stricken? Or secretly relieved?

Alix considered turning the car around and trying to get in to see her, then thought better of it. Most likely, Kim was holed up within her 'castle' while the press laid siege outside. Alix's heart went out to her. Let her grieve this day in peace! There would be time enough to offer condolences (and get her side of the story) in the weeks ahead.

Verifying Miranda's story presented few problems. A quick background investigation confirmed Tonio's presence in France at the time of the outrage. There were hospital records, travel records, financial records. The clincher came when Alix wangled a statement from the French lawyer who had arranged Miranda's stay at Marival, convincing him that diplomatic immunity did not extend beyond the grave. And most convincing of all would be the testimony of Peter Mainwaring.

Peter had flown to New York the day after the story broke to be with Miranda. Shortly after, he called on Alix at her office. It was a curious reunion.

The last time they had seen each other had been at the Gilchrist trial. Alix could hardly forget Peter's bitterness and pain – so much of it directed at her.

To her relief, however, he now appeared thoroughly recovered from his wife's death. The shadows of that dark winter were gone and the Peter she now dealt with was a vibrant and energetic man, full of warmth and humor, eager to be of service.

'The moment I saw Miranda's picture on television,' he told Alix, 'and realized who she was, I had to drop everything and come in case she needed my help. By God, she's a wonderful woman! And DuMesne was a degenerate wretch. He deserved his fate, though of course I feel sorry for Kimberly. Have you heard from her?'

'Not a word. And frankly, I'm mystified. She's locked herself up inside the house, won't see anyone, won't take phone calls, though I've left a dozen messages. She's still in shock, I imagine. And of course, what with the revolution in San Miguel, she can't ever go back. Not that she'd want to – with such a bloodbath going on! That poor unhappy island! I suspect Tonio's death was all the rebels required to topple the regime. Still, it must have been a double blow to poor Kim – losing both husband and country in such short order. She must be living in limbo.'

Peter nodded. 'I dined with them once in San Miguel and sized him up immediately as a psychopath. His wife was terrified of him, and now that he's dead, I expect she has mixed feelings. Living in limbo, as you say. But for that matter, so is Miranda – and will be until this trial is over. If my testimony can be of any use –'

'Oh indeed it can!' Alix said, noting how flushed he became when speaking of his former patient.

He reached across the desk and clasped her hand. 'Count on me,' he said, 'as I'm counting on you.'

'So what's your strategy?' Bill asked early on. 'Insanity? Self-defense? Justifiable homicide?'

'I haven't decided as yet,' she replied. 'I'd appreciate your advice.'

'As I see it' – Bill steepled his hands – 'your basic problem is that of premeditation. She wanted to kill him. She had an opportunity to kill him. She killed him.'

Bill spent the next twenty minutes erecting straw men, then cutting them off at the legs, explaining why Strategy A wouldn't work, but Strategy B was worse, whereas Strategy C – forget it!

'In fact,' he concluded, 'there are two crimes to consider here. Miranda Vee's and the crime that triggered it. Only that earlier crime has never been prosecuted.'

Alix was right up there with him.

'Of course!' she said triumphantly. 'I don't defend Miranda Vee. I indict and convict Tonio DuMesne!'

That conversation had taken place some time before this lazy Sunday morning, with Alix watching through hooded eyes as her husband tiptoed to the closet, selected one tie (sober, conservative), stuck another (rather jazzier) into his briefcase alongside the yarmulke, then tiptoed over to where she presumably lay dozing, pecked her on the forehead, mumbled 'Back around midnight,' then slipped out of the room like a wraith.

The moment the door was shut, Alix's eyes snapped open.

Rats! she thought. Ever since this damned campaign began running full throttle, husband and wife had hardly had an hour together. Certainly, never had a whole day. She resented it.

She particularly resented it since today was Sunday, dammit. When proper husbands lazed in bed, had breakfast with their family, read *The Sunday Times*, played piggyback and Chinese checkers, cut the lawn or shoveled the snow, whichever was appropriate, took the kids to the zoo, ate heavy Sunday dinners, watched *Sixty Minutes*, and at day's end tucked the children in, then went to bed and made love to their wives.

It was Sunday, all right, but only Alix would be covering the domestic routine unassisted. And if she did see Bill at all, it would be at the witching hour, most likely in a routine that was the exact reverse of this morning. He would tiptoe in, get undressed in the dark, wash, then slide into bed like a thief taking care not to wake her. With luck, Alix might merit another peck on the brow. Three seconds later he'd be asleep, exhausted.

She rolled over to Bill's side of the bed and brooded. Already his pillow was cool. Might as well be a single mother all over again, she thought. Only this time with two kids. She had a sense of stasis. Of treading water and going nowhere fast.

Funny, it struck her, how all the principles in her big case were living in limbo. Peter and Miranda, waiting for their fates to be resolved. Kim, still sequestered in her mansion, unable to face the world.

And Alix herself, for all her busyness and overloaded workdays, Alix too was in limbo. Some life! Some marriage! If it still was a marriage. If indeed it ever was.

The depth of her pain surprised her. The truth was – it hurt to admit it – that she loved Bill. A lot. A helluva lot more than he loved her. But not quite enough to sustain a marriage single-handed.

Well, if it didn't work out, this bumpy marriage of theirs, then the hell with the whole business of romance. It wasn't worth the pain, the misery, the doubts, the insecurities. Bill would be the last man of the line.

LONG ISLAND

She was his first love and his last love.

There was a rightness about it, a sense of full circle. Yet the Miranda who filled Peter's heart these days was a far cry from the girl who had won it so long ago. He loved her, yes! loved her still – though she was no longer the wounded doe he had been smitten with when she was Maggie, Missy, Lady X.

He loved her as Miranda (how easily the new name sprang to his lips), freed at last from the snares of the past. No longer an object of pity or pathos, this Miranda Vee – but a magnificent woman: brilliant, confident, mature. Who loved him in return.

For the first time in the tangle of their lives, they could meet as equal partners.

Now. And forever.

He had been lying in bed that Sunday morning in August. In bed eating jelly doughnuts and watching daytime TV – two of the shameful pastimes he had succumbed to since Judi Syme's departure.

Insightful, delightful Judi – who could make a meal out of a lettuce leaf and a federal case out of a jelly doughnut. Incredible how much he had liked her, how little he missed her.

Though it had been a long time in the making, their parting, when it came, was peaceful. No tears, no recriminations, no blood on the floor.

Oddly, the catalyst had been the invitation to the DuMesnes' ball. For reasons of her own, she decided to make an issue of his refusal.

'Damn it, Peter,' Judi had grumbled. 'You're so sedentary these days. You know how much I wanted to go and wear a fabulous costume and kick up my heels and dance all night. But you would rather stay home with a book. It bothers me, the way you're settling into a premature old age.'

'Good lord,' he had laughed. 'I'm not ready for the boneyard yet. Hell, Judi, it's only a party. A lot of rich people in funny clothes. Besides, you're always telling me what a disaster I am on the dance floor.'

'Yes, you are,' she said crisply, and he realized she had been lying in wait for such a moment. Since he had deflected her offer of marriage, she had grown secretive, removed. He suspected someone else was waiting in the wings. Someone younger, more eligible.

'It's not just the DuMesnes' ball . . .' She launched into a litany of Peter's shortcomings. He played a lousy game of badminton, left the lid of the toilet seat up, was getting gray as a Brillo pad, strewed newspapers all over the living room, ate junk food in bed, insisted on wearing that ratty old Harris tweed jacket to the Redfords' last month —

'Whoa there!' Peter broke in. 'If you want to pick a fight, ring up Sugar Ray Leonard. But if there's something you want to tell me, just spit it out.'

Judi studied her toes for a moment.

'We're not going anywhere,' she declared with a frown. 'In fact, we've never been anywhere – and no, I'm not talking about discos and parties. I like you fine, Peter, but you're a gadfly. You flit about on the surface of things, sampling a little of this, a little of that, never settling down, always taking off for some god-forsaken corner of the world whenever real life threatens to bunch up. What are you waiting for, Peter? The feature attraction? In your cool English way, you've made it clear that I'm not it. I think it's time we called it quits.'

She was going to Spain next week to do a film with that hot new comic from *Saturday Night Live*, Nicholas Bly. The opportunity had arisen quite suddenly and it was not to be missed. A terrific script. Young. Hip. Contemporary. 'Like me!' she added.

She wouldn't be coming back to this house. She had decided to buy a place of her own in Bel Air.

'I'm sorry, Peter. We've had a lot of fun.'

'I'm sorry, too,' he said.

'But not very. Or if you are, I wouldn't know it. You're too much the buttoned-up Brit. *"Never let 'em see you sweat."* I bet that's your family motto.'

'Actually, no,' Peter said. 'My family motto is *"Eat Eat."*'

She laughed, after which they said the right things to each other with some measure of sincerity – 'wonderful friend'. . .'dear person'. . .'will always care for you' – then bussed each other's cheeks. The next day, she was gone. The next month, she married Nicky Bly. Who also was young. Hip. Contemporary.

After she left, Peter was surprised to find that his heart was intact. The only injury had been to his pride. Which, happily, proved to be a most resilient organ.

He celebrated his new-found freedom by leaving the toilet lid up, strewing newspapers around the living room, and eating junk food to his heart's content.

Thus it was that on that Sunday morning, he was in bed munching doughnuts, letting crumbs fall where they may, poking through *The Times*, keeping a semi-eye on the telly when the name Tonio DuMesne speared into his consciousness.

Peter sat up with a jolt. So somebody had finally gotten to that bastard! Not soon enough. Immediately, he thought of Kimberly and of that little Lhasa apso of hers. Ding-ling. Well, the pup could live in peace from now on. Along with its mistress.

Over a shot of courthouse steps (and by God! if that wasn't Alix Bryden waving to reporters), the newscaster was giving a quick rundown of events.

Peter watched, transfixed.

The costume ball – yes! the same one he had been invited to a couple of months ago. The scene of the crime – a file photo of a vast Italianate mansion. The 'alleged assassin,' as the newsreader phrased it – a trim figure trailing Alix down the steps, her head covered by a policeman's raincoat. The name – which meant nothing.

Peter was listening so hard his ears hurt, trying to make some sense of the events.

'. . . the victim's neighbor Miranda Vee . . . no known motive . . . a well-known figure in international finance . . . local philanthropist . . . founder of MiraCo . . .'

'MiraCo!' Peter gasped. The name rang a one-hundred-pound bell.

The MiraCo Corporation! It had to be a coincidence! Anything else was impossible!

But so was every other explanation.

MiraCo – whose boss was crazy about Peter's writing. Who

had had him reeled out of Smitty's Bar one drunken evening. No – let's be accurate here, Peter admonished. Who had rescued him from the edge of the grave and sent him off to make a second life in California. A miracle, he'd thought at the time. But no – not a miracle at all!

The blood rushed to his brain. Then the tumblers began falling in place.

He stared, dry-mouthed, as the woman in the raincoat stepped into a waiting car. She turned to wave reporters away. A glimpse.

But Peter Mainwaring had scarcely needed it, for in that instant the puzzle that had been his life was solved.

'My God – it's *her*!'

He thought he would faint, thought better of it, then spent the next half hour trying to get through on the phone.

But Miss Miranda Vee had an unlisted home number, and neither threats nor pleas would get any purchase out of the operators at MiraCo headquarters in New York.

Peter racked his memory. What the hell was the man's name? The blond fellow who had smoked him out that night at Smitty's with that ridiculous hard luck story. The southerner. He would know how to reach 'Miranda.' Indeed, she must have trusted him profoundly to send him off on such a commission.

Cousteau? Bistro? Something French like that. The name was on the tip of Peter's tongue. *Bizet? Bisset?*

'Bisseau!'

He wiped the sweat off his hands and reached for the phone.

A few minutes later he was talking to Jim Bisseau, a half hour later to Miranda herself.

'Will you come to me?' she asked in that low voice he loved so dearly.

'You couldn't keep me away.'

Their first days together they talked and talked, filling in all the years between. Peter told her everything, how he had loved her years ago in Marival, and chosen to leave once she was gone. He told her about Annie, but of course she knew and was glad that he had had those happy years.

Sometimes they didn't talk at all, merely touched each other gently, tentatively, aching with happiness, drinking in endearments and caresses in long cooling drafts, like two parched travelers who had survived a desert crossing.

Often, in the early morning, Peter would walk the dogs along the road to the Villa Fiorentina. A guard was always on duty at the gate, and Peter never sought entry. The grounds had been maintained since the tragedy, the leaves raked, the trees and hedges clipped, yet the house itself gave off an aura of neglect. Or perhaps of sadness. Peter would look up at the mullioned windows and ponder on the fate of Kimberly West DuMesne. She had become a recluse since her husband's death and Peter respected her privacy. He would stand in the road for a minute or two, then whistle for the dogs and move on.

Understandably Miranda never walked in that direction. She had no desire to revisit the scene of the crime.

COBBLE HILL

Alix Bryden was frustrated.

For weeks she had been trying to get through to Kimberly DuMesne, only to be foiled at every step. She spoke to maids, housekeepers, secretaries, anonymous flunkies, each of whom either hung up or foisted her off with some transparent alibi.

Alternately, Madame DuMesne was out, sleeping, unavailable, on another phone, under the weather, resting. In short, DO NOT DISTURB. Alix presumed Kim had had a nervous breakdown.

'I was hoping she'd testify at the trial,' Alix told Bill, 'to confirm what a sadist Tonio was. Who better than a man's wife to make that point? However, as it turns out I won't need her testimony. Did I tell you about the photos from Marival? They just came in, and they're dynamite!'

It was Peter Mainwaring who had informed her of the existence of the Polaroids taken upon Miranda's arrival, then induced Dr Frankl to release them. Even Alix, who had a strong stomach, couldn't look at the pictures without flinching. Together with Miranda's medical records, they provided a devastating indictment of Tonio DuMesne.

'My bet is, once the jury lays eyes on them, they'll want to dig up Tonio's body so they can shoot him all over again. Plus,' Alix clucked, 'all these horror stories coming out of San Miguel one on top of another. Unbelievable!'

Tonio's murder had ushered in the final spasm of the DuMesne dynasty. The following night, in a hasty departure, El Tigre fled to the South of France, taking what was left of the treasury with him and leaving a second cousin in charge. Two days later, the army defected and the presidential compound was overrun by insurgents.

At last, after forty years of tyranny, the secrets of the DuMesne dynasty were revealed to an incredulous public. Overnight, San Miguel became a media circus. Journalists of every stripe vied with each other to serve up the freshest, most scabrous, most delicious, most disgusting revelations. In stories datelined Benedicta, the ghastly mingled with the grotesque, the brutal countermanded the bizarre, while millions lapped up the details with gusto.

Among the disclosures were the torture instruments of the notorious Black Chamber, the death squads, the unearthing of mass graves. Yet alongside these grim reports were tales of celebrity-studded parties and sybaritic luxury, of lunatic expenditures and sexual perversions.

One of the first acts of the New Interim People's Revolutionary Government was to throw open the doors of the DuMesnes' private quarters so that the populace of San Miguel might marvel and learn. Illiterate farmers with red dirt beneath their nails tramped through the marble rooms in a daze of disbelief. Peasant women fingered the satins and sables of Ladorita's top-floor dressing room. Who can forget the widely disseminated AP photo of the wizened papaya vendor from the slums of Benedicta who had donned a gossamer silk teddy over her rags and was grinning her toothless grin? The contrast of gnarled hands and lacy lingerie spoke volumes.

Among the stories that titillated ordinary folk the world over was the discovery of a secret library beneath Tonio's bedroom in Le Paradis. It became the subject of a segment on *Sixty Minutes*, housing as it did what one rare bookseller pronounced to be 'the finest collection of pornography since King Farouk's.'

Like everyone else, Alix gobbled up the details with a mix of disgust and fascination. No wonder Kim was hiding from the world. How dreadful it must be to have your most intimate secrets – your most intimate garments, for Chrissakes! – pawed over by strangers, held up to ridicule before millions. Worse yet, to see the father of your children exposed as a sadist and debauchee? The Butcher of Benedicta, *Time Magazine* had labelled him. Alix shuddered. Poor Kim! She had not deserved such a fate.

Yet each revelation, revolting in itself, was an arrow in Alix's quiver. Each excess, each atrocity a justification of Miranda Vee's act. It would be a foolish prosecutor indeed who would demand the maximum penalty in this case. It would be a heartless jury that would grant it.

Nonetheless, Alix wavered when the District Attorney offered a deal.

'Manslaughter One,' Herb Foster proposed. 'Eight and a third to twenty. Which means she'll serve maybe four.'

'Man Two,' Alix countered. 'No jail time. Eighteen months' community service.'

'No can do, Alix. I've got to consider the magnitude of the crime. After all she mowed the guy down in cold blood. He was a human being, let's remember, not a rattlesnake.'

Ultimately, the decision rested with Miranda Vee.

'You'll probably be out by the time you're forty,' Alix noted, 'and you'll be spared the ordeal of a trial.'

'And if I don't buy it?'

'They'll throw the book at you.'

Miranda hardly hesitated before turning the offer down. Now that Peter had resurfaced in her life, her fatalism had vanished. For a woman charged with premeditated murder, she was full of fight and brio.

'When I was in Chicago,' she said, 'I played commodities futures – oil, soybeans, winter wheat, whatever. I'd try to figure out which way the tide was running, then bet my money accordingly. All or nothing. Win or lose. Well, this time, the future I'm gambling on is my own. Instinct tells me I'm on to a winner, and my instincts have served me very well thus far.'

'And if you're wrong?' Alix asked.

'If worst comes to worst, I'll serve the time without complaint.'

'And I'll wait,' Peter said. 'You see, Miranda and I will be getting married as soon as the trial is over no matter what the outcome.'

The two lovers exchanged a look so tender, so intimate, Alix felt like a voyeur. *Love*, she thought. Even in the shadow of the prison gate. She almost envied them.

'I'll have to put you on the stand, Miranda,' she pointed out. 'You're your own star witness. But first, are you sure you have the strength to relive both nightmares? The one in France *and* the one at the Villa Fiorentina?'

393

Miranda took Peter's hand. 'Lord knows I don't want to, but if I must, I shall.'

On the second day of the trial, Alix was waylaid as she was leaving the Mineola courthouse.

'Why, Dorrie!' Her heart thumped at the sight of her step-mother. 'This is a surprise. I . . . ummm . . .'

Dorrie held out her hands in greeting. Flustered, Alix took them. They were soft and plump and manicured.

'Forgive my sneaking up on you,' Dorrie said tentatively, 'but I didn't know if you'd be willing to see me otherwise. It's been such a long time. Is there somewhere we can talk?'

Alix grabbed her elbow and steered her to a luncheonette a block away. Seated in a booth, the women exchanged edgy smiles while they took each other's measure.

The years had treated Dorrie Bryden well. She was a little blonder with age, a trifle heavier, but still very much the well-dressed society matron, although clearly ill at ease.

'It's good to see you, Dorrie.' Alix broke the ice. 'You're looking lovely as ever. You didn't have to take me by surprise, though. Of course I would have seen you. I never had any argument with you. Never! On the contrary, you always treated me kindly. If not for your efforts' – Alix gave a brusque laugh – 'I'd still be in solitary confinement back in Pride's Crossing, like one of those mad aunts in the attic from Victorian fiction. The family freak. So a belated note of thanks – that's spoken from the heart. And how are the boys? Though they're not such boys any more, I suppose. I saw the notice of Ted's wedding in *The Times*.'

'Did you?' Dorrie responded with an eager smile, happy to have found a neutral subject. 'Yes, a very sweet girl, one of the Forbes from the Nahant branch of the family – lovely people. And we're going to be grandparents next summer. And James – we don't dare call him Jim any more – he's turned out quite a handsome young man. Well, James is at Harvard, finishing his MBA . . .'

As Dorrie rattled on about her sons' accomplishments, Alix listened with a sense of wonder. Pride's Crossing was a world away from her present life. Another planet, almost. She found it hard to think of these men as her brothers.

Though, in fact, she had never had any quarrel with Dorrie's sons, any more than she had with Dorrie. Her only quarrel had been with —

'Your father!' Dorrie delivered the truly awesome F word, the one far worse than Fate. 'As you can guess, that's what brings me here. I feel you should know, your father had a stroke last month.'

Alix's heart skipped a beat.

'Bad?'

'Bad enough. It happened in the middle of an important business deal. Brought on by stress, I expect. The left side of his body has been severely affected. He's lost the use of one arm, he's in a wheelchair. Thank God his wits are still intact, though he's profoundly depressed. He hates being helpless.'

'And the long-term prognosis?'

'We don't know yet.' Dorrie sighed. 'Your dad is pushing seventy, you know. So how long is long?'

'I see,' Alix drawled. But she wasn't sure she saw at all. 'I'm sorry to hear about it. Tell me, did he ask you to come here and make peace between us? Is that it?'

Dorrie lowered her eyes. 'I'm afraid not. You know your father. He can be very stubborn, a regular mule once he's taken a stand. No, Alix dear. Lucius didn't ask me to come, it was my own idea. But I know he wants to see you, even though he hasn't said so in so many words. I can read what's in his heart.'

Alix grimaced. The heart was not an organ she associated with Lucius Bryden. Undeterred, Dorrie forged ahead.

'So I thought it would be helpful if you came to Pride's Crossing. Preferably without mentioning this little chat we've had. In other words, just show up one day as if it were a spontaneous gesture. It would make him very happy.'

Alix fought back angry tears.

'If he had sent for me, Dorrie, then I suppose I would come. As an act of charity, nothing more. But if you think I'm going to "show up" without an express invitation – no way! In all these years, did he ever make a single move in my direction? Did you? Did Ted or Jim? I can only presume you didn't because my father forbade it expressly, that he had declared me a non-person. A pariah. I know how his mind works. He never forgets, never forgives. My bet is if I turned up, as you suggest, he'd have me thrown off the premises.'

'Oh no, Alix! Believe me, darling. He'd be thrilled to see you.' Dorrie reached into her bag, pulled out a hankie and dabbed her eyes. 'In his own way, he loves you dearly. Sometimes I think he always loved you best of all.'

Alix could barely suppress a hoot of agonized laughter.

'You've got to be joking! My father never gave a flying fuck about me. Sorry about the language' – for the older woman had winced – 'but that's how I feel. Not once in my life did he ever hug me, kiss me . . . I was the family leper, for God's sakes.'

'Please, Alix. Try and understand. Lucius is not a demonstrative person. He has difficulty showing affection, but that doesn't mean he's unfeeling. Remember how he used to look forward to your chess games? Well, after the rupture, he never played again. He locked the set up and put it away. I think he was grieving. And he's followed your career, you know, quite avidly. Would he do that if he didn't care about you? I think he's secretly very proud of your accomplishments.'

'He's very proud, period,' Alix retorted. 'Well, if he's so eager to see me, let him ask. Let him swallow his pride and pick up the phone and goddamn ask me to come.'

'He won't. It's very hard for him to make the first move. Please, Alix. Bend a little. You're young, he's old. There may not be much time left. And who knows? Once the door is open, I expect he'd make up for the years between. In the financial sense, too.' Dorrie blushed and pulled on her gloves. She hated talk of money. 'Well, I must be getting back or your father will wonder what happened to me. One last word, though. I want you to appreciate that in coming here to plead with you, I have nothing to gain. In fact, any reconciliation between you and your father actually works against my own children's best interests.'

'Because I might inherit after all?'

Dorrie nodded. 'So you see, I came here only for Lucius's sake. It would bring him peace. I beg you, go see him.' Dorrie's eyes glistened with tears. 'And don't put it off too long.'

My God! Alix stared at her step-mother. *She really truly loves that stubborn cold selfish demanding son of a bitch!*

There was no logic to it. No sense at all. God knows he had done nothing to merit such devotion. *Love!* she thought, with a twinge of envy. Inevitably, she softened.

'Look, Dorrie, I can't go anywhere until this trial is over. But I promise to think seriously about what you've said.'

That night, Alix waited up in the study for Bill who had been upstate all week. He came home around one, tail dragging.

He greeted Alix with a perfunctory kiss on the cheek, went into the kitchen, fetched a pair of beers, then returned to kick off his shoes and collapse into his favorite chair.

'God, but I'm whupped,' he said, pulling the tab on a Bud. 'These fund-raisers take all the juice out of me. How come you're up so late, honey? Don't you have to be in court tomorrow? Not that I'm not pleased to see you. You want a brew?'

'Nope. Just an expert opinion. Sometimes even lawyers need advice.'

She described Dorrie's visit in detail, omitting only the mention of money. Bill could figure out that angle by himself.

'I know you're going to say I ought to see him and bury the hatchet,' she concluded.

He pulled on his beer. 'If you know, why bother to consult me?'

'Because in a way this affects us both. We see each other so rarely these days, Bill. We almost never talk. I'm trying to decide whether to go or not. One part of me wants to put the past to rest. The sensible part, I suppose. But the other part keeps yelling, "Screw him!" What did my father ever do for me except make my life a misery? I owe him zilch, *nada*, nothing!' She stopped in her tirade, and scowled. 'Will you listen to the sound of my voice? Isn't that crazy? I'm still furious with him after all these years. I guess there are some things one can never forgive. Why should I go? So he can tear me up all over again? What's the point? Even if half of what Dorrie said was true, how much he misses me and all that crap . . . You know what got to me, though?' She wiped away a tear. 'That he stopped playing chess. My old man loved chess. Who knows – maybe he did love me in his twisted way, though I have a tough time believing it. I know that I sure loved him! Hell, I idolized him. I wasted my whole childhood trying to win his approval and all I got for my efforts was a kick in the pants. The point is, Bill, in all these years, never once did he send out a feeler in my direction – a birthday card, a Christmas greeting. Never! Okay, I didn't send him one either, but it was his move. Even now he won't make the simplest gesture. Just too fucking stubborn!'

'Look who's talking!' Bill shot back. He opened the second can of beer. 'I don't get you, Alix. You have no qualms about representing every crook and mugger and homicidal zomboid from one end of the state to the other. You've won acquittals for murderers, embezzlers, junkies, con artists, child molesters, swindlers, mafiosi, self-styled "urban guerillas," all without turning a moral hair. Tell me, Alix, do you truly consider your father a bigger villain than Tommy Three-Fingers Manitucci or the Ice-Pick Killer? Sure, you're all heart and compassion when it comes to dealing with the dregs of society. And why not? They don't impinge upon your life. But when the injury is personal, close to home, then it's another story. I'd like to know – what crimes has your father committed? what laws did he break?'

'He broke my heart,' she burst out.

'As I suspect you broke his. Oh, Alix!' Bill was shaking his head in dismay. 'Why even bring it up at this late date? It's ancient history.'

'Not to me. I feel like it happened yesterday.'

He stared at her, then shrugged. 'That's your defense for Miranda Vee, isn't it? In her mind it happened yesterday. But don't compare your father with Tonio DuMesne. Granted he's a mean, stubborn, petty old man, but that's not a capital crime. And he's the only father you'll ever have. Why does everything have to be so black and white with you? Get rid of that grudge you've been hauling around all these years, for your sake if not for his. What'll it cost you?'

'My pride,' she whispered.

'Pride, pride!' Suddenly Bill looked sad. 'Let me tell you something about pride, Alix. I spent all week upstate fund-raising which is a euphemism for sucking up to a broad bunch of special interest groups. I made nice both to union leaders and factory owners. To environmentalists who are worried about the lesser horned owl and urban developers who want to plow under everything in sight. To dairy farmers who want price supports and mothers' groups complaining about the cost of milk. People at opposite ends of every pole. You should hear me, Alix, the way I pander and flatter and pull my sincerity number while trying not to promise the moon. Yet every one of those groups is going to claim they own a chunk of me, or whatever is left of me, if and when I get elected. So don't talk to me about pride, Alix, not when my own is stuck halfway down my throat.' He got up. 'I've said my piece. Make up your own mind, Alix. You always do.'

Bill's argument cost Alix a sleepless night. No denying he had a knack for posing uncomfortable questions, forcing her to face unpleasant facts. It was what made him a good lawyer and a difficult husband.

Though it stung, she had to admit he was right about Lucius. True, Alix had suffered at the time of their rift, but in fact she had not only survived being kicked out of the parental nest; she had flourished as a result. Her family, her independence, indeed her brilliant career had largely been built upon spite, upon the need to thumb her nose at her father.

Hell, Lucius Bryden had done her a favor by disinheriting her. She owed him her thanks. Otherwise, she would have wound up a corporate flunkey in the vast gray empire of Bryden Electronics, more under his sway than ever.

He was old now, frail. She had bloodied her knuckles long enough battling his shadow. What if he died before they had a chance to be reconciled? She could live with anger, but not with guilt. As soon as the trial was over, she would go to Pride's Crossing and by doing so, prove that she was the bigger person of the two. The more mature. The more gracious.

Besides, Alix realized with a shock, she felt compelled to see him in the flesh once more, but whether out of curiosity or affection, she couldn't decide.

The letter was marked PERSONAL. There was no return address. Alix opened the envelope and a check tumbled out. She unfolded the accompanying letter.

It was handwritten, almost indecipherable. A dozen lines, undated, on a sheet of stationery.

Dear Alix,

Forgive me! Forgive me for not answering your letters or taking your calls. Forgive me for hiding from the world. Thank you for all you have done for me, but I doubt if we shall meet again.

I am a broken woman. My life has been shattered. I will be going abroad soon and doubt that I shall ever return. Again, forgive me, dear Alix. Forgive my cowardice. And when you think of me, think of me kindly.

Your loving friend,
Kim

Alix read the letter through twice, touched by the tone of despair. Of finality. 'A broken woman.'

She remembered Kim as she was when they first met at Marival, when Kim had been a sunshine creature: ebullient, guileless, full of dreams. Dear Kim with her innocent belief in perfect love and Prince Charming and happily-ever-after. For a while, when Tonio was courting, it must have seemed that her dream had come true.

Perhaps it might yet, for Kim was possessed of great fortune and beauty. She was still young enough to have the best part of her life before her, to find happiness with a kinder, better man. God knows she had earned it.

Yet she wrote she was 'a broken woman.' The phrase wrenched Alix's heart.

Remarkable – that in spite of Tonio's cruelty and heartlessness and infidelities, Kim should have adored him above everything, that his death had left her so shattered. He must have loved her too, in his crippled way. Loved her profoundly. Else why would she withdraw from the world?

Oh, to love and be loved like that, to discover a true kinship of souls. Peter and Miranda. Lucius and Dorrie. Even Tonio and Kim. So different from her own pragmatic unromantic marriage.

Alix reached for a tissue and blew her nose.

She envied all of them their perfect love.

VILLA FIORENTINA

The reporters had long since abandoned their vigil. The DuMesnes' 'dearest friends' had moved on to Palm Beach or Gstaad. Villa Fiorentina had turned in upon itself.

Wilt Austin, the day-shift gatekeeper, whiled away the hours listening to soft-rock radio. Life had gotten so boring since the 'big bang,' as he called it. Almost as dull as watching paint dry.

He missed the old days when the limos lined up at his sentry box packed with celebrities; when he could go home at night and boast to his wife about having tipped his cap to, say, the likes of Wayne Newton or Chris Evert or the Kissingers.

Nowadays the road was little trafficked, except for the occasional 'ghouls' – mostly teenagers and middle-aged women – who parked on the opposite side to gape at the scene of the crime. And absolutely no one – except for staff, the doctors, and a handful of tradesmen – was permitted past the gates any more.

One bitter winter morning, a taxi from town pulled up at the entrance to disgorge a man in a nylon windbreaker and a pair of faded Levis. Thirtyish with dirty blond hair, he had the weathered face and hands of a manual laborer. He looked about him with a dubious expression – 'This it?' – then paid the cab driver from a slender stash of bills. 'I guess you better not wait. I can hitch a lift back.'

Wilt Austin checked his list to see if they were expecting a repairman, but except for a delivery by the greengrocer, the day's page was a blank.

'Can I help you, mister?' It was an unfriendly question. Strangers had no business on these premises. Except for monkey business, maybe. The world was full of terrorists and outraged citizens of San Miguel who would be only too glad to take a potshot at anyone unlucky enough to bear the name of DuMesne.

The lady of the house had already sent her children away – abroad, it was rumored, to France or Switzerland, and changed their names to Smith or Brown or something equally colorless, while she was about it. Well, who could blame her? You couldn't be too careful when it came to kids.

Now this guy here—!

Out of reflex, Wilt fingered his Uzi, although frankly the fellow looked more like a drifter looking for casual work. And tongue-tied, to boot.

'State your business or get a move on,' Wilt said.

'Yes, sir.' The stranger cleared his throat. 'I'd like to see a Mrs Kimberly DuMesne.'

'Madame DuMesne to you, bud. And you can head straight back to whatever hole you crawled out of, because Madame DuMesne don't see nobody, least of all bums. The lady's in mourning. So why don't you just—'

'I can't do that. Not till I see her. I've come a real long way.' He lowered his eyes, embarrassed. 'The thing is, I'm like – you see, I think I'm her brother.'

'And I'm Arnold Schwarzenegger, so get a move on.'

Then Wilt took a closer look at the upstart, blinked, furrowed his beetle brows and reached for the intercom.

'Wait here,' he ordered, 'while I check it out.'

He carried on a long muffled conversation with someone on the inside, nodded, growled, then addressed the stranger again, this time with a note of respect.

'Your name, sir?'

The man spelled it out. 'That's with two e's, though I don't think it's gonna mean an awful lot.'

Wilt repeated the name on the intercom, then stepped out of his box, and frisked the visitor top to bottom.

'Sorry, Mr Kelley. Regulations. Now in you go.'

At the front door, Kelley was further detained by a tall sleek Englishman who scanned him with radar eyes.

'Do you wear contact lenses?' the Englishman asked.

Kelley shook his head. 'Why would I do that?'

'Millions of reasons,' came the reply. 'Now if you'll follow me . . .'

The Englishman led him down a hallway, up a staircase to an imposing double door on the second story. Now and then Kelley paused briefly to look at a painting or peek into a room, his eyes big as poker chips. At one point he whistled.

'Come along, Mr Kelley,' the Englishman chided.

'Yeah! Wow! This is quite a place.' The voice was hushed.

Apologetic. He wasn't used to being called Mister. 'Like a museum or something.'

The silence was creepy. He suspected there had been a mistake after all, despite what they told him down in Baton Rouge. A guy like him had no business in a place like this.

'Maybe I should come another time. I can find my way back to town.'

Instead of answering, the Englishman handed him a comb. 'Before you go in, a word of warning. Madame DuMesne has been badly shaken up by her husband's death. Indeed, it was a shock for all of us. I used to be His Excellency's private secretary in happier times. Madame has been in seclusion ever since.'

Kelley ran the comb through his hair and wished he'd worn a tie. 'Do I look okay?'

'You'll do. With regard to your forthcoming interview, may I advise you not to speak unless spoken to, nor make any sudden moves. Madame has suffered deeply since the tragedy and I expect you will respect her sensibilities. She's very' – he paused to choose his word carefully – 'very fragile.'

The secretary opened the door and ushered him in.

'Mr Kelley,' he announced.

Although it was daytime, the curtains were drawn and the air was stuffy. The only illumination came from a high intensity lamp that had been placed above an empty club chair. The rest of the room was lost in darkness.

Beyond the circle of lamplight, Kimberly DuMesne was sitting on a low sofa, dressed in black, heavily veiled. In the Stygian gloom, she appeared as little more than a muffled voice, a barely discernible form.

'Please sit down. No, no!' Her urgent whisper grew alarmed, for the stranger was moving across the room, coming toward her. 'Back off! Sit! There under the lamp! Now let me look at you.'

He did as she bade, blinking in the brightness like a deer caught in the headlights.

Kim also blinked. She was unused to the light. All was silence for a moment, then she sucked in her breath.

'Is it true? I can't believe my eyes!'

Could it be true, that this was her brother? But how could it be otherwise! For this man who sat before her was wearing her face. Not her 'best' face, to be sure. Indeed not any of the faces that had been created for her over the years, and certainly not the face she had now. Yet indisputably her face: genuine, authentic. Minus the artful ministrations of Dr Frankl.

This was the face she had had at fourteen. Older, to be sure. More careworn. But still her face as it might have been, had time been allowed to take its toll.

A good face, though not divinely handsome. Attractive rather than attention-getting. The nose was a bit too thick and the lips a trifle thin. (She tried to remember what her mouth had been like before collagen, what kind of nose she had been born with. She would have been an attractive woman – nothing more.) It was like looking at a mirror in a fun house, seeing an image that was both you and not you.

She thought he looked older than his age – *her* age – for the skin was rough and weathered and there were wrinkles about the eyes as if he'd spent too much time exposed to the elements. But the pupils were violet. As violet as the blossoms of the massala tree.

Kim felt a surge of adrenaline.

Her impulse was to throw her arms around him, cling to him, call him brother. With effort, she managed to wrestle the impulse down. She had lived amid deception for too many years; suspicion had become second nature. Perhaps, as instinct told her, this man was her brother. Perhaps not. The thought of being traduced yet again was unbearable.

Kim clenched her fists so tightly her nails dug into her palms. Patience! Self-control! First impressions deceived, she knew from hard experience. Had she not fallen in love with Tonio at first sight? Her White Knight? Her Prince? One lived and learned and took precautions.

In all likelihood, this man with her face, her eyes, was an impostor, a cold-blooded fortune-hunter endowed with nerve and smarts, staking out his wealthy prey. What wouldn't people do for money! She had but to think of Bette for an example of greed.

Or he might be a reporter who, having sniffed out her secret, had wormed his way into her presence and was planning the scoop of the year. With pictures! Kim felt sick. For all she knew, he had a hidden camera on him.

Or perhaps one of Alix's private detectives had dreamt up some elaborate scheme and the fellow before her was an actor hired to play the part. Conceivably the profound 'resemblance' was nothing more than a latex mask and colored contact lenses. She knew the tricks of impersonation.

'Please,' she whispered dry-voiced. 'Indulge me for a moment. If you would shut your eyes and sit very still —'

She rose. Avoiding the circle of light, she stepped behind him and placed her hands on his face. Gently, she traced the shape of his forehead, his cheekbones, felt his flesh beneath her fingertips. He was sweating. It was real skin, real bones. Kim felt a rush. She had the sense of blood calling to blood. This man was her brother, she could swear it. Every cell in her body rang with confirmation.

And yet – and yet she hesitated. The world was so full of scoundrels and thieves. Who were wilier by far than she.

'May I have your jacket?'

He passed it back to her. She turned it inside out, read the label. K-Mart. It smelled of axle grease. She felt the pockets, pulled out the stub of a Greyhound bus ticket. Thieves and scoundrels didn't travel fifth class. No notebook, no camera.

She went back to her seat, the pulse in her neck beating wildly.

'Forgive me for behaving like this,' she whispered. 'But this is so new to me. You see I didn't even know I *had* a brother until last spring. And now I can't be sure if it's really you. I'm sorry. What did you say your name was?'

But when he answered, Kim's final vestige of doubt was laid irrevocably to rest. In a shattering flash of revelation, she grasped the meaning of Bette's last words.

No. Not '*you . . . you . . .*' as she'd believed all these months. 'Hugh . . .' he said, 'Hugh Kelley.'

Their mother's name was Marilu Kelley. She came from a family of farm hands and casual laborers, who had headed west during the depression. They were simple God-fearing folk, the Kelleys, not much for books or learning, but strong and good with their hands. They had come to California in search of a better life. They never found it.

Marilu was sixteen, a pretty girl of no particular accomplishments, when she became pregnant by a soldier stationed nearby. Or perhaps he was just passing through.

No, Hugh didn't know his father's name. Maybe their mother never knew it either. No ma'am, Hugh told his sister, their mom wasn't a stickler for protocol. She was bubbly, though. Flirtatious, full of fun, the kind of gal who lived for Saturday nights. At least, that was Hugh's memory of her.

As for Kim's notion that their father had been killed in Korea – well, maybe. Who could say? It made a nice story.

All Hugh could state with certainty was what his mother told him later, which was that her parents had kicked her out when they learned of her condition. She must have been desperate, he guessed.

Be tied down with a baby? Hell, she was little more than a baby herself. No money. No education. Nothing going for her but a dinky job in a local beauty parlor, shampooing hair and sweeping up cuttings.

The only person to befriend Marilu in her dilemma was a manicurist who worked in the salon. An older woman. A Bette something-or-other. Wisenheimer or Wesenhalter or was it Westovsky? – Hugh never did get the name straight – only the gist of the story. It seems this Bette person had never married, being one of those women most guys give a wide berth – at least according to Marilu. But she'd always wanted a child and some kind of advance deal was made. Perhaps money changed hands. If so, not much.

But when Marilu gave birth to twins, that was more than Bette had reckoned on. She took the girl, leaving the boy for the young mother to bring up as best she could.

It was an unequal struggle. 'The millstone,' she used to call Hugh when he was small. After a couple of years, Marilu threw in the sponge. She was young and attractive, life with a growing boy was too hard. Thus Hugh grew up in a series of foster homes and charitable institutions.

When he was seven, she came around to visit him one last time. He could still remember what she wore – a dress in a red floral print with white collar and cuffs. She looked very pretty. She had come to say goodbye. She was leaving California for a while, but she'd be back. Probably found herself a husband, was Hugh's bet. He never heard from her again.

Even now, at the memory of his childhood, he choked up. He still felt the void, the pain of his loss.

'At least be thankful you had a "mother,"' Hugh told Kim with a grim laugh. 'Someone who cared about you. Jesus, but I was a lonely kid. And all those years I kept waiting for her to come rescue me. Dumbnuts me!'

The sense of early deprivation was lodged deep in his psyche. As a result, his life never took shape. He had left his foster home at sixteen and drifted from then till now. Bartender, oil driller, roustabout, cabbie, a stint in the merchant marine that had taken him as far as Macao and Yokohama. He rolled up his sleeve and showed Kim his tattoo. A broken heart with a blue banner that read MOTHER. 'That was Subic Bay,' he said. 'Sweet Jesus, I must've been awful drunk that night.'

The years slipped by uneventfully. One job, then another; one place, then another; one woman, then another, and not much to choose among them for he was a man with no calling, no family, no roots. Just lucky enough to stay out of jail.

He had been pumping gas in a Shell station in Baton Rouge when a couple of New York investigators tracked him down.

At first he didn't believe them. He thought it might have something to do with a paternity suit from a gal back in Waco.

No, he had never heard of Kimberly West DuMesne, nor of the DuMesne family. Famous, were they? You couldn't prove it by him. He wasn't one for reading magazines and newspapers. But the more the investigators talked, the more alarmed he became.

If what they told him was true, what was the point of it? Why rake up the past?

So he had a sister who had made her way, become a somebody, respected and admired. And here he was – nothing but a bum.

'But weren't you curious?'

Hugh paused. 'Christ, yes! Plenty curious. I know you're gonna think this sounds crazy but . . .'

From earliest childhood, he had been haunted by the sense that his life was unfinished, incomplete. That there was another side of himself, hidden from view like the dark of the moon. His twin. His flesh and blood.

Yet even sitting here in the same room with her, sharing his memories, he wondered if he had done the right thing. Why should he blight her life with the story of his failure? He was a loser. He was incapable of giving happiness to anyone. Maybe it would have been better if he had stayed away. This was not his kind of place.

This house was so big. Scary. 'Like in the movies,' he said. He couldn't imagine that real people actually lived in palaces like this. Least of all people like him.

'I'm a nobody,' he said.

'I'm a nobody too,' she murmured. *Can't sing, can't dance.* The phrase from the past echoed through her mind. She brushed back a tear. 'I was never anything but a face. We're a pair of nobodies, Hugh, but maybe together we'll add up to a whole. Would you like to come and live with me?'

'I guess so,' he said. 'But not here in this house. It's too dark. When I was a kid I was always petrified of the dark. It still gives me the willies. It's nice out. Why don't I open the blinds and let the light in?'

'Please don't,' Kim said. 'I like the dark.'

More than that. She loved it. The dark soothed, calmed, disguised, repaired hurts. The dark was all that was left of her domain. It was better than a sable coat: warmer, more comforting. She could sit in the dark for hours on end, for days on end. Forgetting the past or remembering it, as she chose. Neither seeing nor being seen.

'And me? Are you frightened of me?' she whispered.

'Yes . . . no . . .' His face contorted briefly, then settled into a semblance of a smile. 'No, I'm not scared of you. How could I be? We were born together. We never should have been parted. I knew that even as a little boy. It made me feel like I was a half person.' A lone tear coursed down his cheek. He made no attempt to blot it. 'Maybe that's what set me wandering. What made my bones so restless. But now – being here . . .' He wet his lips. 'Do you believe in fate? I guess I do. What I mean is, I don't think it was an accident, those detectives locating me in that filling station. It was something that had to be.'

Kim burst into tears.

'Yes,' she sobbed. 'I know what you're feeling, because I feel the same way. All my life, I've been waiting for someone to complete me, make me whole. Looking for the one person in the world I could trust. You've been a long time in coming, dear Hugh, almost too long, but no matter. You're here at last. We'll live together. We'll share everything – our hearts, our hopes, our most secret thoughts.'

She reached out of the shadow to take his hand in hers.

'We'll never be lonely again, Hugh. Either of us.'

He took her hand and held it to his cheek, overcome by emotion. They sat for a long moment in the consanguinity of perfect peace. Then he sighed from the depths of the soul.

'Tell me, sister, do we look alike?' Hugh asked.

'We did once,' Kim replied.

'Let me see.'

He swung the lamp around toward her as she pushed back her veil.

'Oh, my God!' Hugh Kelley cried.

MINEOLA

'The State of New York versus Miranda Vee': a defense in three acts, conceived, produced and directed by Alix Bryden.

Act One: *Tonio DuMesne*. In which the jury discovers the nature of evil.

Act Two: *Peter Mainwaring and Co.* In which the jury hears the testimony of various experts.

Act Three: *Miranda Vee*. In which the jury meets the True and Only Victim of certain events that took place in a country road outside Chambord.

As the trial entered its final phase, Alix Bryden had every reason to feel pleased.

Act One had played superbly, with the defense managing to display enough of Tonio's brutality to appall the men and women who would decide Miranda's fate, but not so much that they tuned out. Repetition only dulled the senses, and there were occasions when less was more. Nonetheless when the photos of

Miranda at Marival were passed around, Alix counted the prevalence of white faces and clenched fists in the jury box. Juror Number 8 (car mechanic from Hicksville) looked as though he were about to go ballistic, whereas Juror Number 2 (Syosset housewife) nearly passed out.

Having established who was the true villain of the piece, Alix called in the professionals. Sociologists addressed the question of rape victims and battered women, a top psychiatrist explained the nature of post-traumatic stress and Peter Mainwaring chronicled in heart-breaking terms Miranda's sufferings during the years at Marival.

Then it was time for Miranda herself to take the stand.

'You're going to be the grand finale,' Alix told her during the long hours of preparation. 'I want the jury to live through each moment with you – the good *and* the bad. I want them to fall in love with you a little bit. To care on an intensely personal level. To think of you as, say, *their* wife, or sister or daughter or girl friend. I want each and every one of them to feel not only that they *know* you, but that they have a vested interest in your acquittal.'

When the moment arrived, Miranda was superb.

She looked pretty yet vulnerable in a moss green woolen dress, a small-boned woman with a wistful smile and an untimely streak of white in her chestnut hair.

In a quiet even voice, Miranda described growing up in the working class streets of Chicago, spoke of her adolescent ambition to 'make something of myself,' of the job in Paris where she had learned to speak French and be a lady. She told of going on a bike tour through the château country. She brought the jury with her into the bar as she drank a glass of wine, sang along with Billie Holiday, danced with an attractive stranger. Then haltingly (the jury could share her struggle as each word, each memory seemed to inflict fresh pain), Miranda relived each step of the assault by Tonio DuMesne.

'What was going through your mind as you lay in the ditch?' Alix asked.

'I thought I would die.' Miranda swiped at her eyes. 'I thought I *was* dead. I remember thinking, no one would ever find my body to bury me.'

'You didn't call out?' Alix asked.

'I couldn't,' she whispered. 'He had cut my throat.'

At that point, Juror Number Seven (Roslyn Heights florist) began to sob. Alix waited gravely till he stopped.

Next, Miranda recalled the details of her rehabilitation: the on-going surgery, the constant pain, the profound depression.

As Alix walked her client through the years that followed, there was no varnishing of prose, no verbal extravagances, yet the jury hung on every word.

Though thoroughly rehearsed, her testimony was nonetheless utterly honest, sincere. The tears, when they fell, genuine.

'Would you like a brief recess?' Judge Willis asked, as he himself downed a draft of water.

Miranda said no, but she touched her face, as though to assure herself that it was there, that it was whole.

'What made you choose Vee for your last name?' Alix asked.

'In my mind it stood for victim.'

For years, Miranda had been able to banish all memory of that night, but the cure proved not as total as she had hoped.

She spoke of how her experience with Tonio had left her so terrorized as to rule out any possibility of a normal existence. She was condemned to a life of loneliness. But that was tolerable. Until —

'Tell us about the nightmares,' Alix prompted. 'When did they begin?'

For a moment, Miranda closed her eyes, as though living them anew. Then she spoke of the recurrent dream.

'It was as if it was happening all over again, night after night, each time more vividly. It got so I was afraid to go to sleep, to stay in any one place for too long. I traveled a lot, I tried to leave the nightmares behind me, but it didn't work. They kept getting worse. I thought I'd go mad. And then —'

She dabbed her eyes.

And then she had a moment of total recall and knew her assailant to be Tonio DuMesne. After that revelation, everything else fell in place. She knew what she had to do.

How long had she suffered from the aftermath of the assault in Chambord? Alix asked.

'Constantly, from April 12, 1965 until the night when I shot and killed Tonio DuMesne.'

'Thank you. No further questions.'

But Herb Foster did. They were few but pointed.

'When did you decide to kill Mr DuMesne?'

Miranda hesitated. 'As soon as I realized that he was the man.'

'By which you mean the man who assaulted you in 1965?'

'Yes,' Miranda breathed.

'And knowing who he was, you danced with him?'

'Yes.'

'And kissed him?'

'Yes.'

'And accompanied him to his bedroom?'

'Yes.'

'Intending to kill him?'

'Yes.'

'Did you consider at any point calling the police and pressing charges, or going public with your suspicions and letting the law take its course?'

'No. What was the point? He had diplomatic immunity.'

'Diplomatic immunity. But not immunity from Miss Miranda Vee.' Herb's voice was barbed with sarcasm. 'Tell me, when you picked the name Vee, wasn't it really Vee for Vengeance?'

'Objection!' Alix sprang to her feet.

'Sustained. Get on with it, Mr Foster.'

'And when you got to his room, what happened next?'

'He began to undress. He took his gun off and placed it on a table by the bed. I picked it up—'

'Knowing it was loaded?'

'He assured me it was.'

'And then—'

'And then I shot and killed Tonio DuMesne.'

Satisfied, the prosecutor headed back to his chair, the question of premeditation having been disposed of.

During the breaks, Peter and Miranda would repair to a small chamber near the courtroom and bury themselves in a welter of travel books and maps and history books and luscious brochures.

'*If . . .*' Miranda would begin.

'*When . . .*' Peter would amend.

If . . . when Miranda was acquitted: they would set off on an open-ended journey that would take them around the world, wherever adventure beckoned. Miranda had been to wondrous places in her travels; Peter too had traveled widely. Yet there were still more marvelous places they hoped to discover together.

If . . . when! there would be money enough and time enough for all their desires. Such a journey it would be, one as might befit a modern Sinbad or Marco Polo.

They compiled huge lists of places replete with myth and magic. Names to be savored: Baiã, Timbuctu, Sounion, Cappadocia, Samarkand, Zanzibar.

If . . . when Miranda was acquitted: they would sail down the Nile in a felucca, cross the Andes on mules, travel the Silk Road across the breadth of China, seek the lost city of Meroe, explore the volcanoes of Kauai. Each day the itinerary compounded, grew more fantastic, more outrageous. Walled cities vied with hidden cataracts for the travelers' time; Brazilian rain forests were traded off against remote temples in Nepal.

If . . . when!

Then the bailiff would poke his head in to tell them that the court was back in session.

On the fourteenth day of the trial, the end was in sight.

Alix was summing up, the prosecution would close, and within days, within hours perhaps, Miranda would know her *If* or *When*.

'It's a man's world,' Alix began. 'That's a cliché we've all heard a thousand times and like most clichés it is founded on truth. It's a man's world, you bet it is, especially when it comes to the traditional 'right' of a man to inflict physical violence when the occasion warrants. To commit murder, in fact, with impunity. Let me give you some examples.

'A robber tries to stick up a liquor store. The store owner beats him to the punch and shoots first. Justifiable homicide. Example. A man wakes up in the middle of the night, hears footsteps, gets his gun and catches a burglar in the act. Justifiable homicide. In short, a man is justified in pulling a trigger to protect his shop or protect his home. He's defending the sanctity of private property.

'But what about the woman who kills to protect herself from a rapist? What recourse does she have? What retribution can she demand? Damn little. But I ask you, is a woman's body less valuable than the contents of a liquor store? Is it easier to replace? To rebuild? Is her body not her exclusive property to protect and fight for, using whatever weapons come to hand?

'It's a funny thing how the legal system – cops, prosecutors and occasionally judges – deals with the female victims of violence. The system treats the woman more vindictively than the man who beat up on her. The general attitude is that she brought it on herself. What was she doing out on the street at that hour, anyhow? Or in a bar? Or wearing a sexy dress? A classic case of blaming the victim for the crime. By the way, does anybody ever ask such questions of men? Can't you just hear it?'

she mocked. '"Hey bud, what were you doing out after ten p.m.? And wearing a *tie*?"'

A juror tittered. Alix however didn't smile.

'If the woman doesn't resist her attacker, that proves compliance. If she fights back, she's over-reacting. Why didn't she "relax and enjoy it," as the expression goes, instead of inciting him to further violence? Either way, she's in the wrong. If she's acquainted with her assailant, it's even tougher to get justice done, because too many people think that a woman's *No* really means *Yes* or at the very least, *Maybe*. So the victim gets violated twice: first by her assailant, then by the legal system. What then is a woman to do?

'Tonio DuMesne got away with murder. He murdered my client's hopes and dreams and peace of mind and psyche. And if the corpse he left behind wasn't quite dead, it's only because of the wonders of modern medicine. Tonio DuMesne left Miranda in a ditch to die, while he himself went on to live a very full life, to marry, have children, and enjoy countless women. At least those ones who didn't fight back. For all we know, there may have been other Miranda Vees left at other waysides to die. This was a man, after all, who ran his own private torture chamber. A man without conscience, beyond the reach of any law.

'How little his assault on Miranda must have meant to him that years after he could jest at it, say he had been bitten by a wild animal which he then destroyed. For Tonio, this incident was just one in a long catalogue of crimes, but for Miranda Vee it was the single focal point of her life. It deprived her of the normal blessings of life. For her, there would be no possibility of marriage, she would never know the joy of family life, of children. For more than her face had been destroyed that night in Chambord. Tonio DuMesne had murdered her future.

'The district attorney has argued that this was a vengeance killing, undertaken in cold blood years later. He has told you it could only be justifiable homicide if Miranda truly believed she

417

was in imminent danger. But in her mind, Miranda Vee felt herself to be constantly in imminent danger. It was as though that long-ago assault was a single on-going act. It never stopped. In her waking world, every man was a potential rapist. In her dreams, every night was that night in Chambord.'

Alix cited the psychiatric testimony as to post-traumatic stress syndrome, and how the past enveloped the present. She quoted the academic whose research had illustrated how society was skewed against battered women, on the pretense that men and women were equally matched in terms of physical strength. And finally, most compellingly, there was the defendant herself.

'Is Miranda Vee a dangerous woman? A menace to society? Ask her neighbors, her employees. Ask the board members of all the charities she works for. Ask the stray animals she's always taking in. Ask your instincts, your feelings. Then ask yourself: what if what was done to her that night in Chambord had been done to someone you love. What if it had happened' – Alix fixed the forewoman with a steady glance – 'to you?

'Yes, a man is dead because of Miranda Vee. But when those shots were fired in the Villa Fiorentina, all you could hear was the sound of justice being done.'

Alix lowered her head for a moment, then returned to her seat and squeezed Miranda's hands. But she had seen what she had wanted to see: the tears in the forewoman's eye.

'It's *when*,' she whispered to her client. 'Not *if*.'

The morning after Miranda's acquittal, without a word to Bill or anyone in her office, Alix went to Pride's Crossing.

PRIDE'S CROSSING

Pride's Crossing! Was ever a town more aptly named, Alix brooded as the taxi pulled into the drive.

All the way in from the airport, she had balanced the possibilities the next few hours held, playing scenarios in her head, unsure which she feared more – finding her father the same harsh unyielding tyrant he had always been or finding him broken in spirit as well as in body.

The house itself appeared unchanged. The façade had been freshly painted, the French windows gleamed, though the old magnolia tree by the front door was gone. Such a lovely tree. The first to blossom in spring.

Emotion seized her by the throat. A keen ache for the tree, for the years of absence. Oh! the wrenching power of the past.

Lips pursed, Alix got out of the cab and marched up the steps muttering under her breath: *I will be cool. I will not cry or lose my temper . . . temper . . . temper.*

She had decided against Dorrie's suggestion of turning up unannounced, afraid the shock might trigger a second stroke. Instead, she had taken elaborate precautions to make the visit seem casual, thus giving Lucius the option of backing off without a loss of face on either side.

The previous afternoon, she had called his office and spoken to his private secretary.

'I have to be in Boston in connection with a case,' she said, 'and would like to spend some time with my father. Please let me know if tomorrow at eleven is convenient.'

Miss Milgrim called back within minutes to say that such a meeting would indeed be 'agreeable' to Mr Bryden.

Agreeable! Such an ambiguous word. Faintly warmer than

'convenient' but far short of 'delightful.' Nonetheless, Alix chose to take it as a positive sign.

So here she was ringing the doorbell of her childhood home, forcing her features into the semblance of a smile.

Dorrie herself answered, feigning long-time-no-see. They exchanged greetings, brushed cheeks.

'How nice to see you, Alix! You're looking well,' Dorrie proclaimed in a public voice, while Bridget took Alix's coat.

'Hello, Bridget,' Alix said to the maid. *My God, she must be forty!* 'You've graduated from the kitchen, I see.'

'Yes, miss. Thank you, miss.'

'Your father is waiting in the conservatory,' Dorrie said, 'and I'm sure he's eager to see you.' Then she whispered in Alix's ear, 'Would you like a shot of brandy before you go in?'

Alix shook her head, relieved that the reunion would take place in the sunniest room of the house, rather than in the dark library beneath her mother's portrait. Too many memories.

'Well.' She gulped down a sense of dread. 'Here goes nothing.'

He was seated in a mechanized wheelchair with an elaborate control panel built in, one designed by Bryden Electronics, no doubt. A Black Watch shawl covered his legs. His left hand lay useless in his lap. He looked pale and frail and shrunken. He had trouble focusing one eye, but the other was sharp as ever.

'You'll forgive me if I don't get up to greet you.' His mouth bunched to one side as he spoke, yet his speech, though blurred, was controlled. Was he also thinking *temper temper temper*?

Alix looked about her, awkwardly. Here he was in the flesh after all these years, and she couldn't think what to do or say.

Was she expected to kiss him? hug him? shake his hand? Why now – since she had never done so before? It struck her that she had him at her mercy. This once, he couldn't run from her embrace.

420

But her vocabulary didn't extend to the spontaneous show of affection. Not with him, in any case. He had never taught her the language. The best she could muster was a cordial smile, the kind she employed with juries. So she smiled and pulled up a wicker chair a few feet away. The room was stifling. Alix cleared her throat.

'Hello, Daddy. How are you? It's been a long time.' *A good opening. Simultaneously neutral and trite!*

They sat for a minute in heavy silence, like flummoxed contestants in a TV quiz show.

'Long time,' he rasped at last. 'How does the house look to you? Dorrie had it re-decorated last spring.'

'Terrific!' Alix pounced. 'Though I haven't taken the grand tour yet, but' – *God, this was excruciating!* – 'but I noticed the old magnolia tree is gone.'

'The roots,' Lucius croaked. 'They'd gotten overgrown and twisted, they were undermining the whole structure of the front porch. I had it cut down last year.'

Alix wondered if this was meant as a parable.

'Maybe azaleas would be nice instead.'

He grunted. 'I see you won an acquittal in the DuMesne case. She's a good businesswoman, this Miranda Vee. Very innovative.'

They moved cautiously for the next few minutes over neutral territory – the trial, the house, the weather – inching forward toward each other's turf in tiny conversational steps, like battle-weary soldiers in the final days of war. The few feet of carpet represented a kind of no man's land across which the two factions faced off, each equally armed, equally entrenched.

It remained to be seen whether this initial contact would result in an armistice or a renewed outbreak of hostilities for there were land-mines everywhere.

Alix wondered if she ought to inquire about his health, or if he would deem that an invasion of privacy. She decided to let him pick the topic.

Lucius began to talk about the law. Not in the abstract, as in those bad old days of the sixties, but in terms of Alix's career.

He was so precisely informed on her high profile cases that she wondered if he subscribed to a clipping service. She recalled how he had spied upon her at Cambridge, and felt a ripple of dismay. Old habits die hard. Yet she couldn't ignore the irony of the situation. All those cases she had taken on with the impish glee that they would make her father apoplectic had instead turned out to be a source of parental pride. *His* daughter. *Her* triumphs. There was something almost tribal about it.

She was astonished at the depth of his information.

'I imagine you do very well,' he said at one point. She knew he was probing. 'Especially from those Wall Street swindlers you manage to keep out of jail. I know what top lawyers charge.'

What should she tell him – that half of her business was pro bono? That she was a sucker for every hard luck story that waltzed into her office? That money poured out even faster than it poured in? That they'd taken a second mortgage on the house?

Making half a million dollars a year wasn't quite so stupendous when you were spending a half million and one.

'I do very well,' she replied. 'No financial worries.'

At eleven, Bridget came in wheeling a cart with coffee and biscuits.

'I'll serve my father,' Alix said.

'Very good, miss.'

She remembered how he liked his coffee – lots of cream, no sugar. She poured him a cup, arranged biscuits on a dish, and placed the tray within reach of his 'good' right arm.

'Is this okay?' she asked. 'Can you manage?'

He actually smiled. 'Fine. Thank you, Alix.'

Yet despite his bravado, he maneuvered with difficulty. His hand shook, the coffee cup rattled, the liquid slurped down his chin – all of which Alix pretended not to notice. How he must hate being a prisoner in a chair.

'I'm married now, Daddy. Going on five years.'

'Yes,' Lucius said. 'I read about your husband in *Newsweek* a while ago. He seems an ambitious young fellow. A Democrat, I gather.'

'He is, though I expect you'd like him nonetheless. Bill's very smart. Columbia Law. He used to clerk for Justice White. We live in a brownstone in Brooklyn. Everybody always groans when I say we live in Brooklyn, but it's really quite pleasant. We have two children. Would you like to see their pictures?' She was glad she'd had the foresight to take them. 'They're only snapshots, but . . .'

'Yes, please.'

Alix pulled out the photos – kids, dog, house, herself and Bill. Lucius made vague grandparental noises, but he studied each one closely. Then he fixed his one good eye upon Alix.

'She's a big girl, your daughter. What did you say her name was? Samantha?'

She watched her father doing mental arithmetic, putting two and two together – and getting Sam Matthews. Suddenly her old lover's presence loomed between them, divisive and sinister.

Goddamn you, Sam! Just when everything been going so well!

'A big girl,' he repeated. 'How old is she?'

'Samantha will be thirteen in July.'

'I see,' Lucius murmured.

He handed her the photos.

She shook her head. 'They're for you to keep.'

'Thank you. Perhaps next time you come, you'll bring the real articles. That is, if your business happens to take you to Boston again.'

Alix inhaled deeply. *Here goes*, she thought.

'I lied to Miss Milgrim. I have no business in Boston. I came expressly to see you, Daddy. Because I wanted to. Because we've been apart too long and it's time to bury the past.'

In his good eye, she read a flash of triumph. *See!* his visage proclaimed. *You made the first move!*

'I'm very glad you did.' Were those tears in his eyes or merely the rheum of old age? Yes, tears. Most definitely.

Alix exhaled. 'Well, that's a relief. I'm glad I did too.'

With his one good hand he blew his nose, wiped his chin. Then he nodded.

'I'm a little tired now. If you don't mind, I'd like to take my nap. At noon the nurse comes in to wheel me away. Can you stay the night, Alix?'

No, she apologized. Time was tight. She had to be on a two-o'clock plane back to New York. But there would be other visits, other days. She promised.

Lucius shut his eyes and seemed to drift off. Alix waited a couple of minutes, then gathered her belongings for a tip-toe departure. She was halfway out the door when he called her name.

'Alix,' he said, his voice sharper than it had been.

She wheeled around. 'I thought you'd fallen asleep.'

'No. I was thinking,' he said.

She returned to her chair, the dutiful daughter as he smiled his lop-sided smile. It made him look crafty.

'My dear,' he said, choosing every word with care. 'It affords me great pleasure to welcome you back into the bosom of your family. This change of heart does you credit. Yes, it's time we put the past behind us. You were always my favorite, you know. And now that you're my daughter again, as surely as Ted and James are my sons, you're entitled to a full share of my holdings.'

Alix turned crimson. She hadn't expected him to be so blunt.

'That's not why I came, Daddy.'

'I know it isn't,' he snapped. 'If I thought it were, I wouldn't have offered. For all your faults, Alix, I have never thought you venal. Hot-headed, yes. But not venal. In any case, since by your admission you're doing very well as an attorney, such moneys as I might bequeath you would be more in the nature of a bonus than of a lifebelt. Nonetheless, you have a young family, a husband with political ambitions. I'm not a small-minded person, Alix. Indeed, there's no reason to wait for my death to enjoy the fruits of this reconciliation.'

He was, Alix knew, talking about a great fortune. About Bryden Electronics, and Alix's share of it. About money and power and wealth and prestige. And public office for Bill.

'Let's not discuss it now,' she said. 'Go take your nap and I'll catch my plane.'

'Not yet. Spare me another few minutes.'

He looked at the pictures of his grandchildren, then placed them on the tray.

'Tell me, Alix,' he said in a low voice. 'Did you ever see that fellow again – the one who blew up my plant?'

'You mean Sam Matthews? He had a name, you know. Yes, I've seen him since,' she replied, thinking of that shameful afternoon in a Chelsea hotel. What was the point in lying?

Lucius winced.

'I must ask of you one condition,' he said, 'and then we can go on as nature intended, father and daughter. A very small proviso, really, in light of all there is to gain.'

'And that is?'

'I want you to promise to have nothing more to do with him ever again. Give me your word.'

Alix felt the wind go out of her. Mellow? Change? Lucius would never change. What was this but a verbatim repeat of that scene so many years ago in Cambridge?

At that moment, she didn't know if Sam Matthews was alive or dead, nor did she care. There could never *never* be anything more between her and Sam. She loathed the man as much as she had once loathed her father. And the fact that Lucius had been right about him all along didn't improve the situation.

Theoretically, what Lucius asked was such an easy pledge to make and keep. But he had no right to demand it. No right to treat her with such disrespect, such distrust.

What did Lucius think – that after all these years, some of the Bryden fortune would wind up in Sam's pockets? Or was he only trying to make her admit she'd been wrong? Either way, she could not, would not submit to his will. Pride forbade it.

She got up and smoothed out her skirt.

'I'm afraid I can't promise you that. You'll have to take me as I am.' Then on impulse, she leaned over and kissed her father's brow. A first kiss. And he didn't recoil or shudder or cry out. He seemed almost pleased. So she kissed him again for good measure.

'Keep your money, Daddy. It's immaterial. I don't even want it. By God, but you're a stubborn old bird. No matter. I love you anyhow. I'll come again soon. That's the only promise you can wring out of me. Next time, I'll bring you your grand-children. And maybe, if you like, we'll play a game of chess.'

'Yes,' said Lucius. 'I'd like that very much.'

She blubbered all the way to the airport, then fell asleep on the plane. By the time she got back to her office she felt weak with exhaustion. But good too, as if recovering from a long illness which had once been erroneously diagnosed as fatal.

'Unfinished business,' Peter Mainwaring had described her situation. His words had been a warning. But at last she could close the file. The struggle with Lucius Bryden was over.

The battle with Bill was yet to be resolved.

COBBLE HILL

The weather was perfect for a garden wedding, and the caterers had done their best to make the modest lawn behind the Cairns' brownstone look charming and festive. At the bride's request, the guest list was small – 'to the point of being micro', Alix complained cheerfully. She'd never hosted a wedding before. In fact it was more like a family picnic.

Present were Alix and her husband (who had managed to

sneak a day free from the campaign trail), their children, Peter's mother who had flown in from London for the event, Jim Bisseau, Mr Rabinowitz, and eleven members of the jury (the twelfth had come down with the flu) 'but for whose sympathy and understanding,' Alix acknowledged, 'this would be a considerably less joyful occasion.'

There was a good deal of merriment and a moment of sadness too, when the bride, one arm around her new husband and the other around her lawyer's waist, said that she wished Kimberly West might have been here to share this day.

Alix blinked in surprise. What an extraordinary thing to say, was her first reaction. The widow's presence would have cast a funereal pall upon the festivities. Then she grasped Miranda's meaning.

Of course!

Had Kim not risked her life to save Miranda's on that night long ago, had she not been bold and selfless and gutsy, this union today would never have taken place.

It was thanks to Kim that Miranda and Peter and Alix were standing here at this moment, arms and hearts linked. Thus the past cast its dark shadow on the present. Alix and Miranda and Peter and *Kimberly*. The Marival Four.

Alix was touched by Miranda's gesture: to remember Kim at this moment when her own happiness was consummate – that was the sign of a great lady.

'Let's the three of us drink a toast to her in absentia,' Alix murmured, thinking of another toast, long ago, in a restaurant at Glovier when she and Kim and Bette had drunk to their futures with insolent faith.

Peter filled three glasses.

'To Kimberly,' he said. 'May she find happiness.'

They clinked glasses and drank.

By nightfall, the last of the guests had gone. The kids had fallen asleep exhausted. The newlyweds, who were sailing in the

427

morning to Trinidad, had returned to their hotel to pack. The young woman from the catering service was finishing up in the kitchen.

'Nice people,' the caterer said when Alix gave her the check. 'I bet they'll be very happy.'

'I'm sure they will,' Alix said. Happier than the Cairns, she had no doubt. A few minutes later, Bill drifted in.

'Good wedding,' he said, letting out a notch in his belt. 'And that cake was terrific. If you don't mind, hon, I'm going into the study for a while. I have a shitload of work to catch up on. I'll surface around ten for coffee.'

Alone in the kitchen, Alix had a fit of the blues. *Post-party* depression, she supposed, which was like *post-partum*, only worse, because you had given birth to nothing but grievances.

Weddings weren't ordinary parties, they were significant occasions: times of affirmation, of love and of high sentiment. Not just for the bride and groom, but for all present. And for married people most especially.

Weddings were when men who'd been married for donkey's years suddenly hugged their wives and grew schmaltzy and declared their love for the thousandth time, or maybe the hundred thousandth time, and said how happy they were to be married and that they'd do it all over again.

Not her Bill, though, who throughout the afternoon kept running into the house to take or make phone calls. Her Bill was not a sentimental person. Nor, normally, was Alix.

Still, weddings made her weepy, and that was a fact.

At ten thirty, she put a pot of coffee on a tray, cut two slices of left-over cake and went into his study.

Bill had his feet up on the desk, a legal pad in his lap, and a phone perched between neck and shoulder. He was talking to somebody named Myron, an animated if technical discussion of demographics in North White Plains.

He acknowledged the arrival of coffee by waving a casual two fingered 'thanks' and kept right on talking.

Alix placed the tray on a table, then sat down in an armchair, waiting for him to get off the phone. Or at least wink. But she might as well have been on Mars. At last, the demographic survey complete, Bill hung up the phone.

'Got a cup for me, Alix?'

She handed him coffee and a slice of cake.

He took a huge swallow of cake, spun his Rolodex and reached for the phone. No time even to chew.

'Got a few more calls to make,' he mumbled, mouth full.

'They can wait,' Alix said briskly.

'Why? Something wrong?' he said. Then he peered at her. 'You look bushed, hon. What was it – too much wedding, or too much wine?'

'I followed your advice, Bill,' she said quietly.

'Always a good idea,' he said routinely. His mind was elsewhere. 'Which piece of advice are you talking about?'

'I flew to Boston a week ago Wednesday,' she said. 'I went to Pride's Crossing.'

Bill swung around, clearly startled. *Now*, Alix thought with satisfaction, *now do I have your attention?*

'I've made it up with my father.'

He took off his glasses and rubbed his eyes as if to see her better. Then he beamed.

'Why, Alix! By God, that's good to hear. After all these years! So the reunion went well, did it? No glitches?'

'Extremely well. It was a powerful experience.'

'I bet. And how did you find him?'

'Older, of course. And his stroke has left him physically impaired, but otherwise pretty much the same Lucius Bryden. Still stubborn, manipulative. He'll never change, the old dragon. Though he appeared glad to see me, I must admit. And I was glad to see him. I said next time I came, I'd bring the kids.'

'Well, that's terrific, Alix. But I'm surprised you didn't mention it before. Why wait ten days to tell me?'

Instead of answering, Alix took a bite of cake and frowned. Just a few hours old, and already the frosting was stale. Just like marriage. She pushed the plate aside. When she spoke, it was without inflection.

'He offered me my due, Bill, and I turned it down. Categorically. Over quite a trivial matter, but as a matter of self-respect I couldn't relent. So I'm afraid you can forget about your golden pipe dream.'

He pulled at his ear and looked puzzled.

'What exactly is that supposed to mean? Your due? My golden pipe dream? You're speaking in parables, Alix.'

'Come off it!' she shot back. 'Don't play the naif with me. I'm talking about money. Loot. Dough. Bread. Moolah. The long green. The big bucks. The blessed wherewithal that was going to make me an heiress and you a Senator. That, Bill, is what I meant by my due *and* your pipe dream, which happen to be one and the same thing. Only it's not going to happen. For the second time in my life, I've thrown away a fortune. What I want to know is, have I thrown away a marriage as well?'

'Alix!' Bill was ashen. 'You're talking crazy.'

'Am I? Isn't that why you kept pressuring me year after year? Open up a dialogue with your father, you'd say. Send him a Christmas card, a birthday card. Make *nice daddy* – quick, before he pops off. I think his money was in the back of your mind when you agreed to marry me – hell, maybe in the front of your mind for all I know. Why not? The potential was enormous, especially for an ambitious young man.'

'Is that what you think?' His voice trembled with rage. 'That all I wanted was to get my mitts on your old man's fortune?'

'Yeah, that's what I think. Why else would you marry me? For my beauty? my charm? Give me a break! You could have had your pick of just about every woman in New York. Sweeter, softer women. It's okay, Bill. You don't have to keep up the pretense any more.'

'You idiot!' He slammed his fist down on the desk so hard his coffee cup fell to the floor and shattered. 'I married you because I was nuts about you. Because I thought you were a terrific dame. Smart, sexy, all that jazz. A little eccentric, maybe, a little disorganized—'

'You sure have a poetic way of putting it,' she snapped.

'—and totally exasperating at times, like right now. God knows being married to you is no bed of marshmallows. You can be a very uncomfortable person to be around. But this looney-tune accusation of yours! It's left me staggered. That really hurts, Alix. What kind of guy do you think I am? What's your opinion of me, what's your opinion of yourself, for Chrissakes, if you believe I married you for money? Not even money firmly in hand, mind you, but iffy money. Money on the come. My God, Alix. Are you all that insecure? As for the Bryden millions, I don't give a rat's ass about them! I never did. To me, that kind of bread is unreal, like Monopoly money or the Publisher's Sweepstakes. Your old man wants to contribute a thousand bucks to my campaign, the legal limit, well that's OK with me. I never had expectations in that department. The only reason I ever pressured you toward a reconciliation was that you spent too much time and energy hating him. It was eating you up alive. All I wanted was for it to be over so you could get on with your life. That's the truth, and you can believe me or not.' He splayed out his palms in a gesture of helplessness, a simple man confronted by the eternal mystery of What Do Women Want? 'I don't know what more I can say,' he said humbly.

Alix was confused. Was Bill being sincere in his protestations or was he simply a seasoned campaigner caught up in his own oratory? She wanted to believe him, ached to believe him. But though he had made a strong case, he had omitted the single most compelling argument.

'What more can you say?' she echoed. 'Yes, there's something more. It's not a very big speech, certainly not for a super-sharp lawyer who can extemporize for hours on end on any given topic, from the federal budget to the survival of the spotted owl. The speech I'm thinking of is quite brief. Extremely so. In toto, it consists of three little words.'

Bill sighed and put his arms around her, began stroking her hair, but Alix recoiled. This once, she didn't want sex to take the place of a romantic declaration.

Bill took a deep breath.

'Anyone with eyes in his head can see that I love you, Alix,' he said. 'You surely ought to know that by now.'

She shook her head. 'Put that way, it sounds like a legal argument, a rebuttal.'

'What do you want, Alix? Great flowery phrases? A Hallmark greeting card? Should I spout poetry? compare you to a summer's day? You know me better than that, honey. I never was one for packaged mush.' He gritted his teeth. 'I admit these last few months have been rough on both of us, what with the pressure of the campaign. I guess I've probably been less of a husband than I should have been, time being so tight. Maybe we ought to look into some re-scheduling, organize things so we have more time together. Now let's discuss this reasonably —'

'Say it,' she commanded. 'Stop pussyfooting around and just say it.'

He paused. Shrugged. 'Of *course* I love you, Alix.'

'I make that out to be six words, not three. You want to try again?'

The phone rang. It was Bill's hot line. Only his campaign manager and a few key politicos knew the number.

Instinctively his hand shot out. His expression read *Saved by the bell*.

'Don't answer it,' Alix said.

'I'm expecting an important call.'

'Don't,' she mouthed.

Their eyes locked, BRNNNG . . . BRNNNG. Bill's fingers spasmed with each ring. He was in physical pain. For him, ignoring a phone call was the ultimate act of will.

After the fifth ring, the answering machine kicked in.

'Bill Cairns here,' said his disembodied voice. 'I'm unable to answer the phone at this time. Please leave your message at the tone.'

BEEP.

'Harry McAfee.' The voice at the other end sounded excited. 'Call me pronto about the rally tomorrow morning. I'm at the office. Things are looking good, kid.'

Then the machine shut itself off, leaving Bill and Alix facing each other in near-total silence. The wall clock ticked. A floor-board creaked in the hall. It was an old house, constantly resettling. Bill folded his hands and took a deep breath.

'I love you,' he said softly. 'I love you for reasons that don't always fit neatly into words, but here goes anyhow. I love how you look when you wake up in the morning, all rumpled and fuzzy. I love the way your face lights up when you order a pizza with everything on it. I love you when you wear that pretty blue dress with the funny collar. I love you when you slop around the house in old jeans. I love the way you make lifelong friends with cabbies on a five-minute ride. I love the curve of your throat. I love your silhouette in the shower. Last week when I was in Albany, I saw a woman walking down the street, she was tall with dark hair cut in a sassy flip just like yours, and my heart turned over. I love it when you get all hot and fiery because of some outrage that you read about in the papers, even if it happened in Upper Slobbovia. I love you for being the mother of my son. I love you for marrying me in the first place. I'm not saying all this with the intention of making you cry, Alix' – for she was bawling like a baby – 'or even to prove a point. I don't know that it's incumbent upon you to believe me. Because everything I've said just now is, in fact, nothing but words. We sure know how to deal in words, you and I. Glib. Articulate.

433

Adept at talking people out of one point of view and into another. We know from experience that words can be plain or fancy or symbolic or factual or honest or deceitful or obscure or manipulative or downright lies. As it happens, the words I spoke just now were true.'

She expected him to take her into his arms, but instead, he returned to his desk and sat down heavily.

'I've given a lot of thought to what'll happen if I get elected in the fall. God knows we've talked the matter to death. I'd be in Washington Mondays through Fridays. You and the kids would be here, doing business as normal. I'd come home weekends to re-charge and get some sex in. Well, okay, I thought. A lot of couples live that way, these days. Sometimes it's the price of a two-career household. The thing is, Alix, I'm not sure our marriage would survive it. And so—' He picked up the phone and began to dial.

'What on earth are you doing?' Alix cried.

'I'm calling Harry McAfee to tell him I'm pulling out of the race.'

She watched incredulous as he placed the call. Waited while a phone rang in another part of the city. Her mind was reeling.

Bill was serious. Dead serious. He was willing to surrender the cherished dream of his lifetime for her. For the sake of their marriage. For the love of Alix Bryden – without frills.

'Hello, Mac,' Bill was saying. 'I'll make this short and sweet. Well, short and bitter, to be precise. I won't be going to the rally tomor—'

But Alix had snatched the phone from his grasp.

'What Bill started to say,' she blurted into the mouthpiece, 'is that Bill won't be going to the rally tomorrow *alone*, because I've just joined the campaign. From now on I'm going to be right up there along with him. Got that? So starting tomorrow, be sure to set out an extra chair up on the hustings. I suggest you place it just a little behind my husband and' – she grinned – 'slightly to the left.'

434

'Hey, Alix, that's great!' Harry barked at the other end. 'You'll be one hell of an asset! How come you changed your mind?'

But Alix couldn't answer because Bill was kissing her too hard. Instead she hung up and kissed him back with a passion.

'You're amazing,' Bill said when they surfaced for air.

She giggled. 'Sometimes I even amaze myself. Now this is my plan.' She felt suddenly energized, full of fire. 'As of eight a.m. tomorrow, I'm taking a leave from my firm. My associates can take it over, it'll make them happy. Meanwhile, you and I are going to beat every bush in New York State. We'll raise a bigger campaign chest than you'll know what to do with, including my old man's thousand bucks, canvass every little whistlestop for votes. Oh God, how I love you!' The revelation filled her with delight. 'Believe me, Mr William F. Cairns, no candidate will ever have a more persuasive campaigner in his camp and no US senator will have a more devoted helpmeet. *If* – she thought of Miranda and Peter – 'no, not *if*, *when*! *When* you get elected! I'll simply amaze you. I'll quit practicing law and instead do all the little wifely things I'm supposed to – make cookies, putter in the garden, have the ladies to tea—'

She was off on her periodic *House and Garden* fantasy of Alix Bryden as the little woman in a lacy apron: homey, compliant and modest. To her astonishment, Bill was laughing.

'You left out the antimacassars, Alix. Isn't that part of the picture – where you crochet little antimacassars, whatever the hell they are? You start that crap and I'll institute divorce proceedings. No, love. You'd make a lousy housewife, whereas what I'll really need in my quest is a first-class brain to pick on from time to time. No, my pet, you're constitutionally incapable of ever becoming the "little woman." You're a lawyer. A great lawyer. It's a fundamental part of your identity, and I expect that you'll go right on being a lawyer, no matter what.'

'But how can I, Bill? You'll be in the capital, whereas my clients are here in New York.'

Bill gave her a hug.

'What's the matter, sweetheart? They don't have criminals in Washington DC?'

'Washington. Of course!' Suddenly, Alix was gloating. 'Do you know something, Bill? Last year DC had the highest homicide rate in the country. And as for white collar crimes – why, baby, it's paradise. My bet is, Washington has more crooks per square foot than Little Italy had during Prohibition. And you know something, Bill? I'm about ready to expand beyond criminal law. I've always been interested in doing environmental law, consumer law, class action suits, the kind of stuff Nader's been doing . . .' Alix stopped to catch her breath. Whole new horizons were opening. Then she laughed.

'Will you listen to me? Words, words, words. What do you say we sublimate our lawyerly impulses and go to bed and make love?'

'Yeah!' said Bill Cairns, ever the poet. 'I'll buy that.'

TONIO'S ROOM

'You didn't kill Tonio.' Peter slipped a shawl about his bride's shoulders as they stood on deck that first night at sea.

'Please, Peter!' Miranda said, watching the coast slip away. 'Let's forget about the past. This is our honeymoon.'

'You didn't kill him,' Peter said. 'I've known that all along.'

In the ship's lounge, the orchestra was playing Cole Porter. 'What Is This Thing Called Love.' The music floated out toward them, tart yet poignant. It was a tune she used to play on her phonograph late at night in Marival. Years ago when they both were young.

She listened for a moment, then turned to her husband.

'What makes you say that?'

Peter sighed. 'Because I know you. You're not a murderer. You're too decent, too gentle.'

'Me *gentle*?' Miranda laughed softly. 'I'm one of the toughest women in the business world. The Iron Maiden, they used to call me in Chicago. Ask anyone, they'll tell you the same.'

'I said *gentle*,' Peter stressed, 'not *fragile*. If you'd been fragile, you never would have survived. Though I grant that you've grown very skilled at deception since Marival. The product of all those years in the business world, I gather. Every time I'd hear you give that set speech in court, about how you shot and killed Tonio DuMesne, it was all I could do to keep from getting up and shouting *Not so! Not so!* It astonished me that no one else caught on to what you were doing. Not even Alix.'

Miranda shivered in the chill of memory.

'I haven't a clue what you're talking about,' she said.

'Oh, yes, you do. You see, darling, in all matters pertaining to Miranda Vee, I have perfect pitch. I can tell when something you've said rings false. Alarms go off. Your confession in court, for instance, or your pretending just now that you don't know what I'm talking about. You can fool Alix Bryden, you can fool all those jurors, but you can't fool me. I know you too well.'

Miranda took Peter's hand and gripped it hard. Then she sighed. 'You're right, Peter. I *was* lying. Don't tell Alix though. I wouldn't want to spoil her pleasure in having gotten me off. She was brilliant in court.'

'You were too, darling. You pulled it off superbly. But why? I think I can guess the reason, but I'd rather hear it from you? What really happened that night? No secrets between us, Miranda. We've lived with too many already.'

'So we have, love,' she murmured. 'But you must promise that what I'm about to tell you is for your ears only. And then we shall never talk of it again.'

*

That night too, an orchestra had been playing, while a happy raucous crowd laughed and flirted and danced the hours away. Up in Tonio's room, however, the only sound was of his breath coming thick and fast. That and the throbbing *vrmmm vrmmm vrmmmm* of the rhythm section, like far-off voodoo drums.

Tonio had taken off his gun, placed it on the night table, then, eyes glittering, lain down on the bed and beckoned to her.

'I'm at your mercy,' he said with that mocking laugh of his, permeated with contempt and cruelty. 'Come and undress me.'

He shut his eyes in expectation of sexual pleasures.

This was it! The moment she had been waiting for. All she had to do now was pick up his gun, squeeze the trigger and put paid to years of suffering. Spare him? Whatever for? Had he spared her that night when she had been at *his* mercy?

Justice demanded that she seize the moment. Such a chance would never come again.

In her mind, she reached for the gun. In her heart, she reached for the gun. Only her hand stubbornly refused to obey.

She couldn't. For the life of her she couldn't do it. The thought of a bullet ripping through flesh, smashing through bone, shedding human blood made her ill.

The act was too dreadful, too obscene.

She was not a murderer. She was a healer, a tender-hearted soul who couldn't bear the sight of a bird with a broken wing, who wanted to adopt every draggle-tailed kitten and feed every hungry mutt that crossed her path.

She couldn't kill an animal, let alone a human being. She would sooner die herself than take a life.

In that instant, she knew she had to get out of there – fast. *Move, move! Out of this room, out of this house.* Before what happened at Chambord happened again. Only this time, Tonio DuMesne would truly kill her – and that would be the end of it.

Move, move! But her knees had turned to rubber. She felt dizzy. Off balance. The floor beneath her feet pitched and rolled like a raft in white water. She was terrified that she would stumble and fall. That he would jump her.

Then the door to the hall burst open.

Miranda turned to look. Her eyes almost bolted from their sockets.

'You!' Tonio sat up in bed. 'What in hell are you doing here?'

Looming in the doorway was the figure of a woman, a vision so resplendent as to numb the senses, set the mind reeling.

It was Kimberly West. White upon white upon white. A brilliance so blinding, so ethereal, it was as though Miranda was staring direct into the sun at the blaze of noon. The platinum hair, bleached to almost total whiteness, was piled high and crowned with a diamond tiara. She wore a gown of rich silk brocade, festooned with satin scallops. Wound about the throat were ropes and ropes of pearls, creamy as soap bubbles, plump as plovers' eggs. Another stream of pearls cascaded down her bodice like a white waterfall. The milky arms were piled from wrist to elbow with diamond bracelets, and shimmered with the dazzle of a thousand carats. The face – perfect and pale as fine porcelain – was incandescent beneath a gossamer veil.

She was not the girl Miranda remembered from Marival. This apparition was more beautiful, less real. She was flawless, immaculate beyond what might be deemed humanly possible. The only touch of color was her eyes. They blazed with a violet fire.

Here, in this improbable playhouse filled with saints and sinners, Kimberly West had chosen the role of a virgin bride, the ultimate symbol of purity.

For a moment, this vision stood in the doorway transfixed, as were they all for it was an astonishing sight.

Why, she's mad, Miranda thought. *The poor creature has lost her senses.*

Tonio was the first to recover.

'Go back to bed, *mon ange*. You're pathetic.'

She seemed not to hear. Instead, this glittering zombie began moving across the room toward Tonio, utterly unaware of Miranda's existence. The mad eyes were focused on her husband.

All of a sudden she put her hands to her ears and screamed.

'Beast!' she shrieked. 'Monster! You killed Maxim,' the words tore from her lips like shouts of pain. 'You killed my lover.'

'And you . . . you whore,' he spat out with venom. 'You're a joke. Look at you, you cunt! The so-called virgin bride. Sleeping with riff-raff. Spreading your legs for that rabble-rousing swine. I have half a mind to kill you too. Now go back to your room before I send for your keeper.'

'Stop!' Miranda was beside herself with horror. 'Please! I beg you both to stop!'

But the two were caught up in a drama that had nothing to do with her, in a hatred so thick it was palpable.

Kimberly tore a rope of pearls from her throat and flung them at him with all her strength. They skittered across the floor in a white cloudburst. The next thing Miranda knew, Tonio had vaulted across the room and lunged at his wife full throttle.

'Bitch!'

He smashed his fist into her face. There was the crack of breaking bone. Then he punched her again. Kimberly reeled.

'My face . . . my face . . . !' she was screaming. 'Oh God! What have you done to my face!'

As Miranda watched in horror, the years and years of plastic surgery began to crumble and implode. The mouth caved in, one eyelid collapsed, the cheekbones shifted, the very flesh seemed to melt and contort and fall away and dissolve like wax before a searing flame.

Miranda couldn't believe what was happening. It was grotesque. Terrifying. Like Miranda herself so many years ago, Kimberly had become a woman without a face.

Tonio too reeled backward in horror.

'My God!' he choked. 'You . . . you . . . *freak*!' He turned his head away, unable to look at what he had wrought.

Swift as a deer, Kim ran past him to the night table. Her fingers closed about the gun. With her one good eye, she fired point blank at Tonio. And fired and fired. Tonio fell to the floor at her feet and still she fired. Six shots. Till the barrel emptied.

Then, stepping daintily around his body, she sat down on the bed and stared into space.

The sound of the shots roused Miranda from her paralysis. She caught her breath, pulled her head together.

She went to where Tonio lay, knelt beside his body, raised his eyelids, checked for a pulse. There was remarkably little blood. Yet Tonio was dead. As dead as road kill.

It took a second for the irony of the situation to strike her like a knife in the heart.

Kimberly West had done in fact what Miranda had done only in her imagination. One might almost say, she had killed Tonio DuMesne *for* Miranda. In her stead.

If there was any justice on earth, if there was a God in heaven, Kimberly should not pay for this crime.

She went over to Kim, took the gun out of her hand, then stroked her hair gently.

'Leave here,' Miranda said. 'Go back to your room. There is nothing to fear from the law or from me. You were never here. What happened tonight never happened. I'll handle everything. No one will ever know.'

'But why?' Kim was blank. Uncomprehending.

'Because I owe you for one midnight swim in Lausanne. I owe you a life for a life. And I always pay my debts. Now go!'

'So she let you take the blame?' Peter said broodingly. 'I would have thought better of her.'

'She was in no shape to protest. She was shattered – not just her face, but her mind. Who knows? Perhaps she had suffered more from Tonio than I ever had. Besides, at that time I felt I had nothing much to live for. Nothing but mindless acquisition. And you see, I'd killed Tonio a thousand times over in my heart.

Which is almost like doing it in the flesh. Anyhow, the law is satisfied as to how Tonio DuMesne met his death. And so am I. And so must you be.'

Miranda's story had moved Peter profoundly. 'What a woman you are!' he said. 'But what, I wonder, will become of Kimberly?'

Miranda shook her head. 'We may never know, but that's just as well. The past is over for me. And the DuMesnes belong to the past. Meanwhile, we have the future before us.'

'But the past served its purpose,' he said. 'For it brought you to Marival and to me. I loved you then, so long ago. I love you now and I will love you forever. Full circle.'

'So it is.' Miranda gazed across the sea to the limitless curve of the horizon. 'Our lives have come around full circle.'

MARIVAL

AT THE WATER'S EDGE, A WOMAN SITS OVERLOOKING THE LAKE. SILENT. BROODING. HER CLOTHES ARE DARK. HER FACE IS HIDDEN BEHIND A MASK.
IT IS KIMBERLY WEST DUMESNE.
BUT SHE IS NOT ALONE. HER BROTHER SITS BESIDE HER.